Sláine
the Exile

Sláine the Exile is the first action-packed verse in the Lay of Sláine Mac Roth, son of the Sessair. This epic new series follows the young warrior's life into manhood as he struggles to come to terms with his warrior's gift – the Warp Spasm. Sláine gets his first taste of battle and a chance to prove his bravery when he is chosen to take part in a raid against a rival tribe. But with fate guiding the future of young Sláine, his life will become a lot more dangerous as he strives to fulfil his destiny and become a warrior worthy of legend!

More from Black Flame

CABALLISITICS, INC.
HELL ON EARTH
Mike Wild

FIENDS OF THE EASTERN FRONT
OPERATION VAMPYR
THE BLOOD RED ARMY
TWILIGHT OF THE DEAD
David Bishop

ANDERSON, PSI DIVISION
FEAR THE DARKNESS
RED SHADOWS
SINS OF THE FATHER
Mitchel Scanlon

Sláine created by
Pat Mills & Angela Kincaid.

Sláine
the Exile

The Lay of
Sláine Mac Roth
Book One
By
Steven Savile

BLACK FLAME

For Sven
A friend when I had none
A father when I needed one
The very best man I know
A Celt at heart – this one is for you
With love

A Black Flame Publication
www.blackflame.com
blackflame@games-workshop.co.uk

First published in 2006 by BL Publishing, Games Workshop Ltd.,
Willow Road, Nottingham NG7 2WS, UK.

Distributed in the US by Simon & Schuster, 1230 Avenue of the
Americas, New York, NY 10020, USA.

10 9 8 7 6 5 4 3 2 1

Cover illustration by Max Bertolini.

ISBN 13: 978 1 84416 387 8
ISBN 10: 1 84416 387 3

A CIP record for this book is available from the British Library.

THE FIRST TRISKELL

MOTHER

One
Death or Glory

THERE WAS HONOUR in death just as there had been glory in life.

The old king walked proudly among his people for the last stime, offering a smile for the maidens of the Sessair, stopping to embrace each of the mothers who had strewn garlands at his feet so that he might walk on flowers to his death. He saw beauty in every face, in every wrinkle and crease that marked mother, maiden and crone, although the beauty was nothing more startling than lives lived, and lived well. He tousled the hair of the lads and joked with the men of the Red Branch as the warriors said their own farewells.

These were his people.

Fierce love for them flowed in his veins.

He had served them body and soul for seven years. For seven years he had been beloved of Danu, the Earth Goddess. For seven years. But all things must end. Flesh and bone must return to the dirt. It is their way. They are not owned by the soul, merely borrowed from the earth. He had served the Goddess and in doing so served his people. Now, at last, he would be allowed to rest. It would fall to a younger man to care for the Sessair.

He smiled when he saw her, in the shadows, watching his sacrifice. They would be together soon, for eternity. He would serve her in death as he had in life, as her husband, her lover, her protector, her champion. He would be her king. Danu smiled for him and the love in her eyes broke his heart. She was a woman truly worth dying for: a Goddess. Her smile lent him the strength he needed to join the druid, Cathbad, at the foot of the huge funeral pyre.

The air reeked of linseed oil. The oil had been soaked deeply into the ash and rowan of the pyre, ensuring that the wood would blaze when lit. The fierce heat would consume him. Soon, in a matter of hours, there would be nothing left of him. He would exist only in the memories of his people. He would live in them forever.

He knelt and held out his wrists to the druid, exposing his pulse.

"This is my blood," the old king intoned as Cathbad drew his bone-handled knife the length of his forearms. He held them out at his sides as if they might become wings and grant flight. His blood ran down his arms, splashing on the dirt.

"Calum son of Cathair," the druid cried, his voice thick with emotion. "King of the Sessair, arise and go into the endless summer night to be joined with your bride, Danu, Goddess of the Earth. Let your flesh become as one with the Land of the Young. Let the vitality of your blood feed the ground beneath our feet while your spirit flies unfettered in the skies above. Your vigil is over, son of the Sessair. Go to your great reward."

The druid set the crown of antlers on the old king's head.

The burden weighed his head down. It went beyond the physical. The old king became an aspect of the Horned God himself, by wearing the crown of antlers.

He rose unsteadily and turned to look one last time upon his people. He recognised every face. He knew these people and their lives. He knew what frightened them in the darkest hours. He knew what drove them, and what hopes they harboured closest to their hearts. His gaze settled on Macha's boy, Sláine. He was a plain-faced lad, a little awkward around the elbows and knees where he hadn't quite grown into his body yet. Growing up could be cruel on the young, desperate as they were to own their muscles. In that, he was just like any other boy his age. It was his eyes that set him apart. The lad met his stare. He was brave, stubborn and stupid, all the things a child was supposed to be, but more than that, the old king realised looking at the boy and seeing, for the first time, the man he could become. He was touched by the Goddess; it was plain to see if you knew where to look. The lad was special. The knowledge steeled his resolve. His people were protected.

He bowed his head and lay on the sacrificial slab. His blood spilled into the channels that had been carved in the stone, drawing out the pattern of the triskell. It was the Goddess's mark.

The druid bound him hand and foot with leather tethers. Cathbad had his instructions. He was a good man. He would do as he had been bidden. Calum would be dead before the first flames touched his body. He nodded to the druid. He was ready to die.

But there was no merciful release.

A swift cut across the throat with the bone knife silenced his screams before they could be given voice. He would not be allowed to humiliate himself in death. He would not be allowed to bring dishonour to his rule.

He would burn alive, in silence.

He tried to call for his wife.

Blood gurgled in his throat.

He knew fear as the druid touched the smouldering brand to the treated wood, igniting the conflagration. The pyre went up with a soft crump that gave way to a harsher cackle. As the first licks of flame seared his flesh the old king stared at his trusted druid, the man he had called friend, the man who had served as advisor and confidant, and saw at last the hunger that ate away at his cadaverous face. He felt the malice in his black eyes and understood the depth of the druid's hatred. He was burning and the world faded into an agony of black as the flames took him.

Sláine watched the man burn with grim fascination.

The man's strength was incredible.

He didn't cry out – not even once.

Not even as the flames shrivelled away his hair and charred the flesh from his skull.

Sláine watched the destructive dance of the flames. There was something distinctly primal about the naked savagery of the fire. It consumed all things equally. He couldn't take his eyes from the dying man as he bucked and writhed against his tethers.

The druid moved around the pyre, beseeching Danu to claim her husband's spirit even as his mortal remains merged with her body once more.

The old king's silence was unnerving.

The people around Sláine cheered Calum's name. The death of the old king was cause for great celebration. He had served his people and earned his release.

Sláine felt none of their joy.

His father, Roth, had tried to explain the ritual to him but it made no sense. Why would the best of them choose to die instead of lead them? He saw a good man dying. He wanted to be like his parents and rejoice in the sacrifice but he couldn't. He felt empty.

His father laid a reassuring hand on his shoulder.

It wasn't until he turned away from the flames that it began to make sense. He saw a maiden with garlands in her hair – the same garlands, he realised, that littered the cracked and broken path leading to the pyre – holding out her hands to embrace the spirit of the dead king as it rose from the funeral bier. Death was not the end, not for the King of the Sessair. Death marked his ascendancy from the Land of the Young into the Summerland. In death he rose to his rightful place at the side of the Goddess.

The maiden inclined her head to regard Sláine thoughtfully.

Then she smiled.

She was beautiful.

He stepped forwards, drawn to her, but she shook her head and turned, leading the spirit of her lover as she skipped into the darkness beyond the trees. For a heartbeat, it was as if her smile had stopped the hands of time, but it snapped back brutally as a single voice rang out: "The king is dead!" Cathbad's cry cut through the cheers and for a moment silence reigned.

"No he isn't," Sláine barely whispered. His father's grip tightened on his shoulder.

"Aye, he is laddie, but that's just as it should be. He was a fine man, so what say we mourn him in a manner befitting his greatness and raise a jug to the old king?"

"I just saw—"

Roth hunkered down in front of his son. "Listen to me, Sláine Mac Roth, in a minute we'll be walking up to the bier to pay our last respects to Calum, are you going to be all right or do you need your ma to take you home?"

Sláine stiffened.

"I am not a little boy anymore, father." But of course that was exactly what he sounded like.

"I reckon you're right. Come on, son, let's say our goodbyes and see about getting drunk, shall we?"

Together, they made their way to the dead king's side. The line was slow, the mourners taking their time to say their own private farewells. Calum had been a popular leader, although he had remained a warrior at heart right up until his last days. He tempered his strength with compassion and wisdom, although he was never less than ruthless with those who threatened the Sessair. He was, in every way, their king.

There were whispers, of course, about who would be a worthy successor. A few favoured Kilian, although many feared the consequences of his temper. Others championed Druse against the doubters who argued the need for a Red Branch warrior to lead the tribe. There were others, Cuinn, his brother Ansgar, Grudnew, Orin and Phelan, all men who believed they embodied the future of the tribe.

Long before Sláine knelt at the dead king's bier, the druids retreated to the nemeton to confer. When they emerged again it would be to name the new king, such was their power. They were the kingmakers, guardians of the earth, and the voice of the Goddess. They were, in many ways, the Sessair.

Black smoke burned from the nemeton's chimney. When it burned out it would signify that a choice had been made.

The singing and dancing began again, and with it, the drinking. It was a time for celebration. Even Tall Iesin, the storyteller, had come home to pay his respects to the old king. Iesin sat cross-legged on a dolmen, a beautifully carved stone that had toppled onto its side, and picked out the chords of "Llew Silverhand". The ballad of the legendary hero was a crowd-pleaser; it had all the aspects of a great story, adventure, romance, danger, passion, earth magic and the crawling horrors of madness and betrayal. A few voices sang along. Drinkers gathered around the storyteller as he wove his magic. It was a fitting send-off.

The first drops of rain fell as Sláine dropped to one knee and bowed his head. He mumbled a few words: a short prayer to the Goddess.

Roth took a handful of earth and cast it over the blackened remains of the old king. "To the earth returned."

Sláine savoured the sensation of the rain running down his neck in silence. In the most basic of ways the sensation proved he was alive. The world touched him.

"Be happy in your new life, my King," he said finally and pushed himself to his feet. He cast a glance over his shoulder towards the trees, but neither the maiden nor Calum's ghost were watching.

"Fine sentiments, lad," Roth said. "Come, let's send the old bugger off in style, shall we?"

The rain grew heavier as the day wore into night but it did nothing to dampen the enthusiasm of the revellers. They drank, they sang, they danced, they toasted the dead king, and as the darkness came more than a few slipped off into the woods, emboldened by the heady mix of drink and lust. It was ever thus: sex and death, death and sex, the two were inextricably intertwined.

Nine months from now, more than a few babes would come into the world owing their life to the dead king's wake.

It was natural. There was nothing like the physical act of sex to reaffirm the most basic truths: that you were a living breathing beast, that the blood pumped through your veins, that you were potent, vital, and virile.

Black smoke still hung in a thick pall over the nemeton.

No decision had been made.

The duration of the decision process caused some discussion over the dwindling cups as the men of the tribe got down to some serious drinking. Tales grew taller and more outrageous. Claims of prowess took on epic proportions as every last one of the Red Branch embroidered stories around their heroics. If they were to be believed, each and every one of them had wrestled giant earth wyrms, and cracked open a leviathan's skull, scooped out its rotten brains and fried them for breakfast. Tankards banged on tabletops demanding more ale. The stories grew ever more outrageous. Sláine sat beside his father, watching the men as they made fools of themselves with their boasting. Even a youngster like Sláine could hear the hollow ring of their lies.

It was all bravado, he realised, listening to the stories. No one dared deny the deeds of others, so they fabricated heroics of their own, layering boast upon boast, while somewhere near the bottom the truth was decidedly more mediocre and far less heroic.

More drinks were drunk, belches belched, toasts toasted and lies laid down. Most of them wove around Calum in some way. The boy knew that the warriors' tall tales he was hearing in the round hall were the beginnings of what would become the old king's legend. They needed his exploits to be larger than life so that he could live on in life as majestically as he would in death. In their own way they were making him immortal.

"Even death couldn't hold him." The words came out before he could stop them. He wanted them to believe him. "It's true. I saw his spirit disappearing into the trees with the Goddess even as his body burned."

"Good one, lad," Ansgar said, slapping him on the back. "I can see the old bugger doin' just that. Always was one for thinkin' with his little head when he got his blood fired up." The warrior laughed at his own joke, but around him the laughter began to take a darker turn as the cups ran dry and tempers frayed.

"He was twice the man you'll ever be, Ansgar Mac Caw," Sláine's father said, shaking his head in disgust.

Ansgar's brow furrowed with the effort of thought. Not exactly handsome to begin with, the effect made it look as if someone had stuffed a bag with rocks and painted eyes, nose and mouth on it.

"You're asking for a world of hurt to come crashin' down on your shoulders, Bellyshaker."

"Oh aye?"

Ansgar lurched to his feet and staggered forwards. He swung a clubbing fist at the side of Roth's head but missed and went sprawling across the reed floor where he lay in a stupor. After a minute, he spluttered something that sounded like "urrrgh", gurgled and lapsed into unconsciousness. That brought a different kind of laughter from the drinkers as their good humour returned.

Roth was the first to notice the white smoke. He slammed his tankard on the table and smacked his lips loudly. "Come on, lad. They've made up their minds." He pushed back the bench and rose unsteadily to his feet. Sláine ducked in under his father's shoulder to stop him from falling as they walked to the nemeton.

★ ★ ★

The protectors of the faith made them wait, filing out of the nemeton one by one, each bearing some symbol of the Goddess: a tree branch, a sprig of mountain heather, feathers from a crow's wing, a pot-bellied earthen figurine and a garland of spring blossoms.

Sláine studied their movements. It was plain to see, even from the way they walked, that the priests of Danu were half-men. They moved without any of the natural grace or power of a Red Branch warrior. Their bones were brittle. He knew that all their strength resided in their link to the Earth Power. They were conduits. They tapped the very magic of the Goddess herself. They fed off the earth, touching the essential mysteries of nature. They claimed that their link to Danu made them favoured of the Goddess, chosen children, and that in turn made them more powerful than even the mightiest warrior. Sláine pictured a stone axe cracking a few druid skulls. The image raised a smile to his tight lips. It was hard to argue strength with a stone axe buried in your head.

Cathbad raised a hand for silence. In his other hand he held the mask of the Horned God, the masculine aspect of the land's magic.

The druids circled around him, falling to their knees and lowering their eyes to the dirt of the earth. They laid their talismans at their feet.

The rain added a sense of the elemental to the ritual.

They waited.

Cathbad called on the men who would be king, beckoning them to stand forward. Sláine looked at his

father. Even at this late juncture there was still a chance
that a new claim could be staked.

Roth made no move to join the claimants.

Kilian, Druse, Cuinn, Grudnew, Orin and Phelan
stood before the druid awaiting judgement. Only Kilian's face betrayed any trace of emotion. The warrior's
pride was plain for all to see. Sláine knew that he was
the obvious choice. His father had schooled him in the
relative merits of the would-be kings.

"Are these all who would guide and serve as protector of our people?" Cathbad intoned, turning slowly in
a circle. He cast ash from the holy fire on each of the
cardinals, north, south, east and west, letting the powder
disperse on the four winds. The ash was from the rowan
tree, one of the sacred woods. "Blessed be our protectors, beloved of Danu; may the Goddess look upon the
Sessair with grace and favour in the days ahead. May
she grant our new king strength when strength is called
for and wisdom when wisdom is lacking. May the new
king of the Sessair have the bearing of the mountain
and the relentless nature of the stream, carrying us forwards into the sea of tomorrow. Let him flow around
obstacles and stand undaunted in the face of our enemies. Let the essences of the earth, of river and
mountain, embody our leader."

One by one, Cathbad walked the line of men, marking them with a thumbprint of white ash on the
bridges of their noses.

"Who is the river?"

None of the men answered.

"Who here stands as the mountain?"

Still no one spoke.

"Who here is rightful heir to Calum Mac Cathair?"

Cathbad walked the line of men again. This time he paused behind Grudnew. No one dared breathe as the old man laid a cadaverous hand on the new king's shoulder.

Grudnew remained unmoving as the druid placed the mask of the Horned God over his face.

While all eyes were on the new king accepting the horned mask, Sláine looked along the line of men, at those passed over. His father had taught him that the measure of a man was in how he took defeat. Sláine found it a fascinating notion that the greatest strength came in the mastery of failure and not in the simplest successes. Kilian flinched physically as Cathbad proclaimed: "The king is dead! Long live the king!" to the raucous cheers of the gathering.

Sláine made himself a silent promise:

He would be the mountain.

He would be the river.

Two
Beltain's Fire

BELTAIN PROMISED TO be a rare treat. With a new king, the traditional celebrations took on an added air of importance among the men of the Sessair. Grudnew would light the huge Beltain bonfire, and with it, signal the beginning of the games. Murias was abuzz with anticipation. The men drove themselves hard. They ran, they sparred, and they tossed cabers and hurled spears, forcing themselves into greater and greater feats of prowess. Their spears sank into the earth a step further on, they crossed the finish line a step sooner, and they punched harder, climbed higher, and dived deeper. They forced themselves to do everything better because to do less was to fail. Grudnew was an unknown entity. He had not curried favour or promised alliances as Kilian, Orin and Phelan had. He hadn't fallen into the first – and perhaps most fatal – trap of kingship: elevating fools because of friendship. He kept his own council. He watched the men, judging them on their abilities, allowing for their weaknesses and seeking out the strengths in others to complement and compensate for them.

Every king gathered his faithful to his side. Every leader had his chosen ones. Grudnew was no fool. He

understood that the men he chose to surround himself
with stood as the foundations for his reign. It was
through them that the Sessair would find greatness, not
through him. He was one man. They were the heart of
the tribe.

And so the competition for Grudnew's favour would
be fierce.

Each man approached the games with the sure and
certain knowledge that his place in the tribe depended
very much on his showing in the coming games.

No warrior wanted to be humiliated before the new
king.

The children's games were no less competitive, and
the young men of the tribe no less eager to prove
themselves in the eyes of the men. The games were a
trial, a trial of strength, of guile, of technique, and, as
with their fathers' games, only the most exceptional of
the youths could hope to triumph.

"If that is the best you can manage, Sláine Mac Roth,
you might as well stay in bed come games day!" Cullen
of the Wide Mouth sneered. His own spear had fallen
six inches closer to the mark than Sláine's, just as his
clachneart had sailed another foot before the stone
embedded itself in the dirt, and his caber turned a
degree closer to true. Núada and Cormac had yet to
throw but it didn't matter, neither could hope to match
Cullen's spear for distance or accuracy.

They didn't. Núada's landed a full fifteen feet shy of
Sláine's mark. Cormac's was closer, but not by much.

Sláine trudged up to reclaim his spear.

He dragged his feet.

He wasn't used to being second best.

"Another throw?" he asked, working his spear free.

"Why bother? We all know how it will end." Cullen held his hands up, fingers just wide enough apart to signify the shortfall between their spears. "Or do you enjoy losing?"

Cullen of the Wide Mouth had been swaggering around the settlement for weeks, boasting about how he would walk the path of heroes and be crowned champion of the games just as his father would emerge victorious in the senior tournament. Sláine was loath to admit it and with good reason. Cullen was almost a full year older than Sláine and the other lads. This made him a step faster and stronger, and he already had the endurance of men twice his age. He was also every bit as cunning and ruthless as a weasel. Few doubted he would follow his father into the Red Branch when the time of the choosing came.

For all that, his talent hadn't earned him any friends. Cullen was a dour spirit who solved his problems with his fists. He saw little joy in life outside fighting. He was a natural bully and saw his strength as proof of his divine right to make life a living hell for anyone who couldn't stand up to him. Of all the young men of the tribe Cullen of the Wide Mouth was the one Sláine Mac Roth had least time for.

Sláine saw Wide Mouth for what he was: a bully, a liar and a cheat.

That was how he had earned his name.

Fionn had caught him out in a series of vile lies involving his younger sister, Elspet, and made sure that everyone knew exactly what kind of a gutless liar Cullen was. Cullen had blackened Fionn's eye for it but it didn't matter. The name stuck because Cullen was incapable of giving an honest answer; his mouth was so wide he couldn't even speak straight, that's what Fionn said. In the eyes of the Sessair Cullen would be a man soon, but he would not be known as a good one.

These would be his last junior games – and a new king would be watching.

Sláine wanted nothing more than to humble the wide-mouthed braggart. Nothing would give him more pleasure.

"I'm done here. I'll let you have a taste of victory, Sláine. Even you ought to be able to outdistance these losers."

A murder of crows flew in a thick bank of black overhead, circling over the rooftops of the village while the boys threw again. Sláine hurled his spear a full six feet beyond the scar in the earth that marked where Wide Mouth's spear had fallen. There was no satisfaction in it. Cullen wasn't there to see it. Sláine collected his spear and threw again, and again, both times surpassing Cullen's last throw.

Dian, Cormac's younger brother surprised them all, coming out of the mountains at a sprint to be crowned King of the Mountains. It was a brutal race across six miles of crofters' paths and dirt tracks through the wild country, across the fields of wheat and rye and up into the heather-purple mountains, taking in three peaks and traversing rugged mountaintops. Dian was smaller and lighter than the other boys, and though normally not as fast, the nature of the course made it perfect for his slight frame and long legs. He ate up the ground, leaving a blustering Cullen of the Wide Mouth in his wake.

Sláine ran, arms pumping, chest heaving, gasping for breath, his eyes fixed on Niall's back. His lungs were bursting and his legs burned like fire but somehow, no matter how hard he pushed himself, Niall always managed to stay a few feet ahead of him. He collapsed over the finish line in fourth place with Núada, Fionn and Cormac bringing up the rear. Sláine rolled over onto his back and looked up at the clouds. His chest heaved on deep dizzying breaths. He heard Cullen laughing but he didn't care. The day was far from over.

"Come on, son."

A face swam in front of his eyes, obscuring the sky. His mother, Macha, held a cup of water to his lips. He struggled to sit up, leaned on one elbow and drank thirstily. With the nimbus of sun and sky surrounding her head Macha could have been the Goddess herself. Her hair, black like a raven's and oiled, cascaded down her back. She was beautiful, but in a different way from the maiden he had seen all those months ago. She cradled him as he swallowed mouthful after mouthful of water.

"It was a good race, lad," his father said, coming up behind them. "That young Dian ran as if the spirit of the wind had taken hold of his legs. Unbelievable. There's no shame in losing to him. He's still light and small: built for speed. Your muscles have bulked up more; your frame is meant for explosive bursts of strength and power. The spear throwing'll be a different proposition entirely, lad. Technique and strength of arm will win it."

There was very little to separate the seven boys after the first three events. Cullen had won the caber toss, and come second in the other two events. Dian had won the mountain marathon but had not placed in either the caber or the clachneart. Sláine had won the clachneart, hurling the sixteen-pound stone eight feet further than Cullen of the Wide Mouth.

Sláine forced himself to his feet. He walked unsteadily over to Dian and slapped the youngster on the back.

"Good race," Dian said. He hardly looked winded. He was breathing lightly and grinning with the exhilaration of victory. Sláine couldn't help but grin along with him. Dian was the last boy that anyone would have expected to win an event, making his win all the sweeter for its surprise.

"Aye, not bad," Sláine agreed. "Nice to see Wide Mouth humbled, that's for sure."

"We aim to please. Another mile and it might have been a different story though."

"Good job there wasn't another mile, then, eh?"

They walked together to the rack of spears, picking out the weight and length that best suited their arm. Cullen was already there, putting himself through a series of warm-up exercises to work the kinks out of his shoulder muscles. Sláine mimicked some of the older boy's movements. He breathed deeply, drawing his focus into himself. He couldn't allow himself to be distracted by anything. His world narrowed down until it consisted of the spear in his hands and nothing more. Gobhan, a Red Branch warrior, acted as judge for the spear throwing. He heard the sharp intake of breath from the crowd as Cullen launched his spear and the appreciative sigh as it sailed through the sky. He didn't need to see the throw; he knew it was long. It didn't matter. He couldn't change what happened to Cullen's spear so there was no point worrying about it. Instead he concentrated on regulating his breathing, maintaining a shallow regular rhythm, and keeping his mind clear of everything except for the throw. Catcalls and appreciative claps rang out. It was a good throw. It only meant that his had to be better.

Cormac was up next, and again judging by the crowd's response, it was a good throw, although not as long as Cullen's.

Fionn's flew true, but Núada's and Dian's throws were greeted with little more than polite ripples of applause from the spectators.

Sláine stood and walked to his mark.

Gobhan said something – he wasn't listening. The world had ceased to exist. It all came down to his hand and the spear in it. In a few seconds even that would cease to be.

He scuffed his foot in the dirt, marking the point he wanted to launch off his lead foot and send the spear flying. He turned away from the run, looked up, feeling the wind on his face. It was slight, a cross-breeze blowing from left to right. It was fast enough to affect the throw if he launched the spear too high. He needed to

throw flat and hard. He paced out nine steps – enough
to lend the throw some momentum, not enough to tire
his legs after the mountain run. He turned. Sláine
closed his eyes, visualising the snap and throw before he
made it: low, hard, bouncing and skimming across the
grass, not stabbing into the earth abruptly. He nodded,
rocked back on his heel, and started his short run. He
almost missed his mark, forcing him to adjust his balance and throw all of his weight onto his front foot as
he loosed the spear. He skidded as his footing betrayed
him but it didn't matter, the spear was away. The power
was all in the shoulder, the trick to beating the wind lay
in keeping the spear-tip flat, that would negate the
weapon's natural instinct to launch up into the sky and
arc down sharply. He couldn't readjust his balance and
ended up flat on his face in the mud. Gobhan's hand
went up. The throw was good! It didn't matter that he
had fallen; he hadn't crossed the mark. He lay there,
watching the spear. It flew low and hard.

Cullen's laughter rang out harshly.

Sláine held his breath, silently urging the spear to fly.

And it did.

Cullen's laughter choked in his throat as he realised
that, despite his fall, Sláine's spear was in danger of
matching his own.

Cheers went up as spectators urged it on, yelling:
"Fly! Fly!"

And it did.

He held his breath, trying to force it on with the
sheer strength of his mind. His lips mouthed the beat of
the crowd's invocation: Fly! Fly!

His eyes widened as he realised how close to perfect the throw was.

Sláine drew himself slowly to his knees, unable to take his eyes from the spear as it began to waver. He willed it on another precious foot.

The spear dipped sharply and stabbed into the dirt, quivering.

The cheers were deafening.

Sláine pushed himself to his feet.

He closed his eyes to savour the moment, knowing that he had outdistanced Cullen's spear by more than twenty paces. It wasn't just that the throw was good – it outdistanced even the best throws of the warriors. It was an incredible feat, one, most certainly that would draw the attention of Grudnew and the warriors of the Red Branch. It couldn't have been better. He held out his arms and spun in a slow circle, drinking in the crowd's adulation. He could lose the games now – it didn't matter how good Cullen of the Wide Mouth was, how many events he won. Nothing he could do would come close to matching Sláine's powerful throw, and judging by the look of seething hate on Wide Mouth's face both of them knew it.

To add insult to injury, Dian came running up and wrapped Sláine in a fierce embrace. Cormac and Fionn joined the bear hug, the four boys dancing and shouting and spinning around in a circle, unable to hide their delight. Núada and Niall bundled into them, sending all six of them sprawling across the floor, laughing and whooping and punching the air.

When Sláine looked up, King Grudnew was standing over them. "Graceful," the new king said with a wink and held out his hand to help him up.

"It was incredible," Dian blurted, unable to contain himself.

"That it was, young man; much like your triumph over the three peaks. The future of the tribe is in such good hands. There are good days ahead, but for now there is a tug-o-war waiting for you lads, is there not?"

The tug-o-war came down to Cullen and Sláine in the end. As with everything the boys did it was a close-run thing. They weren't evenly matched in terms of sheer brute strength and muscle, but with the adrenalin still surging through his body Sláine gave Wide Mouth the fight of his life. The rope straddled the river, a boy on either bank, heels dug in to the earth and stubbornly refusing to budge. Roth and Macha led the cheers for their son. Sláine's feat with the spear had won him a lot of support. To Sláine's ears it sounded as if no one was cheering for Cullen.

He wrapped the rope around his shoulder and looped it around his wrist.

The nature of the games changed. What had been healthy rivalry took on a darker edge.

Cullen didn't wait for the signal from Gorian, War-lord of the Red Branch. He pulled viciously on the rope, unbalancing Sláine a moment before Gorian's arm came down and the contest began in earnest. Sláine fought to regain his balance. The rope burned against his shoulder and hands, and his feet took him closer to the edge, slipping and sliding in the mud even as Wide Mouth's anger drove him on. Sláine found his footing and somehow managed to arrest his slide. He dug his heels in and clawed first one and then a second step back. With Cullen on the back foot the pull could have gone either way. Their faces betrayed the strain. Cullen grunted. Sláine growled. Cullen roared. Sláine howled. Neither gave an inch. Their arms trembled violently and the sweat stung as it ran into their eyes. Still neither Sláine nor Cullen gave an inch of ground up to the other.

Then, from somewhere, Cullen Wide Mouth found the strength he needed to up-end Sláine and dump him unceremoniously in the river.

The crowd applauded but it wasn't the wild adulation they had afforded Sláine. It burned him; that much was plain to see. Cullen turned his back and stalked off towards the wrestling circle for the final event. He didn't give Sláine's floundering a second glance.

Sláine swam to the bank. This time it was Fionn who offered him a hand to help him clamber out. All of the boys had taken a dunking during the tug-o-war. Dian sat huddled on a stone bench, wrapped in a fur and shivering. Núada and Niall flapped their arms and stamped their feet, trying to work the chill out of their bones. He saw some of the village girls clustered together, heads down and giggling as one of them turned quickly away from his gaze. Grinning, Sláine shook the river out of his hair. He unwound a leather thong from his wrist and bound his hair up in a long ponytail.

It all came down to the final event, the wrestling.

Sláine drew Dian to one side, away from the others.

"Paint me, like a demon."

Dian grinned. The boy's smile was infectious.

"Come on, quickly, before they notice we've gone!"

They ran back towards the village together. The first series of bouts would give them about quarter of an hour to craft their horrors on Sláine's skin. The warriors of the Sessair daubed themselves in woad before battle, depicting the very pits of the Underworld on their skin. The intention was to put the fear of devils into their foes. Dian was a deft artist; his brushstrokes were precise, his art haunting. He drew a spiral vortex across Sláine's left cheek and the face of some nameless demon in the centre of his brow, talons reaching down and digging in to either temple. The right cheek was transformed into an endless knot that curved away down his throat and across his chest. It lacked subtlety and finesse but it was impressive. The knot spread into a huge Celtic cross, and behind it Dian sketched a warped warrior in the full grip of a mighty spasm. As Sláine's chest rose and fell the warped one grew as if seething with earth power.

Fionn burst in on them and stopped dead in his tracks seeing Sláine, slowly rising to his full height. The effect of the woad tattoos was startling. He looked like something risen with vengeful fury from Cernunnos's underworld.

His knowing smile undid the illusion.

"They're waiting for you, you've drawn Wide Mouth and he's ranting about how it should be a forfeit because you aren't there."

"Well let's go put him out of his misery shall we?" Sláine said.

The three of them strode through the village and out to the tournament fields. Heads turned and seeing Sláine, eyes widened. He walked tall, proud, Fionn and Dian at his side. He ignored the whispers. His eyes sought out Cullen Wide Mouth, who could easily have been renamed Cullen Slack Jaw when he saw his opponent striding out of the crowd to face him.

Sláine didn't say a word.

He strode into the centre of the fighting circle, bowed to Brand, Wide Mouth's maternal uncle, who served as judge, and dropped into a tight crouch, circling, circling, lips curled back in a feral snarl.

Cullen stood on the edge of the circle, staring at the beast that was Sláine. He moved hesitantly, dropping into a crouch and scuffling forwards, fingers clawing at the dirt.

The pair circled each other warily, each weighing the other up, looking for a weakness. Sláine's bone-white grin was stark against the blue woad. He curled his lips back in a feral snarl and slapped his own face. Then he winked at Cullen, knowing that Wide Mouth's temper would get the better of him. It was almost too easy to goad him into losing his concentration.

Cullen slapped out at the side of Sláine's face but Sláine rolled around the blow, coming to his feet six feet from where he had been, and threw his head back, howling at the sun.

To a man, the spectators were silent. No one dared utter a word for fear of breaking the spell the combatants had cast over the scene. It was almost like watching a dance, such was the grace and fluidity of the boys as they feinted, blocked and rolled around blows, neither gaining the upper hand for more than a few seconds at a time.

Sláine reared up, luring Cullen in. Wide Mouth lunged, throwing himself forwards, off balance. Sláine drew in a huge breath, feeling the surge of earth power infusing his blood as he gave in to his anger. It gave him strength beyond anything he had ever felt in his life. When he came down on Wide Mouth's head it was with all the ferocity of a cudgel of stone, slamming both fists into the hard bone of Cullen's skull. The blow sent Wide Mouth reeling, spitting cracked and broken teeth as he tried to gather his wits about him. Wide Mouth struggled to get his legs under him. His left leg twitched uncontrollably. He was beaten, badly, but his body refused to lie down. All that remained was for Sláine to move in for the coup de gras. There was nothing pretty about it. He reached out, grabbing a handful of Cullen's hair and pulled him off balance. Brand moved to intercede but Sláine was determined to win, not be given victory. He spidered sideways, scuttling on all fours and keeping just beyond the judge's reach, forcing Brand to drop a strip of white cloth between Sláine and Cullen. The cloth signified the end of the fight.

Sláine saw it fall and ignored it.

The power of the earth roared through him. He was the mountain. He was the river. He was Sláine. No one would take this victory from him!

He roared forwards, spitting and hissing like a man possessed.

Wide Mouth was too disorientated to do anything but slump into Sláine's forearm as he brought it crashing into his face. Blood sprayed from Wide Mouth's broken nose as the cartilage ruptured and smeared across his face. Brand grabbed at him, but before the warrior could haul Sláine off he finished it with a scything kick that took Cullen's legs out from under him and left him on his back in the dirt, groping out desperately for something to hold on to as his world spun away from him.

Wide Mouth wasn't just beaten; he was humiliated.

Sláine stood over his fallen enemy, blood singing through his veins.

Brand made to grab him as Sláine threw his head back and roared, beating his fists off his chest.

The crowd had fallen utterly silent.

They stared at the painted Sláine as if he was indeed the warped demon Dian had depicted him as.

Sláine put his boot on Cullen's chest and pinned him to the dirt, claiming his victory.

"Crom's balls, that was harsh," someone said, finally.

Then someone else said, "Was that Roth's boy? He's got a hell of a temper."

And someone else said, "You bet he has. That lad'll make a hell of a Red Brancher."

Sláine smiled. He had done it. They had seen him. They knew what he had within him. He walked away, leaving Wide Mouth sprawled in the dirt, with his arms and legs splayed out like some cheap whore begging for business.

He walked through the crowd, seeking out his king.
They people parted around him. A few patted him on
the back as he passed. None stood in his way. He could
hear woodland sounds, forest sounds, earth sounds, all
around him – the crowd was so quiet. These weren't
tranquil sounds. He heard nature coming alive. He heard
predators stalking and killing succulent prey. He felt
empty inside: dead. The thrill of the earth's power had
left him a hollow shell of a man. He walked woodenly
through the press of people, unwilling to believe what
had happened – what he had done. It was as if a dark
spirit had found its way into his skin and turned him
into a stranger. He didn't know himself. He could see his
friends looking at him, although none of them looked
at him the way they used to. Now their eyes were
clouded with fear. They had seen what he had done to
Cullen of the Wide Mouth. He knew what they were
thinking. They were thinking that if he could do that to
Cullen what was he capable of doing to them?

The worst thing was that he couldn't find it in himself to blame them.

He would have been thinking the same thing, in their
place.

It frightened him.

Sláine found Grudnew standing with Gobhan and
Gorian. He dropped to one knee and bowed his head.

"Well, Sláine Mac Roth, you are full of surprises," the
king said. "You fought well and the honour is yours. Rise."

"He fought like a dog," Gobhan spat derisively. Sláine
didn't rise to the bait. Gobhan was only looking for an
excuse to bring him down a peg or two.

"That may be so," Gorian agreed, "but he walked away victorious. I would trade grace for a butcher's instinct in my warriors every day of the week."

"Is that what you are, lad? A butcher?" Grudnew asked, studying Sláine.

"No, sire. I am the mountain. I am the river," Sláine said earnestly.

The new king smiled. "You'll do well, lad," he said after a moment. "Now come on, stand up. A man doesn't debase himself longer than he must, even before a king. Let the sycophants bow and scrape. Warriors stand tall."

"Sire."

Sláine stood. His hands trembled. He wasn't frightened. It was a peculiar thing; with the threat long gone his body finally allowed the fear to catch up. He looked at his hands, fascinated by their treachery.

"That's an interesting design," Gorian said as Sláine straightened. "Quite elaborate." The warlord pointed at the warped figure emerging from behind the endless knot. "What is it? Some kind of warped demon of the aether?"

"I don't know, lord. My friend drew it. I wanted him to make me look scary."

"Oh, he did that, son. You're a sight to drive the fear of the Horned God into a soul, take my word for it." And as he said it Sláine heard the honesty in Gorian's voice. The warlord wasn't mocking him. He felt pride colour his cheeks, and was grateful for Dian's woad taking the sting out of the blush.

"Thank you," he said.

The old warlord leaned in close. "You gave young
Cullen a sound beating, lad. Today was supposed to be
his day. It didn't work out that way and you are the reason for that. He isn't going to thank you and I doubt
very much that he will forgive you, either." Sláine nodded and started to say something. Gorian held up a
finger. "Don't think we haven't seen him lording it over
you boys," Gorian interrupted. "We aren't blind and we
aren't fools. We know exactly what he's like, just as we
know exactly what young Dian is like, and Fionn, and
you for that matter. We look at you and we see the
future, lad. It behoves us to pay a great deal of attention
to your exploits. Believe me, you took the wood right
out of his pecker. If he's anything like his father Wide
Mouth's going to nurse that grudge. So take care of
yourself, boy."

Sláine saw Brand helping a dazed Cullen to his feet.
Wide Mouth had never been particularly easy on the
eye but Sláine had left him with a face even his mother
would find it difficult to love. Cullen lifted his head and
stared straight at Sláine. The animosity in his glare was
venomous.

Sláine knew that Gorian was right. Sláine had humiliated Cullen. He knew Wide Mouth well enough to
know that he wouldn't rest until he had returned the
favour.

He didn't have to wait long.

Wide Mouth dragged himself to Sláine's champion's
feast. He hadn't cleaned the blood from his face. He
walked unsteadily into the roundhouse and pushed his

way through to where Sláine sat, beside Grudnew and Gorian, claiming the hero's portion. Thick meaty juices ran between his fingers as he tore at the succulent rack of lamb. He licked his fingers, smacking his lips even as he tore another hunk of meat free from the bone. The meat was cooked to perfection: crisp on the outside and pink and juicy at the core. It peeled away in his fingers and melted in his Mouth.

"You have no right!" Cullen bellowed, slumping against the side of a table and needing its support to keep from falling. "You cheated! You broke the laws of combat by delivering blows after the white flag. You are a coward and a cheat, Sláine Mac Roth, and I demand my right as winner of the games. I demand the hero's portion."

Sláine tore another strip of meat from the bone and tossed it onto the floor at Wide Mouth's feet.

"Your share of the spoils, Wide Mouth. Eat it. Lap it up like a dog. Go on, get down on your knees. Eat the scraps from my plate, loser. It is all you are good for, grubbing around in the dirt, begging."

Cullen snarled as Fionn, Dian, Cormac, Niall and Núada all moved to stand between their friends.

"Enough," Cormac said.

One of the Red Branch warriors caught hold of Wide Mouth's arm and held him firm. "Aye, the lad has the right of it, son. Get yerself away home. No good's gonna come of this here fight."

"I don't need you to tell me what to do, old man. Get your hands off me!"

"Calm down, laddie, yer don't want this gettin' any uglier than it already is."

"Oh just shut up you drunken fool. This is between me and him!" Cullen levelled an accusing finger at Sláine. "Do I need to come up there and get you, coward?"

"Did I damage your brain with the pounding I gave that thick skull of yours? Do I need to come down there and beat you again? I will if you want me to. I'll beat you to a bloody pulp so you never walk again if it will make you shut the hell up." Sláine laid aside the stripped bone and tore another rib free from the rack.

"Enough, children," Grudnew said, the calm authority of his voice cutting across theirs easily. He was not amused. "In defeat, you need to learn grace, Cullen Mac Conn; in victory you need to learn humility, Sláine Mac Roth. There is more to being a great warrior than winning your battles. A great man carries himself with dignity. He doesn't stoop to name calling and throwing his fists around. He doesn't humiliate his foe; he befriends him so they need be foes no more. You both have a lot to learn, but that is unsurprising. For all your exploits on the games field today you are still children. You will learn, and I would wager that there are plenty of people willing to beat that learning into you, if needs be. Look at your friends. Right now each one of them is more of a man than either of you. You might have beaten them on the tournament field, but in life they have the measure of you. They have shown great courage in putting themselves between you. You could learn from them. Now, both of you, out of my sight before I decide it is time for your first lesson."

Roth Bellyshaker grabbed Sláine by the arm and hauled him from the roundhouse. Conn was no less gentle with Wide Mouth, dragging him so that his feet barely touched the ground.

"Just wait 'til I get you home, boy!" Roth growled, shoving Sláine in front of him. "Making a show of our family in front of the king!"

Then, when they were out of sight of prying eyes, Bellyshaker wrapped his arm around Sláine's shoulder and said, "You did yourself proud today, my boy. You took down a stronger, faster opponent and he'll not forget the beating you gave him in a hurry. You caught the king's eye; he marked you, lad. Do you have any idea what that means? The king's marked you, six months from the time of the choosing, the king has singled you out. Do you think it was a coincidence that Gorian was talking to you? The man's the Warlord of the Red Branch, son. The bloody warlord! When you were out there they saw something in you that they liked. Then you had to go and show them something ugly. You better get a grip on that temper of yours before it gets you in even more trouble."

"Yes, father," Sláine said, remembering the intoxicating touch of the earth power as it seeped into his body, remembering the feeling of strength it promised, and yearning to feel it once more.

Three
The Choosing

IT WAS THE first day of the trinox Samoni: the three nights of Samain.

They called Samain the feast of the dead. Feis Samain. At Samain, the barrier between the world of the Sidhe and the mortal world was at its thinnest and most fragile. These were the days in which old ghosts returned to their familiar haunts. It ought to have been the stuff of nightmares but it wasn't. It was a time for remembering. A time for celebrating those lives that had gone before. It was a time for reflection.

And, they whispered, if you were lucky, a time to remake old acquaintances.

More practically it was the time between times, between the death of summer and the birth of winter, outside the ordinary turn of the seasons. Tithes were paid to the king from the harvest and the king himself settled the Ugarta. These were tribal taboos, old scores that demanded the sovereign's hand in settlement because the claimants couldn't find satisfaction between themselves. Some were held over from Calum's reign, others were new to Grudnew's. The king would seek to settle many with a bountiful feast and even more bountiful ale. A full year had passed since the marriage of

Grudnew to the Goddess, crowning him King of the Sessair.

It was also the birthday for the men of the tribe, marking the turning of another year.

Today Sláine became a man.

The Choosing began at noon. He would learn his fate soon enough, as would the others. Sláine woke early and sat on the edge of his cot, watching the sun rise orange on the horizon. He hadn't slept well the night before. He was restless, nervous. He wanted nothing more than to be accepted into the Red Branch, to be a true warrior of the Sessair. But doubt gnawed at him, and for good reason. It had been six years since Gorian allowed an apprentice into the Red Branch. Six years. Why should they embrace him where they had overlooked so many others?

His mother had risen early and left to work the fields before dawn. His father was still in his cot, snoring loudly.

He crept out of the house without waking the old drunk.

The morning air was crisp and sharp, and the sky was glorious. It was going to be a good day.

He found Núada and Fionn kicking a ball back and forth between them. The ball was Cormac's. His father had made it out of a pig's bladder and cased it in rawhide. Grinning, Fionn punted the ball to Sláine.

"We're waiting for the others," Núada said. "We thought we'd get our minds off the Choosing with a game. Cormac's fetching Niall and Dian."

"Yeah, knocking ourselves senseless ought to do it," Fionn agreed.

"Here's Wide Mouth," Sláine said, seeing Cullen round the corner. The boy's face hadn't healed well. His nose had set flat, the nostrils splayed wide. The broken nose made his nickname all the more ironic. "The morning just gets better and better."

Cullen tossed a stone underarm and caught it by snatching down on it overarm as he walked. On the fifth snap he spun and hurled it away over the rooftops.

"You up for a game?" Fionn called, side-footing the ball across the street. Cullen flicked it up with the toe of his left foot and held it there, balanced on the flat of his boot for a while before he hoofed it across the street to Núada. He didn't look at Sláine. Not even once.

"More fun kicking you lot than watching you kick each other," Wide Mouth said, wandering over to join them while they waited for the others. Dian, Niall and Cormac turned up later, Dian still knuckling the sleep from his eyes.

"Rules," Fionn said. "Straight run, from here to Lugh's Spike, anything goes. The one holding the ball at the top of the Spike is the winner. Ready?" The others nodded. "Good. Happy birthday, lads." And with that he punted the ball high into the sky and started chasing after it.

Sláine followed the arc of the ball with his gaze, breaking into a gentle run. Their goal was nearly eight miles away through streets and town squares, across fields, hedges, fences and streams, skirting the edge of the forest and then up into the hills to the Spike itself.

Fionn had picked a nasty run deliberately. It played to all of their strengths but more importantly it preyed on all of their weaknesses.

The ball bounced and rolled ahead of them. Cullen whooped as he ran, pumping his arms powerfully. He had put on a burst of speed to make sure he was the first to the ball. As ever, it was all for show. As long as the game was still within Murias he wanted to be seen to be winning, especially today. With the Choosing coming up he wanted it fresh in everyone's minds that he was the best of them.

Núada took him down hard before he had covered sixty paces clutching the bladder. It was a crunching tackle. The ball went bouncing away towards the ditch where Niall scooped it up and set off like a startled deer.

Wide Mouth staggered to his feet and cracked a punch off the side of Núada's skull, but Núada laughed and rolled with the blow, coming to his feet five steps out of Cullen's reach. He saluted Wide Mouth and bolted after Niall. Cullen hared off after him.

The morning was fresh and blustery. It wasn't cold but the bite of the air was nothing short of harsh in his lungs as Sláine swallowed breath after deep breath. Sweat rimed his skin. He felt a hot flare of pain run the length of his left leg from ankle to groin, tearing through the muscle, and pulled up short. He hobbled forwards tentatively, each step drawing a fresh needle-sharp stab of pain as he put his foot down.

Grinning like an idiot, Niall hoofed the ball over the fast-flowing River Dôn.

"Oh, you just had to, didn't you?" Dian groaned, throwing himself into the water. The others splashed through the river behind him, fording it at a shallow point. Even so the water splashed up around their chests. The undercurrent was fierce enough to sweep both Cormac and Cullen off their feet and carry them thirty paces down river before they managed to drag themselves out and up the bank on the far side. Niall ran an extra three-quarters of a mile to the rope bridge because he was afraid of being swept away.

Despite the pain, Sláine kept pace with Dian, near the back while the others fought over the ball with kicks and curses and flying fists. An elbow split the skin above Fionn's right eye. Blood made it impossible for him to see properly but that didn't slow him down. Fionn dragged Núada into the dirt, tackling him from behind. He threw himself forwards, wrapping his arms around the smaller boy's waist and dragging him down. Sláine claimed the loose ball, drop-kicking it over two hundred paces further on down the road. He loped on easily even as Wide Mouth dashed passed him. Dian was first to the ball. He put his head down and pumped his arms, running flat out.

Sláine didn't push himself any harder than he had to.

The winner wasn't the one who possessed the ball the longest – it was the one who drove it over the finish line. It was as simple as that. It didn't matter if he didn't touch the ball right up until the foot of Lugh's Spike, just as long as he was the one carrying it over the goal.

His thighs burned as they ploughed through the stubble of the wheat fields. He had to time his final charge just right. The Spike loomed imperiously, less

than a quarter of a mile away. He hurdled a fallen log.
Pain lanced through his leg as he came down on the
hard-packed earth. He ran through it, forcing himself
on. With the Spike less than one hundred paces away
Sláine gave one final burst, putting everything he had
into catching his friend. Even so, he never would have
caught him without the intervention of a jag of rock
protruding from the dirt floor. Dian's leading foot came
down on the splintered stone, turning his ankle
viciously. He skidded through and tripped over his own
legs as they tangled up around themselves. Dian's mistake came when he threw a hand out to stave off his fall
– instinctively, he let the ball go.

Sláine surged forwards and punted the ball with his
foot, setting his eyes on the goal, sixty paces away.

He had timed his surge to perfection.

Sláine kicked the ball forwards twice more, chasing it
desperately, his focus solely on the pig's bladder as it
bounced away in front of him. Forty paces. He ran,
chest heaving, head rolling from side to side as he
plunged on for the finish. Thirty paces.

He scooped up the ball.

Twenty.

His heart felt as if it was about to burst in his chest.

Ten, nine, eight.

He threw his head back giving every last ounce of his
strength to driving himself over the line.

He knew that he had won. He threw his head back,
savouring the triumph.

And his legs were cut out from under him by a scything tackle from Wide Mouth, two-footed, hammering

in just below the knee. The challenge snatched defeat from the jaws of victory. Sláine went down running, six paces from the line. He tried to haul himself forwards. He couldn't move. The agony was incredible. For one sickening moment he thought his leg was broken. No matter how desperately he willed the rogue limb to move it didn't. He had no control over it.

He rolled over onto his back only to see Wide Mouth's ruined face leering down at him. The pain was excruciating and made so much worse by the humiliation of Cullen wrestling the ball from his grasp. He was helpless to do anything but watch as Wide Mouth walked the last few steps to victory and slammed the ball down in triumph.

Sláine was forced to lean on Fionn's shoulder as they walked into the town square for the Choosing.

His leg wasn't broken. Indeed the only casualty of the game was his pride.

Together the pair moved awkwardly over to join the line of boys and girls. Sláine looked up and down the line at the faces of his friends. Their lives would be shaped for better or worse over the next hour.

Murias came out in force to witness the Choosing. The candidates' parents lined the square, anxiously waiting their children's fate. The Choosing reflected on them almost as much as it did on the youngsters. They would, after all, take immense pride in welcoming a new warrior of the Red Branch into their family. Other trades, although less coveted, were no less important to the survival of the tribe. For the want of a nail the kingdom was lost, that was the adage. There was sense to it. An army needed food as much as it needed steel. It needed fur and wool, and leather and grain. It marched on its stomach and on its feet. What good was an army that hadn't eaten? An army that's feet were blistered and chaffed raw by poor boots?

One by one the masters came into the square and walked the line, examining the lads and lasses as if they were sides of meat waiting to be dressed.

Few words were exchanged.

Sláine had long suspected that the decisions were actually made long in advance of the actual ceremony and this torture was little more than a relic hung over from centuries of ritual.

That was why the Choosing was so vital.

It was a way to assure that the lifeblood of the tribe was replenished: the butchers, the bakers, the chandlers, the farmers, tanners, and every other trade under the sun. They were all in their own way as important as the warriors. Of course, the warriors themselves would never have admitted that.

The masters almost certainly met in private to decide what trades were under-represented and needed fresh blood – they would have been fools not to – and while they were at it, decide who amongst the youngsters were best suited to the various trades.

The only question was who they had chosen for what purpose. That was what the ceremony was all about. It gave ritual to nothing more mystical than a calculated decision process.

Fionn was taken early, chosen by Tall Iesin, to the delight his family. Whispers ran along the line. No one knew if the bard had the right to claim an apprentice. They weren't even certain he was Sessair. He came and went as he pleased, trading news for food, song for drink and stories for a place to lay his head come night. He had been alone for as long as any of the boys had known him, and now he had chosen Fionn.

That he had selected Fionn out of all the boys set the wolf amongst the proverbial crows. What did he see in the boy that he had never seen in a candidate before? What made Fionn worthy?

They had no answers because there were no answers.

The honour of being chosen as apprentice to the great storyteller was second only to being called to take the Red Branch. And some would have argued the reverse: that the Red Branch was second only to the bard. Fionn was beaming as he left his friend to await his fate.

Núada found himself pressed into service with Rioch, the tavern keeper. This was something of a surprise choice, but reasoned out it made sense. Núada was quick of thought and good with numbers. He would be able to help Rioch with the brewing and the stables, as well as the tabs run up by drinkers, and because he was a brawler at heart, he'd be useful when it came time to collect those tabs when the drinker's credit ran dry. He didn't seem unhappy with the choice, although he had harboured hopes of being apprenticed to Grudnew's personal bodyguard.

Bluth the Blacksmith's strong hand came down on Niall's shoulder. It was an obvious match that met with the approval of Niall's parents in the crowd. They swarmed around their son delightedly as he walked alongside his new master on the way to the smithy. Grinning, Bluth had to send them on their way so that he might have a few moments alone with his new apprentice – he appeased them with promises of shared ale at the Feis Samain later that night.

A few moments later, the cordwainer, Milo, claimed Cormac.

Cullen, Dian and Sláine stood alone in the square. There were no more masters to come. They had been judged and found unworthy. The thought sank like a smooth sided stone to the pit of the young Celt's gut. Roth wore a face like thunder whereas Macha just looked distraught. The boys didn't move. The ritual of the Choosing demanded that they stay there until sundown on the final day of tri-nox Samoni. They promised to be three lonely nights while the others celebrated their indentures.

That wasn't the worst of it though. Without a trade they were outside the tribe. They would be forced out of Murias to become exiles. No man of the Sessair was allowed to beg and without a trade that is exactly what they would be reduced to doing. Travelling from homestead to homestead begging for work and a roof for the night.

Sláine turned slightly and saw Cullen staring at him, hatred blazing in his eyes. It was obvious that Wide Mouth blamed him for their fall from grace. Their public feud had undone their ambitions. The stupidity of it galled him. Wide Mouth had come marching into the roundhouse demanding justice – well he had it now. They both did.

But Dian being out here didn't make sense. He had nothing to do with their fight. Indeed, Grudnew himself had praised the youngster for standing between his two friends when both Sláine and Wide Mouth had lost their heads. That deserved a reward surely, not exile?

Whispers began after another spell. Sláine knew that they were talking about him. Their words didn't carry. They didn't need to. He saw their meaning in the eyes of the speakers: pity.

He wouldn't be the object of anyone's pity.

He held himself taller, drew his back straighter, and kept his eyes fixed firmly on an invisible spot in the middle distance where nothing existed. They could keep their pity. He was Sláine Mac Roth. He had no need for it.

Cathbad, the druid, shuffled into the square, his twisted frame bent almost double as he moved towards the boys.

Sláine didn't know what to think. Life as a druid was not the life he would have chosen for himself even an hour ago, but now Cathbad's arrival offered a slim hope of salvation. He could give himself to the service of the Goddess. He even started to believe that he had always dreamed of that oneness with the earth, that that was reason for the sensation of raw power he felt surging through his body when he lost his temper. So it was doubly hard when the old druid walked up to Dian, wrapped him on the knuckles with his rowan staff, said, "Follow me, boy", and turned his back.

There was to be no last minute reprieve for either him or Cullen of the Wide Mouth.

As the afternoon wore on into dusk all hope left him.

The last thing he wanted to do was cry but it was impossible not to. He bit down on his lips and focused on that nowhere right in front of his eyes as the tears streamed down his face.

No one laughed at him.

They shared his grief because they knew no one was going to come.

The crowd had thinned down to nothing as the first hour stretched into a second and then a third without anyone coming to claim the boys.

Sláine had cried himself out, mastering the weakness that was emotion. He didn't sniff, didn't moan. He just stared into space. Wide Mouth was devastated and made no effort to hide it. He no longer stood. He waited out the final hour of sunlight on his knees, beseeching Danu to forgive him and find a place for him in her heart. It was pitiful to see the proud boy reduced so easily to a wreck of a man.

A man.

They would be men when the sun sank below the horizon – no longer boys. And as men they had no place in the tribe.

Cullen looked up with red-rimmed eyes.

"It's all your fault," he spat accusingly at Sláine. He kept his voice low, harsh, so that it wouldn't carry any further than it had to.

Sláine didn't bite. He knew what Wide Mouth was doing. He hoped to provoke Sláine into a fight and by doing so show the few remaining watchers that Sláine was the canker that needed to be cut out of the Sessair. It was a pitiful attempt to make him look like the innocent victim in all of this, but there was no innocent victim. Both were party to their own downfall and both of them knew it.

Still there was a vindictiveness about Cullen of the Wide Mouth that defied reasoning. It wasn't just spite. It went beyond that. Wide Mouth derived glee from his own malice. He revelled in it. His behaviour now was only a hint of the man he would become. It made sense that Grudnew would not want him as part of the tribe. Who wanted a vicious moron in the heart of their family? Sláine was being punished for goading Wide Mouth when he had beaten him. What was it the king had said, "a warrior needed to learn humility"? What was more humbling than exile from his people?

"Look!" someone said.

Sláine didn't.

He didn't want to know what was happening. He wanted Danu to open the ground up around him and swallow him whole, ending his humiliation.

Someone else cheered.

"Blessed be!" Macha cried out, barely able to restrain herself. He sought his mother's face in the line of faces but saw instead the glowering figure of Gorian, Warlord of the Red Branch, striding into the square. He held in his hand two ties of red wood. The warrior walked up to Wide Mouth.

"On your feet, man. We prostrate ourselves before no man. We are Sessair! We are proud! Unbreakable." He held out one of the ties. "Do you take the Red Branch, Cullen Mac Conn?"

Wide Mouth nearly ripped it out of Gorian's hand, much to the delight of the few onlookers. "Yes," he said, drawing himself up to his full height. "Yes, yes, yes, yes."

"The boy seems happy."

"With good reason."

As Gorian turned to Sláine, a smile touched his lips. "And what of you, Sláine Mac Roth? Do you take the Red Branch?"

"Would you have me?"

"Aye, man, I would."

"Then why did you not come earlier to claim me? Is this pity now? Do you save me from exile because none other would take me?"

"Don't be a fool, son," Roth Bellyshaker shouted from the sidelines. "Take the damned branch!"

Someone else laughed.

"No one else claimed you because you were mine. Make no mistake. I chose you and your friend here a long time ago. My choice was well known among the masters. There is no room for pity in the Red Branch. We are champions, Sláine Mac Roth. We are the finest of the Sessair. Now, will you swallow your pride and take the branch? I will not ask again."

"Aye, I'll take it," Sláine said, reaching out to take the ties from Gorian. The warlord surrendered the branches with a slight smile.

"A wise choice, young man."

Sláine held the branch tightly, hardly able to believe what had transpired. All thoughts of his wounded leg fled from his mind as he followed Gorian towards the roundhouse.

At sundown Cathbad lit the Samain fire, signalling the arrival of the first night of the trinox Samoni.

The young men gathered around it, Sláine seeking out Núada and Niall. Fionn and Cormac joined them a few minutes later. They all bore the same huge smiles. "We aren't boys anymore," Fionn said, pointing up at the moon. It was full in the sky. He was right; night had begun in earnest. They were men now.

Cullen of the Wide Mouth stood slightly apart, watching the flames.

Sláine moved away from his friends and went to stand beside Wide Mouth.

"What do you want, Mac Roth?" Cullen asked without turning. He warmed himself at the fire, rubbing his hands briskly.

"A new beginning. We aren't children anymore, Cullen. Tonight we've become men. We've taken the Red Branch. You heard Gorian, the Red Branch are the finest of the Sessair. Let's make a clean start of it, eh? Bury our childish grudges and move on?" He offered his hand, holding it out to be shaken.

Cullen stared at Sláine's outstretched hand as if it was an adder poised to strike. His lip curled slowly into a sneer. "You think a handshake will undo all you've done to me?" Instinctively, Wide Mouth's hand went up to touch his ruined face.

"No," Sláine said. "It won't undo anything, but hopefully it will serve to begin something new. After all, we are Red Branch. That makes us brothers."

Cullen thought about that for a moment and then took Sláine's hand and shook it.

"Danu help us all," Wide Mouth said with a grin.

Neither saw the spectres of Grudnew and Gorian watching them approvingly from beyond the circle of the fire's light.

"See, sire. A little humiliation is good for the soul," Gorian said, turning his back on the boys. It had been a calculated risk, but after the beating Conn's boy had taken at Beltain something needed to be done. These two were by far the best of the youngsters, the most gifted athletes with the most fiercely determined spirits. There was an unquenchable fire that burned inside them. Together they would forge this celebrated brotherhood. They would become legends.

Perhaps one day they would be crowned kings in their own rights.

Alone, left as they had been going with the constant prodding and goading, one would almost certainly have killed the other before the season was out. They couldn't have allowed that to happen, but they couldn't simply sit the boys down and tell them that. Boys tended to have thick skulls and needed the learning beaten into it. So they had cooked up the idea of letting them stew, see if they couldn't work out themselves what they stood to lose, and why they stood to lose it.

"Every once in a while you are quite wise, my old friend. Far better this than banishing such young men. Judging by the silent language of their bodies I would say that just this once you were quite right."

"Aye, sire. It looks like they've put childhood behind them and realised that they are men now."

"Much as we did, eh?"

"Much as we did," Gorian agreed, "although I still haven't forgiven you for bedding Ailis."

"Ah, who needs forgiveness," Grudnew chuckled, "when you can make a woman squeal like a stuck pig?"

"And then there was Maeve and Una. And Cait. And–"

"Yes, yes, you've made your point. But you know what I believe? Men should never let a woman–"

"Multiple women–" Gorian interrupted.

"–come between them," Grudnew finished as if he hadn't heard him.

"Come on you old dog, let's go join the celebration shall we? There's good ale to be drunk. Rioch's tapped a fresh keg and he's even brought out the honey wine."

They moved over to where Tall Iesin was picking gently over his long-necked bouzouki. It was a beautiful instrument, made from a single hollowed out piece of rosewood. His fingers moved lithely up and down the fretted board, picking out the chords of the "Ballad of Tam Lin". Fionn sat at his feet, keeping rhythm on his bodhran. The music was rich and sweet but it was nothing compared to Iesin's voice.

The crowd was rapt by the twists and turns of the tale. Children gathered around Iesin, their faces turned up to look at him as he sang, their hushed expectancy quite beautiful to see.

Gorian and his king found a spot a little removed from the children and settled down to listen to the balladeer as he carried them to the land of the Sidhe where Tam was a mortal man, who, after falling from his horse, was rescued and captured by the Queen of the Fairies. The horror of the ballad unfolded slowly, until Tall Iesin held them in the palm of his hand, playing them as expertly as he played his bouzouki. His voice dropped to a hush as he told them that every seven years the fairies paid a tithe to Hell of one of their people, and Tam was fated to become that tithe on that night: on this night, because it was one and the same.

"And pleasant is the fairy land,
But, an eerie tale to tell,
Ay at the end of seven years,
We pay a tiend to hell,
I am sae fair and fu o flesh,
I'm feard it be yself.

"But the night is Halloween, lady,
The morn is Hallowday,
Then win me, win me, an' ye will,
For weel I wat ye may.

"Just at the mirk and midnight hour
The fairy folk will ride,
And they that wad their true love win,
At Miles Cross they maun bide."

Roth Bellyshaker came pushing through the listeners, bearing three flagons of ale. He stumbled but like an expert drunk didn't spill so much as a drop. Belching, he settled down beside Gorian and Grudnew, face flushed with more than just pride. The man had already drunk his fill, and without doubt would drink it twice more again before the night was done. Loosing another belch, he offered them a flagon each.

"To the lads," Bellyshaker said by way of a toast, and downed a frothy mouthful of ale.

"To the lads," Grudnew echoed. The king drank deeply, wiping the creamy foam from his mouth.

"Aye, to Cullen and Sláine," Gorian said, tipping his own flagon back and draining it. He smacked his lips appreciatively. "Good stuff this. Rioch knows his brew, that's the honest truth."

"It is, indeed," Bellyshaker grinned, "an' I should know, I've sampled enough of it over the years, if you get my meaning?"

"Oh, we do. We do," the warlord assured him.

"Them boys will do you proud," Bellyshaker said, shuffling around on his backside to look at Sláine and Cullen over by the fire. It made a change not to see them at each other's throats.

They were as thick as thieves – up to no good no doubt. He knew exactly what scheme he would have been hatching in their place, having just become men and all. There were more than a few bonny lasses in Murias, very easy on the eye.

"I am quite sure they will."

"Aye, they're the future, right. Headstrong, passionate, reckless, and still young enough to care about it all. I remember being like that. Now what have we got eh?

I dunno about you, but I've seen too much to want to stay sober most days."

"We were just talking about the same thing," Grudnew said wryly. He laid a hand on his warlord's shoulder. "Gorian was reminding me of the many times I, ahh, took a shine to one of his lady friends."

"You always were a randy little whoreson," Bellyshaker laughed. "Those were the days, eh, my friends? Back when we were young and stupid and ready to take on the world."

"I was a spirited youth with a weakness for a pretty girl," the king grinned. "There's no crime in that."

It was Cullen's idea that they blood themselves together.

It was a rite of passage. It would set them apart from the others.

They were men now after all, warriors of the Red Branch. So what if they had never raised an axe or sword in anger? It didn't matter. They ought to live like men if they were expected to die like them. They spat in their palms to seal the bargain with a handshake and set off before either of them could change their mind.

They were men in all ways but one and that could easily be remedied with enough coin. That was the gift of the moon. In one day they had gone from children to fully-grown men in the eyes of the tribe.

They slipped away from the celebration.

"You got a coin for Brighid?"

Brighid was a daughter of the Goddess. She served the aspect of the Maiden in the Temple of Danu. She tended to the needs of the men of the Sessair with skill and, blessedly, without the attachment of love. A silver coin bought her companionship for the night so that the men could offer their devotion to Danu, the Earth Mother by sinking into her warmth. It was hardly a king's ransom for her gift, and judging by the faces of the men after they had given devotion she was gifted.

Brighid's hut was on the outskirts of the village, removed from the prying eyes of the wives of the Sessair. Any closer would have been bad for worship.

They chose Brighid because she was comely but not in an intimidating way. There were other daughters of the Goddess so pretty that a single look could stop a man's heart. Brighid was older, and they hoped kinder. Neither wanted to be humiliated for a second time that day.

The music of Feis Samain was distant, a haunting melody in the dark night. It wrapped itself around them, a familiar thing in these unfamiliar moments.

Sláine was nervous but he wasn't about to let on about it to Wide Mouth. He felt his heart hammering against his breastbone as he knocked on the door of her hovel.

Brighid answered the door before he had time for second thoughts.

"Ah, two beautiful young boys come to see old Brighid, eh?"

"I… we."

"Now don't be shy boys," the Daughter of Danu said with a gentle smile. "We're all friends here, right? You looking for a little companionship?"

"We've come to offer devotions to the Goddess," Wide Mouth said earnestly, stepping forward and bowing.

"Well that's mighty good of you boys."

"We aren't boys anymore, ma'am. Today's our coming of age," Sláine said, feeling awkward and clumsy as he spoke. He wished he'd taken a leaf out of Bellyshaker's book and gotten himself well and truly drunk before coming to pay his devotions.

Brighid looked the pair of them up and down. "And you want to become men in the only way that counts, am I right? So who's first? Or are both of you strapping lads wanting to do this together?" She laughed, seeing how utterly horrified they both looked at the notion. "Well I guess you better work it out between yourselves, my big strong boys. Come to me with your coin when you're ready. I'll be waiting with a smile and welcoming arms." She reached out and touched Sláine's cheek, fingers lingering tenderly. "You are such a beautiful, beautiful boy," Brighid said wistfully, withdrawing into her hovel.

"I'm first," Cullen said, even before the door was closed. Old angers ghosted behind his eyes.

"Why'd you imagine that?" Sláine said, standing between Cullen and the Daughter of Danu's painted door. He crossed his arms.

"By right of victory," Cullen said. "I won the ballgame and I was the first to take the Red Branch. You can't deny that you were beaten both times, Mac Roth. It's only right I claim the right to bed her first."

"I don't think so," Sláine said slowly, testing the limits of their uneasy friendship. "We were children then, now we are men. Nothing separates us as men. We need a fresh challenge."

"The hell we do, I won fair and square and you know it."

"If you can pass me you can go in," Sláine said, dropping into a crouch.

"Don't make me hurt you, Sláine."

"Wouldn't dream of it. Hmmm… Maybe I can fix your nose this time," Sláine said, grinning even as Cullen launched himself at him.

Sláine took a half step forwards and dropped his right shoulder, stepping into Wide Mouth's charge. The move up-ended him. Sláine wrapped his arms around Wide Mouth's waist and lifted him bodily off the floor. He finished by dumping Cullen unceremoniously on his backside in the dirt.

He opened the door and stepped through. Brighid lay on a bed of furs, tallow candles burning a sweet scent that left him feeling a little dizzy after only a few breaths. Her chemise of white lace was held in place by a pewter pin in the shape of a butterfly. He closed the door behind him and slid the bolt into place.

"Ah, my beautiful boy, come to me, my sweet." She patted the skin beside her. "There is so much for you to learn but we have all night."

He sat beside her, all embarrassment gone as her hands touched him. She unclasped the butterfly and the front of her chemise fell away, leaving her naked to the waist. Sláine stared. Brighid smiled; it was a haunting expression on her pale skin. She pulled his jerkin over his head and drew him closer into an embrace. Her hand set against the flat of his chest, Sláine felt the beat of his heart as it quickened.

"What do I–?"

"Hush now, my beautiful one, let our flesh talk. Let our bodies find their own language." She took his hand in hers and laid it gently on her breast. Sláine felt his breath catch in his throat as he thrilled to the touch. Her skin was perfect, although not smooth, far from it. It was made up of thousands of tiny creases, each one earned and owned by life lived to the full. He cupped her with both hands, losing himself in the sheer swell of sensation. Her red curls fell down across her face. She moved to brush them away but he stopped her. He wanted to see her like this, like lovers do. "I have such delights to show you," she whispered. "You are favoured of the Goddess, Sláine Mac Roth, but you should know that she collects beautiful things." She squeezed his hand. He felt her flesh stiffening against his touch.

Brighid leaned forwards and kissed him, her mouth closing over hers, and he lost all sense of self. As they moved, touched and kissed, he was unable to tell where he ended and she began, such was Brighid's skill.

"Let me make a man of you," she breathed.

And he gave himself to her completely.

Four
Pranks

SAMAIN MIGHT HAVE signified their ascent into manhood but they were not so grown up that they didn't take delight in pranks. Indeed, their apprenticeships opened a whole new world of possibilities for their jokes, and those new possibilities in turn brought more delight.

The old druid, Cathbad, was the butt of their first and most elaborate charade.

It was a simple lie and its success or failure depended very much upon the integrity of the druid. An honest man would walk away untouched but a liar would find himself humbled.

To honour his reign, King Grudnew had ordered the construction of a new Great Hall, almost twice the size of the current roundhouse. It was a sign of prosperity, a very visible message that could be passed from village to village – Murias thrived beneath Grudnew.

Twenty good men had been digging out the foundations for over a week. It was back-breaking work. From dawn to dusk they shovelled earth and clay, banking the waste high while the children wheeled it away in barrows. It was the sight of all that clay that gave Dian the bright idea of hiding some "ancient treasures" in the unbroken ground. He could imagine the salivating Cathbad declaring the find a great discovery even as he proceeded to translate the gibberish the boys had painted onto the "old" tablets. No doubt it would be some great wisdom that only he had the knowledge to fathom.

"Do you think he'll fall for it?"

"The pompous old fool wouldn't dream of admitting he doesn't understand something," Dian assured them. "He'll proclaim them works of antiquity, no doubt hidden there by followers of the Carnun, Horned God, and promise to unlock their secrets and we'll all get to have a good laugh at his expense."

"Nice," Cullen said approvingly. Anything even vaguely humiliating always received Wide Mouth's seal of approval.

Dian had been learning his letters for several months and had a passing fair knowledge of Ogham script. Enough, certainly, to convincingly forge a few shards of wisdom.

Cormac, Niall, Cullen, Fionn, Sláine and Núada laboured painstakingly over the actual painting of the stones, trying to replicate perfectly the scratchings that Dian had made in the dirt. Dian's own images were more elaborate, quite stunning representations of the Horned God himself and images of some wild hunt where the beasts had risen up to chase the men from their forests. The imagery was all very deliberate. He hoped that Cathbad would leap to a certain set of conclusions.

"They're close enough they might be letters but they aren't any letters old Cathbad will have seen before."

"So whatever he says is a lie?"

"Whatever he says is a lie," Dian agreed.

The friends waited for cover of night before they crept down to the building site. The clay tablets were heavier than any of them had expected them to be. They scrambled down into the pit, digging away as quickly and quietly as they could and hiding the various fake relics across the length and breadth of the site. With the moon waxing, they re-covered the tablets and crept back to their beds to sleep out what remained of the night.

Sláine returned to Brighid's bed to take a new lesson in the skill of giving devotion. There was so much he had to learn of the ways of the flesh and, for a coin, she was a willing teacher.

"You'll make a good husband and a skilful lover," the Daughter of Danu whispered in his ear as he slipped into sleep. It was all pillow talk but it was pleasing to hear. He had never thought of himself as being someone's husband but the time would come, he knew, when he had to make a choice from the girls of the tribe. Who would it be? He had no idea. Eabha had a pretty face, but wore her fat a little too comfortably for his tastes. Eilis on the other hand had the taut form of a hunter, her muscles as hard as her face. Isibeal always smiled when she saw him and Keeva blushed whenever he came within ten paces of her, but none of them set a fire blazing in his heart. None of them made his blood sing; not the way Brighid's touch did. He fell into a dreamless sleep, savouring the feel of her hand on his bare chest.

He woke twice in the night. The first time he thought he heard voices, women talking softly. The second time he saw Brighid on her elbow looking down at him. She smiled and kissed his lips.

"Sleep, my beautiful boy," she whispered.

And he did.

For two days the young men went about their duties, desperate for their forged wisdom to be discovered, but either the diggers passed over their finds without taking a blind bit of notice or they were digging in the wrong place.

On the second morning, Tall Iesin left Murias, taking Fionn with him. He promised to be back for Beltain with new stories gathered from the furthest corners of the Tir-Nan-Og especially for the boys. They gathered at dawn to wave Fionn off. He looked so small as he shouldered his pack and set off with Iesin, but then the balladeer made dwarfs of giants with his lanky frame. Fionn was almost running as he hustled to keep up with his master. It was an odd feeling watching their friend leave. They had never been apart before. Sláine found himself wondering if they would actually recognise their friend when – if – he ever returned. Things, he knew, would never be the same between them again. Where there had always been seven, now there were six. It felt as if a part of his life had been torn away and that he was never going to see it again.

He didn't know how to cope with what he was feeling, so like any man he threw himself into his work and simply ignored it.

Fionn's departure was the first sign that they really were men now – or if not men, at least they were no longer children.

On the third day the cry went up for Cathbad to come, quickly. The town was abuzz with rumours in a matter of minutes. Something had been found at the new site but no one knew exactly what. The old druid grumbled as he emerged from the nemeton, his face set like thunder. Dian followed a step behind him doing well to keep the smile from his face when they passed Sláine and Cullen standing on the corner by Rioch's inn. Wide Mouth pulled a face. Sláine turned his back on the pair of them, he was laughing so hard. Cathbad's sour humour soon changed as he saw the clay tablets the workmen had unearthed. Three were crude, nothing more than scratchings of something not dissimilar to Ogham script, but the fourth was a work of art. He licked his lips appreciatively and demanded it be carried with haste and reverence to the nemeton where he might peruse it in peace. Cathbad turned his attention to the cruder tablets. He clucked and tutted, and hemmed and hawed over the possible meanings of the letters. Grudnew came, followed by Gorian. Sláine and Cullen of the Wide Mouth followed five paces behind the warlord.

"What is it, man?" the king demanded, hunching over the tablets.

"The voices of the damned, sire," Cathbad breathed. "From the past, come to share their secrets with us."

It was almost too perfect.

"Are you sure?" Grudnew asked sceptically.

"I do not question you on matters of kingship, sire. I do not expect to be questioned in matters of the spirit. When my fingers brushed the tablet I caught a trace of the author's anguished cry. His words, recorded here, are of great import, recorded in haste as all around him crumbled to dust."

"Fascinating," Gorian said, "and you can actually read his words?"

The druid twisted his birdlike body and craned his neck around to look up at the warlord, thinly veiled hostility in his ancient eyes. "I can, warrior. Can you?"

"Perhaps you will share their wisdom then?"

"No," Cathbad said sharply. "The knowledge is for the king's ears only." He tapped a grimy fingernail at one of the spidery symbols. "See this mark here? It is a portent, and this one beside it bears the king's name. Now do not question me again, warrior. There is more to this world than your philosophy allows for. Steel is no match for stone, and stone is of the earth, of the body of fair Danu herself."

"You talk a lot of rot, old man," Gorian said, shaking his head.

"Hold your tongue, warrior!" the Druid spat, lurching up from his crouch.

Grudnew laid a restraining hand on his friend's shoulder. "I would hear these words, my friend."

"Then you are a bigger fool than I took you for," Gorian muttered in disgust.

"Do not overstep yourself, Gorian. Now, druid, perhaps we should find somewhere more private?"

Rubbing his hands with undisguised glee, the druid nodded. "Yes, yes, yes, my king. To the nemeton, there I have another treasure from Danu's belly to show you. Together with these tablets it sheds much light upon the trials our tribe will face over the coming years. It is truly a gift from the Goddess, sire."

Grudnew raised an eyebrow curiously. "Then the sooner we see these wonders, the better."

"Yes, yes, yes, sire. The sooner we see them the better."

"No," Grudnew said, "not we as in you and I, druid; we as in the warlord and I."

"But—"

"Mark me well, druid. Any observation on a threat to the wellbeing of the Sessair is for Gorian's ears. He, every bit as much as I, stands as protector of our people."

"But these words are from your wife, the Goddess herself. They are not for his ears any more than a midnight promise between lovers is for a stranger's."

"I'll brook no argument from you, druid. Now, lead the way. Time is wasting and I am eager to hear your words."

"Perhaps you aren't such a fool after all," Gorian said as they followed the crook-backed druid to his holy house. "Sláine, Cullen, stay here."

"But we—" Wide Mouth stopped mid-objection as Sláine elbowed him in the side. "Yes, master. Right here."

"You're learning, lad," Gorian said, disappearing into the nemeton behind Grudnew and the Druid.

"Not fair," Cullen grumbled sourly as the door closed, shutting them out. "Dian's in there. He gets to see it all."

"And he gets to tell us all about it," Sláine said.

"Well there is that." Wide Mouth sat down with his back against the wall of the nemeton and began plucking stems of grass from the dirt and rolling them between his fingers. When Cullen found a blade he liked he gripped it in both hands between thumb and forefinger, and blew, transforming the simple grass into a high-pitched whistle. He grinned up at Sláine.

A few minutes later they heard uproarious laughter followed by a foul-mouthed rant and then more laughter.

The door slammed open and Dian came charging through it, laughing uncontrollably even as he hurdled the low fence surrounding the nemeton.

"Do you reckon they found Dian's signature on the picture?" Cullen asked, getting up and dusting his hands off on his breeches.

They watched Dian disappear down the lane.

"Looks like it, doesn't it?" Sláine's grin was infectious. He slapped Wide Mouth on the back. "Come on, best make ourselves scarce. I bet old Cathbad's none too happy."

"I can't wait to hear what future he predicted for the king."

"Then we better catch up with Dian."

Word of the druid's humiliation spread quickly through the town. Cathbad was feared but he wasn't liked. Anything that brought him down a peg or two was welcomed by most of the inhabitants of Murias. Their stunt hadn't just undermined the pompous old druid, it had seriously humiliated him.

Cathbad wasn't the only one to be on the receiving end of one of their pranks. A few nights later it was Rioch's turn. Núada made sure the side door was open so that when the other boys drove one of Piaras's cows down from the pasture they were able to lure it inside the inn and coax it up onto the second floor. They set a small plate of honey on the landing and crept out.

Come morning Rioch's howls of frustration rattled the inn's windows.

No matter what he tried the animal wouldn't go down the stairs. He tried sweet smells, driving it with a board, pushing it, kicking it and screaming in its face. The cow just settled down on the landing and looked up at the innkeeper with a baleful stare.

It took eight Red Branch warriors to get the frightened cow back down the stairs, along with Piaras muttering about how the dumb animals will go up stairs but they won't come down again, because of their weight and how they might fall.

Piaras himself was the butt of another joke less than a week later, when he woke to find that his entire herd had been dyed blue with woad.

Breaking into Grudnew's roundhouse was Dian's revenge for the trouble the others had gotten him into with Cathbad.

"Fair's fair," he said, grinning as he held up a sprig of poison oak. "In and out. All you have to do is rub the poison oak inside the king's loincloth and he'll be scratching like a pox-ridden doxie for weeks. So, who's game? Cullen?"

Wide Mouth shook his head. "Uh hunh, no bleedin' way. I may be ugly but I'm not stupid."

"Ugly and a coward," Sláine said. "Give me the poison oak. I'll be back before sundown."

"You're mad!" Núada said, more than a hint of envy in his voice. There was an edge of recklessness about Sláine that the others admired even though, more often than not, it was that recklessness that landed him in the most trouble.

He wrapped the poison oak up in a small oilskin and stuffed it inside breeches, careful that none of the flowers were loose. The last thing he wanted was to be itching for a week.

The trick was to make it look as if he belonged there. If he acted suspiciously Grudnew's guards would become suspicious. He walked along the banks of the River Dôn looking for a good place to ford it. There was only one place that was safe to cross. That was where he had crossed the river in the first place. His plan had been to swim to the far side, skirt along the treeline and come into Grudnew's roundhouse from the back, out of sight of the guards. It was a simple enough plan but simple or not he had already found one rather considerable flaw in its logic.

The River Dôn was fast flowing and deep enough to be difficult to negotiate, even for a strong swimmer. And it wasn't just a river – it was an entire landscape of stagnant pools, shingle and rocks waiting to break the flesh of those stupid enough to try and cross, pebbles that massed to from beaches, and sand that banked up against the meanders. The Dôn itself snaked down through the dark heart of this water world, a white water rush.

The only good fording place was too far away to allow him to sneak up unseen by Grudnew's guards and on this side of the river he had no cover. So he had no choice, he would have to risk the deep water and that required precautions if he didn't want to be swept away and broken on those angry rocks that jutted out of the Dôn like the teeth of some vast sea monster.

Sláine moved deeper into the trees, out of sight of prying eyes while he foraged for things that might somehow help him cross to the other side. For the first few hundred paces he moved along parallel to the water's edge but he couldn't find what he was looking for so he was forced to move deeper into the woods, away from the trail. Branches hung down low, snagging at his clothes and hair as he pushed through them. He pushed on. The white water rush of the river faded as he moved further into the forest. Then he found it: a huge tree trunk smothered in moss and wrapped in thick creepers.

He silently thanked Danu and unravelled the thick vine from where it clung to the tree trunk. He coiled it up, slung it over his shoulder and headed back towards the water.

It took him another ten minutes to find a boulder big enough to anchor him without weighing him down as he battled the current of the Dôn. He made a cradle out of the vine and fastened it around the boulder, tying the loose end around his waist.

The shallows along the riverbank were low enough for him to splash along in without risking being caught unawares and swept away. It widened as he followed its curve, but the curve itself served to slow the current. He found the perfect spot, masked by the far bank and the roundhouse itself, and plunged away from the shingle into the swirling water. The shock of cold was fierce. He gritted his teeth and sank lower, until the icy water washed up around his shoulders.

Five paces in, he was glad of the boulder.

For all his preparation, Sláine had underestimated the river's power – it lifted him bodily and carried him twenty floundering paces sideways. Without the boulder's weight to drag him down he would have been carried away. As it was Sláine scrambled around, splashing up great plumes of water until he got his feet under him. An entire tree had been uprooted, stripped clean and washed downstream during a flood. The branches broke up the water, forming rapids.

Sláine plunged forwards again, the white water cuffing him around the ears. The surge and splash were deafening. For a full five seconds he was completely under. He surged up to the surface, sucking down huge mouthfuls of air. He forced himself deeper into the river until he felt the shelf beneath his feet begin to creep upwards again. He risked fighting to get his head well up above the waterline just long enough to be sure he was passed the middle. The sooner he was out of the river the happier he would be.

He pushed on.

In six paces the water was around his waist and he was coming out on the other side. His feet sank into the shingle as he struggled out of the water.

He clambered up onto the bank and collapsed onto his back, gasping as the sun dried him off. He didn't move as a mosquito landed on his arm and began to feed greedily, sucking the blood out of him. He let the insect have its fill and watched it fly off drunkenly.

Sláine dragged himself onto his stomach and forced himself to stand.

The river had pummelled him. Every muscle ached. Every ache was driven in bone deep, but he was on the other side.

He fumbled with the knot of vine around his waist, picking it loose. He let it fall and crept up behind the roundhouse until his face was pressed up against the daubing on the wattle wall.

He couldn't risk going in around the front so he was going to have to pry open the shutter and squeeze through. Sláine pulled the long-handled hunting knife from the sheath in his boot and worked it into the crack where the shutter joined the frame until he found – and cut through – the catch securing it.

Grinning, he popped the shutter open and squirmed through, dropping awkwardly into the king's round-house.

He was in the bedroom.

It wasn't dark, as he had expected it to be. Candles burned. A tapestry was half-woven on a loom. The shuttle was dangling on the thread, still spinning.

Grudnew's huge cot was piled high with animal skins and pillows of down. It was big enough to sleep a family of six. A curtain at the far side of the room was drawn over the king's changing room. Sláine pushed back the curtain and slipped inside. It took him a few minutes to find the chest containing Grudnew's various loincloths, and a few moments more to smear the poison oak inside the materialcups. The poison oak disintegrated in his fingers. He closed the chest and slipped out of the changing room.

He walked over to the loom. The shuttle had stopped spinning. That was the first thing that he noticed. He didn't move. He breathed deeply. His nostrils flared as he caught the faintest musk of perfume.

Sláine let his fingers linger on the loom and turned slowly. That was when he saw her, cowering in the corner. At first he thought she was one of the Sidhe, a fey spirit slipped through from the Otherworld. Her skin was pale; white where it should have been tanned from the wind and sun. Her hair was dark, black where the shadows of the candlelight failed to lighten it.

He stared, dumbstruck and slack-jawed.

She was a thing of beauty.

No, beyond beauty – she was a thing of heaven, proof of the Goddess's hand in the perfection of creation.

She looked at him with wide frightened eyes.

Sláine stared. It wasn't often you met divinity without dying first – although he had come mighty close to that in the river.

He held out his hand to her.

She shook her head and pushed back against the wall as if hoping to disappear into it.

She was a new day rising. She was a perfect clear blue summer sky. She was the pinpoint silver of the stars at night. She was the first flower of spring. She was the last leaf of autumn. She was the savage sea and the towering cliff. She was raw heart-stopping beauty.

"My name is Sláine Mac Roth," he said, hoping that it might coax beauty into talking. She shook her head again, her hair falling in front of her face. He stared at her lips as they parted slightly with her frightened breath. He wanted to kiss those lips. He wanted to kneel down at her feet and worship. He wanted to offer her all the devotions her body deserved.

He knelt and tried to take her hand, but she opened her mouth to scream and he backed off with his hands raised, palms out, trying to show her he meant no harm.

"I'll go," he promised. "Just please, don't breathe a word. Don't tell a soul I was in here. They could hang me for this." As soon as he said it he regretted giving beauty his name for surely she would betray him to the king. "Sorry. Sorry. I just–" but he didn't know what he wanted to say. He couldn't find the words to express the confused mess of feelings surging around inside him.

He edged back to the wall, hands in front of him all the way, turned and scrambled back out through the window. He landed with a thump, rolled and came back up to his feet. Without thinking about it, he pushed open the shutter and leaned back through. She was standing by the loom, the shuttle in her hand. Her azure eyes met his and he fancied he saw the ache in them even from here. "You have placed a claim on my heart, beauty," he said, flashing her a dangerous grin.

"No," she said, coming over to the window. "It cannot be."

With that she closed the shutter, barring it behind him.

There was no point calling out to her – any noise would only attract Grudnew's bodyguards. Sláine gazed at the shuttered window and smiled. She had talked to him. He kissed his hand and pressed it to the wooden shutter. "I'll be back," he promised, his voice barely a whisper. It didn't matter that beauty wouldn't hear his words; she could surely hear his heart.

He crept cautiously up to the curve of the round-house and peered around it. There were two guards but their attention was turned towards Murias. All he had to do was skirt the compound and come out a little further down the road and no one would be any the wiser. With one last backwards glance he dropped down into the gulley that ran alongside the river and shuffled forwards in an awkward crouch until he was far enough away to be safe.

He didn't return to the others. With night coming he went in search of Brighid, almost banging her door down. The fear was bright on her face as she opened the door. In a single breath the Daughter of Danu relaxed and opened her arms to him. "Oh my beautiful boy, what's wrong?" She kissed him tenderly as he fell into her embrace.

"I... I..." But he couldn't tell her. Instead, that night, as he offered his devotions to the Goddess it wasn't

Brighid's face he saw beneath him as he buried himself in the warm flesh of the Earth Mother, it was Beauty's.

Even when he closed his eyes.

"What's wrong?" Brighid asked again, hours later.

It was too dark for him to see her face.

"Hold me," he said after a while.

They lay in silence until he found the courage to talk.

"I saw the Goddess today," he whispered, barely daring to give voice to the words.

"You did?" Brighid said, smoothing his hair back from his brow. "Tell me about it. I would hear all about my mistress."

"It was Dian's fault."

"Ah, isn't it always?"

"I crept into Grudnew's roundhouse, to smear poison oak in his loincloths." Brighid laughed. He liked the way she laughed. She laughed with all of her body.

"Oh my."

"She was in there. She was beautiful, Brighid. No, not beautiful. That's the wrong word. She was different. She was unlike anyone I have ever seen, but you know that, surely? You have seen the Goddess."

"Oh my sweet beautiful Sláine, that wasn't the Goddess. That was Niamh," Brighid said, the amusement gone from her voice. The darkness couldn't hide her sadness as she spoke.

"Heaven?" Sláine asked, misunderstanding. Niamh was the old world for heaven.

"Grudnew's chosen bride. She was raised by women in Rath Grainne, I think, and brought to camp not three moons since. No man has ever seen her. No man will until she is wed to the king. There is to be a huge ceremony."

"I have seen her," Sláine said simply.

"And you must never see her again, my beautiful boy. To do so can only bring you pain. Promise me, you will never see her again." She leaned over him. "Promise me, Sláine."

He made the promise, but like so many midnight promises shared between lovers it was made to be broken.

Five
Warrior's Dawn

I<small>T WAS</small> D<small>IAN</small>'s idea to repeat the poison oak gag on an unsuspecting Cullen, smearing the prickly herb inside his breeches while he slept and then delighting in Wide Mouth's discomfort as he itched and scratched his way through the best part of the day.

Sláine made the mistake of laughing as Cullen rooted around in his crotch trying to ease the poison oak's sting.

"You're hopping around like a whore in heat, Wide Mouth. You got some little love bug you didn't think of mentioning when you were getting deloused by the druids last week?"

"Shut up, Sláine. I know it was you. I'll make you pay for this you miserable sack of shit. You mark my words."

"Trembling in my boots."

Today was the day their training began in earnest. The past few months since having taken the Red Branch had been spent on exercises aimed at working on general fitness and stamina. Gorian drove them hard, pushing the boys beyond the limits of endurance to the point where mind and body wanted nothing more than to break. Then still he goaded them into doing more.

The drills were repetitive, running, lifting, carrying, running, lifting, pushing, pulling, carrying and running some more.

Over and over and over again.

From sun up every day for the last week they had laboured on the new roundhouse, building muscle by lifting huge blocks of stone and carrying them into place for the masons to lay into the complicated mesh they were constructing. The physical labour was a welcome change from the endless running.

It was all about turning the soft flesh of youth into the iron muscles of a fighter. They hadn't lifted a weapon since being sworn into the warrior's sect.

"Just shut up." Something in the way he said it made Sláine do just that.

It had been raining the night before. The soil was still damp underfoot.

Murdo, Gorian's youngest brother strode towards them carrying three tathlum.

Sláine walked away to a tear in the ground where the clay was exposed, wet his hands on the damp grass and scooped out a handful of red clay. He worked the clay into a paste and smeared it into his hair, working it up into red spikes.

"You look like a fool!" Cullen sneered, but that didn't prevent him from walking over to the same tear and spiking his own hair with red clay.

"You boys look like real Red Branchers now," Murdo said, kindly. "Just like your father's in the grip of a mighty warp-spasm."

"Not that Bellyshaker ever had a spasm that wasn't brought on by the beer," Wide Mouth muttered.

"Enough of that, Wide Mouth," Murdo said, tossing the young warrior one of the three tathlum. He handed the second to Sláine. Each tathlum consisted of two balls joined by a leather tie. "You know what these are made of?"

"Stone," Sláine said, stating what he thought was the obvious.

"No," Murdo said. "Brains mixed with blood and lime to make 'em set hard. We favour the brains of our enemies."

"Better than our own brains," Cullen agreed.

"Now then, see that tree over there?" The offending oak was more than sixty feet away. "Watch and learn, boys. Watch and learn." Murdo whipped the tathlum around in a vicious arc above his head, once, twice, and on the third pass loosed it. The hardened brain balls spun through the air, seeming to chase each other as they flew, tangling around the tree. "Now you do it."

It was easier said than done. Cullen tangled his tathlum around his arm and nearly knocked himself senseless as the lime-hardened brain ball slammed back into the side of his head.

"You're meant to let go of the damned thing," Murdo said, shaking his head.

Sláine's first effort wasn't much more successful. It whistled out of his hand and flew straight for Murdo's head. Murdo was standing twenty paces behind Sláine at the time. Cullen howled his delight as Murdo was forced to hurl himself out of the way of Sláine's wild throw.

The morning progressed with more of the same.

Sláine was the first to hit the tree, and a throw later he succeeded in wrapped the tathlum fully around its bole.

The afternoon was spent working on the various feats Murdo demonstrated. The warrior was incredible to watch as he launched himself into the Salmon Feat, leaping more than his own height, straight up, from a standing start. He had Cullen join him to demonstrate the Shield Feat. Wide Mouth braced himself, holding the huge shield as if it might bite him, while Murdo launched himself under the shield's rim, kicking up so that the protection was nullified. As the shield flew upwards Murdo leapt, catching it so that he could use its protection as he delivered a deathblow to Cullen.

Sláine applauded Wide Mouth's death.

"Think you could do better?" Cullen grumbled, nursing a bruise from Murdo's practice sword.

"No doubt," Sláine mocked. "Give me your shield and we'll see, shall we?"

Murdo came at Sláine, and even knowing what the warrior intended it was impossible to stop him from knocking the wind out of him as he hammered down on the upraised shield.

"Not so full of yourself now, are you?" Cullen sneered, his anger festering. Sláine knew Wide Mouth well enough to know he should have ceased with the constant jibes, but he was angry with himself for constantly failing Murdo's challenges and he couldn't help himself. He had to take his frustration out somewhere, and Cullen was convenient. Sláine wasn't used to always coming up short when challenged. It wasn't a feeling he enjoyed, and it certainly wasn't one he wanted to become familiar with.

★ ★ ★

Most of the next few days went much the same way, with Cullen failing and growing increasingly frustrated with Murdo's urging him to be more like Sláine, to try to match Sláine, to watch how Sláine mastered his body. His ears burned with the word: Sláine, Sláine, Sláine, Sláine, Sláine.

It didn't matter what he did, Murdo always saw something better in Sláine's effort.

It galled him.

He failed repeatedly when forced to attempt the Chariot Feat, stumbling as he ran along the chariot's yoke pole. Sláine, of course, succeeded at the second time of asking, his balance honed by the weeks of bending himself double to kiss Murdo's backside. Cullen hurt himself badly on the fifth fall. His trailing arm caught and stuck in the wheel arch and was broken in three places as the chariot rolled mercilessly onwards. Sláine had the gall to laugh, even as Murdo prised his hideously contorted arm out of the trap.

For two more weeks there was little he could do except work on his body form and balance, standing for hours at a time on first one leg and then the other, walking balance beams and shadow fighting. His arm was slow healing. Frustration ate away at him as he was forced to watch Sláine move further and further ahead of him.

Murdo taking Sláine aside to share with him the Spearrach Carden manoeuvres was the final straw. The spear had always been his chosen weapon. Spearrach Carden, or the thicket of spears, had all the grace and fluidity of a deadly dance. Exponents were highly skilled with the gáe bolga – a bellows spear with a serrated head of thirty barbs that had to be cut out of a victim. It was a brutal weapon, the most brutal of all the tools at the disposal of the Red Branch.

Mastery of the gáe bolga meant that the wielder could turn a single weapon into an apparent forest of spears, allowing the warrior to face down a huge force single-handedly. Such brute killing power was not the weapon's only grace. In the right hands it was incredibly accurate, and the barbs made it lethal more often than not.

"Sit," Murdo instructed. They did. "Now, I want you to think about this: when down, unarmed, what is a warrior to do but die? It's a rhetorical question, boys. The answer is fight back. A Red Branch warrior is never predictable in the lengths he will go to in battle. Victory is all. Go on, take the spear with your foot."

Cullen struggled to grip the shaft of the gáe bolga between his toes. He looked across as Sláine succeeded in not only lifting the spear but also in propelling it forward with ferocity. He snarled, his eyes narrowing to slits and lips curling back so far that his teeth jutted out like a row of jagged dolmen caving in on each other.

"Come on, Wide Mouth, you've got to be quicker than that or your enemy will gut you. Watch Sláine."

Watch Sláine. Watch Sláine. Precious fegging Sláine Mac Roth.

Even the name was enough to make his blood boil!

Couldn't they see that he was every bit as good as Sláine? If he hadn't mangled his arm… As it was, he was a laughing stock. He couldn't do anything right. He saw the others laughing at him when they thought he wasn't looking, and it was Sláine's fault.

It was all Sláine's fault.

He did it without thinking.

He saw Sláine moving off, following Murdo. His back was turned.

Cullen picked up the gáe bolga from the floor with his good hand and stared down the barbed tip at Sláine's retreating back. He was unarmed, but that didn't matter. It would be an accident, an unfortunate accident. Sláine would be gone from his life and he'd never have to hear Murdo or anyone else saying: "Why can't you be more like Sláine, Cullen?"

He took three steps and threw, hurling the barbed spear at Sláine's back, and he knew, even as it left his hand, that his aim was true.

He heard it rather than saw it.

The barbs of the gáe bolga gave the weapon a distinctive whistling sound as it flew.

Without thinking, Sláine turned to see what was happening and that slight movement was enough to save his life. The head of the spear tore into his arm, scraping past the bone and out the other side in a spray of blood. A searing wave of agony ripped through him. He staggered back, clutching at the shaft of the gáe bolga with trembling hands. His vision swam, the horizon canting dangerously away from him as his balance betrayed him to the pain. He lurched sideways, the movement jarring the teeth of the spear and tearing a scream from his mouth. He couldn't think for the fire in his body. He stumbled three paces back, feeling his legs buckle beneath him.

Even as he began to fold, he felt it touch his blood: Danu's fire, earth power, the berserker rage. It bubbled up inside him, and he embraced it.

When he looked up Cullen was running at him with an iron sword brandished above his head.

He had no weapon.

Unless…

Gritting his teeth, Sláine tore the gáe bolga from his arm, each barb slicing through his muscle and tendon, and grating down the bone of his arm. His scream was terrible. Blood fountained from the ragged wound in a huge arterial spray. He embraced the pain and used it to feed his anger.

Cullen's face loomed huge and ugly in front of him, grinning stupidly as Wide Mouth hurled himself forwards in a poorly executed salmon leap.

"I'll bury my blade in your guts," Wide Mouth raged, all sensibility fleeing beneath the eagerness of loathing. He lunged, and when the sword's tip lanced wide of the mark, he swung it around and around as if hoping to decapitate Sláine with one of the wild blows. Sláine ducked under the erratic swings, struggling to staunch the bloody wound with his fingers. His blood – lots of it – leaked between them.

Feeling the life bleed out of him, Sláine surrendered completely to Danu's fire and felt it warp through his entire body, like lightning surging up out of the earth herself. The pain was excruciating but quite unlike the agony of the wound. Every ounce of his flesh screamed as it twisted and distorted, deforming his body into monstrous proportions. The flesh around his wound overlapped, fusing with the fierce heat of the earth's power, the blood sizzling and hissing as it evaporated against his bulging skin. As every muscle screamed and every hair stood erect, Sláine became one with the power spasming through his body. He roared, a deep, vast, primal scream that echoed all the way back to the centre of Murias, and charged Cullen of the Wide Mouth.

He heard the coward's screams but couldn't understand his words.

"Danu's blood, he's warped." That was Murdo's voice cutting across Cullen's screams for – for what? Mercy? There would be none of that on the field today!

"Freak! Cut me down and my entire family will see you strung up from the centre of the town square, your guts out to feed the crows," Cullen blustered, back-peddling. He held the sword out like some kind of talisman as if it might somehow protect him from the warped one's rage just by simply being there between them.

Sláine batted it aside as if it was nothing more threatening than a buzzing gnat.

"My father will avenge his son," Cullen half-pleaded, half-threatened.

"He isn't losing a son, Wide Mouth, or at least he won't be when I have finished cutting you. He'll be losing a daughter." The words came out of him in a rush, charged with the raw rage of Danu's eternal fire drawn deep from the Earth Mother's molten core.

He felt the muscles straining beneath his skin, felt his skeleton stretch and twist, the bones elongating and warping even as he lunged forwards.

"Now, you die, Wide Mouth."

Rejoicing in the battle heat, Sláine rammed the tip of the gáe bolga into Cullen's stomach and twisted it so that the barbs cut deep, anchoring themselves in the loops of his gut. Cullen's eyes flared as wide as his mouth ever had, shock and pain registering in them as Sláine yanked the gáe bolga back out of him. The barbs hooked up the slippery grey ropes of gut and dragged them out of the gaping hole in Wide Mouth's stomach.

Grinning manically, Sláine rammed the spear back into Cullen's guts, angling it upwards, killing him even as he clawed desperately at the hole in his body and the loops of intestine spilling out. In a rage, Sláine worked the gáe bolga back and forth so that the spear's teeth bit and tore at Wide Mouth's lungs, his liver and finally his heart, and then he pulled it free of the corpse.

Savage glee sang in his blood.

Sláine threw Cullen's body away like a bairn tired of its rag doll. He stood over the broken corpse. Death wasn't enough. The power in his blood cried out for more. It demanded sating. He tossed his head back and roared again, beating his clenched fists off his chest.

Conn of a Hundred Battles saw his boy's slaughter from across the training field.

He stumbled and fell to his knees, the grief overwhelming as he saw Cullen's broken body spin away from the warped one. Murdo was too far away to help

him. Cullen was dead. That was the ultimate price for
stupidity. Conn had seen it all: seen his boy hurl the gáe
bolga at Sláine's back, seen him charge the unarmed
boy with a sword, and seen him cut down for his
treachery.

He deserved to die but that didn't mean there wasn't
a price to be exacted from Mac Roth.

There was.

Blood for blood; honour demanded nothing less.

He pushed himself to his feet, unstringing his sword,
and walked across the training field. How was he
going to tell Corinne that her blessed boy was worm
food? It would break her. Sláine's head would be no
consolation. Death begat death but it didn't appease. It
left an ache that was contagious. He couldn't think
about it; couldn't allow himself the luxury. His world
funnelled down to two things: his sword and Sláine
Mac Roth. There would be no mercy. Conn of a
Hundred Battles would have vengeance for his son.
He would scoop out the murderer's brain and use it to
make a tathlum. Warped warrior or not, Conn was no
innocent. He was a killer amongst the elite of the Sessair. Sláine would die, and all because of the stupidity
of his boy.

"He's mine, Murdo!" Conn bellowed as the trainer
sought to restrain his son's murderer.

"They'll be digging an extra-wide grave!" Sláine
raged, and came running at him, roaring wordless
sounds at the top of his lungs.

"You'll pay for his death," Conn promised, kissing his
blade as he readied himself to meet the charge.

A moment later the training field was swallowed by screams: screams of anger, screams of pain, screams of horror, screams of fear, and screams of agony fading into sighs of death.

The rage subsided but its ghost was slow to fade.

Sláine stood over the dead.

A detached part of his brain knew that he was responsible, that these lives had ended because of him, but that part seemed so far away, dislocated from him in a way he couldn't begin to explain.

There was blood on his hands. His arm hung limply at his side. Trying to move his arm sent a wave of nausea through him.

"What have I done?" he barely breathed the words.

He realised that Murdo was talking to him. He had no idea what the warrior was saying. It didn't matter, his voice was soothing.

Warriors gathered around him. A babble of voices demanded justice. Conn's kin argued for his head. Sláine felt his anger rising quickly. He knew that he could kill them all. It would not be too many.

Six
Prophecies of the Druid

Two Red Branch warriors dragged Sláine between them. Murdo walked in front of them.

The atmosphere in the town was tense.

Conn's kin were demanding their right to retribution and they wouldn't be satisfied until Sláine was pinned down on to the headsman's block and his skull was rattling around in the basket.

He was thrown at the feet of Grudnew.

Word spread quickly. Women came running from their homes, wringing hands on washcloths and pulling up skirts as they rushed, desperate not to miss a thing. Men marched down from the high fields and the plains of Airghialla. The druids came from the nemeton – all but Cathbad and Dian who were tasked with caring for the dead.

Grudnew waited in silence, his face impassive.

Sláine did not say a word.

When Conn's brother, Raif, read the charge they expected the youngster to beg for his life. He didn't. He didn't move. He didn't even look up.

Grudnew stared down at him.

"Well, lad, what do you have to say for yourself?"

"He's a warped one, sire. Got no control of himself. He killed my nephew and my brother, cut them down in cold blood."

"I wasn't talking to you, Raif of the Bloody Axe. Your time to speak will come." Grudnew surveyed the faces around him. "Would anyone speak for the boy?"

Murdo stepped forwards. "I would."

"Go on."

"As my eyes are my witness, Conn's lad, Cullen, betrayed his friend on the training field. I was too far away to prevent it. Cullen threw a gáe bolga at young Sláine's back and when it failed to bring him down, he hurled himself at an unarmed man with a sword."

"Is this the truth?" Grudnew asked Sláine – who still hadn't moved. He nodded slightly. "Go on, Murdo."

"The spear lodged in the lad's arm. He had no weapon save that so he tore it out of his own flesh and used the assassin's own tool to cut him down. It was a righteous killing, sire. The lad was defending himself. He did nothing to incite Wide Mouth's anger."

"Lies!" Raif snarled, coming forward. "He cut down the lad in cold blood! He's a monster touched by the warp! You saw it, Murdo! Why protect the beast? I'll whet my axe in his thick head and then you can feed his meat to the damned pigs for all I care!"

"Silence!" Grudnew bellowed, wheeling round on Raif. "You will talk when I tell you to, not before. Now, Murdo, finish your account."

"Not much more to tell, sire. Wide Mouth's father, Conn of a Hundred Battles came blustering up demanding his blood right, and again attacked the lad, forcing Sláine to defend himself or perish. He was in the blood rage when he dispatched Conn but it wasn't unjust."

Grudnew nodded thoughtfully. "Anyone else here see a different version of events? And before you open your mouth, Raif, I mean see as in with your own eyes." He waited but no one spoke up. "So this is how it is, both speakers claim the lad Sláine was in the grip of an almighty warp-spasm when he did the killing. That means the spirit of the Goddess was inside him and he was not in his own mind. Who am I to punish an act favoured by Danu herself? My beloved lady knows her own mind far better than I do, but I know well enough not to question her. This is my judgement: Sláine will face the tests of the druids. If he truly is favoured of Danu he shall walk away from the testing as a blooded warrior of the Red Branch and there will be no recriminations. Should he fail the druid's test, he dies. Do I make myself clear?"

"Abundantly," Raif of the Bloody Axe grumbled. "You are a coward, not a king. Calum would never have sheltered the murderer of an innocent man. He was better than that."

"Hold your tongue, Raif, before you say something you don't live long enough to regret. Your kin started this, but it ends here, now. Go against me and I'll have no qualms about cutting your tongue out and wearing it on my belt. Understood?"

"Understood," Raif sniffed, and then hawked up a wad of phlegm and spat into the dirt by Sláine's feet. He craned his head and rolled it around his neck slowly, cracking the bones in his neck. He turned his back and left.

Grudnew shook his head. Everything about that last little show promised that it was far from over. He was going to have to deal with Raif, and more likely than not, the rest of his nasty little clan.

"Up you get," the king said, not unkindly. He offered Sláine his hand and hauled the youngster to his feet. "Your fate's in Cathbad's hands, better hope he doesn't hold too much of a grudge after that prank you boys pulled with those supposedly ancient tablets. Could have been worse – you could have smeared his loin-cloths with poison oak."

Gobhan and Searlas pushed and prodded Sláine towards the Great Cairn.

Murdo walked behind them, talking quietly to himself.

The fact that the druid had chosen to try Sláine in the Great Cairn was ominous. Of all the places he could have selected, Cathbad had decided upon the most sacred place in all of Eiru – the place where the Goddess began her work of creation. To the unknowing eye it was little more than a grassy hillock with a huge cairn of flat stones stacked on its summit. A huge stone served as a door to the immense burial chamber beneath the hill, and there were whispers of other darker places in the deeps below the ancient crypt.

It was a place of power, a place worthy of fear.

The wound in Sláine's arm had opened up again and was bleeding freely by the time they had walked beyond the nemeton to the huge burial mound.

Cathbad stood beside the huge stone doorway, waiting for them. Several other druids gathered around him, ready to serve in Sláine's trial, including Dian. "The druids'll see to you, lad," Murdo said, inspecting the tear. White lines of fat surrounded the bare meat of his upper arm. "It ain't pretty but you might get lucky. All depends how good their healing skills are."

Sláine nodded.

That strange feeling of dislocation persisted.

He knew where he was and what was happening, but it was as if it was happening to someone else and he was watching from a distance ever so slightly removed.

"Thank you, Murdo."

"Don't thank me, lad. Go prove me right. Anything else is a waste of more life."

"What's going to happen to me?"

"Haven't got a clue, but judging by the look on your friend's face, nothing good."

Dian looked ill. His skin was ashen and he was shaking. Sláine tried not to read anything in to it but it was difficult not to. They had made Cathbad look like a fool, exposing him as a charlatan in front of the king. Now his life lay in the hands of the old man. It was a perfect bitter circle of irony – perfect enough for Sláine to appreciate it even though he found himself caught in the heart of it.

"You, boy, are to be judged by the dead," Cathbad said gravely. His wizened knuckles whitened around the rowan staff he leaned on. Malice burned in his eyes. "They will not be lied to. The king may fall for pretty words and the promises they hold, but the dead know the darkness of a man's soul for that is the world they live in. They will examine you and if they find you wanting they will take you. There is no glory of the Summerland for a murderer, Sláine Mac Roth. If the dead find you guilty your afterlife will be one condemned to eternal torment and suffering.

"You will be chained within the darkness of the Great Cairn for three days and three nights without sustenance, until sunrise on the fourth day, Midsummer's dawn. The door will be sealed. You will not be allowed to emerge before the trial is complete. If you are innocent Danu herself will care for you, as your defender claimed. You will know it is done when a single branch of red morning sunlight falls on your face. You will be alone – although the bones of heroes past will sit vigil on your trial – if you are innocent you will leave the Great Cairn alone. If you are guilty the spirits of the dead will drag your soul kicking and screaming into the Underworld, such is your doom, Sláine Mac Roth."

Sláine nodded, he had expected no less. "My arm?"

Unmoved, the druid said: "It seems your trial has already begun. You will receive no healing until your innocence is established."

"That's outrageous!" Murdo objected, rounding on Cathbad. He made to grab the druid by the scruff but Cathbad's rowan staff came rapping down on his hands, hard.

"That is Danu's law. The Earth Mother will care for him or she will damn him. It was you, was it not, that pleaded his case, claiming the intervention of the Goddess in the slaughter?" Cathbad leered at the warrior. "You only have yourself to blame. Now, take him inside. I grow weary of explaining myself to heathens."

Sláine was thrown into the darkness. He staggered but refused to fall. He held his head high as Dian entered the tomb.

"I am to be your gaoler," his friend said, steering him towards a set of rusted manacles set into the far wall. "Forgive me."

"What is there to forgive?" Sláine asked as Dian secured the first cuff. There was a lock mechanism of some sort. It held firm as he tugged on it. Dian secured the second cuff, jerking his wounded arm upwards in the process. The agony was exquisite. The cuffs were set high, so that the prisoner was forced to stand, adding an extra level of pain to the trial.

"What happened? I mean—"

Sláine hung his head. He couldn't look his old friend in the eye. "Wide Mouth tried to murder me in cold blood. He threw a gáe bolga at my back." He nodded at the bloody wound in his arm. "Something happened to me, Dian. I lost control of myself. I killed him but it wasn't me. I felt myself disappear and some beast rise to the surface, warping my skin and bone as it claimed my flesh. Am I a monster? Is that what I have become?"

"Lug, so it is true what Murdo said? You're a warped one?" There was a peculiar reverence in the way he said it.

"I don't know. Carnun's balls, I just don't know. I'm frightened, Dian. I lost control of myself there. It's happened before, but not like that. Not so that I lost myself so completely."

"You better pray to Danu you are, my friend, otherwise there is no way you are walking out of here alive."

The young initiate took hold of Sláine's arm and pressed around the wound, causing it to open up again. Blood ran between his fingers. "There's little I can do," he muttered, more to himself than Sláine as he pulled a metal torc from his own arm and secured it on Sláine's, above the wound. He tightened it as best he could, staunching much of the blood. It wasn't perfect but it would slow the bleeding enough to at least give him a chance of not bleeding to death.

He watched Dian clamber up onto the side of a tomb and release a single crystal from its setting in the ceiling. A weak chink of light picked out a cobweb on the far wall. It revealed more than Sláine wanted to see. The floor was strewn with bones.

"When the light blinds you, then its time to come out. Don't die, eh? I've buried one friend already this week. It wasn't exactly fun."

"I'll do my best," Sláine said wryly.

"No food, no water, can't even sit down. You know this is because of what we did, don't you? He wants to break you."

"Then I shall have to do my best to disappoint the old goat."

"Come on, boy!" Cathbad called from outside the cairn. "We'll seal you in there with him if you don't hurry!"

"Sorry... I've got to go." Dian backed away. "Coming, your holiness. Coming."

They rolled the stone across the doorway and sealed him in the darkness with the ghosts of the dead and the rats.

He lost all sense of time in the darkness.

At first he was strong.

At first he was stubborn.

At first he believed he would survive.

But all that changed as the darkness brought his ghosts back to haunt him. There would be no respite.

Sounds drifted up to him, rats chittering, and darker, fuller sounds that his imagination painted as the dead coming to drag him down to the Underworld. He closed his eyes but it made no difference to the sounds, they haunted him just as completely. At times he heard a longer dragging sound and a deep grumbling moan. At other times voices incapable of forming words, left to rasp guttural and incomplete sounds of pain and despair. He imagined it was Cullen down there, trapped some-where between the Summerland and the Underworld, cursing him for condemning him to that vile limbo. In his head those sounds took on the more desperate edge of humanity. His mind swelled with the torments of that exile, his victim denied both heaven and hell.

The voices were his, he realised at some point. He haunted himself, accused himself, betrayed himself.

He tried to think of his friends, picture their faces in his mind, but he couldn't see them. He saw only Cullen and his dead father.

Madness lurked in the darkness of the burial chamber.

He couldn't find it in himself to feel angry.

He was surrendering, giving up.

He had killed both men. He deserved his fate.

Oh yes you do, warped one. Vile thing. Monster. You deserve death. You deserve suffering. You deserve your pain. Nothing more. Nothing less.

He knew that the voices of the dead spoke the truth. He deserved nothing more than pain.

So he gave himself to it.

Smells reached him too: dank must, rot, decay, and occasionally, like a ghost in the all-consuming dark, the pestilent reek of disease.

He suspected then what lurked in the depths beneath the Great Cairn.

Madness. That's what lies in here, warped one: the madness of a betrayer, the madness of a murderer, of a cold-blooded killer. The madness of– He silenced the voice. He needed to listen, to hear.

Not all of the Goddess's children were perfect, beautiful creations.

There was Avagddu, her firstborn: Avagddu, the vile personification of disease, decay and stupidity. Avagddu the essence of corruption, canker and treachery. Avagddu was a thing of the dark places. It shunned the light and contact with the Goddess's other children.

It couldn't be Avagddu.

Couldn't be.

The druids wouldn't shelter the monster.

They wouldn't.

Sláine pulled on his bonds but the chains were firm. He was trapped. He listened desperately for anything, any sound that might betray the beast.

Uncountable time slipped by.

More sounds haunted him and his mind began drawing wraiths to flit across the contours of the crypt.

Hunger ate at him.

His mouth dried up, his tongue cleaving to the roof of his mouth. His head swam. The darkness offered nothing for him to fix on, no detail to help him focus his balance. Instead it was a turmoil of ever-shifting black. His legs buckled and he sankdown but the chains wouldn't allow him to fall. The slump triggered a wave of nausea and a sunburst of pain from his wounded arm. The pain gave him something to focus on. Sláine latched on to it desperately. There was a world of pain. That was what it all came down to.

He imagined he heard the beasts prowling beneath him, imagined the diseased form of Avagddu trying futilely to find a way to the surface.

"He's in your mind, fool," Sláine told himself – or tried to. His voice died in his throat. Only shapeless words emerged, cracked and broken beyond recognition even in his own ears.

He lost himself in the darkness. Time drifted. He obsessed over his own ghosts, remembering over and over the look on Cullen of the Wide Mouth's face as he rammed the gáe bolga into his guts, hearing again the taunts of Conn of a Hundred Battles and the screams, and the screams. He couldn't shut out the screams. He moaned in the darkness, a pitiful sound that was only barely human.

He felt something brush up against his leg.

He heard the squeak of rats and surged upwards trying to lash out, but the chains restrained him.

Rats.

Rodents were scavengers. They stayed close to their food sources. He remembered the picked-clean bones he had caught glimpses of as he had been brought into the chamber.

The next time he felt the rodent brush up against his leg he stamped his foot down on it making sure the rat knew he was alive. The rodent's spine crunched beneath his foot. He had no desire to become lunch.

Fire burned in his arms and his back but even that numbed as his circulation dried up.

He lapsed in and out of consciousness.

He remembered Cathbad's words of how the dead would judge him, how the dead would find him wanting, how the dead would drag him kicking and screaming into the darkness of the Underworld.

He felt his blood slowing in his veins.

He imagined them, the dead, circling his body like vultures, waiting for the death rattle that could only be a few breaths away.

He felt his flesh hunger.

He looked up at the crack in the roof, willing the sun to come alive for him, for it to be over.

He faded again, head snapping up suddenly alert, unsure what had startled him.

In the blur where his eyes refused to focus he saw a bone white smear and painted it in to the head of some fell beast risen up from the Annwn, too impatient to wait for his passing.

Then he saw the single shaft of light on his hand. He looked up at the ceiling and saw the dust motes dancing in the thin beam of light. His fingers tingled. He closed his eyes trying to focus on the sensation, not at all sure what it meant. He flexed his fingers, stretching them open. His middle finger broke the beam of light. It was like touching lightning. A jolt of raw power surged through his body, causing his back to arch and his body to spasm in agony. It burned briefly but all the more intensely for it. His head swam. Even such a miniscule infusion of earth power was intoxicating. His body ached for more. Sláine stretched up, trying desperately to reach the light with more of his hand. He closed his eyes, succumbing to the agony and the ecstasy of it.

And it was both.

The power flowed through his fingers and down his arm, infusing every nerve and fibre as it searched to earth itself through him. His body bucked beneath the onslaught. His heart strained in his chest. His blood sang in his veins.

He had forgotten what it felt like to connect with the earth but here, in this most sacred place, he was reminded – and that reminder was brutal in the extreme.

His cries were terrible. He felt the monster rising inside him, felt the sudden and forceful surge of base instincts, to rut, to hunt, to kill, to feed, swelling up inside him like a siren from below – the call irresistible.

Sláine surrendered to it, and it was good.

A connection grew, slowly at first but he felt it building.

He felt the tie between his flesh, his spirit, and the earth itself. He felt Danu's strength flooding into his veins, and it refused to be tethered. It was power capable of shaping mountains, mere ropes could never hope to harness it. He pulled at the heavy iron chains binding him, testing their limits as well as his own. His arms trembled though not with weakness. It surpassed anger. He became the mountain, resolute, indomitable, and indefatigable. He became the river, decisive, driven, a torrent that refused to be quelled. He sacrificed himself to the power of the Goddess as it swarmed through him.

In a momentary lapse of reason he saw visions of who he might yet be if he walked from this tomb. They danced before his eyes, hallucinatory bursts of light and sound as his head swam with the earth sense. He saw the health of the land, and encroaching on it, the sickness of the Sourlands eating away at the lush pastures and rolling hills, devouring the very body of the Goddess — and it sickened him.

It sickened him enough that he knew it could not be allowed to happen, not while he lived and breathed. The earth power was inside him, a part of him, as much as his blood was. He was a child of the Goddess. Sláine thought of that ghostly maiden he had seen two summers gone, leading the dead king into the trees. He would not fail her.

He held his head high and leaned into the chains, all of the power in his shoulders and upper arms braced by his legs for one final massive push.

He felt the anchor pins straining. The sound of iron grating on rock betrayed their weakness.

It was surrendering, but it needed more.

His arms spasmed uncontrollably, the pressure so intense it came close to buckling his joints.

Raging, Sláine summoned every last ounce of strength and surged away from the wall. It was done. The sheer power of his final press was enough to rip the anchor pins out of the limestone wall.

The chains clattered about his feet. He staggered forwards, the shaft of sunlight finding his face, and as he breathed in he felt the fears of the mortal world fade away. He was the land. He was the mountain. He was the river. He was eternal.

He broke the ropes, banging his wrists together until the hasps shattered and the locks sprung open, and left them on the floor with the bones.

He knew, without needing to see, which of the stones was actually the door. He picked his way through the bones, breaking them underfoot in his urgency to be out.

"Lug be praised!" Dian cried, seeing the huge door-stone brushed aside as if it wasn't there.

Cathbad squinted and scowled at Sláine as he emerged, triumphant, from his trial.

The young Sessair warrior was changed by his ordeal.

He stood taller, his muscles more prominent, but wrong. His entire musculature was deformed.

"So it's true," the surly old druid muttered. "Sláine Mac Roth really is blessed of Danu." He shook his head in disbelief.

Others seemed less surprised by the young man's survival. King Grudnew appeared to be particularly happy with this latest turn of events. He turned to his warlord. "I'd say he's proven himself worthy, wouldn't you, my old friend?"

"Without doubt, the Goddess touches him, sire. That makes him more than worthy."

"Druid," Grudnew commanded, watching Sláine discard the door-stone. "The trial is satisfied, wouldn't you agree?"

"The boy is alive."

"No, druid, the man is alive. He has lived through your barbaric ritual and proven the right of Murdo's claims, that he is indeed gifted with the warp-spasm just as the greatest warriors of the Red Branch ever were. Right proven by your own trial absolves him of the deaths of Cullen Mac Conn, and his father Conn of a Hundred Battles. All shall know his innocence – and there shall be no hint of retribution lest the speaker would face my wrath. Am I understood?"

"Indeed, sire. It is clearly and plainly, and in all other ways, understood."

"Good, druid. I sense that great things await young Sláine Mac Roth. I would have you read him and divine what you may from the remnants of the earth power still surging within him. Gorian, I think it wise you escort Cathbad over to young Sláine and then see Bluth about fitting Sláine with a hero harness – if the old wisdom has not been forgotten."

"As you wish, Grudnew." Gorian turned to the druid and, leaning in close, slipped an arm around the old man's shoulder. "Come then, old man," his voice dropped to barely more than a whisper, "let's listen to you spin some lies in an attempt to sound portentous and impress our king. I trust you will make them good. No doubt you'll try to implicate the lad in some unknown future ill. Once a killer always a killer, eh?"

"Get your hands off me, warrior," Cathbad hissed, pulling free of Gorian's embrace.

"Not denying it then?"

"I revere all life, warrior. I serve Danu with my every breath. She has seen something in this lout. I pray that she reveals it to me so that I might know her purpose and help steer the boy. That is all. There is nothing to deny."

Gorian didn't believe a word of it. A fool could see the disappointment on Cathbad's mottled face as Sláine emerged from the tomb. He had wanted the lad to fail or at least emerge humbled and begging for mercy so that the druid could claim back some of his lost pride. He had been an idiot to proclaim Dian's drawings the wisdom of the ancients and vainglorious to pretended to be able to read them. There was no doubting that the old man still harboured a grudge. In Gorian's experience a petty man with power was a dangerous man, and for all that the druid tended to the spiritual wellbeing of the tribe, his was still a position of power, power that commanded respect. He had long ago proven himself petty enough for his dislike of young Sláine to cause the warlord concern.

The last of the empowering warp-spasm still flowed through the young warrior's veins. Gorian stood beside him. "Come, Sláine. You have proven your innocence. Walk into the sun where you belong."

"Aye," the druid decreed. "The innocence of Mac Roth is not in doubt. Danu herself has taken a hand in his affairs. He is judged worthy. Now come to me, Sláine Mac Roth. I would consult with Danu over your destiny, come to me boy."

"I am a man," Sláine said stubbornly.

"That you are," the old druid said placating. "Forgive me."

Sláine emerged fully into the dawn's early light, and walked up to the druid. Cathbad laid a wizened old hand on his forehead and lapsed into a curious muttering, half-words slipping from his mouth. A moment later the druid threw his head back and cried, "I see a hero swinging a crimson axe, I see red-mouthed screams, I see huge mounds of fallen, I see smashed shields, I see ravens gnawing at enemy necks on the field of slaughter… I see a… a curious rat-like dwarf? I see pain. I see a world of hurt." The druid lapsed into silence. When his eyes met Sláine's there were tears in them.

"A promising future, lad." Gorian said.

But of course there were repercussions.

Grudnew's claim that it all ended there, that morning, was nothing more than wishful thinking. Seven of Cullen's kin came out of the night, torches in hand. They circled his home in silence. With a nod from one, they touched their flames to the wattle and daub walls and the thatched roof, and the place went up in smoke. They moved back beyond the ring of fire and the flame's punishing kiss.

Macha came out first, in her night shift with a fur pulled over her head. She looked small, frightened, as she slumped against the wall of the neighbouring house and coughed up great lungfuls of smoke and phlegm. Bellyshaker staggered out behind her, his face flushed with the red sting of ale. He lurched around in almost comical circles, flapping his arms ineffectually at the flames as if he hoped to wave them away.

The cordon of the seven vigilantes closed around the burning hut.

One delivered a heavy blow to his father's temple with the butt of an axe, sending the old man sprawling in the dirt. The vigilante knelt to check if Bellyshaker was breathing. Evidently he was.

Sláine watched the scene play out.

He knew they had no intention of letting him leave.

They held him responsible for the lives of their kin. They would extract a blood price in retribution, as was their right – or as would have been their right, if Grud-new hadn't snatched it away from them.

Sláine found it hard to believe they would be willing to watch him burn to death. That was a barbaric fate if ever there was one. Of course if they hadn't been so stupid they might have realised that his mother wasn't screaming hysterically and trying to get back into the burning house to save him, which she would have done if she had thought he was in there.

He watched it all from the roof of a neighbouring house.

He had known they would come. They were cut from the same cloth as Cullen of the Wide Mouth.

There was no way they could allow the deaths to go unanswered. It would be akin to accepting that their blood was wrong, that Cullen was a treacherous back-stabbing weasel and Conn was just too stupid to admit it. To do so was to admit that the same flaws were inherent in their blood. It would never happen.

There would be a reckoning, Sláine promised them all, watching the vigilantes as they moved around, catching glimpses enough to know exactly who had come to do him harm. He promised himself that he would remember their faces until they had breathed their last, and then he would forget them completely and utterly.

His mother's cry tore at the very fabric of the night.

Macha stumbled towards one of the men. From a distance it looked as if she was pleading with a friend, someone she knew, most certainly, but the man's hand came up and down, hard, and she went sprawling in the dirt, her nightshift gathered high around her waist, mud spattering up the soft white flesh of her thighs.

The vigilante stood over her and spat, a wad of phlegm hitting her in the face.

Sláine felt something inside him snap. It was a powerful thing, like the unfettering of a restraint that had otherwise held him in check. Suddenly it was gone. He rose to his feet and bellowed, a tribal war cry, beating his fist off his bare chest to incite this primal anger. Backlit by the dancing flame he looked like some demon from the Underworld come to wreak pandemonium. He held his father's axe above his head and leapt down from the roof. As his feet came into contact with the earth, a huge surge of energy shocked through his system from his feet, rising up through his legs to his body and seeming to burst like black fire out of his skull.

He demanded retribution in blood, and there was nothing the vigilantes or anyone else, including his parents, could do except watch in horror as he gave himself over to blind fury and claimed what was rightfully his.

He killed all seven that night. Seven. It was bloody and brutal, and savage: a dance of death as naked in its savagery as any battlefield had witnessed. They came at him as one, but in his berserker rage Sláine relished it, goading them into their own deaths. Seven fell to his axe.

He did not think it too many.

Spent, he lay on his back looking up at the heavens.

The dead lay around him.

The fire burned on, his home reduced to ash and smoke.

Grudnew knelt beside him, his face troubled.

"What happened, lad?"

The last ripples of power drained from his fingertips back into the earth.

"They came in the night, seven of them. They burned down the house. They would have burned me alive. You said it ended here, today, and you were right, it does. They are dead. They won't come looking for vengeance again."

"Because they are dead," the king said, understanding his meaning well enough.

"Exactly," Sláine agreed.

"You're a hard man, Sláine Mac Roth."

"I am not the one who sought death this night, sire. I merely helped those who were looking for it, to find it."

Seven
Lies Drip From Dead Tongues

SLÁINE WAS IN a black mood. He had been ever since Gorian laid out the battle plans for the upcoming raid and learned that his task was to steal cows. It was humiliating. Stealing cows. He was being treated like a boy despite the fact that he was every bit as strong as any of the others – and if he went into a berserker rage, more so than all of them. He should have been in the thick of the fighting, not skulking around on the fringe trying to sneak into the cattle pens to liberate a bunch of milkers.

He knew it was because they feared him. Feared what might happen if he surrendered to the warping power of the earth and could no longer tell friend from foe in the battle frenzy.

So, they had him sneaking around the battle like a damned thief and tried to placate him by telling him how vital it was that he succeed, that their winter supplies depended upon him.

All he wanted was to be treated like one of them, to be a man, an equal.

The fighting was ferocious.

The Red Branch came sweeping out of the hills in two broad phalanxes that swept away all before them. Ten chariots, thirty horsemen, and fifty naked warriors daubed in the blue woad they used to drive the fear of the daemonic underworld into their foes. The thunder of hooves and war chariots was lost below the whooping and hollering of the warriors as they fell upon the town.

It was slaughter.

The men of the town barely managed a token defence, but that almost certainly saved their lives. The Red Branch warriors were not murderers. They were warriors, the very best the Sessair had. They killed as the need dictated, not senselessly. They killed today for food, to ensure their own survival during the harsh winter that Cathbad had predicted.

Gorian's scheme was executed to perfection.

They came at dawn, sweeping down out of the hills and breaking right and left around the town like a huge mouth waiting to snap shut. As the men emerged, food still stuck in their beards from the nightly feed, the mouth of the trap sprang – and it had iron teeth.

Screams of terror followed blood. Women watched their menfolk cut down even as they reached for weapons. It was harsh. The heat of the battle inspired the blue-painted warriors to feats bordering on evil. They tore the tongues out of the dead, cut out their eyes, and maimed their faces so that they would bear their injuries into the otherworld. Their sex granted the women no immunity from the suffering. They threw themselves at the painted men, gouging at faces and eyes with hooked fingers, clawing up bloody runnels only to be beaten back, silenced with a knife across the throat.

In all, it took less than an hour's quarter to subdue the town.

The place would never be the same.

Ghosts owned the town.

Even with the dying still unfinished, the place was smothered in blood and pain, and it stuck to the heart in a way that prevented those left behind from breathing. It would die now, just as the men had. If they wanted to live on the women would be reduced to the humiliation of begging, although some would seek out the temple of Danu and offer their bodies for food and shelter. Others would end their own lives that night, mourning. In the days to come grief would prove a killer to match the iron of the Red Branch.

Sláine skirted the slaughter. He watched it, with mute fascination. The Red Branch was awesome, irresistible. He ducked beneath a hedge, and crawled on his hands and knees to the tethers binding the heifers and the older milkers. The animals were skittish, frightened by the sounds and smells of the battle.

He used a rope to gather up ten of the animals and drew them away from the smell of blood.

He slapped the lead cow's rump and moved her on. The others followed. Sláine cast a backwards glance to be sure he hadn't left any stragglers, and was surprised to see the blue woad-smeared Gobhan Mac Tadg pressed up against the side wall of a roundhouse. The warrior clutched a sack in one grubby hand and a knife in the other. Sláine watched, horrified, as Gobhan picked his way through the dead, tilting back their heads and opening their mouths to see if their tongues had been

claimed. If he found one that hadn't he reached into the
corpse's mouth and cut it out. There was no honour to
the man. He scavenged the kills of better men and in
doing so avoided the fiercest of the fighting, marking
him out as a coward as well.

Sláine turned his back on the man.

After the passion of the fight the men returned to their
Dun and sated themselves in a glut of food, ale, and a
very different kind of passion.

They gathered in Grudnew's new round hall, only
recently completed, where all were seated equally at the
king's enormous round table. Sláine saw the irony in the
druid's chair, placed as it was over the exact spot where
Dian and the others had buried the fake tablets. The
king most certainly had a sense of humour. The walls of
the new hall were adorned with the skulls of some of
the Sessair's greatest foes. It was more than merely a dec-
orative touch. By using the skulls, they denied their foes
a place in the Summerland, turning them into restless
dead. It was the ultimate price to be paid for standing
against the Red Branch.

Food over-spilled the tabletop, dripping with grease
and steaming in the fat of its own juices. A huge wild
boar had been spitted and roasted over an open fire, its
skin crackling and its fat spitting in the flames.

Gorian held the silvered skull of Paidrag the Fair to his
lips and drank deeply of the red wine before passing it
on to the warrior on his right. The old king, Calum, had
had Bluth plate Paidrag's skull so that they might drink
in his humiliation over and over in every victory the

Red Branch toasted. Today was no exception. It had been a rousing success. Not a single warrior had fallen and the winter famine the druid had warned of was staved off.

The warriors drank their fill, passing the silver skull around the table. Sláine, having not blooded himself in the fighting, was the last to drink.

Grudnew stood up and leaned forwards, pressing his fists onto the table. "Who here claims the hero's portion from today's battle? Who today is the mightiest of us all? Let us take a count, shall we?"

Warriors spilled the contents of their sacks onto the tabletop, heads rolled across the floor. Gorian claimed fifteen heads. Murdo nineteen. Sláine watched as Gobhan Mac Tadg waited until all of the others had made their claim, and then stood up and emptied two sacks onto the table, one of heads and another of tongues.

The warriors took in his number with something approaching awe. He had delivered easily fifty heads and tongues, more than double any other man.

"Thirsty work today, eh boys?" Gobhan smirked. "I killed fifty today and I didn't think it too many. I claim the hero's portion as bravest of them all, but lads, it is no shame to be bettered by Gobhan Mac Tadg."

"That's a mighty count indeed, Gobhan," Grudnew said. "It's with great honour that I proclaim you hero and invite you to claim your portion."

Gobhan rose and tore an entire leg off the spitted boar and tore at it with his teeth.

"Good stuff, lads, tuck in, even you, young Sláine. There's no shame in not blooding yourself in battle, lad."

"And you should know," Sláine said without thinking. "You're a fire without smoke, Gobshite."

"Watch your tongue boy, or I'll add it to my pile." Gobhan chewed loudly, licking the dripping juices from his lips.

"Well, it'll be the first you've won today," Sláine sneered.

"You want to die, pup? It can be arranged, here and now if you are in a hurry."

"Go easy, Gobhan," Murdo said, laying a restraining hand on the older man.

"Take your hands off me. I'll have this out with the boy. I want an apology, and I want him salting meat with the women in the kitchens all winter."

"Apologise to a coward? I don't think so, Gobshite. I saw you scavenging the battlefield, cutting out the tongues of other warrior's kills. You're craven. You don't deserve the honour of the hero's portion. You don't deserve to sit at the same table as these men. You disgust me."

"Lies!" Gobhan roared, leaping over the table, sword drawn. "You want to challenge me? Face my wrath, boy. Taste my iron."

"Leave him be, Gobhan," Murdo said, his chair scraping back as he pushed himself to his feet.

"Oh no, I will not be dishonoured. I killed these men."

"Did you hell," Sláine mocked. "Did anyone actually see you kill a single man, Gobshite?" He looked at the assembled warriors, challenging them to defend the liar. "Well, did you? Any of you? Surely someone must have seen your heroics? It's hard to kill fifty men without anyone seeing you do it."

"You talk too much," Gobhan said, and swung. Sláine reacted instinctively and snatched up a huge carving knife from the table, burying it in Gobhan's chest even as the warrior swung for his head. He ducked under the sword and stepped sharply to the left, planting his elbow on the back of Gobhan's neck as he stumbled forwards, and pushing him down into the fire pit. His face began to crackle and burn but the warrior didn't make a sound. He was already dead.

Silence engulfed the round hall. Sláine stood over the dead man.

"He…" Sláine started, trying to defend himself.

"It's all right, lad," Gorian said, standing beside him. "The man's reaction betrayed him for the braggart he was. Had he claimed nineteen no one would have doubted him, but fifty… It is as you said, to kill fifty unseen is impossible, even in the heat of battle. You did well here, Sláine, you kept your head standing up for what was true and honourable. You've proven yourself as one of us."

"Aye, that he has," King Grudnew echoed the warlord. "And in doing so, you blooded yourself. Take the liar's tongue, boy. It's only fitting."

Eight
Skull-Swords

Rumours of raiders came to Murias that winter: creatures out of the Fir Domain.

The descriptions were unreliable, exaggerated by fear and made almost mythic in monstrosity as word moved from mouth to mouth, becoming more and more horrific. Inevitably that didn't matter. What did was the headcount. People were dying, too many people: people under Grudnew's protection, people who looked to Murias for leadership. They paid tribute and tithe for both.

Grudnew bore the burden with difficulty.

All his life he had been taught that life was sacred.

What Grudnew heard was that fell beasts were plundering deep into all of Eiru, unafraid. That alone did not auger well. For one, it did not instil confidence in the fringe borderland territories. Fear had them dispatching riders to Murias, the second leaving before the first could possibly have arrived, so desperate were they to impress their urgency upon the king. They begged Grudnew to unleash the Red Branch and drive the creatures back into the hell that had spawned them.

Tensions ran high in the capital, and tempers flared.

Word of the increasingly audacious raids came with unerring regularity. Over the course of a month the creatures hit many of the villages close to Murias.

Initially, Grudnew held back from the expected swift strike in retribution.

He counselled caution. If there was one thing he knew it was that a reckless king costs lives.

Instead he chose prudence, watching, listening to the riders as they reported on the raids, and building a more thorough picture of the invaders and their motivations.

But there was only so much watching he could do before people started to call it weakness and after weakness, fear.

The fundamental rule was that a king governed by respect. If his people did not feel safe they would not support him, and there would be no foundation to his power, it was that simple.

It was prudent to be cautious but there was a fine balance to be met. His people needed to be able to trust that he had their best interests at heart in every thing he did, even inaction, but his caution could soon be misinterpreted as fear. Fear could spread like a canker undermining faith at every turn, bringing with it turmoil, bitterness, and distrust.

Grudnew was afraid, only a fool would not have been, but it was a healthy fear born of respect for the threat they faced. Word of the attacks came from as far a field as Aileach the Bold's heart, Cruachu, and Ulaid the Mighty's capital, Rath Grainne. That two of the three Sessair territories reported such terrors was disturbing, that they should reach Airghialla the Fair was inevitable.

People were looking to Murias to see how the king would deal with the threat they faced.

He knew that however he reacted he would fail some of them.

Some of his people would die, and whatever he did, others would blame him. It was the cost of being king.

He made his decision; a decision that he would have to live with.

The Red Branch would ride forth.

"Wake up!" Sláine shouted, emptying a bucket of ice-cold water in his father's face.

Roth spluttered and came awake, cursing and shaking as he lurched out of his chair. His feet tangled beneath him and he sprawled out across the floor, pants around his ankles.

"Wah?"

Sláine looked down at the old drunk, with a mix of pity and disgust. Bellyshaker hadn't managed to completely extricate himself from his clothes as he rolled home, blind drunk, and had only succeeded in falling asleep in a chair where he'd soiled himself during the night. He stank.

"You're no father of mine, fat man. Gorian commanded us to the hunt, come dawn, and you, you can't even pull your damned pants up. Drink yourself to death if you must, but don't force us to watch you do it. I hate you."

Bellyshaker grunted but didn't move. His lips blew bubbles of spittle.

Sláine stepped over him as if he wasn't there, digging a good firm kick in before he took the old man's axe and slammed the door. He went to join up with the others. He wouldn't excuse his father, he promised himself. Not this time. The old man was a disgrace. He had let his body run to seed and only functioned with more alcohol in his veins than blood. It was a sorry sight. Every day it became more and more difficult to remember the great man he had been. That was the worst of it, the drinking was killing both aspects of the man – the wreck he was and the hero he had been. It was more than Sláine could bear to be a party to.

It was a hunting party.

They were supplied for seven days; that would give them time to scout out the surrounding territories and sniff out signs of the hellish beasts supposedly ravaging the countryside.

The axe felt good in Sláine's hand. The old man had called it Brain-Biter but it had been a long time since the axe had done any biting of brains or other body parts.

"Alone?" Murdo called, seeing Sláine.

"He's too drunk to stand so I left him where he'd pissed himself," Sláine said.

"You shouldn't speak that way of him, lad. He was a fine man once," Gorian said, mounting up.

"Once," Sláine agreed, claiming a mount from the stable boy. He grabbed a handful of mane and hoisted himself into the saddle.

"Drink's a foul enemy, boy, I pray you never have to battle it."

"And be like him?" Sláine shook his head. "I'd rather die."

"I suspect your father would as well," Murdo said, spurring his horse forwards.

They rode on in silence, forty-nine of the Red Branch, each of them thinking of the fiftieth, lying at home in his own filth. It wasn't a fate they would have wished on their worst enemy.

They divided into three parties on the plain of Airghialla, thinking to take in more ground, and Danu willing, come back from the hunt with something more to show for their efforts than whispers of ghosts and monsters. The landscape was wild, embodied with a savage grace that matched the Celts; untamed, unfettered and free. High grasses lashed at the horses' fetlocks as they cantered across the plain. Far to the left savage granite cliffs denoted the edge of Airghialla, the right bounded by an apparently endless rank of denuded trees.

Sláine travelled with Murdo and eight other men, tracking back towards the Great Cairn and south towards Airde Mogha and Falias. They rode hard for two days. The brothers, Liam and Lomman, led the way, Lomman moving on foot, reading the signs of nature for the mark of corruption. At night the wind keened so mournfully it was easy to imagine where tales of the banshee were born. It was the curse of the Great Plain. The longer they searched the more convinced they became that there was nothing out there with them, meaning that the entire adventure was little more than a wild goose chase.

It galled Sláine that Brain-Biter wouldn't get to taste the monster's blood but the anger wasn't his own. He

was curiously detached from it. It didn't boil his blood
in the way that Cullen's betrayal had. It didn't ignite his
flesh or blind his reasoning. It was somehow less intimate and yet more powerful for it. It grew day by day.
He felt it more when he walked, his feet coming into
contact with the ground. Some part of him knew that
it was the earth herself talking to him, feeding him with
images of the corruption that defiled her. He could feel
Danu's thoughts as clearly as if they were his own. She
hungered to be free of the abomination that trod on
her flesh, turning it sour. She wanted the despoilers to
suffer the way she suffered in their presence. She
wanted them to die just as she did, one foul step at a
time. He was her instrument. That much he had known
since he emerged from the burial chamber. He was her
weapon to wield just as Brain-Biter was his.

There was nothing they could do but turn around
and head home.

She came to him while the others slept.

He knew her.

Even before he opened his eyes, he knew her.

How could he not?

It was the maiden with the garlands in her hair. It had
been more than two years since he had seen her leading Calum Mac Cathair into the trees but it didn't
matter, she was impossible to forget. It was not that she
was pretty, although she was, nor was it that she was
lithesome, although she was as supple as a willow, and
as pretty as the flowers tangled in her hair. It was the life
that suffused her, the sheer and complete vitality of her.

He had never seen it in another living soul. It marked Danu for what she was: a Goddess.

The sight of her made his blood sing.

She smiled at him, giggled, and skipped away into the shadows, beckoning for him to follow.

He hesitated and then levered himself onto his elbow, watching her move. The sway of her hips captivated him. He knew that it was purely sexual. It felt much the same as when Brighid undressed him with her eyes even as she played him with her fingers. He smiled as she turned to see if he followed. She beckoned again, teasing him with a tantalising glimpse of flesh, her leg, inner thigh and the swell of her hip, and disappeared into the moonlight shadows.

Sláine counted to ten and followed.

He crept slowly through the camp, careful not to wake Ansgar as he moved past the warrior's bedroll. He caught a glimpse of her pale skin as she danced just beyond the fringe of dark. He followed, giving himself over to her dance. She led him a tantalising chase into the edge of the woods, hiding behind trees, peeking out when she needed him to see her. For an hour, he followed nothing more substantial than her giggles, her voice haunting the last moments of deep night.

It was a game.

She led him; he followed.

She allowed him glimpses to draw him on, left her gown draped over the bough of a tree, her garland in the thorns of a bush further along, and then, as the sun rose lush and orange in the sky, he caught up with her.

She stood before him naked and beautiful, her smile all the invitation he needed to approach.

The maiden took him in her arms, her lips finding his, her hands guiding his, and brought him down to the grass, opening her legs to him. He felt the moistness of the early morning dew as he knelt, lips kissing as he offered devotion.

"Oh my beautiful boy," she breathed, as his fingers found her. "Look." And he did. For a second he didn't know what he was looking for but then he saw it — smoke on the horizon. He followed it with his eyes, seeking the source. "You needed to see, to understand," she whispered, kissing the side of his face even as he pushed her off, the sickness of certainty settling in his gut. "You're too late, my love, always too late."

He understood where she had led him, and why. They were on the ring of low wooded hills overlooking Murias. The thick black smoke came from the town, burning. Sláine started to run even though he knew she was right, he was too late. His legs tied up as he charged down the hill. He didn't have a weapon. He had left the axe on the grass by his bedroll. He didn't slow down, not for a second. He forced himself to run, driven on by the anger he felt surging through him. Images of more flames, of innocents burning, of the despoilers pillaging and raping the earth, turning it sour, superimposed themselves on Murias. It was her doing. He saw what she wanted him to see. She forced him to understand that it was about more than his home, his parents and his friends. It was about The Land of the Young and the Goddess, and the very power of the earth itself, being soured by the evil of these fell beasts.

The flames leapt high into the morning.

The smoke was thick and choking.

Sláine battered his way through it, drawn by the screams of the dying.

"Mother!" he yelled into the smoke. "Father!" But the only answer was another scream. He stepped over the body of a young boy, not even five summers old, his arm bent unnaturally across his back, face pressed down in a puddle of blood. He didn't know the boy. It did not matter. These were his people. He felt his anger rising.

You're too late, my love, always too late.

"No," he said, although the denial was useless. He walked through the carnage where once there had been happy families. Bodies lay in tangles of bloody flesh, mothers dead, their arms wrapped protectively around dead children.

The screams drew him deeper into the smoking ruin of Murias.

"Face me!" He bellowed the challenge, daring the beasts to come charging out of the smoke and take him.

They didn't.

They had other sport to occupy them.

Terrified screams came from the burning building in front of him: a woman's voice counterpointed by the shrill cries of children. He couldn't tell how many. It didn't matter. Sláine didn't allow himself to think; he plunged recklessly into the leaping flames but was beaten back by the intense heat before he'd made two steps inside the door.

The flames hadn't spread into the neighbouring roundhouse.

"I'm coming! Work your way to the back of the house if you can!" he yelled, running around the side of the burning building. The flames hadn't spread all the way through the building but even so the walls were beginning to warp and buckle beneath the heat, and it would only be a matter of minutes before something gave and the whole structure came down.

Sláine yanked at the window shutters, tearing them savagely from their hinges, and clambered through the tight hole.

The heat was unbearable, the smoke so thick it made his head spin just breathing it in.

He was in a bedroom.

"Where are you?" he shouted and was answered by a feeble cry from deeper in the house. He couldn't be sure it was anything more than the spirit of the fire luring him like a siren. He had to believe it was the woman. He had no choice. Sláine reached out to open the dividing door but despite the fact there was no fire, the metal handle seared his hand as it closed on it. Wincing, he looked around the room quickly, but there was nothing of much use. Then he saw the thick fur rug at the foot of the cot. He draped it over his head and shoulders and battered down the door.

The flames sucked back through the opening in a powerful backdraught that bowled Sláine off his feet. It was only the sheer thickness of the rug that saved him.

The roaring tongue of fire stripped the fur down to the coarse hide but didn't burn through it. Moving instinctively, Sláine threw the ruined rug over the rising fire and stepped into the middle chamber, using the ruined hide as a bridge.

A woman and two children huddled in the corner, petrified by the rapidly spreading conflagration.

"Quickly," Sláine called above the snap and cackle of the fire. He reached out for her. She pressed her back against the wall holding out her two bairns for the warrior to take. He hoisted them up, one in each arm.

The ceiling above them buckled, the tying joist splintered and dumped its load. In a second the flames intensified, spreading across the doorway he'd just brought down. He backed up a step. There was no other way out. He didn't have a choice in the matter. "Come on, woman!" he yelled and plunged through the flames. He had to move quickly, running to the bed where he wrapped the youngsters in the bedding as protection from the rising heat. "You're fine," he promised them as he carried the children to the window. "Out, now. I'm going back for your ma." The older of the two nodded and helped his brother out through the window.

Sláine didn't wait to see them out.

The fire stung as he forced himself to go back through it once again. The woman stood on the other side of the sheet of flame, staring in mute horror at the all-consuming fire. There was no way she was moving, not by herself. Sláine didn't wait for her to move. He grabbed her, threw her bodily through the flames and then ran through behind her.

She fell, sprawled across the floor, gasping for breath
and kicking out at the flames that had caught her skirts
and burned up her leg. Sláine threw himself on her,
smothering the fire before it could do any serious damage. A criss-cross of burns scarred her bare leg but she
would be all right.

"Up," he said. "Your children are outside. They need
you to hold yourself together, woman."

She nodded, gathering her wits, as he boosted her up
through the open window and followed her out.

She ran across the street and swept her bairns up in a
huge embrace. She turned to him, tears staining her
soot-smeared cheeks, to say thank you, but he was
already gone, moving on down the street.

He was going home.

He saw one of the monsters coming out of a burning
building.

It didn't look much like a monster, save for its face.

It looked disturbingly like a man, in fact.

The thing certainly had the musculature of a man, the
arms and legs, but its face was masked like some huge
shoggy beast.

Masked, Sláine realised.

It was no beast.

Some wore masks to hide what they were, but not
this man. He wore a mask to become what it made
him. It was nothing more than a guise worn to ter-
rorise, in the same way that the Sessair warriors painted
themselves with woad. The creature wore a horned helmet, the design mirrored in the antlered stag-head

loincloth it wore. His leather shield bore the stain of the sinister triskele, a perversion of the Goddess's triskell (mother, maiden, and crone); the triskele symbolised wrath, despair and ultimately, doom. Its sword bore a silver skull for a pommel.

The triskele marked the skull-sword warrior for what he was, a follower of Carnun come to defile Danu's sanctuary. The Horned God was a hungry master, never satisfied with his lands, but then how could he be, with the vile practices of his worshippers leaching the very essence of the earth's power from its dirt and turning the land sour with their greed.

Now they had come to Murias and Airghialla the Fair.

They would not sour the Goddess's flesh, not while he had a breath in him.

The beast saw him.

He could have sworn he saw the thing smile through its foul mask as it brought the skull-sword to bear.

Sláine matched its grin with a manic one of his own.

"Come on then, ugly. There's dying to be done," he mocked, cracking his knuckles.

The skull-sword rushed him, seeking a quick kill. Sláine stood his ground and in the moment before the blade could cut his legs, he sprang, leaping like a salmon. He landed lightly on his feet as the beast struggled to regain his balance. The skull-sword spun, lashing out with its blade, cutting high this time, expecting another leap where Sláine dropped low and swept his leg out, kicking the skull-sword's feet out from under him. The beast fell back, his sword spinning out of his hand. Sláine stood over him, and then placed his foot on his throat, stamping down until the airways were crushed and the dead skull-sword's corpse had ceased spasming. It was a clean kill. Sláine claimed the beast's sword and ran for home.

You're too late, my love, always too late.

The maiden's words followed him.

He tuned out the screams as he ran. He couldn't save them all, not before his own: his mother and father. He ran, gasping and coughing as he choked on the smoke of the burning homes, and skidded around the corner.

Six skull-swords ringed his home. The flames had already caught in the thatch. Two more threw bottles of naphtha stuffed with oil-soaked rags into the house even as his mother bolted out of the front door.

He ran towards her, sword out, swinging, screaming as he ran.

It was too far.

You're too late, my love, always too late.

Blind panic seized him as Macha saw her son and started to run towards him. He saw the fear in her eyes, saw the skull-sword loom behind her and ram his foul blade through her back even as his drunken father stumbled out of the round house and was clobbered insensate by the skull-pommel of one of the masked warrior's swords. Sláine was three steps too late to save her. Her hands came up, closing around the sword's tip protruding from her breast even as her legs buckled beneath her. Macha's eyes met his, pleading for him to save her, but he couldn't and she knew it.

Worse, he knew it.

She stumbled forwards and fell short of his arms.

The skull-sword levelled its blade, keeping it between them as if a piece of iron could possibly save the murderer from the fate he had earned for himself.

Sláine felt something snap inside him. He hurled the stolen sword, taking his mother's murderer through the chest. The momentum of the throw punched the skull-sword off his feet. He hit the floor dead, but he hadn't paid. He hadn't paid nearly enough.

Sláine felt the kiss of the earth's power coil through him like an angry serpent, its forked tongue driving thought from his mind in place of the twin demands of blood lust and fury. He felt this righteous anger explode. His rage was primal.

"Come on boys, I'm unarmed, let's see what you've got. Can you get to me before I get to them swords?"

As they came at him, Sláine stretched down, fingers closing around the dead man's blade and drawing the second one protruding from his chest. He rose, twin blades weaving a hypnotic dance as he moved forwards menacingly. "Not fast enough." Five killers remained. It was not too many. It was not enough. Not for him. Not now. Not enough to sate the fury burning inside his skin.

They came at him as one, five in a line, their hideous masks making them appear to be a drunken blurring of the same killer weaving in and out of focus.

"I don't need no stinking swords," he snarled. "You die too easily that way." He hurled both blades simultaneously, taking two of the skull-swords in the guts even as they tried to throw themselves out of the path of the deadly blades.

Sláine arched his back, the vertebrae stretching ago-nisingly as he did so, his arms warping into huge trollish knuckle-dragging appendages as the earth power rav-aged his flesh, thickening his skin, distorting bone and cartilage into something monstrous. His cheek and jaw distended, as he reached out for the first of the butch-ers.

The skull-sword was like a rag doll in his arms as Sláine tore him limb from limb. He beat another to death with the bloody stump of the dead warrior's arm even as the last man fled in terror.

Sláine ripped the hair mask from the dying man's face and rammed the head of the ball joint into his face over and over, destroying all sense of shape and feature, and turning it into a bloody pulp. Blood gurgled as the skull-sword sucked in a last breath and bubbled out as a death rattle.

It was not enough.

The last man cast a panicked look back over his shoulder. Sláine grinned and chased the coward down. "Let me give you a hand," he mocked, smacking the man across the face with the dead man's hand. The skull-sword staggered back, stumbling. He hit him again with an open-handed slap, and then he reversed the arm, turning it into a fleshy cudgel and beat the skull-sword senseless with it. The warrior tried to fend off the blows but was powerless against Sláine's warped strength. He didn't stop until the skull-sword was beaten beyond anything recognisably human and still he continued, driving the head of the bone into the warrior's face, splintering the bones, cracking open the eye sockets, pulverising the nose until it was all one bloody raw mess and the man was dead.

Sláine lurched to his feet, looking around for something to kill.

He saw that Roth Bellyshaker had crawled across the dirt and was hunched over, cradling his mother's body to his chest.

His anger failed him, turning into despair.

He stumbled up the street, the world blurring more and more with every step. He fell to his knees beside his father.

He had killed them all.

He did not think it too many, but it was not enough.

THE SECOND TRISKELL

MAIDEN

Nine

The Sins of the Father

HIS GRIEF WAS absolute and inconsolable. It was a sense of loss that a young man like Sláine couldn't hope to comprehend, and it afflicted the entire community. The slaughter of women and children had been indiscriminate. Murias had suffered horribly at the hands of the skull-swords, although the warlord, Gorian, was certain that there was more cunning involved than a few renegade bandits ought to have been able to muster. It smacked of organisation and planning far beyond that required for a simple skirmish. That meant that there were more of them out there, somewhere, watching how Grudnew and Gorian reacted to their threat.

He couldn't stop blaming his father. The man's drinking had been the death of her. Had Bellyshaker been able to stay away from the ale for even a night she might still be alive. It was unfair thinking because of course had the old man been anything other than a drunken sot he would have ridden with the Red Branch to hunt the outlanders and Macha would have died alone instead of wrapped in the arms of her husband and her son.

It didn't matter that it was unreasonable.

Grief didn't demand reason. It demanded a scapegoat. It demanded answers that weren't there. It demanded retribution.

"I want the corpses taken to the nemeton," Cathbad told the warlord as the pair of them walked through the ruined town. The smell of blood was still strong in the air, so strong that even the smoke and char of the wood couldn't mask it completely. The warriors had returned home at sundown to find the devastation. The first hour had been hellish, men running through the streets, calling out the names of loved ones only sometimes to be answered. The sky cried for their loss, its grey matching their grief. "A slab has been prepared. I will drag the truth out of their bones, my lord. Believe me, even the dead cannot hide from my mistress. They will tell us all we need to know to avenge our loved ones," Cathbad explained. His usual supercilious sneer was replaced by a look of grim determination.

Regardless of whether the druid truly had a gift, or if he were going to find the answers he so obviously needed, Gorian didn't doubt for a moment that the old man was going to try and raise the dead if needs be to find them. For all that he disliked the old man, he couldn't help but respect that. That was the kind of strength they would need to survive the coming days.

"It will be done," he promised, his thoughts turning to young Sláine. "How is the boy bearing up?"

"The warped one is strong, Gorian. He understands that it was Danu's will that he should bear witness to the slaughter. We have talked. He told me of a maiden with garlands in her hair that led him a dance through the trees. I think he knows in his heart that it was the Goddess that led him to the hillside so that he saw the smoke. He doesn't deny it, even though it marks him for something special if the Goddess has taken an interest in him. You and I both know that events shape us. He will grow from this."

"Aye, druid, but into what? I don't know what to believe when it comes to Danu and your mysticism, old man, but I do know that the lad is hurting. Macha was an arm's length away when the bastard cut her down. Put yourself in the lad's place for a moment. He has to contend with the minutes wasted saving Bethan and her pair. Had he not heard her screams – or if he had chosen to ignore them – Macha would be alive now. In his head he bought their lives at the cost of his mother's. That's a bargain none of us would willingly strike. So of course the boy's hurting. We all are, but we were helpless to change circumstance. The warriors were still five leagues away. Grudnew's guards made good account of themselves but they were outmatched and outnumbered. Had we been here things would have been different. So every one of my men lost someone and blames himself for not being there when he was needed. It's different for Sláine. Sláine was here. While the rest of us torture ourselves with how things might have been different had we been there, Sláine has to cope with the reality that he was there and couldn't save Macha. He couldn't make a difference. He saw it and yet for all his strength he was helpless. His mother as good as died in his arms, Cathbad. He didn't come across her in a ditch."

"How I wish I could change the way of it for him. No son deserves that," the old druid agreed, "but the lad must know he did make a difference. He saved Bethan and her two boys, and they weren't the only ones. Alone he did what the king's bodyguard could not, he slew the outlanders. Without him our losses would have been much greater."

Gorian bent down to retrieve a tarnished silver disc that he saw half-trodden into the mud. It had come from the belt of one of the corpses they had dragged out of a burning building. The metal was still warm to the touch. He turned it over in his fingers, hoping it would reveal some mysterious secret, but its smooth sides had nothing to tell him.

"I know that, old man, but I'm betting it doesn't make a blind bit of difference to Sláine. As far as he is concerned he failed his mother. If I was him, I would be punishing myself in a thousand different ways, and I'd be looking to hurt Bellyshaker, too. How could I not be? I had failed the one person I would have saved even if it meant damning the entire town in the process while my father just got drunker and hoped the world would go away with the ale."

"You paint a black picture of the inside of the boy's head, warlord."

"I fear for him, Cathbad. Touched by the warp, the way he is, he is already different, set apart from everyone. With his grief unfettered, who knows what tortures he is capable of inflicting upon himself."

"I will send Dian to find him, they have a bond. It will be good for them both, I think, to share their grief."

Gorian nodded. "Aye, the lad needs friends now more than ever before, so thank you. I'd send word to Iesin if I had a clue as to his whereabouts."

"Word will spread fast enough, warrior, it is its nature. Tall Iesin will be home before the turning of the season, and with him, young Fionn."

"Stop reading my mind, old man, it's most disconcerting." Gorian grinned. It was the first time a smile had touched his lips since returning from the hunt.

"There's no great magic in it, Gorian. You're a decent man. You wouldn't be what you are without caring for the men who serve you. I don't need a geas to tell me young Sláine's wellbeing is forefront in your thoughts."

"Well stop it anyway."

Sláine needed answers – better ones than he could give himself.

He had thought he understood.

That was the bitterest irony.

He had thought she had led him to the hillside to save them, but she hadn't–

You're too late, my love, always too late.

She had lured him there to witness the attack, not prevent it, not to save lives but to see them lost.

He needed to know why, but the simplest of questions have the most complex of answers.

Why?

Why would Danu do that to him?

A world without answers was one devoid of limits and boundaries, and a world without boundaries was one without safety or the promise of justice for its people.

His mother's killers were dead, killed by his own hand. There was no comfort to be had in that. There was no comfort in knowing that he had crushed them, not when he knew there were more of them out there with their skull-pommelled swords, and their monstrous masks. Just thinking about it made his blood roil and his mind rage. He wanted them dead, every last one of them. He wanted them gutted. He wanted to turn the plains of Airghialla into a vast sea of blood, their blood. He wanted to bathe in it, wanted to do to them what they had done to him. He wanted to go to their homes and root out their family trees with his axe, and wanted to string their tongues from his belt. He wanted to so badly it hurt.

He knew in his heart of hearts that Danu had led him home. That wasn't his question when he thought about the maiden. What he couldn't understand was why she had done so if it wasn't for him to save his mother? Why go to the trouble of leading him through the dance in and out of the trees, the coy glances and the tantalising glimpses of flesh to lead him on, if not for him to strike back against the butchers? Surely the Earth Mother didn't delight in his grief? Surely she didn't seek to cause him pain? What kind of cruel bitch would she have to be to take delight in forcing him to witness his own mother's death? No, there was a reason, a why, and he wasn't seeing it. Still, her words haunted him:

"You needed to see, to understand." He felt her shade kissing the side of his face even as he tried to push the memory of it away. "You're too late, my love, always too late."

He couldn't bear it.

He wandered in circles, hearing his mother's laughter around every corner, hearing her words spoken yesterday, last week, last year, coming back to him as clearly as if she was there talking to him. He followed the sound of her voice. He saw people looking at him, saw the pity in their faces, saw the grief they shared, and couldn't bear it. His feet took him out of Murias. He didn't know where he was going until he was almost there.

He went to the hilltop where Danu had led him, where she had kissed him, where he had seen the smoke she had brought him there to see.

He didn't know what he hoped to find there but he felt drawn to the place. When he realised where he was going he started running. He plunged through the long grasses and the whipping and scratching brambles and shrubs, forcing himself through the thickening undergrowth, his eyes always on the hilltop.

A bird flew low, black wings ruffling the leaves of the first tree, halfway up the hill: a crow.

He ran beneath its perch.

Twenty feet further he was forced to catch his breath and push himself from tree trunk to tree trunk.

He saw more of the beady-eyed black birds lining the high branches, watching his passage with curiosity.

Grunting, Sláine ran on, pushing through a tangle of choking weeds and emerged, staggering, into the clearing on the crest of the hill's top where Danu had ripped his world apart.

The maiden wasn't there, not that he had truly expected her to be.

The Gods did not dance to the desires of their children.

Sláine turned in a slow circle, looking down over Murias in the distance. His home looked small, broken.

A crow cawed as if in agreement.

Another black bird answered it.

Sláine turned to see the boughs of the ringing trees weighed down with hundreds of crows, their oily black wings giving them nightmarish leaves.

They stared down at him, their yellow eyes judging him and finding him unworthy.

"Why?" he asked, spinning around faster. "Why did you bring me here?"

He was answered by a flurry of feathers as the crows took wing, swooping and swirling around the hilltop, black wings battering at him as if trying to drive him back, over the edge. Sláine covered his face with his hands as the beating intensified. The caws were raucous, dizzying. He staggered beneath the battery and then there was nothing, not a wing beat, not a sound as the birds found fresh perches.

Then there was laughter.

He lowered his hands to see an ugly crow-faced hag laughing in his face. She cackled at his pain; mocked him.

"Why?" she goaded, her voice a thick rasping caw, spreading her arms to the sound of ruffling feathers, stretching her oil-black fingers. "Why? Why? Why is there ever a why, my beautiful boy? Why me? Why you? Why her? Why them? Why like this? Why now? Why here? Why is there ever a why more important than this? This is your why, my sweet Sláine Mac Roth: death makes us stronger."

Her yellow eyes blazed with a hatred that encompassed all living things. The black feathers of her brow rose as her beak clacked. She threw back her head and gave voice to a mighty caw that caused the crows in the boughs to take wing once again, scattering them to the four winds.

"You are tempered by tragedy, not broken by it. All of your kind is. You are tiny frail things, like chicks fresh from the egg, and only the bitterness of life makes you stronger. A life of pain makes a hard man. It is the fire that toughens you for the life you will lead."

"What life? What do you plan for me, crone?"

"Everything, my pretty little boy, everything, and whether you understand it or not is not important. You are stronger now. That is my doing. The last of your childhood is gone. That is my doing. In death you become the man I need you to be. That is my doing. In death you become my axe, my beautiful sharp axe to cut the sickness out of my body before it festers. That is my doing."

"And if I refuse?" Sláine asked stupidly and stubbornly, jutting his chin out. "What if I ignore you?"

"You cannot, just as you could not save your mother when I told you it was too late. I speak the simplest of truths: you love me, Sláine Mac Roth. Your heart was mine from the moment you laid eyes on my fairer self. Otherwise why follow her recklessly into the dark last night? Surely not because you thought she needed saving? You wanted to show her your devotion, didn't you?" The crone snickered harshly, her voice breaking into a cruel caw caw caw. "Now you see the ugliness that lies beneath her skirts, it isn't all daisies and daffodils. She is no innocent little girl and you would do well to remember that. Even knowing that, even seeing this, is not enough to quash your love for the maiden with the pretty little flowers in her hair, is it? You are a man, and like all men, when it comes to it, no matter how we temper you, you are weak against the inviting fragrance of sex. Pitiful really, the way you need to rut like animals but my sister selves ever did have a sense of humour."

She loosed another primal caw that echoed all across the hilltop before she disappeared in an explosion of wings.

It was as if she had never been there.

Sláine sat a lonely vigil through the night, waiting.

The maiden never came, although he dreamed – while he thought himself awake – of her, the smell of honeysuckle and heather and the melody of her laughter that broke and scattered like black winged birds into the hideous unending *caaaaaawwwwwww* of a huge crow.

He awoke with a start.

It was dawn.

He stumbled and staggered back down the hill, fighting his way through the scrub and brush. The brambles bit and stung. He constantly caught himself looking over his shoulder, trying to spy crows high in the branches overhead. Sunlight broke through the filter of leaves, casting a scatter of gold discs across the dirt like the fabled coins scattered at the end of the rainbow.

Every boy knew that there were three aspects to the Goddess: mother, maiden and crone. There was little doubt that the crow-faced crone he had met was the Morrigan, Danu's third aspect. That's what she had meant by goading him about her sister selves. Mother, maiden and crone were all reflections of the same sacred female. The Morrigan and her harbinger birds brought death. She was the darkness.

He stumbled on.

She was right. Even now, having seen her, having tasted her foetid breath on his tongue, he still knew he would follow the maiden blindly to whatever fate she intended for him.

He burst free of the trees and tripped, falling and rolling down the hill, tumbling as he fell. He came to rest on his back, winded from the beating the hillside had given him. Sláine stared at the sky, watching a single crow wheel overhead.

"Death makes us stronger," he told himself, knowing the truth of it.

He lay there making shapes out of the clouds. It was a childish thing to do, but it felt right to him. He reached out a hand into the grass, tangling stems between his fingers as if gripping another hand. "I see a huge wyrm, see, there." he pointed up at a curious cloud formation. "What about you? What do you see?"

No one answered him.

He made a decision as he lay there, cloud watching. He would go home. He would sit with his father, share his grief, and make peace. He needed to. They both did. His mother would have hated them fighting like this, her two boys. He would make this right between them.

Resolved, he let go of the grass, held his hand to his nose and breathed deeply of its fragrance. Its tang brought him back to himself. He rolled over onto his elbow and pushed himself up.

It took him the best part of an hour to wander slowly back into Murias.

The town had changed.

He felt it.

He wondered if others did, or if it had only changed for him?

He was conscious of people watching him every step of the way. He could feel their pity. A few called his name, but he ignored them.

He was going home.

He never made it that far.

Roth Bellyshaker came rolling drunk out of Rioch's inn. He lurched from right to left, weaving a path as slurred as his singing as he tried to stay on his feet.

It was the singing that burned Sláine. The old man was tying his tongue around some miserable half-arsed shanty, barely getting half the words out. Sláine clenched his fist without consciously realising that was what he was doing. He took two steps towards the old man, brought his hand up and hit him hard, hammering his fist into the side of Bellyshaker's head.

The drunk staggered back three steps, stumbled sideways another, and shook his head. "Wha–?"

Sláine surged forwards, delivering a clubbing left to his jaw, three fierce jabs into the centre of his face, rupturing his nose and splitting his eye, and a thundering uppercut that lifted his father off his feet. "How dare you! How dare you be drunk! She's not two days dead and you're pissed out of your skull! I could kill you! I could kill you!" he delivered a punishing kick to Bellyshaker's side, lifting him six inches out of the dirt, and another doubling him up so that he drew his legs up to his chin trying to protect himself. A third curled him into a ball. "That bloody drink! She died because of you, you drunken bastard! She died because of you! And you are singing like you haven't got a care in the whole goddess forsaken world! You make me sick!" he felt the rage beginning to warp his flesh, the roar of the earth's need to strike, the need to punish his father, to avenge his mother on the drunk's body.

"Her favourite... her favourite..."

"Shut up you piece of—"

"Song... her favourite song."

Before it could rise, before it could fully rule his flesh, Sláine mastered the black anger and fell to his knees, tears staining his cheeks as he stared at the mess he had made of his father's face. He clenched his fists as he sobbed.

A lone crow settled on the eaves of Rioch's inn, watching as Núada came out into the street and knelt beside his friend.

"Come inside," Núada said.

Sláine shook his head, choking on the sobs that forced their way out. "I... I... could have killed him. I saw him and I lost it. I..."

"Shhhh."

"No… I have to… I couldn't stop myself, Núada. I saw what I was doing but I couldn't stop myself. I wanted to kill him… I came here to make peace and the moment I saw him… I wanted to kill him." he shook his head. How could he explain the red rage that had taken hold? How could he explain the way the anger drove him out of his own head – or rather turned him into a spectator within his own head? He couldn't. He held up his bloody fists in explanation. "I did this but it wasn't me. It wasn't…"

He pushed Núada away and stood, lurching as drunkenly as Bellyshaker ever had. He saw, for the first time in his life, fear in his friend's eyes and he knew that he had put it there.

The druids called a meeting of the survivors: a council of war.

They gathered on the green outside the nemeton, a full three hundred people. The talk was uncomfortable. They muttered darkly about the Goddess having left them. Some claimed that the druids were impotent against this new evil of the masked warriors. A few even questioned the Red Branch's role in their betrayal, having left them – offered them – like some sacrifice. It was nonsense and most knew it but the words stung just the same. Doubt was like that; it wormed its way inside and festered.

Dian supported old Cathbad as he moved awkwardly out of the nemeton. The druid appeared to have aged twenty years in the days he had locked himself away with the dead skull-swords, such was the strain on his body and soul. He raised a hand for silence, hushing the murmuring voices. Gorian was there, with the Red Branch standing side by side with the king's bodyguard and the druids before the citizens of Murias.

Cathbad lowered his gaze, gathering himself, and then looked up. He looked at each and every face in the crowd, faces he knew so well.

"Friends," he said, his voice shaky with disuse. "An enemy unlike any we have faced walks amongst us. An enemy–"

"How do you know?" someone called, interrupting him.

"Do you know this? Is it some form of ancient wisdom you discovered?" another heckled.

"Silence!" Gorian barked, levelling a warning finger at the speaker. "I am sorry, Cathbad. These are trying times. Forgive the fools this one interruption. There won't be another, I assure you. Please go on. I for one would know the enemy I face."

Cathbad nodded, shaken by the challenge to his authority. That they mocked him, even now, cut deep, but his words would end their mocking. He took no delight in the knowledge. "My thanks, warlord. As I was saying, we face an enemy far greater in strength and cunning than any we have faced down before. I have used my arts to divine what may be learned from the dead, although I fear it will prove precious little over the coming fight. They are warriors known where they come from as Drunes." He waited a moment, letting his words settle. "They serve the enemy of the Goddess."

He knew he had them then. "They give devotion to Carnun, the Horned God himself." A ripple of superstitious fear ran through the watchers as they gasped at the mention of the Horned God. "They are his soldiers."

"Can you be sure?" It was Grudnew, the king – an interruption even Gorian would allow. Cathbad turned to face the king.

"Yes, sire. I have communed with the Goddess and she has shown me their lands, and many of their heathen ways. Their lands were much like ours, once, lush, with plentiful game. They supported livestock and yielded rich harvests but now the soil is sour, crops wither and choke and livestock sickens and dies with barely enough meat on its bones to feed a few mouths. The people, like the land and their livestock, suffer. Villages are dying out, starved by the infertile land, and refugees flock to towns incapable of feeding them."

"A grim picture, druid. What ails the land? Is it these Drunes who somehow make it barren," Grudnew asked. "Or some other?"

"Their masters, the Slough priests, draw the vitality out of the land to feed their purpose, and that of their master, Carnun. What that purpose is, the dead would not reveal, sire. His grip on them is fierce, even in the afterlife."

"You think they seek to turn our lands sour like their own?"

"I fear that they are being forced further and further north in search of fertile earth, my lord. Whether the aim is simply to sour the soil or to leach the essence out of it for some secret task, I know not. I fear not the purpose so much as I do the result. I see fields of dead bones planted like spring crops. I see fat-bellied crows picking over the remains of friend and foe. I see a blood red sky." Cathbad lapsed into silence.

"You have given us much to think about, druid," the king said, "much indeed. What of their grim mien?"

"A mask, my lord, although for what purpose I am not sure. Made of hair, it covered the face of otherwise normal men, making monsters of them."

Grudnew nodded.

"You have done well, druid. There is more to fear in the unknown than there ever is in an enemy named. You have my thanks."

"Did the dead truly speak to you, master?" Dian asked, as they retreated into the quiet sanctity of the nemeton.

"No boy, I have long known of the Drune lords and their vile masters. I just never thought to see their taint spread this far."

"Then why the charade? Surely you could have identified the dead in the field?" Dian was shocked by the idea that the old druid would so willingly stage a performance, making something mystical out of what was a very mundane truth.

"A lesson, my young learner. What is more valuable, the easy truth laid bare or the more difficult truth, hard earned?"

Dian thought about it for a moment. "Their value is the same, they are both the truth."

Cathbad smiled at that. "You're a quick thinker, laddie. I like that. If I were to simply tell you something, how long do you think you would remember it?"

"For as long as possible."

"That is saying nothing. Whereas, if you learned something for yourself, how long then do you think you would remember it? It's like walking, if I tell you to do it, I can describe it as controlled falling over and that won't help you walk, but that is exactly what it is. If you stand and take a step and fall and get back up again and take two more steps you will learn. Agreed? On the other hand, which is more powerful, knowledge handed from father to son, a legacy, or knowledge gifted from the divine?"

"More difficult," Dian conceded. "The divine must surely be the ultimate truth."

"Indeed, so, outside when I said the Goddess had spoken to me?"

"You were claiming the ultimate truth."

"I was indeed." Cathbad nodded.

"Yet Danu did not speak to you?" Dian asked, clearly horrified by the lie.

"She seldom does, but that does not make the wisdom we hold here in the nemeton any less precious does it? If she spoke to our brothers in years past, they are still her words, are they not?"

"They are," Dian said, seeing where Cathbad was leading the conversation.

"So the knowledge handed down can also be the ultimate truth, you see? That is why we gather it and hold it dear, boy. That is why you must study and learn. The Slough priests, the Drunes, the Sourlands are all real. I have known this since I was your age. That is our true power, lad, we know the truth. The rest is performance. That is the only magic of it."

They walked a while in silence, Dian thinking on the old druid's lesson, beginning to understand.

"When did the Goddess speak to you?" he asked later.

"Once, when I was young."

"What did she say?"

"That is a story for a different day."

Ten

Heaven's Gate
or Hell's Teeth

SLÁINE WAS FURIOUS. He wanted nothing more than to break something, and right at that moment that something was the man standing in front of him telling him he was being left behind, again. The fact that it was his king only made it worse. He felt his rage rising. His lip curled into a sneer.

"Listen to me, boy," Grudnew said, gripping him by the shoulders to shake some sense into him. Sláine shook the man's hands off and raised his fist to strike.

The King of the Sessair faced him down, a look trapped between anger at his temerity and sympathy for his pain etched onto Grudnew's face.

He shook his head. "This is why I can't bring you, lad. You're a liability. You're angry. You aren't thinking. If another man raised his hand to me I'd have it cut off. I can't trust you not to do something stupid."

"It's my right!"

"Aye, lad, it is, and I'm taking it away from you. There's no easy way to do this. You're stuck between the Mountain and Crom himself. Damned if you do, damned if you don't. I understand your need for retribution. I truly do, lad, but I cannot put it first. Your anger won't help the others fighting with you, not on this hunt. This one requires a cold heart. We cannot sur-render to fury. Most importantly, lad, we cannot let you surrender to your anger. A warp spasm taking you at the sight of Macha's killers could damn every man around you. Would you want that?"

"Why should I care?" Sláine said, petulantly. "Just as long as the skull-swords die miserably, vengeance will be mine. I can live with that."

"Well, I cannot. So, you can either back down and stay home of your own will, or I can have Gorian place you under house arrest. Just know that wasting good men to keep you locked up will no doubt jeopardise what little chance of success the rest of us have of avenging your mother."

Sláine's face twisted. "You hate me so much?"

"I do not hate you, lad. In any other fight I would have no other stand at my side, but in this brutality is not what I need. I need ruthless cunning, stealth, the prowess of the hunter not the strength and brave heart of the warrior. So what will you do?"

"What choice do I have?" Sláine asked.

"I will give you justice, Sláine Mac Roth. You have my word," Grudnew promised.

"Well that makes me feel so much better," Sláine muttered. He turned his back on his king and walked away.

He knew he lost sight of the path to his higher soul in a fog of bitterness and anger. His head swam with a swarm of dark thoughts. Justice demanded an eye for an eye, a cut for a cut, no more, no less. He wanted more than that. The need that coiled around his heart craved it. It wanted to exterminate the skull-swords, every last one of them. It thought of nothing beyond purging Tir-Nan-Og of their taint. Sláine saw visions of himself reaching in and ripping their spines out from their shuddering corpses, cracking their skulls open and playing ballgames with their brains, and taking bites out of their warm hearts while they still beat. He breathed deeply, savouring the vision even as it shattered beneath Grudnew's refusal to allow him his vengeance.

He thought about following them, but knew it wouldn't work. The Red Branch had men capable of picking up the faintest spore. They would know he followed, and what then? Would Grudnew have him beaten? Imprisoned? Exiled? Killed? To defy the king of the Sessair was treasonous and for all the understanding Grudnew spoke of, the man was still king. He would brook no more defiance from him.

It wasn't a foregone conclusion that the trackers would pick up his scent; even dogs lost the scent in water. The answer lay in the River Dôn and its fast flowing current. The mighty river and its white water rapids were not the unbreachable defence Grudnew imagined them to be. Sláine had mastered them once. He could do it again.

He knew that they would be watching him, expecting him to do something reckless, so he walked, pacing every street and alley in Murias, visiting old ghosts. He stood on the corner where Macha had died, looking for her blood in the hard-packed dirt but already the rain had washed it away or the earth itself had leached it up, feeding on her as it would any other nutrient offered up to it. He visited the croft where she told him Roth had first pledged his troth, a stone where she sat him on her knee and told stories of Finn and Llew Silverhand, the legendary heroes of their people. He dug up a handful of dirt and cast it over his shoulder, as any dutiful son in mourning would, mouthing a silent prayer for Macha's soul.

He visited the places she loved, seeing her there even though she was not, and knowing she never would be again. He did everything they would have expected a grieving son to do.

His actions were a charade, but even so he began to hate the game for the emotions it stirred within him. Every new landmark added fuel to the fire that burned inside him. Only vengeance would quench it.

They were buying him time to think, to plan.

He thought about one thing and one thing only: crossing the river and following the hunters.

Dian found him an hour after the scouting party had ridden out.

The young druid was sombre as he settled down beside his friend. The riders had finally disappeared from sight.

"How are you doing?"

"How do you think?" Sláine asked, still staring at the spot where the last of the riders had been just moments ago.

"I think you're planning on doing something stupid. You've got that look on your face."

"That's why I love you, Dian. You know me so well," Sláine said, picking at the dirt with his fingers.

The young druid shook his head. "What are you going to do?"

"You mean apart from the obvious?"

"The obvious being hunting the skull-swords down and killing them, I take it?"

"That would be the obvious, yes," Sláine conceded.

"Don't do it, Sláine, please. Grudnew's been good to you, you know that, but you are putting him in an impossible situation. If you go against him like this he'll never be able to forgive you. He isn't just Grudnew the man, he is King Grudnew. The man might understand your grief but the king cannot countenance such an insult from his warriors. The Red Branch is unquestioningly loyal. He won't be able to forgive you, Sláine."

"He won't have to."

"You're not thinking straight. Just wait, please, for me. Wait.

"The king made you a promise. Give him a chance to honour it."

"You mean sit here and twiddle my thumbs while they chase around like headless chickens without the slightest inkling as to what they are hunting?" Sláine shook his head emphatically. "No. Do you know why?" He didn't wait for his friend to answer. "I'll tell you why. Because I can feel them out there, Dian. I can feel the skull-swords feeding off the Goddess's body. When I dare give my anger its head I can feel all sorts of things crawling across Danu's dirt."

"That is your grief talking."

"No, it isn't. I can feel them. They are parasites. They leach away at the earth power, their poisons feeding back into it, tainting it. Their presence is a canker eating at her flesh. I know that now. I could follow them to the ends of the Land of the Young and beyond if I wanted to. There is nowhere they could hide. All I have to do is surrender to the anger, let the earth power rise within me, and then I would be able to give the Goddess what she wants."

"What does she want?"

"Vengeance," Sláine said.

"That is not Danu's way, my friend," Dian said, sadly.

"You think not? You forget that it is the Morrigan's way, and that she is an aspect of the Goddess. You doubt me? Then tell me why she led me back in time to see my mother die? Why she said it was necessary for me to see it if it wasn't to cut that canker out? Answer me that if you can."

But Dian had no answers.

They sat side by side in silence, each of them thinking about the other's words and the implications they held.

"I want to be alone," Sláine said after what seemed like an age.

Dian studied his friend's face. "Nothing I've said has gotten through, has it? You're still dead set on some stupid crusade of self-destruction."

Sláine looked his friend in the eye. "We've both grown up a lot haven't we? Both changed. There was a time when you would have been the first to raise your fists and fight, now look at you."

"And there was a time when you would have lis… Who am I trying to kid? There has never been a time when you listened to anything I had to say. Just don't ask me to lie for you, I can't do that, not anymore."

"Like I said, things have changed."

Sláine checked the knotted rope for the third time. It was secure. He cast one last look over his shoulder towards Murias, knowing even as he turned his back on the wattle and daub houses that he was turning his back on the only life he had ever known. The moment he launched himself into the water he knew there could be no turning back. Still, well aware of the consequences, he dived, submerging beneath the awesome crush of the white-tipped rapids.

The sudden shock of cold slammed the breath out of his lungs and left him gasping and swallowing water.

He was in trouble in seconds.

He floundered, trying desperately to claw his way to the surface but the undertow dragged him down. He flailed and splashed, coughed and spat, and swallowed water as he opened his mouth to scream and the river came rushing in to suffocate him.

He was drowning.

He lashed out at the water, clawing at the riverbank even as the undertow relinquished its hold on him and the river sent his body tumbling end over end through the rushing water, playing with him. It bounced him off protruding rocks even as he choked on the air and water in his lungs, sucked him back under the surface and bullied him deeper, down and down and down. The mud had turned the water black, blinding him so thoroughly that it was impossible for him to tell if his eyes were open or closed. Sláine felt himself spinning and tumbling. He couldn't tell if he was upside down or the right way up. He had no idea where the air was, which way to strive for. He groped out trying to catch something – anything – of substance but the river had him.

It wasn't about to let him go.

Instead of fighting it, he surrendered to it, accepting death's cold kiss.

Instead of those icy lips he felt something else brush against his skin, something solid, fleshlike – a leg? A hand? It was impossible to tell what through the muddied waters. He flailed out for it blindly, suddenly desperate not to die.

He felt it again, whatever it was, like hands guiding his back, pulling him around.

He rolled with it, helpless to resist as he felt a delicate hand slip into his. His eyes stung as he opened them. Suddenly, through the muddy darkness a wide-eyed alabaster pale face swam into view. A face quite unlike any he had ever seen before. The eyes were bright with a sickly greenish luminosity; and the skin hideously translucent – he could see the blood in the veins beneath the surface, pumping. It had a mouth, but beside the mouth were three short slits, cut horizontal to each other: gills. The creature bared its teeth, sharpened fangs like jagged rusty nails hammered into its jaw. Its gills flared.

Sláine struggled to pull away but the delicacy of the creature's fine-boned hand belied its vice-like grip.

The thing had him and it wasn't letting him go.

He twisted and kicked, but the creature refused to relinquish its hold on him. Instead, it grinned a raffish grin, and leaned in as if to kiss the young warrior.

He swallowed more water as he screamed into the river.

Its lips closed around his but there was nothing erotic in the gesture. Sláine was powerless as the creature breathed him in, sucking the water up from his lungs and taking it into itself before expelling it through its gills. His body shuddered violently beneath the punishing kiss. He felt the strength drain out of his limbs. He tried to turn his head away and break free of the kiss but he couldn't.

The creature had him.

The creature kicked back against the current, dragging him easily with it. It was a thing of the water. He had heard talk of such creatures, mermen and selkies. Half man, half fish, and seal like creatures of the deep capable of shedding their skin and walking beside men in the air. Tall Iesin spun wondrous tales about them. They had lured Grymm Wavestrider to his death with their siren call; he remembered that suddenly, a brilliant hallucinatory fragment of memory. The pirate's ship had floundered on the sound, lured into the shallow waters by the selkies' seductive crooning.

Then suddenly he was choking on air – beautiful fresh air – as the creature dragged him out of the river and up on to the riverbank.

"Not your time. No no. The mistress will not let you leave her, little manling." The selkie's voice was a sibilant hiss as it drew out the "s" of mistress, the word rushing with all the melody of the river itself.

Sláine collapsed onto his back and sucked in huge gulping gasps of air as the creature slipped beneath the white water and disappeared with virtually no splash.

It took him what felt like forever to master his breathing, longer still before he felt strong enough to look around and see where the current had dragged him. He was disorientated, dizzy. He rolled over and was violently sick. After another minute of retching up brackish water he drew his knees underneath him and forced himself up into a crab-like crouch. As he looked up and saw the wattle and daub walls of Grudnew's roundhouse a single thought passed through his mind: Niamh.

Vengeance and lust were both passionate aspects of the Goddess.

The selkie had dragged him out of the river less than fifty feet from the king's home, behind the barricades and the guards.

Niamh: heaven.

She had only ever said four words to him but still she had placed her claim on his heart. Sláine remembered his promise to Brighid and knew, even as he did, that there was no way he could keep it. He had to see her again.

Niamh, heaven, Grudnew's chosen bride – the girl who would be Queen of the Sessair when she finally came of age and the king took her.

Surely this was why the Goddess had sent her selkie to save him? Danu herself had brought him to Niamh's door.

"It would be rude not to go in," he said to himself as he stood, and what was worse, he believed it. His body ached where the river had battered it. Sláine moved tenderly, favouring his right side. He felt out his ribs. A dart of white-hot agony lanced through his side as his fingers pushed at a splinter of broken rib. He pulled his hand away quickly. "Just to say hello."

He crept up to the side of the roundhouse, crouching beneath the shutters. He listened at the window for a full five minutes, trying to make out any sounds of movement from inside.

He knew what he was doing, of course, at least in part. He was angry at Grudnew for robbing him of his revenge, angry at himself for being beaten by the river, angry at the world for his mother's death. He wanted to hurt the world, the king, and most of all himself.

He couldn't hurt the skull-swords any more. Instead he wanted to hurt the king in the same way that Grudnew had hurt him, by denying him the right to something that was his.

He cracked open the shutter and clambered through. He dropped to the floor silently, looked around the empty room and called, "Hello, gorgeous. Guess who?"

She knew who he was even before the clumsy oaf was halfway through the window.

No one else had ever dared invade her prison.

It was Sláine Mac Roth.

Niamh had heard her betrothed talk of him often. According to Grudnew the warped one was the future of the tribe, although watching the brute spill into the bedroom it was hard to see exactly why. There was something special about the young man, it was in his ice-blue eyes and reflected in his smile. He had a dangerous smile. It was the kind of smile that could get a young woman into trouble, and a young man for that matter.

He looked up, as if sensing her scrutiny and flashed her that roguish grin of his. He was attractive in his own way. His skin was dark with a weather-beaten tan, his cheeks shadowed with two days' worth of stubble, and his eyes, oh but his eyes were something else, the penetrating ice blue of a bird of prey. They were ruthless and paradoxically swollen with a world of hurt. She felt as if they stripped back every layer of her flesh to get to her soul as he looked at her. He was, she knew suddenly, more than he seemed to be.

"Ah, no fair, Niamh, you're cheating."

"You're a fool, Sláine." She couldn't help herself; she smiled. "He'll kill you if he knows you've been here."

"I'm sure, but between you and me, how could he ever find out it? I mean, I am certainly not about to tell him, and I can't imagine you'd want to confess to my clandestine visits, would you?"

He moved towards her, and winced, his hand cupping his side protectively.

She saw that he had taken a battering from the river.

"You risk a lot being here, Sláine," she said softly, enjoying the truth of her words. He risked more than a lot; he risked everything. And why? For her? How could it be? He had barely set eyes on her. She had no idea how she was supposed to fathom the inner workings of a man's mind. They were unpredictable, vain and violent creatures given to extremes, brooding introspection and cock-like strutting and preening.

"I didn't have a lot of choice," he said. "The river brought me here. I was hell bent on pursuing your husband—"

"He's not my husband," Niamh interrupted, more forcefully than she intended. She couldn't help it. Grudnew was a powerful man, but in the years she had been the king's "prisoner" she had come to despise her gaoler. She hated being beholden so completely to him for her existence. She hated the fact that her life had been lived so removed from the rest of the tribe. Calum had picked her out when she was eight, and had her taken away from her parents so that she might be pure and unsullied when the new king claimed her. She had no friends. She hadn't seen her mother or father for nine years. She remembered the last time she saw her mother, Brighid. She had knelt, cupping Niamh's face in her hands and placed a tender kiss on her forehead.

It is a great honour our king is giving you, dear heart. That's what she had said, and she had meant it. Her mother never would have lied, not knowingly, but it was hard not to resent that "great honour" as it had turned her into just as much a prisoner as any common criminal – more so in that she never came into contact with other people apart from her husband-to-be.

That was until this clumsy warrior had stumbled into her prison.

She felt something then: a rush of blood to the head as he smiled at her. Niamh couldn't help but return it. For the first time in years she felt like someone, a living breathing young woman, vital and full of life, not simply a ghost trapped inside her shell living a non-life like one of the half-dead.

She went to him, closing her hand around his and drawing it away from his wounded side so that she might see. He was bruised, the skin mottled purple where blood had leaked out of his veins.

Even with this brief contact the young Sessair warrior made her feel alive. It was a dangerous sensation.

The frisson of her touch stirred something inside Sláine.

He didn't recognise it at first. He simply enjoyed the sudden charge he felt shivering through his body.

"What in the name of Danu have you been doing to yourself?"

That was considerably more difficult to answer than it should have been. He grinned sheepishly, hoping it said everything even though it said nothing. "I got into a fight with the river." He spread his hands wide, wincing even as he did so. "As you can see, the river won."

Her fingers probed at his side, lingering over the swelling that had risen to protect his damaged rib. He tried not to show how much it hurt.

"Stop being such a man. You're allowed to actually breathe you know."

He hadn't realised he had been holding his breath. He laughed at himself, the wind coming out of him in a sharp hiss as her fingers caught the sharp edge of broken bone.

"Mother, maiden and bloody crone!" he gasped, pulling back from her touch.

Her laugh was joyous.

"What's so damned funny?"

"You," she said, "big bairn. All huff and puff but you're nothing but an overgrown child when it comes down to a bit of pain. Come on, let's get your wound dressed and bound. That'll give you an excuse for being here should one of my beloved's soldiers find you." There was something about the way she said beloved that didn't ring true to Sláine's ears.

As she bathed and tended to his wounded side Sláine grew more and more certain what that first frisson he had felt at her touch meant. It was a silent agreement between them: a secret pact.

Niamh pressed a poultice against the bruise. It stung but he wasn't about to make a sound. He bit down on his lower lip and stared straight ahead at the wall. He was Red Branch. He would not allow himself to be mocked by a woman, no matter how enchanting she was.

He caught her hand as she wound the bandage around his chest.

She looked up at him.

She was a delicate thing. He remembered at first mistaking her for one of the Sidhe. It was not an unreasonable misconception. Her features were so fine, sharp even, giving her the haughty aspect of one of the fey folk. He tangled his fingers in her hair and savoured the way her lips parted in a slight surprised sigh as he tilted her head back. Her tongue flickered across her lips nervously.

"Don't worry," he said reassuringly. "I've done this before."

She laughed at that, leaving him no option but to kiss her to shut her up.

Sláine gave himself to the kiss, tasting her on his tongue.

She was different to Brighid. He hadn't really expected her to be the same, but her tongue was more urgent, more desperate and far less assured than the Daughter of Danu's but for all that it was more intoxicating.

The difference, he knew, would be his downfall.

At first it had been lust, pure and simple, and glorious.

They were like animals, reduced to the most primal level of action and reaction. They touched, probed, explored and satisfied each other in ways neither had imagined. He found himself drawn to her again and again, knowing that any night the warlord and the king might return from their mission but he didn't care. For now he came to Niamh with impunity. He sought her company to satisfy the aching need inside him that had been there ever since the skull-swords came to Murias.

For a while he lost himself. She became the lifeblood coursing through his veins. She became the fire he needed to survive. She became the one thing he had missed more than anything since his coming of age: a friend. She gave him love and from that he drew strength.

This was why the selkie had saved him, he thought, and he truly believed it. Danu had guided the creature to save him for no other reason than to see this love born and to bear fruit.

He gave himself to her, learning every inch of her body, every curve and crease of skin, every sweet fragrance and moist secret.

In those hours they were together he found heaven, but emptiness always returned when he was alone.

He found himself imagining that they might be together like this forever, that he might find happiness in her arms. It was a stupid and naive dream and it was shattered the moment Grudnew's guards hammered down the bedroom door and found them caught up in the heat of the delicious act.

The men dragged him out of the bed, not caring that he was naked. "Cover yourself up!" one of them shouted at Niamh.

"Don't talk to her like that!" Sláine objected, earning a swift cuff across the mouth that split his lip. He tasted his own blood and felt anger surge up from nowhere to overwhelm him, but before the warp-spasm could take him the second soldier drove the butt of his axe into the back of Sláine's skull, dropping him to his knees as easily as if he had been nothing more than a rambunctious child. A second blow sent a wave of blinding pain through his head and had the world dissolving before his eyes.

They hit him again and again.

Distantly, he heard screams and voices, Niamh's screams, and somewhere amid the swarm of voices, Grudnew's outraged command to beat him to death.

Eleven
House of Chains

CONSCIOUSNESS RETURNED brutally. His body was a fire of pains.

He was chained to the pillory in the square. Five guards stood watch. One of them saw he was awake and levelled a savage kick at his side, driving his boot into his still tender ribs. Sláine gasped and slumped against his bonds.

"Not so mighty now, are you, warped one?" someone taunted.

Sláine lifted his head to see who had come to torment him. He had expected one or two people but a line stretched as far as he could see, and at the front of it, relatives of Conn and Cullen Wide Mouth come to goad him now that he was no threat.

"I've petitioned the king for the right to wield the headsman's axe. Believe me, boy, nothing would give me greater pleasure."

It went on like this for hours, Sláine fading in and out of consciousness to the taunts of people come to harangue him. He had never imagined he could be the target of such undiluted hatred, but he saw the truth in their eyes the truth, they were frightened of him. This outpouring of hatred was nothing more than their fear finding a way out of them.

He wished he could have found it in himself to pity them, but he couldn't.

As the day wore on he found himself wishing more and more desperately that he could find a way to ram that fear right back into them, with a hatchet, axe or sword if necessary.

He saw his father lurking on the edge of the crowd and wondered spitefully if the old man was happy now.

Then he thought of Niamh and realised that he would never see her again. The thought opened a channel directly between his and the Goddess's flesh, his anger acting as a conduit for Danu's magic. He felt the first faint surge of the earth's power and surrendered to it.

"I don't think so, warped one," one of the guards said, quite matter-of-factly, clubbing him about the head until he slumped senseless against the pillory. His chains were the only things keeping him from sprawling into the dirt.

Dian came to him after dusk.

There were only two men guarding him. His wardens bowed deferentially to the young druid as he approached them.

"I would have a moment alone with the prisoner," Dian said, his voice flat. Sláine looked at his friend, feeling a surge of hope. Dian had come to save him. He would find a way to make everything all right.

The guard shook his head. "The warped one is to talk to no one before his sentencing; the king's orders."

"That is barbaric, soldier. The prisoner is an old friend of mine. I would prepare him to meet the ruler of the Underworld. He is paying for his crime in the mortal realm, would you have him bear his shame into the afterlife? Perhaps you would condemn him to an existence as one of the half-dead?"

"No but—"

"Don't shame yourself by finishing that thought soldier. Give me a few minutes alone with my friend. You may watch over us, of course, but I would have a little privacy. The ritual of preparation is not usually one for living ears."

"Of course, holy one." The guard nodded. "Come on, Hrothgar. Let's go to the fountain and quench our thirsts for a few minutes, shall we?"

"Aye," the other guard said.

Dian watched them leave and waited until they were far enough away before he whispered, "I begged you, Sláine. I actually begged you not to do something stupid and you have to go and rut with the king's chosen bride. Are you insane?"

"Quite probably."

"What in Danu's name were you thinking?"

"I wanted to hurt him," Sláine said honestly. "I wanted to take something precious from him because he had robbed me of my retribution."

"You and your stupid bloody retribution. What good has it done you, eh? You're an idiot, an absolute bloody idiot."

"Have you come here to berate me or to help me, Dian? I don't need a lecture about keeping it in my breeches. I've got rather more pressing things to worry about, like the axe Cullen's rat bastard of an uncle is sharpening. I don't intend to die here."

"I don't see how you have much say in the matter," his friend said. He reached into the folds of his cloak and withdrew a small finger-sized phial. "Drink this, it will ease your passage into the underworld."

"What is it? Poison? I'm not taking my own life."

"It will save you the pain and humiliation of the headsman's axe," Dian urged.

"You act as if I am already condemned."

"You are. Grudnew will not let you live after this. You know that. The king is a proud man. You have made a fool out of him, cuckolding him in his own round-house."

"So, you haven't come to save me then?"

"There is nothing I can do, save what I have already offered: a quick and painless death. It is more than many folk would afford you, Sláine. You are not a popular man."

"Well, as much as I am grateful for the offer, I'm going to have to refuse."

"You always were a stubborn idiot, may Cernunnos have mercy on your soul."

"Now that's a pleasant thought. I have to say I had hoped you'd come to do something more useful than read me my last rites. Pity."

"Pity is what got you into this mess. I should have made damned sure that you couldn't do anything stupid when Grudnew bade you stay behind. I won't go so far as to say it is as much my fault as it is yours, but

I bear a burden of guilt. That is my shame. Farewell, my friend. Travel safely into the long dark night." And then, despite the sombreness of the moment, he grinned, "And say hello to Wide Mouth for me." He pressed the phial into Sláine's hand. "Just in case you change your mind," Dian said.

There was no talking to him, so Dian left Sláine to wallow in his self-inflicted misery. Friendship or not, there was no way of helping him. Grudnew would not – could not – allow his affair to go unpunished, and the very act of punishment demanded exactly what that punishment had to be. Grudnew punishing Sláine meant that Sláine's indiscretion was being recognised by the king. It was a vicious circle. It couldn't be brushed under the rug. If the king recognised the crime there could only be one outcome: the headman's axe. Dian knew that it was impossible for the king not to recognise Sláine's dalliance with his chosen bride. To do so would have been the ultimate weakness. No king could afford that.

Sláine clutched the small glass phial his friend had brought him.

It was deathly cold in his hand.

Just thinking about it made him feel ill.

There was nothing reassuring about it.

Suicide was not the way.

There had to be another solution, but he couldn't for the life of him see it. It couldn't end like this. Danu had saved him for a reason. He needed to keep telling himself that. To die now, like this, was nothing short of stupidity.

"But then," he muttered grimly, "who said the fool had to make it out alive?"

There was no such guarantee, not even in Tall Iesin's stories. Sometimes the fool died for no good reason other than to make the point that they were fools in the first place.

He was alone. He didn't know if the guards were actually gone, or if they had simply backed off into the darkness. He felt no accompanying surge of hope with the realisation. They had left him because they knew he had no fight left in him and fully expected him to drink Dian's stinking poison.

He wouldn't give them the satisfaction of taking the coward's way out.

He would face his judgement and be damned if that was what the fates had in store for him. He was not a coward. He was determined not to die like one.

He closed his eyes.

When he opened them again, much deeper into the night, he was not surprised to see a beady eyed crow perched on the thatched rooftop of the nearest house, studying him. Sláine stared down the bird. "Come to gloat have you, bitch?"

The bird cocked its head and cawed loudly, almost as if it was laughing at him.

His head lolled. He didn't have the strength to worry about the damned bird. Let the crone send her pets to watch him die, and let them go back to her with disappointing news.

"This fool's not about to die, you tell your mistress that!" Sláine grumbled.

"Oh, really?" said a voice out of the darkness. He couldn't see the speaker but he knew the voice: Grudnew.

Sláine's hand tightened instinctively around the glass phial. He knew exactly what Dian had risked in bringing it to him. He could only imagine what the king would do if he thought retribution was about to be spirited out of his hands by the druid's poison.

Grudnew stepped out of the shadows. "Those damned birds always give me the creeps. There's just something about them. I don't trust them and I don't like them."

Sláine didn't say a word.

The glass phial felt huge in his hand and he was certain the king knew it was there.

"So what am I to do with you, young man?"

Still Sláine didn't say a word.

"Come dawn I must return, do you understand what that means?"

"That I have a few hours before the axe falls to pray for a miracle."

"That's about the size of it, laddie. It's a pretty pickle you've got yourself into, for sure." Grudnew knelt beside Sláine so that they might be eye to eye. This was not an official visit from his king. This was the compassion of a good man torn up by the stupidity of a child. "I've always liked you, you know that, but you've given me no choice. You have shamed me, the woman who would have been my wife, and yourself. Make no mistake about it, there are no winners in this mess, lad, only losers. Everyone touched by your stupidity suffers. Of all the women in Murias you had to rut with my chosen bride? I can't believe it was love, and I refuse to believe it was something as base as lust, so that only leaves some stupid sense of self-righteousness. That's what it was, wasn't it? You wanted to hurt me because you thought I had done wrong by you. You stupid, stupid boy. Did you really think I would never know?"

"I didn't think."

"That's the damned truth, isn't it? Your grief is no excuse for this betrayal of trust, Sláine. You must understand that. No king could hope to retain the respect of his people after what you did. To cuckold a king..." He shook his head sadly. "I should have you hanged, drawn and quartered by a team of oxen come first light, but out of love for your mother I'm offering you an alternative: exile." The king paused, letting the full implications of his offer sink in. "It isn't redemption. It isn't even a reprieve, not really. If you return to Murias your punishment will be waiting for you. The insult won't be forgotten, but the Land of the Young is vast and there is no reason we cannot live on in ignorance of each other. If you choose to run, I make you this promise: I won't send hunters after you. It would be pointless. The chances of finding you out there would be next to impossible. You've been trained by the best we have. You could evade them if you set your mind to it, so why bother with the charade? I'll make no bones about it, laddie. If you choose exile over death you'll be turning your back on everything you know. You'll forfeit your place not just among the Red Branch but also among the tribe. You'll never see your friends or family again, you'll be dead to them, but you will be alive. It's not much, but it is more than I should offer you, Sláine. So, tell me, what do you chose?"

Sláine held out his hand and opened it, offering the king Dian's poison. "I choose life."

"Good."

Sláine expected the king to free him of his bonds but he didn't. He stood, brushing the dirt off his knees. "My parting gift to you, Sláine Mac Roth. Use it wisely."

Then the king was gone and he was alone and just as helpless as he had been before Grudnew's visit. He didn't understand until he heard voices a moment later.

"The dead man deserves a few hours to compose himself before the long walk. Give him some peace. He isn't going anywhere."

"Yes, my lord," the guard said in a way that made it clear he didn't agree with his king's assessment of what their prisoner deserved.

He heard them walk off together, their footsteps getting fainter and fainter until they had faded away. He dropped the phial, grinding it underfoot. It wasn't an option.

He pulled at his chains.

They were no less constraining for the lack of guards.

He pulled at them again, harder, until the metal cuffs bit into the soft flesh of his wrists, drawing blood as he strained against them. There was absolutely no give in the metal. He felt his anger rising. What was this? Some last cruel trick to punish him by getting his hopes up? To make him think he might survive only to have his own weakness humiliate him again? Could Grudnew be so cruel? Were they standing in the darkness even now watching his futile attempt to escape his chains?

He surged to his feet, pulling with such sudden ferocious motion that the entire pillory lurched a full inch up out of the dirt. He threw his fists forward again as if punching out at invisible phantoms. The pillory jerked another inch out of the dirt. He punched again and again, feeling his anger spiral with each swinging blow at nothing. The chain grated and squealed against the hasp securing it. He hated the sound more than anything – it was the sound of captivity. It was more hateful even than the crow's mocking caw.

He staggered beneath the sudden surge of earth power that coiled up from the dirt through his feet and up his legs like fire. The sudden flame of power was enough to drive him out of his mind. He roared up against the chains, tearing the pillory clean out of the earth much to the crow's amusement. The bird cackled away merrily as Sláine tore at the chains with his bare hands, peeling them off as easily as a snake sheds dead skin.

He dropped the rope of metal chain at his feet.

Sláine cast one last lingering backwards glance in the direction of Grudnew's roundhouse. In a half-haze of anger he thought of what the king had said: all of them had suffered because of his stupidity. An image of Niamh suffering unseen tortures flared within his mind. He could hear her screaming. The answering roar of his anger was overwhelming. He hurled the wooden pillory like a javelin through the air and heard it clatter away in the dark as it came down. The sound was like icy cold water in the face – it brought him back to the here and now, banishing stupid ideas of tearing down Grudnew's home wattle by wattle and rescuing Niamh like some helpless damsel. The anger leaked out of him, leaving him frightened. Suddenly he was nothing more than a lonely man on a lonely street, with the first chirps of the dawn chorus breaking out all over the town.

The birds' cries sent a shock of fear coursing through him.

It couldn't be dawn, not yet. It was too soon.

Knowing that he would never see his home again, Sláine ran for his life.

Twelve
No Place Like Home

H E DIDN'T STOP running until the shadow of Lugh's Spike had disappeared behind him. Even then he ran a hundred paces for every fifty he walked, constantly looking back over his shoulder.

His only thought was to put distance between himself and Murias.

He was reduced to scavenging scraps when his trapping skills let him down. For six hours one morning he stalked a roe buck, moving with as much stealth as was humanly possible so as not to startle the animal before he could get close enough to bring it down. It promised a feast and a thick cloak to ward off the encroaching winter, but promises were no good for filling the stoMach or warming the flesh. A misplaced foot cracked a brittle twig and sent the terrified animal bounding off through the trees faster than Sláine could ever hope to follow. Cursing, he slumped to the floor and punched the dirt in frustration. It wasn't a problem yet, but in a day or two his hunger would become crippling and then it would be more than just a problem.

He couldn't sleep. Every noise had him jumping at shadows. He couldn't trust Grudnew's promise that he wouldn't send hunters to bring him down like an animal for escaping. To trust the king would be tantamount to swallowing Dian's poison. If he let his guard down and moved slowly, not worrying about his back-trail, one day he would wake up to the barking of the hunting dogs and the hunter's steel. No, his world had been reduced to two absolutes: he could not go home and he could never stop running, not if he wanted to stay alive.

The next day he caught a scraggy hare, skinned it and roasted it over a makeshift fire. There was barely enough meat on it to sate his gnawing hunger, but he licked his fingers of every last fatty morsel, stripping the bones with his teeth.

It was one of the better meals he managed over the next three weeks, although the one he took most satisfaction over was a crow he brought down with a slingshot. The stone cracked the bird's skull cleanly and even though there was next to no meat on the creature, the thought of feasting on one of the crone's pets pleased him no end.

The weather turned as he neared Craig Rhiwarth.

The rain was uncomfortable, and made bedding down for the night so much more of a chore. He needed to find shelter substantial enough to hold off the elements or at least capable of being used to bivouac down under and weave some kind of lean-too roof across. He wasn't in a position to be picky if he wanted to stay alive. Of course, he knew it would only get worse as the winter wore on.

He made a decision then. He couldn't avoid people forever, not if he wanted to see the next summer. Instead of skirting the next village he approached the wooden stile of the first of the outlying farmer's fields and went looking for good honest work in return for food and a bed. He was greeted by suspicion as he hailed the steel-haired man corralling a flighty sheep.

"Need a hand?" Sláine called.

"Not particularly, sunshine," the farmer said, wrestling with the animal as it kicked and struggled in his grasp. "Not enough work around here for one, let alone two. Assuming that's what you are after, right?"

"Aye," Sláine said. He looked over his shoulder. It was a subconscious reaction. The farmer wasn't an idiot. He caught the gesture and read it right: guilt.

"Looking for someone?"

"No one I want to see," Sláine said truthfully.

"Ain't that always the way." He pulled back hard on the sheep's scruff, showing the animal who was in charge. "You might want to try the widow Bedelia, two homesteads over, closer to the river. Her husband passed on over the spring and me and some of the boys saw to the ploughing and sowing of her fields as a mark of respect for her fella. Like as not she'll be welcome of a strapping lad like yerself to do the fetching and carrying for a bit. I remember what it was like when my Damhnait died five years back. The place was so big and empty without her around to nag at me. I started talking to myself and telling myself I was talking to her, only she weren't there to hear it. I can't really imagine what it would feel like to be the woman left behind, dependent on the charity of others."

"Much the same, I would imagine," Sláine said. "Lonely. Thank you."

Sláine carried on walking along the road towards the village of Craig Rhiwarth. He could see the homestead the sheep farmer had talked about. It was unremarkable. The grain stalks appeared ripe for harvesting. Perhaps he would find some honest work and a roof for the winter after all. He cast another lingering look back over his shoulder, knowing even as he did so that he needed to break himself of the habit.

On closer inspection he saw that some of the wheatsheafs had begun to rot. He broke the head off one of the better stalks and ground the grain between thumb and forefinger. The husk cracked easily. The kernel of grain itself had already begun to soften. It wouldn't be long before the remainder of the harvest spoiled.

He found Bedelia doing laundry down by the river, soapsuds up her arms as she grated the lye and scrubbed the rough spun cloth against a wooden washboard. She looked up, the smile slipping from her face when she saw him.

"Can I help you, stranger?" Her voice was husky. It reminded him of that quality Niamh's took on as they fumbled towards the bed, thick with passion and thinking only of the ecstasy of the flesh to come as he sank into her. He shook off the memory, feeling uncomfortable with the way his thoughts were leading him. He smiled.

"I was hoping I could help you, actually."

"Oh yes?"

"I was talking to a sheep farmer two homesteads over. He said if I was looking for work I could do worse than come see you, assuming you are Bedelia?"

"I am," she said, "and Donagh was right. I could use a man around the place to bring in what's left of the harvest before it spoils."

"I saw," Sláine said.

"You have an odd accent. I don't recognise it."

"I'm not from around here," Sláine said.

"Just passing through, eh?"

"Something like that," Sláine agreed.

"Your trade?"

"I was a warrior, now I am a wanderer."

"Is that a fancy word for bandit?"

Sláine smiled a crooked smile. "Ah, if I was a bandit I am thinking I'd be a piss-poor one. I mean, take a look at me, an axe, a worn-out pair of boots, and precious little else save my dazzling wit and repartee. I am an honest man, willing to work for my keep. That's all that is important, surely?"

Bedelia stood, smoothing down the folds of her skirts. Streaks of water and suds smeared the material and no amount of smoothing was going to make them miraculously disappear. "I can't afford to pay you," she said, unable to look him in the eye. "Since Orin died things have been difficult. I can offer you a warm bed, and food, not the best of either, I'm afraid, but better than nothing."

"Seems more than fair, seeing as I am in need of both."

"Then we have a deal?"

"We do."

★ ★ ★

Sláine worked like a demon for the next week. It was backbreaking toil but it had its rewards. There was nothing like honest graft for purging the mind. His days were filled with the repetitive cut, cut, cut of the scythe and the bend and lift of the wheatsheafs, separating them out from the chaff. It was a return to physical labour. His muscles burned from the exertion but it was a gratifying pain. He was working muscles his training with the Red Branch had begun to neglect as its focus shifted to weapons and combat.

The best thing was that he could see his progress as more and more stalks were scythed down. It would take another week at least to clear the field. More of the crop was going to spoil. There was nothing he could do about it. He had to content himself with the knowledge that without him the entire crop would have gone to waste.

He made himself useful in other ways, too. He was the man about the house, carrying out much needed repairs. At night he slept by the door, as far from Bedelia's blanketed-off bed as he could get and still be in the same room.

He enjoyed Bedelia's company. She was quick witted, with a sense of humour and was very easy on the eye. She rarely talked of her husband. Had he wanted to be a farmer he could have done a lot worse than the widow. As it was he found himself stealing glimpses as she scrubbed the floor and stirred the broth, imagining her body moving beneath her shift. She caught him at it more than once but had the good grace to chuckle rather than reprimand him, which of course only encouraged him to wilder flights of fancy. He watched the gentle sway of her hips as she walked, the slight jounce of her teardrop breasts, the curl of her smile, and the toss of her hair. It was no hardship to watch, he found himself thinking more than once. She was different to Niamh, and Brighid. She moved differently, not as lithe as Niamh, nor as soft and round as Brighid; different but no less appealing, he thought, watching her hike up her skirts and chase a chicken across the yard. She had good strong legs.

He laughed as she scooped the chicken up only to have the bird flap its way out of her hands and leave her scratching her head wondering how it had escaped.

"Want me to crack its skull? I'm a dab hand with the sling."

"I can manage," she said, chasing the chicken until she was breathless and laughing at the bird's instinct for self-preservation.

"I can see that, Bedelia. Think it knows you want to choke it?"

"Oh shut up and do something useful, will you?"

Sláine hunkered down and came at the flightless bird from the other side, shepherding it into Bedelia's hands.

"We make a good team," she said, wringing the chicken's neck. The bird's wings flapped violently for a spell as the life fled from it.

There was something about the way she said it that gave her away; a vague sense of longing in the way she shaped the words. It had been too long since she had been part of a team, he realised, and she missed it.

The pair of them had quickly become friends. It was inevitable given the fact that they were alone and that she had been starved of affection and male attention for so long. Suddenly he had walked into her life, paid a little attention to her, sat at her table, laughed with her and listened to her, and she enjoyed it.

Sláine winked at Bedelia.

That night they ate well, boiled potatoes and white meat, and bread made from the grain he had reaped.

With the grease still on his fingers from the last mouthful, Sláine reached across the table and took her hand in his.

"Don't go getting all serious on me, Sláine Mac Roth. I've already had one husband die on me." Although she said it jokingly enough he knew there was more than a grain of truth to it. Bedelia was terrified of anything approaching intimacy with another man for fear of being hurt all over again.

"Me? Serious? Oh ye of little faith."

"What do you call this then?"

He grinned.

"Well obviously I am trying to charm you out of that dress and have my wicked way with you."

She turned away, blushing furiously. She didn't say a word, just stood up and led him by the hand to the small cot she had blanketed off at the back of the homestead. She touched his face tenderly, putting a finger on his lips to stop him from breaking the silence. For a full minute she just looked at him. Then she drew him into a fierce kiss.

He wondered if she was imagining her dead man in his place but the urgency of her tongue betrayed her: this was all about Bedelia. This was about sating a hunger.

He slipped one hand around her back, pressing her close to him so that he could feel her heat, and the other he tangled in her hair.

The kiss didn't end, it melded into another and another until their movements turned frantic and they were pulling at skirts and trousers, desperate to feel the burn of skin on skin. Her dress was cinched with a laced girdle that cut high beneath her breasts, accentuating her curves. Sláine fumbled with the lace, tugging at the bow and unthreading the drawstring. He shook.

"Nerves," he mumbled.

Bedelia shushed him, closing a hand around his and drawing the string out. The dress fell at her feet.

He stared at her nakedness; drank it in. The knotted pewter cross at her throat drew his gaze. It was a beautiful piece, but then it paled beside its wearer.

"Say something," she breathed.

Sláine smiled as she laid a hand on his chest.

"Beautiful."

The coupling was desperate – quite unlike anything he had ever experienced before. Niamh had been more passive, letting him dictate the rhythm of the sex, and Brighid more skilled and assured, guiding him in his devotions. Here he was neither leader nor follower, they were equals and their hungers more than matched each other. Bedelia craved the physicality of the contact as if his touch made her come alive. She drew him into her and wrapped her legs around him, bucking against his thrusts and gasping as she sank her nails into his shoulders, drawing blood. The pain added a peculiar pleasure to the rutting, spurring him on far more than her cries did.

It was over almost before it had begun.

They collapsed back onto the pallet, naked and spent, their breath ragged, their flesh bathed in commingled sweat.

"You know I only intended to plough your fields, perhaps we need to renegotiate our arrangement," he said, earning a cuff around the ears.

"Pah! I'm beginning to think I pay you too much. I wouldn't go asking for a raise just yet."

It felt good to laugh.

He could belong here if he wanted to. It wouldn't have been any great hardship to wake up with Bedelia in his bed every morning.

He found himself imagining what it might like to be a husband – at first his pretend wife bore Bedelia's face but it quickly became Niamh's.

Niamh.

It had been less than a month and already he had begun to forget how her body felt next to his, and her face in his mind had become less distinct and more idealised.

"I won't forget you," he told the memory.

"I should bloody well hope not," Bedelia said beside him as she rolled over and fell asleep in his arms.

Happiness was fleeting.

The villagers talked.

Gossip of a new man at widow Bedelia's homestead was rife.

They commented on the closeness of the couple, tutting at their obvious intimacy as if it was something to be frowned upon. "Her old man's not even dead a year and she's taken up with the first fella that so much as looked at her," one of the fishwives muttered disapprovingly. "It's a damned disgrace is what it is," another crowed. Only Donagh seemed happy for Bedelia.

That was what happened when people had little going on in their own lives to amuse them.

Sláine heard all of their questions but had no intention of answering them: where had he come from? Who was he? What did he do? He wasn't a farmer, even if he worked the fields, that much they knew. A few speculated that he was a mercenary, after all he had the build of a warrior and carried an axe, others that he was a deserter from a northern army, and more than once he heard someone say he was nothing more than a pretty-faced vagabond come to leech off the kind-hearted Bedelia, to bed her and break her heart.

Let them speculate to their hearts' content, he thought, splitting a thick log in two and then splitting it again into quarters. He dumped the chopped wood into the wicker basket by his feet. It didn't matter. He was, to all intents and purposes, exactly what they claimed. He had no home. He was a wanderer.

He had no need of their approval and so long as Bedelia's name wasn't dragged through the dirt they could gossip all they wanted.

He concentrated on the logs.

He felt himself growing a little stronger every day he spent working the farm. It was good honest labour and it worked up a hell of an appetite. Alas, Bedelia hadn't been lying, the food was basic fare at best, but it warmed his stomach going down and she enjoyed cooking for him.

The sex, however, was far from basic. Released, Bedelia was an uninhibited lover. She delighted in his body and he delighted in hers.

Winter drew in, the rain replaced by the first snows. The ground hardened to the point where it turned away a shovel's blade. He busied himself with other tasks, mending fences, making a chicken coop, and repairing the thatch on the homestead's roof. He enjoyed the simplicity of his new life. He had never imagined something so simple could satisfy him but he was coming to understand that he was not the man he thought he was.

He hadn't felt the rush of the earth's power in his blood since he rounded Lugh's Spike, and that felt like another lifetime.

He was actually beginning to think in terms of life being perfect right up until he saw Donagh lurching up the bridal path, out of breath from running all the way from the village. He had been splitting logs and still had his axe in his hand. It slipped through his fingers when he saw the old farmer's face.

"It's you isn't it?" Donagh asked, clutching at the fence post to keep from falling. "You're the warped one on the run from Murias?"

Sláine staggered back as if he had been punched. "How?"

"They're here – they are looking for you – five hunters from the Red Branch. They are telling everyone you are a traitor to your king and that they mean to drag you back to Grudnew for execution. You've got to run lad, now."

He looked back at the homestead where Bedelia was cooking his dinner.

"I need to say goodbye."

"No you don't, lad. You need to run."

"But—"

"She'll understand, lad, trust me. I'll see to that. Now get yourself gone. I don't care what you did or didn't do, I ain't about to have her burying two men in a year. She ain't that strong."

Sláine knew exactly what he meant.

"Where are they now?"

"In the town, asking around. Sooner or later someone is going to put two and two together and they'll point the hunters this way. Enough people hate the happiness of others to make that a certainty. You'll need to skirt the village completely. Best bet is over the river and through the forest toward Dun Barc. I'll tell them I saw you heading off two days ago in the direction of Dun Keif."

"Thank you."

"Danu be with you."

"That's what got me into this mess in the first place," Sláine said without the slightest trace of amusement in his voice. He shouldered his father's old axe and looked back one last time at the homestead, thinking he could see Bedelia's silhouette in the window. He turned his back on her.

He hated himself as he started to run but he knew he could live with it. He hated himself for so much else already.

* * *

Sláine earned a crust as a mercenary in Dun Barc.

It was not a rewarding experience. He hooked up with a clan chief in a petty dispute over territorial rights and the spoils from a raid, adding his axe to the chieftain's small army. It should have been good to swing Brain-Biter again and crack a few skulls, but all it succeeded in doing was reminding him what he had lost in leaving the Red Branch. When the warp-spasm overtook him during a skirmish Sláine knew it was time to move on. He saw the fear in his comrades' eyes. It hurt him. These were men he had come to call friends in the short time he had known them, drinking together, whoring together and fighting together. He had thought they shared a bond of brotherhood. He ought to have known better. There was nowhere in the Land of the Young that he could truly claim to belong, not anymore.

Each day was an exercise in survival. The next would have to take care of itself.

He deserted long before the conflict was settled.

He didn't care, it wasn't his fight.

Spring came. A new spring deserved a new day beginning.

"Looking for work?"

Sláine studied his would-be employer. The man was a small weaselly individual with close-set feral eyes and a twitching nose. The man was unpleasant and quite possibly dangerous. He harboured no illusions. Whatever the greasy creature was about to suggest, it was almost definitely illegal.

"What have you got in mind?"

One benefit from the dubious nature of the deal was that it promised to pay well. The man's nose twitched through a series of contortions. There was little about his appearance that inspired either trust or confidence. His oily hair was combed flat against his scalp although a cow-lick at the crown refused to lie down, but his clothing was cut well, befitting a man of no small means, and it was one of the finest weaves Sláine had ever seen.

"Ah, nothing too exciting I'm afraid. I'm looking to move some goods from Breiddin to Crumlyn. It's a long road, and often seen as easy pickings by bandits. I'm looking to discourage that line of thinking with some big strong boys guarding the caravan."

There was obviously more to it, but Sláine wasn't about to push his luck. He needed to head south and Crumlyn was about as far south as you could go without leaving the Land of the Young.

"I'm listening."

"Not much more to tell. I need someone handy with a weapon – sword or axe, I'm not fussed – who can ride and has a few other, ahhh, talents."

"Talents?"

The trader chuckled. "You make it sound like a dirty word, lad."

"For all I know it could be, it isn't as if you're owning up to what those talents might be, now is it?"

"You make a good point."

"But you're still not going to tell me," Sláine said.

"I am still not going to tell you," the trader agreed. "So, with that settled, do we have a deal?"

He had met men like this before, always in the same kind of circumstances. They withheld a certain vital piece of the puzzle and then feigned bewilderment when the elaborate construction of half-truths they had built came tumbling down.

"What do I get in return?"

"Ah, a pragmatic soul. I like that in a man. I am thinking the job is worth a good-sized purse, shall we say fifty bits?"

Sláine pretended to weigh up the offer for a moment.

"Shall we say seventy-five? It's a long road after all and if it is worth fifty as an opening gambit it must be worth seventy-five."

"You drive a hard bargain, friend." The trader spat in his palm and held out his hand.

"Should have said one hundred and fifty shouldn't I?" Sláine said, sealing the deal. "You caved in far too easily."

"Ahhh, don't feel bad. It's a fair price. I wouldn't go out of my way to swindle you."

"I don't believe that for a moment."

"You cut me to the quick, lad. You know, I can't keep calling you that, what's your name, big fella? After all, we're old friends now, aren't we?"

"I wouldn't go that far. I am Sláine Mac Roth."

"Now that's a fighter's name if ever I heard one. Good to have you on the team, Sláine. I'm Mannix. Well I was born Mainchin but not even my dear departed mother ever called me that. I've been Mannix for as long as I can remember."

"Mannix," Sláine said.

"Right, well, we're shipping out at first light tomorrow. You know where the cider house is?" Sláine nodded. "Right next door is a narrow gate. It'll be open. Come on through about an hour before dawn. We'll be loading up. Don't forget that axe of yours!"

He was not the only guard on the caravan.

There were two others, brothers, Finbar and Fergus, both redheaded, freckled boys with more muscle than sense. Sláine didn't doubt for a minute that they thought they could handle themselves if things got messy, but there was a peculiar softness — at odds with their bulging muscles — about the pair that didn't inspire confidence. He would have wagered half of his purse on the fact that the brother's had never been in a real fight. The eyes gave them away.

"The best of a sorry lot," Mannix said, following the direction of Sláine's dubious stare.

"Doesn't say a lot."

"Well, we've got you, so all's well that ends well."

"If you say so."

There were three wagons, one covered, the other two flatbeds. The horses looked ready for the knacker's yard. He patted one on the neck. The first flatbed was piled to overflowing with crates and sacks, each bearing the mark of a small monk, which he assumed was something to do with Mannix's trading company. The second flatbed was half empty, and carried the team's supplies, bedrolls, cooking tins and other odds and ends for the journey.

Sláine walked around to the side of the covered wagon and reached up to draw back the canvas flap.

"I wouldn't do that if I were you," Mannix said, coming up behind him and staying his hand. "The, ahhh, beautiful Blathnaid was in a foul humour when I looked in on her earlier. Woe betide anyone disturbing her beauty sleep." The trader chuckled at his own pale attempt at humour. "It always amazes me how a good-looking woman can look so damned ugly in the morning."

"So is she the real cargo?" Sláine turned his back on the wagon. He looked up at the sky, feeling the first few drops of rain on his face.

"You could say that. I was asked as a favour to an old friend to see her safely to Crumlyn. I thought it would be convenient to run some other business along the way, so which is the real business, well that's a matter for interpretation, I suppose. Both pay well, that's what counts."

"Not well enough for decent horses though," Sláine said.

They left a little before sunrise. Sláine rode alongside the front wagon, Finbar and Fergus bringing up the rear. They were not the most talkative pair. Over the next four days Sláine heard them manage only a handful of words between them.

"It's going to be a long journey," he remarked to the trader as the wagons rumbled through another tiny hamlet. Children lined the streets, watching the short procession roll by. Mannix threw a couple of jellied treats down to them.

"They always are," Mannix agreed.

Blathnaid did not make an appearance until the fifth day.

She was an interesting conundrum of personality and beauty all jumbled together and reassembled in a manner that ought to have been pleasing but was just slightly out of kilter, making her an almost-beautiful almost-interesting almost-woman. She wore a simple dress, although it was dyed emerald green, a rare colour, marking it as an expensive piece despite its roughness. The only jewellery was a colourful heather-gem brooch, with a dozen fragments of multi-coloured stone. Again it was a simple piece, and heather stone was hardly a precious gem. It was a cold stone. After a few minutes of trying to make conversation with the woman Sláine decided it suited her, muttered something that made him look busy and rode off to the back of the wagon train to watch the leaves bud with the red-headed brothers of mirth.

Finbar and Fergus were no more fun than usual but anything was better than their precious "cargo".

That didn't stop him from watching Blathnaid from a distance. She moved with an economy that surprised him. There was little in the way of excess about her. Everything, even her body's form, was tailored to minimalising things, be it movement, flesh, even the attention it drew. There appeared to be nothing at all remarkable about the young woman, which was, conversely, rather remarkable in itself. It seemed at odds with her role as the helpless maiden. The longer he studied her, the more he began to wonder if it wasn't an act she cultivated. There was almost certainly more than met the eye about their travelling companion, although what, exactly, he could only guess at.

She retreated into the wagon a little further down the road, and didn't come out again until nightfall.

Mannix amused them with tales of his travels while they ate. The trader had been to places and seen things that Sláine had never heard of. In many ways, the trader reminded Sláine of Tall Iesin. He spun a captivating yarn. He told tall tales of adventure, always painting himself in the hero's role. Sláine chuckled at stories of his escape from the clutches of the witches of Drunemeton, and his escapades with a troupe of female players in Caer Lyonesse. If Mannix was to be believed he had bedded the actresses, fended off the unwanted lusts of an amorous lamia and still had the stamina to rescue a chieftain's only daughter from where she was imprisoned in a high tower.

"It was all I could do to convince the old man that I didn't want the girl as my reward. There're only so many notches the bedpost can take, after all," he finished with a grin.

"I can imagine," Fergus said enviously.

"I can't," Sláine said with a wink. "Some stories are far too tall for imagining, that's what's best about them."

"You really are a man after my own heart, Sláine Mac Roth," Mannix said, slapping the young Sessair on the back. "Come on, let's eat."

He continued to watch Blathnaid over the coming days.

There was something about the woman that didn't ring true but he didn't know what it was.

It made him decidedly uncomfortable in her presence, more so when he found himself alone with her.

"You don't like me very much, do you?" she asked. She had a way of tilting her head that made her hair fall across one eye, and then, when she knew he was looking, she would brush it away from her face. It was decidedly theatrical. He had noticed her doing it whenever she talked to the redheaded mirth brothers as well, but she never did it when she was with Mannix. She was obviously flirting although how she could have imagined it made her more attractive he had no idea.

"Am I supposed to?"

"Well it would be nice. We've got a long way to travel."

"We've managed well enough so far without me liking you," he said. "I am sure we could manage a few more miles without too much trouble."

Blathnaid turned away from him. There was nothing for her to see in the darkness beyond the campfire but he wasn't about to tell her that.

She didn't say a word for a full five minutes.

When she finally turned back to face him her eyes were puffy and her cheeks were streaked with tears. He felt like a complete idiot. Flustered, he lurched forwards not sure whether to hug her or try to wipe her tears away, and ended up elbowing her in the face. Blathnaid recoiled, raising her hands to protect her face from any more of his good intentions.

"Sorry, sorry, ahhh woman, I didn't mean anything by it, I mean, nothing to be getting upset over. Me and my big mouth, I open it without thinking, you know? Say the first thing that comes into my mind, no matter how stupid. You looked like you could handle a bit of banter so I—" He was rambling and he knew it. He didn't know what else he was supposed to say.

She looked at him, vulnerable and suddenly attractive, her eyes wide like those of a startled doe and her cheeks flushed.

He didn't think, he leaned forwards and kissed her.

Blathnaid slapped him, a hard stinging blow across the face.

"I was only trying to make you feel better!"

For that, she slapped him again.

He winced, shaking his head to clear the ringing in his ears.

He turned to see Mannix laughing at him, thoroughly delighted by the whole sorry spectacle.

Sláine shrugged as if to say, what is a man to do?

Over the coming weeks he was doubly attentive to Blathnaid. He apologised several times, making such a fuss of her that she finally grabbed him by the scruff of the neck and hauled herself up to within an inch of her face.

"Shut up and kiss me."

It was an offer he couldn't very well refuse.

Thirteen
Simple Magics

THEY HAD BEEN robbed by bandits on the Crumlyn road.

It hadn't been some random attack, a robber looking for an easy mark on the highway. It was quite by chance he had ridden around the back of the covered wagon in time to see Blathnaid giving three sharp owl hoots into the darkness – a signal for cohorts to bait their trap. They had a slick operation going, with Blathnaid infiltrating caravans in her guise as the helpless young daughter of the well-to-do local. It took some prior planning but having someone on the inside assured things went down without a hitch.

Three men and a wagon with a broken axle pulled up on the side of the road, greasy with sweat and thoroughly exhausted. They waved Mannix down.

"Got a problem?" the old trader asked, stating the obvious succinctly.

"Aye, the axle snapped," the shortest of the three said, equally obviously, given the broken stave of wood lying on the side of the road. He was bald and slightly rotund. Beside him stood a curly haired fop with his hands on his hips, and a brute of a man with a face that looked as if it had been trampled by a herd of aurochs. The short one was obviously the leader of the mismatched troupe. "We've been caught a bit short. Don't have an axe to chop down a decent sized sapling to make a new one, so we're stuck here. Don't suppose you boys could help us out?"

"Muscle-boy has a big chopper," Blathnaid called from her wagon. "Don't you, Sláine?"

The brute rolled the orphaned cartwheel into the centre of the road. He dusted his hands off and looked at Blathnaid.

"Hello, lady."

Blathnaid smiled. She turned to Sláine who was still eyeing the three men suspiciously. "Come on, Sláine, anyone can see these honest travellers are in need of your strapping muscles."

So he dismounted and shouldered his axe.

"Go with him," the short man said to the fop. "Help him pick out the right tree."

The fop nodded. "Come, let us find a straight tree to chop down shall we?"

He followed the fop into the trees, pointing out several he thought perfectly adequate to do the job but none satisfied the other man. He followed him deeper and deeper into the woods until he couldn't see the road, the wagons or anything else apart from row after row of trees.

"This ought to do it," the fop said.

Sláine couldn't see what was different about this sapling over any of the others. He shrugged, pulled back his axe and swung, sinking Brain-Biter's blade deep into the wet wood.

Then his head was ringing and the world was spinning, and his legs buckled.

The last thing he saw was a blur that was vaguely fop-shaped peering down at him and then the world went black.

He had no idea how much later it was when he came to. His head hurt. Tentatively, he felt out the lump where the fop had hit him. It was tender to the touch. When he drew his hand away it was wet with blood. He shook his head, angry with himself for being taken so easily – from behind – and the world reeled around him. He lurched sideways, heaving up the contents of his guts. He wiped the mess off his mouth and counted to thirty, breathing deeply.

He staggered back out to the road.

The bandits were gone, as was their covered wagon, and Blathnaid.

Mannix was sitting hunched over with his head in his hands.

There was no sign of Finbar or Fergus.

He sat down beside the trader.

"Blathnaid?"

"Gone," Mannix sniffed, wincing as he raised his head.

"They took her?" he asked hopefully, even now wanting to believe that her obvious betrayal was nothing of the sort. He imagined the fop and the brute dragging her kicking and screaming to their wagon, muttering something sinister about how there was no one to hear her scream.

"Don't be an idiot, big man. She was in on it. The minute you were gone she had a damned poniard to my throat and that brute was clubbing the brothers senseless."

He really should have known, of course. Blathnaid had played him for a simpleton every bit as effectively as she had Mannix and the redheaded mirth brothers. She had been quite skilled, and had never told an outright lie. Rather, she had a way of making men hear what they wanted to hear. She hadn't been coy or overly flirtatious. There had just been something about her that made Sláine want to protect her, or at least that was what he told himself. He wasn't proud that he had been gulled so completely and so easily. It was exasperating.

"I can't believe it… I mean she… I don't…"

"That's what we get for thinking with the little fella instead of this," Mannix said, tapping his temple. The trader had taken a bad beating. His lip was split and a cut had opened up above his eye that refused to stop bleeding. He was lucky, an inch lower and he would have been blinded for life.

Sláine grumbled. He shifted uncomfortably. Everything hurt, his pride most of all.

"Ahhh, the kind heart ever did fall for the fair maiden. Quite ingenious really, when you think about it. Paying me to take her on the wagon, then stealing her, the coin they paid me with, and a hefty lump of interest besides. Quite ingenious."

The more Sláine thought about it, the more he realised it was true. By the time the wagons had passed beneath the shadow of Cader Idris – what the locals called the Giant's Seat because of its peculiar rock formation – Blathnaid had more than wrapped Sláine around her little finger. A few tears – he doubted they were even real – had been all it took. It was another new experience for him. It was only natural to want to believe her, he told himself, nursing the lump on the side of his head. His vision swam in and out of focus.

"I knew there was something wrong about that woman," he said, and then he said it again, as if by repeating it he could somehow undo his lustful folly and make things right the second time.

"That's a bit like shutting the stable door after the horse has bolted, isn't it big man? Don't beat yourself up over it. She fooled us all good and proper, and no mistake. Who'd have thought it, eh? Just going to have to chalk this one up to experience and all that."

A Red Branch warrior did not fall for a pretty face, Sláine berated himself. A warrior of the Red Branch's judgement was never clouded by the remembered taste of a sweet woman on his tongue. Sláine was a warrior, not some lovesick fool. He fought battles with his axe. He cracked skulls, broke ribs and snapped necks. He was clueless when it came to fighting battles won with coy looks and pretty words that made his head spin.

He had been making bad decisions since he had been exiled. It was fast approaching the point where it would be preferable to come to a gassy end on someone's infernal petard rather than continually making a complete arse out of himself. He vowed to steer clear of women: even the soft ones, the voluptuous ones, the bony ones, the chiselled ones, the cheeky ones, the elfin ones, the comfortable ones, the flinty ones, the tall ones, the short ones, the blonde ones, the brunettes, the willing ones, the unwilling, and redheads, especially redheads. All of them, but women in general. They were all trouble.

Mannix just laughed at him. "Trust me lad, the world would be a boring place without them."

"How can you laugh about it, old man? She robbed you blind."

"Ahhh but didn't she make you feel good while she was doing it?"

He had no answer to that.

With the coin gone, Mannix had nothing with which to pay his wages. No money meant no food. It was a vicious circle. Their prospects were further reduced by the fact that Blathnaid's crew had made off with their covered wagon and hamstrung two of their carthorses. It was not the most auspicious of circumstances. Mannix was all for turning back but Sláine was determined to follow the road to their journey's end so they came to a parting of the ways.

"You sure I can't convince you that fame and fortune lies this way, big man?"

Sláine grinned wryly. "I'm pretty sure people I don't want to see lie that way, and I met a wench in Breiddin who was fairly insistent that fame and fortune are waiting in a little berg just outside of Crumlyn. She convinced me, let's put it that way."

"Ahhh, but laddie, do you ever learn? A woman you say? How can you be sure that it isn't a ruse? Fortune's a fickle bugger, more likely than not to try and trick you into doing something rash." Mannix winked. "Good luck to you, my friend. It's been an interesting ride."

"Indeed it has, but for both our sakes let us hope it doesn't get any more interesting."

"Danu's perky tit, I hope you are right, big man. So, if I happen to run into these friends of yours, is there anything you would have me say?"

"That I went the other way," Sláine said.

"I think I can do that," Mannix chuckled.

They parted company with a slap on the back and a shake of the hand.

Sláine walked on a while, scanning the trees for crows. For a while he alternated between walking one hundred paces and running a hundred. It felt good to stretch his legs. It had been too long since he had done anything physically demanding. Riding a horse was soft work. He missed the exertion of Bedelia's farm.

He walked for two more days. He dropped into the habit of muttering to himself. His thoughts turned to his exile and the reasons for it. Two women: Niamh and his mother. Three if he counted Danu, although technically the Goddess could also have been four and five. Women seemed to be at the root of all his problems but according to Mannix that was the way for every man. He wasn't sure he wanted to believe the old trader. They had a lot of appealing qualities, their infinite variety, for one thing. No two women smelled or tasted the same in his albeit limited experience. No two women made love the same either, although he would need to find twin sisters and bed them both to test that theory in any detail.

Sláine rounded a sharp corner in the road, the trail entering the forest it had been skirting for the last three leagues. The shift in the atmosphere was palpable. It put him instinctively on edge. He walked more slowly, paying more attention to his surroundings. The undergrowth grew gradually thicker and less pleasant the deeper into the woods the road went. He turned instinctively to look behind him.

He appeared to be alone on the road but it didn't take him long to realise that wasn't true.

He stopped by a mile marker to break his fast on a mouldy chunk of cheese and a slab of stale bread. It made Bedelia's meals seem like feasts. He chewed the food and swallowed, doing his damnedest not to taste it on the way down.

He knew that he was being watched, but by whom? It occurred to him that the Red Branch hunters might finally have caught up with him. His skin prickled. It was an uncomfortable sensation, what his mother used to call a goose walking over your grave. It was seldom a good sign and he had learned to heed it.

Without being obvious about it, he looked around for any telltale signs that might betray the observer. They were there to be seen, in fact there was an element of conflicting evidence that puzzled him. It was possible that the watcher was not alone. Sláine almost missed one of the most obvious signs: the sudden scurry from the undergrowth of a startled field vole. The little rodent ran blindly into the dirt road, turning in confused circles, its nose twitching at the conflicting scents of Sláine in front of him and the watcher behind. Sláine smiled to himself. He sat in silence, appearing to toy with his food. More subtle signs included broken vegetation where the watcher had pushed his way into the undergrowth. The broken grass was still green, and it hadn't been raining, which meant that the damage was less than a day old. A little off to the left a bramble had been picked clean of berries, another indication that the watcher had settled in for a long wait. At the foot of the bush he saw a faint spray of dirt, the scuff of what was almost certainly a footprint. It had been the gathering of flies that put the matter beyond doubt. They buzzed around fresh dung.

He wondered how long the watcher had lain in wait. Long enough to eat and shit for sure, which meant a few hours at least, perhaps even the best part of the early morning from late last night? It showed a certain amount of patience, something the Red Branch hunters would almost certainly be short on after so many months away from home. The watcher almost certainly wasn't from Murias.

He had his suspicions as to who it was, but why they had gone to such elaborate lengths to snare him he didn't know.

He closed his eyes to listen for anything, even the slightest sound of movement out of place. Nothing. His thoughts returned to women and the fact that they were at the heart of all of his problems. That was when he heard what could only have been a footstep behind him. Sláine forced himself to act as if he hadn't heard anything. He concentrated on the rhythm of his own breathing and the *dub-dub-dub* of his pulse. He tore off a chunk of blue-veined cheese and forced himself to eat it. He heard nothing for a full five minutes, but he didn't need to.

There were other ways the watcher betrayed himself. Sláine remained on edge, alert. Sláine felt certain the watcher would make himself known sooner rather than later, otherwise there was the possibility that he might move on, reducing the watcher's chance of coming up on him unawares.

A foreign smell reached his nose. He breathed it in deeply. It took him a moment to place it. When he did, he smiled and opened his eyes. There was only one person he had smelled that perfume on recently and it was not a him at all. He waited, and still the watcher didn't reveal herself.

"You might as well come out. I know you are there, Blathnaid," Sláine said after a few minutes. "I can smell your bath oils. I've seen some remarkable things since I left Murias but I have never known a squirrel to wash itself in the oil of orchids gathered from the floor of the Burren. Something to think about next time you want to sneak up on a hunter."

"Aren't you just the clever barbarian, muscle-boy?" the woman muttered, abandoning all pretence of stealth. She stepped out of the undergrowth not ten paces from where he sat. She no longer looked the innocent maiden, having swapped her flowing skirts for practical breeches and a figure-hugging hide waistcoat over a simple shirt. Her hair was bound up in a bun and held in place by a short black-wood pin.

"I like to think I am full of surprises."

The fop and the brute came up behind them. There was no sign of the short one. Sláine assumed he was hiding in the trees somewhere, most likely with an arrow trained on him just in case he should decide to make any sudden moves.

"So." Sláine turned to look at the fop. "Can I assume you've come to hit me on the head again?"

The fop smirked. "Sorry about that, but you know, given the circumstances, us robbing you and all that, it seemed like a sensible precaution. No hard feelings, eh?"

"None. It wasn't that hard." He winked at Blathnaid conspiratorially. "But just between you and me, you ought to know that I'll pay the compliment back one day."

"Is that a threat?" the fop bristled.

"Nah, a threat sounds more like this: I'm going to cut your bollocks off and make tathlum out of them, you steaming pile of stinking offal. You see the difference?"

The fop lunged forwards, ready to go toe to toe with Sláine. Sláine grinned, enjoying the chance to make the man look like a fool. "Come on then, girly man, let's see if you can take me face to face." He moved up into a tight fighting crouch. His hand touched Brain-Biter's shaft; it was reassuring to know the old axe was there should things get serious and he actually needed it. The pair circled each other until Blathnaid's voice cut across their posturing.

"Now, now boys, stop flexing your muscles. There's so much sweaty manhood in the air, a girl could positively swoon."

"I don't like you," the fop sneered, cracking his knuckles. It was a petty little gesture that was meant to seem threatening but just came across as pitifully inadequate.

"That's all right, girly man. She does," he nodded towards Blathnaid. "That's what matters." He let that sink in for a moment. "Why else do you think she had you wait around for me? I guess you boys weren't doing it for her so she thought she'd bring in a real man."

"Your arrogance is incredible," Blathnaid said but she was smiling as she said it.

Sláine sketched a mocking bow. "It's not arrogance, m'dear, it's natural superiority. Admit it. It gets your blood pumping, doesn't it?"

"You're insufferable, muscle-boy. I'm beginning to think it was a mistake coming back for you," Blathnaid said but for all her protests he saw that she was still smiling.

"Probably," Sláine said. Despite his realisation that all of his problems began and ended with women, he began to think that it could be a fun mistake. "But what is life without some fun?"

Sláine threw his lot in with Blathnaid and her rag-tag bunch of bandits.

It wasn't as if he had a vast array of alternatives.

It didn't matter that they were not particularly effective bandits. The group offered security, food, companionship and, despite his forswearing the supple delights of the female form, Blathnaid. He quickly discovered that their deceit with Mannix had been their first successful robbery in over a year, and the booty they had claimed quickly dwindled when the short one, Coyle, put a cunningly concocted sleeping draught into their evening meal and made off with their ill-gotten gains while they snored. How ironic, Sláine thought. They hadn't even managed to hold on to the booty for a night. This, he quickly came to understand, was indicative of their entire operation.

Last autumn the fop, Íhomar, and the brute, Keegan, had spent a month in gaol while Blathnaid struggled to raise the ransom to buy them out, because they had been caught, drunk, at the scene of a robbery.

"You truly are pitiful," Sláine said, shaking his head as he pictured the pair, paralytic over the barrel of mead they'd found in the back of the ambushed cart.

"It was good stuff," Keegan said. His voice rumbled around in his gut before emerging like an earth tremor. "And robbing is thirsty work. Heck, it was almost worth being locked up for." He chuckled, thoroughly amused by the memory.

They were planning a raid on a caravan they had gotten word of. It was coming up the road from Crumlyn, supposedly loaded with wares. The temptation was too much for them to resist despite the obvious dangers of attacking a likely guarded wagon.

"You have to be the worst robbers in all of Tir-Nan-Og."

"We took your shambles, didn't we?" Íhomar said as if that proved his point beyond a shadow of a doubt.

"No great feat," Sláine said. "The red-headed mirth brothers were hardly a match for your obvious guile, and you sucker-punched me on the back of the head."

"Are you being funny?"

"Do I sound it?" Sláine said.

Like everything else they put their hands to, it went horribly wrong.

There were six fully-armoured guards riding alongside the wagon. Sláine recognised their type. These were hard men used to mixing it up. They wouldn't be out of their depth if things got a little rough. The front two wore thick pelts around their shoulders and blue woad tribal markings on their cheeks. They carried iron swords, which surprised him – metal was soft. It always bent in the end, unlike stone. He patted Brain-Biter reassuringly. This, at least, was in their favour. Perhaps if they got lucky the guards' swords would get bent out of shape from beating the life out of the fop, Íhomar.

Blathnaid stepped into the middle of the road, playing the victim. Her clothes were torn and smeared with dirt, her hair bedraggled, one braid undone, the other tangled with brambles as if she had been dragged through a hedge backwards. The boys had done a good job of roughing her up. She looked the part.

Sláine hunkered down behind an outcrop of granite to watch Blathnaid lie through her teeth. She was, he decided, very good at it. He made a mental note not to trust a word she said to him.

"Ho!" the lead rider called, his horse rearing up as he pulled back sharply on its reins.

"Please, sir," Blathnaid called, stumbling theatrically as she took another step forwards. "We were attacked by bandits. My father… my father is dead. They killed him. I don't know what to do."

The rider turned back to the caravan and gestured two of the other guards forwards.

"Bandits, you say? Where?"

"Here," Íhomar said, stepping out from hiding.

"And here," Keegan rumbled, joining him from the other side of the road. The brute looked menacing with a huge wooden club in his hands.

Sláine winced, so much for the element of surprise.

Blathnaid screamed; a pureblooded scream of absolute stark terror.

The noise had all three horses shying, one of the guards tumbling from his saddle, another getting his foot caught in his stirrup as the horse bucked and reared, kicking out. The animal fled in panic, dragging the hapless guard through the dirt.

Sláine chuckled but his amusement quickly turned to dread as the remaining guards dismounted and drew their swords, steel ringing out coldly as they stepped forwards to meet Íhomar and Keegan.

Blathnaid fell to her knees in the middle of the road, whimpering, "Save me... save me."

"Hush, woman," the guard said. "We'll deal with you later." The two others stepped in behind him, forming a tight triangle of steel.

Sláine almost felt bad about not going down to join them, but it was a fleeting sensation that lasted for about as long as it took for the fop to be skewered and the brute to be emasculated. It was not a pretty sight. He died staring at his own manhood lying on the floor like a bloated worm.

"Is there anyone else following you, woman?"

Blathnaid shook her head. "You saved me... how can I ever thank you? What can I do?" She was still on her knees, looking up imploringly at the guard. She did a very good job of ignoring the blood on his sword. "Just tell me."

"You can start by shutting up."

She did.

"Nostrum, read the scene. I'd like to know if there are any more surprises out there."

The one called Nostrum sheathed his sword. He walked slowly in a sweeping circle, crouching occasionally to examine something more closely. The man wouldn't have to be particularly adept at reading the road to know that they were a set of tracks short. Keegan's heavy feet left deep heel and toe impressions, while the fop's slightly rolling gait left side-heavy prints, Blathnaid walked on her toes, and then there were Sláine's, even heel and toe depressions. They all left distinctive tracks. Nostrum walked backwards, lightly, on his heels. He nodded twice to himself as he came to a halt directly below Sláine, precisely where he had abandoned the road for his current perch.

Sláine watched the man, studying how he moved. A thoughtful warrior could learn a lot about his enemy just from watching him move, for instance if he favoured a certain side or ticks or any of many other hints that were there to be read.

The man moved well. There was a grace to his movement that belied his size.

"At least one more, Bragg." He pointed up the hill at the outcropping of granite that Sláine was hunkered down behind.

"He's gone," Blathnaid blurted. "He was my man, we had a fight. He ran when those ruffians jumped our wagon. He's probably run all the way back to Poulawack by now."

"Oh, do stop lying, woman. Do you imagine for a moment that I believe a word that comes out of your mouth?" Bragg said, cuffing Blathnaid across the face. She rocked back on her knees, spitting blood.

I wouldn't if I were you, Sláine thought.

"Poulawack," Blathnaid repeated, stressing the word. She couldn't help herself. She glanced up the hillside to where Sláine was hiding. Sláine cringed inwardly. Thanks for that, nothing like making my life easier. The fact that she didn't weep pitifully but rather had the presence of mind to repeat her message to the man in hiding was all a battle-hardened veteran should need to know she wasn't what she seemed.

Sláine knew that she was trying to tell him that she would meet up with him back at the village. Poulawack was almost exactly halfway between where they were and Crumlyn. A safe distance away, but not so far that they would never find each other again.

Bragg slapped her again, hard enough to send Blathnaid sprawling in the dirt.

"When will you learn to listen, woman? I said shut up!" He turned to Nostrum. "Go find the fool and kill him. I don't want any loose ends."

Sláine didn't wait around to be "tidied up".

Sláine moved quickly and quietly, but took great pains to be sure his track was readable.

He wasn't in the mood to be tracked by more enemies. The ever-present threat of Grudnew's hunters was
more than enough to worry about.

He wanted Nostrum to catch up with him, but under
his own terms.

One truth Gorian had instilled in all of his Red
Branch warriors was that you didn't want an enemy at
your back. Sláine led the guard a merry dance through
the undergrowth. Time and again, Sláine thought bitterly, the distance kill would have been easy with a gáe
bolga. The guard might have been a skilled tracker but
he was a terrible sneak. More than once he stepped out
against a starkly contrasting sky, the sun at his back,
making him a perfect target. Unfortunately Sláine had
no such long-range weapons, but he was far from helpless. He had Brain-Biter. His father's old stone axe was
hungry to crack some skulls.

As the hunt wore on Nostrum grew more and more
reckless, running in places in his haste. Sláine could
only wonder what kind of taskmaster would inspire
such an unthinking need to please in his men. Sláine
led the man further and further away from the safety of
his comrades. The weather began to change around
them, growing decidedly colder. At first faint wisps of
fog curled up from the ground but within half an hour
a thick rolling mist was coming off the grass. The mist
formed haunting shapes out of the trees and low dragging   branches,   distorting   everything.   The
shadow-shapes corresponded with no known beast of
reality but that only made them more unnerving. For a
moment he thought he saw the antlered silhouette of

Carnun, the Horned God. The chimera sent a shiver
the length of Sláine's spine. He offered a silent prayer to
Danu as he doubled back on himself, knowing that
soon the mist would be so thick he would be able to
stand on Nostrum's shoulder and breathe in the man's
ear without the guard having the slightest inkling he
was there until the very last second.

Sláine scanned the shadow-shapes, looking for one
that best suited his purposes. He picked one that looked
vaguely human – a combination of shrubbery and
thick-boled tree, a knot of which looked disturbingly
like a crooked nose – and wedged Brain-Biter in place
so that when Nostrum neared he would see man and
axe in one deceptive illusion. He moved away, hunker-
ing down to settle in for the long wait, praying the
illusion would hold long enough to fool his erstwhile
hunter.

He heard Nostrum come stumbling and tripping
through the mist less then a quarter of an hour later.
Sláine didn't dare breathe. He watched the man freeze at
the sight of his shadow shape and then draw steel, ready
to fight. It was an eerily silent fight. Nostrum rushed his
imagined foe and thrust his sword violently into the
unyielding wood. There was a moment of unreality as
he obviously thought he had felled his quarry and wondered why the man wouldn't fall before he realised his
mistake. Sláine felt no grief that the man's final thoughts
were of failure. Most people in his experience died the
same way, coming up against the ultimate leveller. He
stepped up behind Nostrum, grabbed him by the head
and snapped his neck like a twig.

He took the man's purse. He didn't bother counting the coins. He was sure that there would be enough to see him through while he waited for Blathnaid to find him in Poulawack.

He didn't want to imagine what would happen to her when Nostrum failed to return.

Sláine rubbed his chin, feeling the whiskers that were growing in.

Not for the first time he longed for a good sharp knife and a tablet of lye to lather up and clean himself with.

The road didn't allow for such luxuries.

He realised that she wasn't coming back. He wondered, not for the first time, where she was. Had she become Bragg's lover, using her charms to wheedle her way out of trouble and into his bed? For her sake he hoped not. A man like Bragg would almost certainly be a cruel mate. Then again a little cruelty was almost always better than the alternative: being worm food.

He had spent a month in Poulawack, working his way through the coin he'd lifted from Nostrum's corpse. He was flat broke. He found himself some work as a heavy for a moneylender, Gosta Vern, and his wife Maeve. It was an ideal arrangement for a while. Vern needed muscle, of which Sláine had plenty. Sláine needed money and who had more of that than a moneylender?

He watched Vern work.

The man had an uncanny knack for guessing exactly what was the lowest number of coins someone would accept for their golden torcs, silver brooches and other trinkets but Sláine quickly came to realise it was no supernatural gift. Vern had a highly polished bauble he placed strategically on his desk, between himself and the borrower. As he made his opening gambit, he would look down at the bauble as if considering what exactly he was about to offer, and he would gauge the reaction in their eyes without ever appearing to actually look at them. It was ingenious. People were far less suspicious and guarded with their reactions when they thought he wasn't looking. Time and again Vern made a killing just by watching the reflected dilation of would-be borrower's pupils.

Vern was an oddball. He didn't trust others with the safekeeping of his money, and had a taste for the little luxuries of life, like silk over wool. He paid a small fortune to bring in the most exotic clothes from outside the Land of the Young and never wore them, preferring his grubby old coats and his dirt-smeared shirts. He would take in markers and issue IOU's for goods he imported through various traders like old Mannix, inflating the price by as much as six times so that he fleeced as much profit as possible out of every deal. He was a character, all right. One night Sláine woke to the bang of the back door and a bitten-back curse. Vern had been out by cover of moonlight burying bags of his money in the back yard. It was funny really, the moneylender swore blind he owned the money, but Sláine knew better: the money owned him.

Occasionally Vern sent Sláine out to collect when debtors reneged on repayments. These visits were not something he particularly enjoyed. Word got round that

Vern had a new heavy, and after Sláine had battered eight coins of interest out of the miller, Tooker, locals began to be a lot more circumspect when it came to settling up in time.

He knew he couldn't stay in Poulawack indefinitely but it was home for a while.

He found himself walking through the streets, savouring the feel of the rain on his face. It made him feel alive. The curious dichotomy of the wet and the summertime's heat was seductive. He exercised hard, running until the pain hit his sides and the breath tore at his throat. The running became a ritual, as if by forcing himself to run further and faster he could somehow leave all the pain and the sadness of exile behind, but of course there was no escaping it.

On the eve of Mabon, the fall equinox, Sláine found the maiden with the garlands in her hair. He wasn't the least bit surprised to see her. Their lives seemed to be inextricably tied so it was only natural she would come to him again. This time she was sitting beneath a weeping willow making a chain of flowers to wear as a crown.

His heart soared at the sight of her.

She was every bit as beautiful as he remembered. More so, even: the fall of her hair across her face, the shallow rise and fall of her breast as she breathed, the grim determination in her eyes as she worked the delicate stems into interlocking links. Danu looked up and smiled at him. It was more than simple beauty. The maiden had an aura about her; an intimate warmth that made the recipient want nothing more than to fall down and offer devotion to the Goddess, body and soul. Sláine's head swam. He wanted so desperately to scoop her up and sweep her off her feet, to feel her slender-fingered hands against his chest even as he buried himself in her kiss and her flesh.

And then: You're too late, my love, always too late.

The maiden had lured him up to the hillside to witness the attack on Murias. In her own words he had needed to see it, not to prevent it, not to save lives but to see them lost.

He needed to know why.

Why had she done that to him?

He fell to his knees.

"Why?" His voice cracked.

The Goddess's eyes moved over him, from his hands clenched as if in prayer, to his chest and up to his face. He saw for the first time that she had peculiar bird-like eyes. They made his heart feel as if it would stop beating in his chest. He almost welcomed the sensation. This close Sláine could feel the intense heat coming off her body. He licked his lips, mouth suddenly parched. It was impossible to master a coherent thought in her presence. Images of bare skin leaked into his mind, memories of Brighid, Niamh, Bedelia and even Blathnaid, naked and willing, offering themselves up to him: the wetness of their flesh, the urgency of the coupling, the sheer physical release they offered. He was giddy with the power surging through his blood and bones. It had been so long since he had truly felt the earth's serpent coiling within him, and it wasn't through anger or pity or even abandonment. It was her, Blodeuwedd, the maiden: the beautiful, innocent, aspect of Danu. It was always her.

How could he ever surrender that willingly? How could he give up the devotion of the flesh the Goddess craved?

He couldn't and he knew it.

"It's an enchantment," the maiden said, "a simple magic but no less wonderful for it. Each of the flowers represents a quality I want in my future husband. They are all different. Tonight when I sleep wearing the crown I will dream of my true love."

He didn't recognise all of the blossoms but there was a surprising variety of blooms in the maiden's floral crown.

"I had no wish to punish you, my beautiful Sláine. You must believe that." As she said it, he really did believe her, but then as Mannix had always said, he was a fool for a pretty face. She put the crown of flowers on his head, and kissed his brow. "Dream of your true love tonight, Sláine Mac Roth. Let this be my gift to you, and my apology."

And he did.

He dreamed of himself walking through a leafy door into a chamber deep down in the belly of the earth where Danu waited for him, naked and willing.

"You came," the maiden said, her voice inside him, filling him completely. "I knew you would."

The walls of the chamber were the deep rich red of succulent clay, filled with moisture and unable to contain it completely.

He said nothing.

Creatures of the forest gathered at the foot of the huge bed, squirrels, badgers, voles, mice, roe deer and a single horned stag; all of Danu's children. He was an outsider here.

"No my love, you are not an outsider. This is where you belong, with me, inside me. I am hungry, my beautiful one. I want you."

She held out her hand to him, drawing him onto the bed with her.

The maiden wore a sheer gown, so thin that every contour of her flesh — the rise of her hip and fall of her breast — was plain to see. He savoured the sight of her, surrendered to it. The others, Niamh, Brighid, Bedelia, Blathnaid, were pale shadows beside the maiden, flawed and imperfect. He had no idea why he had been chosen — or even when — that was unimportant.

He fell into her arms. He felt the power of the earth enter him, inciting him to lose himself in the wild abandon of passion. Everywhere their bodies touched danced to the thrill of earth power, burying him alive in a landslide of sensation.

"Oh my beautiful boy," she whispered in his ear.

Fourteen
Captured

"WAKE UP, YOU sorry son of a bitch!" The sharp end of a boot thundered into his side, lifting Sláine bodily from the ground.

He grunted and rolled over.

He had fallen asleep beneath the maiden's tree.

The dream left him.

He opened his eyes to see an unusually ugly face leering down at him.

"There's a pretty penny on your head, warped one. Strikes me the king of the Sessair wants you very badly."

He grunted again but before he could move Ugly had hammered another kick into his gut and a third between his legs, reducing the world to a sunburst of pain. When his vision finally settled down he saw a guilty-looking Gosta Vern standing beside Ugly, wringing his hands. The moneylender nervously scrunched up a roll of parchment.

"Sorry, lad. It's business. Nothing personal, you understand. Word came from the north that Grudnew had put a bounty on your head. Hunters were showing this drawing of you around the village. Someone was going to earn a pretty penny off your scalp, so Maeve and I figured why not us?"

Of course it's personal, Sláine wanted to scream. How could it be anything but?

"I hope I am worth it," Sláine said, wincing as he tried to move. Why was Grudnew pursuing him so relentlessly when the old man had promised to turn a blind eye if he ran? It didn't make sense to him, but of course it did. The Sessair King had been humbled. To hold his head up he had to be seen to be doing everything possible to bring Sláine to justice. Grudnew didn't really care if he was caught, only that it looked as if he cared to his people, which, in a ridiculously roundabout way meant doing his utmost to bring Sláine down. It didn't matter that it was a charade, it was every bit as deadly as the real thing. It would end though. The king's death was sealed the day he took the throne. Seven years. That was a lot of looking over the shoulder, and a lot of running. Understanding it didn't make him feel any better about his current predicament.

Ugly put the boot in again.

"Best not move, lad. The hunters were pretty specific about their king wanting you alive, but Welkin here, well he's got no compunction about sticking a knife in your face if things start to get nasty."

"Just give me an excuse, warped one," Ugly sneered.

"Are you in a hurry to die, ugly?" Sláine spat. He didn't recognise the thug but assumed Vern had hired him as his replacement. It made sense, since a money-lender would always need muscle.

A fifth kick from Ugly sent Sláine scrambling across the dirt. He roared in pain. Anger flamed beneath the agony, a brilliant red flare that latched on to the residual magic in the earth from where the maiden herself had sat weaving her crown of flowers. It surged into his veins, warping his flesh as it struggled impossibly to bind the sheer immensity of Danu's power. He surged to his feet, arms outstretched ready to throttle the life out of Ugly and the moneylender.

"They mentioned that, as well," Vern said, quite matter-of-factly. Sláine saw the moneylender slip the crumpled picture back into the folds of his grubby coat and pull out a small, thin, stick. He put the stick to his lips and blew sharply.

It felt like a gnat's bite on his neck, a sudden painful sting. A blush of heat followed the initial bite. The heat intensified quickly. Sláine felt his heart lurch and his vision blur nauseatingly. Reflexively his hand slapped up at the sting, pressing the poison-tipped dart deeper into his warped flesh. His legs buckled beneath him even as he lurched forwards another step, and he collapsed into Ugly's waiting arms.

"Good job the old man wanted you alive," Ugly goaded, "because killing you would be too easy."

The world rolled around Sláine, the ground rushing up to meet his face. He felt the sheer violent delight of the earth power ripping out of his skin. The energy of raw lightning twisted his body, contorting it. His muscles tore free of bone and tendon. His back arched, the bones in his spine stretching as the warp took full frightening hold. There was nothing he could do. He had no control over his own body. His legs refused to move. For all their size, his arms flopped uselessly at his sides. The power raged impotently within him with no hope of release. The toxins suffused his system, leaving him alert, enraged, seething with pent up earth power, and completely and utterly helpless.

Ugly walked around him, kicking him once in the back and a second time in the side of the face, splitting his cheek open just below the eye.

Vern looked down at Sláine, his nose twitching. The moneylender's eyes darted left and right. "No hard feelings, Sláine." He repeated. "Welkin, get the cart. Let's get this over with."

"Plennnn arrrrrd eeeeelins," Sláine lisped, struggling to form the words.

It was obvious Vern understood the threat well enough. The moneylender backed away from Sláine despite the fact that the drugs had him paralysed and incapable of extracting any kind of reckoning for Vern's duplicity.

"Evidently," Vern said, backing up another step. He looked down distastefully at Sláine's distended body, "which makes you a problem for another day. Today you are my cash cow."

They manhandled Sláine into the back of the flatbed cart, rolling him onto his side in case he vomited. "There we go, don't want our investment choking to death on his on puke, do we Welkin?" His head lolled awkwardly on his neck. He couldn't even see the sky. "Just in case you think about getting frisky along the road," Vern explained, dosing up a second dart with the dregs of the poison draught. Sláine grunted but couldn't move. "Would you like to do the honours, Welkin?"

"With a ridiculous amount of pleasure," Ugly said, taking the dart from the moneylender. He crawled into the flatbed, hmmming and ahhhhing as he looked for the perfect stop to jab the dart in.

"Gerrr ovah wif."

"Yes, yes," Ugly promised. "Won't hurt a bit. Well, maybe a bit."

"Anywhere," Vern said, "it doesn't matter."

"Oh, I know, I just want to do it properly." Ugly grinned and rammed the tip of the dart into Sláine's armpit, puncturing deep into the sweat glands. "That should do it."

The sky dissolved into a haze of pain and Sláine blacked out.

When he came to the cart was jouncing and judder-ing down the rutted track.

He tried to lift his head to get a look at his sur-roundings but his body was having none of it.

The broch was a solitary gaol on the outskirts of Crumlyn, where the land met the wild raging sea.

Even among prisons, the place was harsh.

It had been erected on a geological phenomenon known as a stack: a vertical pillar of rock cut off from the body of the mountain by centuries of erosion. Only the broch was built on the last column of a triple stack, three huge pillars cut off from the land by the churning sea. Once, years ago there had been a series of rock arches but the chalk had succumbed to the elements and collapsed. Now the series of pillars were only joined to the head-land by a rickety wooden drawbridge.

The broch was a canker against the otherwise wild beauty of the natural world; an unnatural pinnacle on the high plateau, the crumbling stone walls of the prison overlooked nothing and everything, depending upon your perspective. It was an imposing spectre, a constant reminder of the austerity of justice. Algae and barnacles crept their way up the walls, tendrils of green and white eating into the brick and mortar.

They had Sláine trussed up. Ugly pushed him forwards onto the wooden bridge. It lurched violently beneath his feet. It was not a pleasant sensation. The bridge swayed sickeningly with every step he took. He didn't look down. It was a long way to the rocks below.

"Go on, take a good look at the rocks," Ugly goaded. "Wouldn't want you to fall and hurt yourself, now would we?"

He prodded Sláine in the back.

Sláine stumbled forwards.

The drop was vertiginous. He concentrated on looking forwards, not down. The prison was like something out of nightmare territory. The wind plucked at him, bullying him every bit as forcefully as Ugly's poking and prodding. A huge brute of a creature stood waiting for them at the other end of the bridge. The guard had shaved his head apart from a furious topknot and a jagged bolt of lightning just beneath the temple. He towered over Sláine, arms as thick as ham hocks from a Beltain feast, legs like the stumps of felled oaks. His face was flat, his brow simian, nose broken repeatedly so that it resembled nothing more than a slab of rib-eyed steak pressed up against his face. Only two teeth remained in his sneer. He crossed his huge ham hock arms and stared them down as they approached.

"We've come for our money, Nudd," Vern called. "Tell your master to crack open his coffers."

The guard grunted and disappeared into the broch, emerging a minute later with a runt of a man dressed in black robes smeared with streaks of egg and bacon fat, and other meals that had missed his mouth. The man in black rubbed his hands together delightedly at the sight of Sláine's captivity.

"Oh, yes, yes, yes, you did well, Gosta, very well indeed. How much was it we said, thirty coin?"

"We said fifty, Kendrick, as you very well know. Don't try to swindle a swindler, there's a good man."

"Yes, yes, right you are," the man in black muttered. "Fifty coin for the warped one. Come with me." He turned to the hulking Nudd. "See our new guest is safely accommodated, Nudd. Put him in with the dwarf and Black Axe while I see about paying the good Master Vern here. Splendid. Splendid."

Vern disappeared into the broch behind Kendrick.

Nudd grunted and grabbed Sláine by the scruff of the neck, pushing him into the old prison.

"Don't say goodbye then, Sláine," Ugly mocked.

"Why? Our relationship isn't over. One day you'll wake up to find me sharpening Brain-Biter with your bones."

"Big words as ever, Sláine. I'm going to miss you."

The broch was dank and oppressive inside, the cells crowded in on each other, the walls slick with mould and the white of sea salt crusting over the damp stone.

The iron bars of the cell doors were riddled with rust and the straw scattered across the floor as insulation had seen better days. In fact the whole place had seen better days. In another life it had almost certainly been a stronghold erected to keep out marauders from Albion, across the savage sea.

"In here," Nudd grunted, taking a huge iron key from the chain around his waist and sliding it into the lock. There was an ominously heavy clunk as the bolt fell into place. The door groaned pitifully as Nudd dragged it open, its rusted hinges protesting. He shoved Sláine into the cell. Sláine stumbled and collapsed into a heap in the centre of the floor, his face pressed painfully into the rotten straw, the needle-sharp splintered ends digging into his chin and cheek. Nudd slammed the door and locked it. There was no lonelier sound than the second clunk of the lock coming down to trap him in the dark.

He felt a curious toe nudge his side, and then again, a little more insistently.

"What?"

"Alive then, always a good sign, eh, Bodb?"

Sláine rolled over to see the speaker, a pug-faced dwarf with wrinkles and folds of dark shadow where he should have had a chin and neck. The little man had a bulbous nose and stringy silver-grey hair. The gap between his quivering top lip and his runny nose was almost as long again as his nose itself. He wore a grey hood with long floppy ears. It took Sláine a moment to realise that the ears were not a part of the dwarf's hood, but were in fact his real ears.

The lighting in the cell was curious. It was lighter than he had expected, with salt and mould giving the cramped room a curious luminescence, and there were windows, lots of them. It wasn't the dank oppressive dungeon he had expected, but then, given the environs it was hardly likely any prisoners would be escaping through them. No one would be stupid – or desperate – enough to throw themselves on the mercy of the sea.

"You must get really bad headaches," Sláine said, pushing himself up onto his elbow.

"What do you mean?" the dwarf asked, quizzically.

"Ears that big must hear everything, even ants farting, it's got to drive you crazy."

From the darkness, Bodb laughed. "I could get to like you, young man."

"Oh shut up, Bodb," the dwarf grumbled. He prodded Sláine again, "So, what did you do to get yourself locked up in the salt lick of creation?"

Sláine sat up. "Long story, little man."

"Well it isn't like we don't have time on our hands, so come on. Tell us your life story. We're all ears." The dwarf waggled his ears at Sláine.

"I can see that," Sláine said, grinning.

"I can see this is going to be the beginning of a heart-warming friendship," Bodb said, coming to sit down beside Sláine.

Sláine assumed he was the Black Axe that Kendrick had mentioned, even though the weapon was nowhere to be seen.

Black Axe wore a long blond braid and whiskers. Sláine noticed that his muscles had begun to atrophy. It wasn't surprising. Life cooped up in a cell would have a debilitating effect on even the mightiest warrior. He didn't for a moment think that Bodb's skill with his eponymous weapon had diminished in the slightest. A warrior didn't forget. The axe was nothing more than an extension of his arm. Sláine nodded to the old warrior.

Nudd still guarded the door. The cell was actually an antechamber with three smaller cages at the back.

"Oh don't worry about tall dark and gruesome. He's as simple as a lugworm," the dwarf assured Sláine, seeing the direction of his gaze.

For all that it was a long story it didn't take long in the telling.

In the end it all boiled down to a single moment of stupidity. Still, he told his story, including the first time the warp-spasm had gripped him and Cullen of the Wide Mouth's part in his downfall. His audience sat rapt, hanging on his every word. The dwarf's ears pricked up at the mention of Vern and his dubious practices. He was like a dog sniffing around scraps. His nostrils flared at the mention of gold. The little rat-like man was thoroughly enthralled with the idea of reading people's eyes in a metal trinket while fleecing them and then, as he put it, "being stupid enough to bury your treasure in the garden." Then, with a sudden look of predatory cunning, "You do remember where Master Vern's garden is, don't you?"

"Let me guess what you are in here for."

"That's me, Ukko, greatest thief in all Eiru." The rat-like dwarf assayed a mocking bow, his nose almost dragging on the floor.

"You can't be that great, seeing as you are locked up in here," Sláine pointed out.

Bodb chuckled. "I really could get to like you, Sláine Mac Roth."

"What's not to like," Sláine said.

"It was just bad luck," Ukko grumbled. "Could have happened to anyone."

"If you say so."

"Yes, I do."

"No need to be so defensive about it."

"I'm not defensive. Why be defensive about bad luck? It's not like I was stupid enough to dip my wick in some other bloke's chosen bride and think I could get away with it. Or, you know, moaning because I happen to be this legendary colossus with the strength of twenty men and truly dreadful taste in women."

"Do you have a point, you little rat?" Sláine scowled.

"Somewhere, I am sure. It evades me just now but I will come to it."

"I'm sure you will," Sláine said.

"One day."

Nudd brought food: gruel; wet, thin, runny gruel. Prison food.

Just the sight of it made him long for Bedelia's cooking, which was not something he could have imagined when she was actually cooking for him.

He hadn't realised how hungry he was until he smelled the lukewarm food and his stomach reminded him it existed. He couldn't remember the last time he had eaten, two or three days earlier, at least.

Sláine spooned it into his mouth.

He was so hungry that he actually managed to convince himself it tasted good.

He grunted his appreciation, licking the wooden spoon clean.

Bodb and Sláine traded war stories over the meal, each one gorier than the last as the two sought to out do each other.

"Soth! Does it always have to be about your axes being red and reeking with the offal of slaughter? I mean surely there is more to it than rivers of blood and your enemy's screams," Ukko grumbled, covering his ears. "It's enough to put an honest dwarf off his food."

"Good job you aren't honest then, eh?" Sláine said, spooning down another slop of gruel.

"Come to think of it, all these bloody exploits are better than hearing you constantly lamenting the slew of women who've left you, warped one."

And so it went, the three of them sparring with words instead of blows. The little dwarf mocked the warriors and in turn the warriors lampooned the runt of their pack. It was a curious form of bonding.

Nudd came to them as the sun went down.

"Lights out," the huge simpleton said, pointing towards the three individual cages at the back of the cell. Ukko moved first, scampering back into the middle cage and pulling a fur pelt down to black out the whole front of his cramped prison. Bodb stood, dusting off his hands, and shook hands with Sláine.

"We'll continue this tomorrow, Mac Roth."

"That we will, Black Axe," Sláine said. "I have stories from Dun Barc that will melt your ears."

"I look forward to them, and maybe I will share the tragic events of Glenn Kathra with you, if you are lucky. Now that is a story and a half." Bodb winked. The warrior retreated into his own small cell, on the left of the three, leaving the final one for Sláine.

Sláine ducked inside the cage. Nudd came up behind him, barred the door and fastened the lock securely, shutting him in. The cage was tiny, big enough for a hard wooden cot, a wash pot and a footstool. He pulled the pelt down to give himself some privacy. There were no windows and with the pelt pulled down the darkness was absolute. He felt his way over to the cot and lay down on the hard wooden pallet. It was as uncomfortable as anything he had ever lain on. Sleep didn't want to come. He was tired but after not moving for so long and being pent up, he was too frustrated to sleep.

For some unknowable amount of time he just lay there, looking up at the dark where the ceiling ought to have been. It was never quiet, this dark. Outside, the waves crashed against the base of the chalk pillar, wearing it away one wave at a time. The susurrant rush of water and the break and fall away of wave after wave was constant.

He rolled over, pulling the blanket up over him.

It felt odd, being this far removed from the earth. He couldn't feel any undercurrent of its power. For the first time in as long as he could remember he felt utterly alone. Even so, at the back of his mind was the nagging doubt that Danu, in any of her aspects, Blodeuwedd, the Morrigan or Ceridwen, would leave him be.

Through the bars he heard the muffled sound of snoring, the *snnnnnnrrrrrrk pssssssssssshhhhawwwww* of Ukko's flapping lips as the dwarf slept the sleep of the righteous.

Sláine, on the other hand, tossed and turned for most of the night.

The voice was haunting, elegiac, its tune a threnody of bittersweet lament.

Sláine lay in the darkness listening to it.

He had no idea who the singer was, or what sins had led her to the broch, but her voice was pure and heart-breakingly beautiful.

He found himself wanting to go to her, to sit before her, and listen. Her words wormed their way inside him. Sláine crawled out of the bed and stumbled for-wards in the dark, drawn by the song. He reached through the bars of his cage, trying to force back the locked beam but there was no moving it. He moaned. The song's lure was irresistible. He needed to find the singer.

Sláine rattled the doors of his cell but they wouldn't budge.

He heaved at the bars but there was no give in them.

The song… There was something about the song.

He had to be with the singer, to kneel at her feet.

He had to…

Sláine pushed away from the bars and staggered back to the bed. He fumbled around in the dark for the blanket, tearing tufts from it and blocking his ears with them. Even muffled the lure of the song was powerful; too powerful for him to resist.

He tumbled out of bed and landed hard on the floor, tufts of wool sticking out of his ears. He scrambled across the dead straw to the bars of the cage door and rattled them, keening desperately.

A hideous blood-curdling scream rent the night asunder. Fear had made the scream so utterly sexless that it was impossible to tell if the screamer was male or female.

When the scream finally died there was only the sound of the waves crashing over and over again against the base of the stack.

Sláine fell to his knees, desolate at the loss of the song.

Finally, he slept on the floor at the foot of the cell door, curled around the ruined blanket.

Sláine awoke to the grunt and grumble of Nudd wrestling with the beam barring his cage door.

The simpleton heaved it back and pushed open the door to let him out. Sláine blinked back the sunlight. He had slept through since... since the song.

He lurched to his feet and stumbled out of the cell.

"Who was that singing last night?"

He grabbed Nudd by the arms and tried to shake him but the simpleton was an immovable mass.

"Who was singing?" Sláine pushed but Nudd just brushed him aside, opened Bodb's cage, and then moved on to Ukko's. The dwarf emerged rubbing his red-rimmed eyes and yawning.

"What's the racket? Some of us were still trying to sleep."

"Did you hear it last night?"

"Hear what?"

"The song? Did you hear the woman singing?"

"I didn't hear nothing. I was out like the lights, dead to the world, dreaming sweet dreams of making love to fat women on bleedin' great piles of gold. It was marvellous."

"How could you not? With those ears of yours! Bodb, what about you, did you hear the song?" Sláine called but Black Axe didn't answer.

"See," Ukko grumbled, "I wasn't the only one trying to sleep."

Sláine didn't like it, he didn't like it one little bit. Snatches of the song came back to him, and then that blood-curdling scream. He pushed past Nudd and in to Bodb's cage.

The place stank of piss and blood; twin reeks of the body laid bare. They were a vile combination, natural and yet so unnatural. The piss reeked, bitter, sharp and pungent, and beneath it lurked the iron tang of blood.

Bodb of the Black Axe was in the corner, pressed up against the wall. His corpse was emaciated beyond recognition, but it could only be him. Bodb was a withered husk. There was almost nothing human left where the man had been. Only the eyes and the whiskers couldn't lie.

Sláine knelt beside the corpse, taking Bodb's hand in his. The skin felt like cured leather, although there was a peculiar waxy quality to it in places. He turned it over, examining the back of Bodb's hand as if it might offer a clue to his hideous demise. There wasn't a single sign of injury anywhere on the old warrior's corpse, no matter where he looked.

It looked as if the old warrior's very soul had been sucked out of his body. There was nothing but a shell left behind.

"What kind of creature could do this?" Sláine asked.

No one answered him.

Fifteen
Freedom

"ARE THERE ANY more prisoners in here?" Sláine demanded. "Come on, Nudd, speak up. Someone or something sang that damned song last night. I heard it. Ukko, stop skulking back there. You've been here how long? Have you ever heard another prisoner in this place?"

"Umm well, now that you mention it, you know, oh great and warped one, it is a prison, so what are the odds of their being umm well, you know, prisoners in here?"

"Oh, I could hit you so hard." He stopped himself, mid-blow.

"You saw that, Nudd? He was going to hit me!" Ukko squealed, pressing up against the wall. "Hmm, you know Bodb borrowed some stuff off me, I really should get that back. It's only fair. I mean it is mine. Yes, let me just get my things back."

"Stay right where you are and keep your hands to yourself, you ratty little thief, unless you want me to smack seven shades out of you."

"I didn't do anything. All I did was talk about getting what's rightfully mine back. You heard that, Sláine, right? Soth! Everyone wants to hit me! What did I ever do?"

"Shut up, Ukko. I am trying to think." Sláine glowered at the rat-like dwarf.

"Well that ought to take the rest of the morning, so I think I'll just sit down here and have a nap. See if I can't find those fat women again. Soth! I love fat women. So much more to get a hold of and love." Ukko made a show of plumping himself down in the middle of the antechamber and closing his eyes.

Sláine kicked him out of sheer bloody frustration but Ukko just grumbled and rolled over, feigning deep sleep.

"I hardly know you but I could cheerfully throttle the life out of you already," Sláine said. Ukko answered with a full-throated snore, his lips flapping together.

Sláine returned to Bodb's corpse, hoping there was something, some clue he had missed the first time but of course there wasn't. The old warrior had been drained completely but it was impossible to tell how it had actually been done. His gut told him it had to be something to do with the singer and that it had been Bodb he heard screaming. There was no evidence but that didn't matter. He knew, instinctively, and no one was talking to him.

Nudd dragged Bodb's corpse out of his cage and hauled it away. Out of sight, out of mind seemed to be the notion the simpleton was working on. Perhaps it was true for him, like a guppy swimming around in circles, each time thinking that bit of the rock pool was a new place to explore. Sláine had no such luxury. He remembered all too well the lure of the damned song, and couldn't help but shiver at the realisation that but for the barred door of the cage the withered corpse could have been his own. It sent a cold shiver through him,

A little while later the sweet tang of burning flesh reached his nose. Nudd had burned Black Axe's corpse. That didn't set Sláine's mind at rest.

Ukko snored on.

"I know you are awake, you miserable little bag of bones," Sláine said exasperatedly.

"No you don't," Ukko said without moving. "You just think I am. I could be fast asleep with those fat women."

"See!"

"No, my eyes are closed and I am asleep. Now leave me alone would you."

"Doesn't it worry you in the slightest? We were eating and joking with him last night and he's gone in the morning."

"I try not to get attached to people. It saves all sorts of problems when they find out I've robbed them," the dwarf said, still not opening his eyes. He let out another tooth-rattling snore.

Sláine went to the window and looked out. All he could see were the white breakers of the sea. He grabbed the bars and hauled himself up another six inches but it didn't reveal anything more telling. He paced the small cell, scuffing up the straw with his feet. He went over to the barred door and shook it. "Is there anybody there?" he called out into the endless corridors of the broch.

No one answered him.

He slumped down against the wall, knowing in his gut that darkness would come, and with it that damned song.

They slouched towards nightfall.

Being held captive dragged time out desperately. There was only so much pacing, thinking and mocking that Sláine and Ukko could do.

Sláine made preparations.

Using the ties from his boots and the fur lining, he made muffs to block his ears. He tested their efficacy by getting Ukko to yell insults in his face. The little man was delighted to be of assistance. He jumped up and down yelling a stream of colourful invective in the barbarian's face, taking far too much delight from it until Sláine pointed out that he couldn't actually hear what he was saying. That little revelation put a dampener on the dwarf's spirits.

Finally satisfied that the makeshift earmuffs actually worked, Sláine hid them under the blanket in his cell and waited for Nudd to lock them up for the night.

He didn't have to wait long.

Nudd came just before dusk. The simpleton went through the ritual, dropping the bar into place, but this time there was no forlorn clunk of the lock mechanism. Nudd rattled on the bars to show the cage was locked even though it wasn't, not properly.

Sláine curled up on the cot, reaching under the blanket for his makeshift muffs.

He lay there in the darkness, waiting.

After a while he found himself imagining that he could hear his lovers' voices masked within the swirl and crash of the waves. It gave him a curious sense of comfort despite the fact that they weren't actually there. He found himself listening out for Niamh and Bedelia, and thought for one fleeting moment that he actually heard Blathnaid.

Then he heard it, the first aching note of the song. He knew the singer immediately and couldn't believe he hadn't recognised her voice last night. He pushed himself out of the hard cot. He knew the door was unlocked so he simply reached through the bars and lifted the beam. He pushed the cage door open and stepped out into the antechamber. The first bars of moonlight spilled across the rotten straw. He lumbered forwards, his feet moving wholly independently of his thoughts. All he could think was that he needed to find the singer of that haunting melody.

Nudd had left the main antechamber door open.

He could hear the dwarf's snark and watched as he snored on, oblivious to the song.

Sláine pushed it open and stumbled out into the corridor, clutching the muffs in his trembling hands. He was powerless to resist as her voice gently rose and fell, weaving a hypnotic pattern around him. He felt a longing deep inside him more powerful than anything he had known, even in the arms of Danu's maiden aspect, Blodeuwedd.

"I'm coming," he called, following the sound of her voice deeper and deeper into the dark heart of the broch. He past row after row of empty cells and stumbled down stairs raddled with woodworm and damp rot. The walls around him shifted from the clean

limewash, mould and salt of above to a sickly
subterranean slime as the song drew him beneath the
level of the sea, and deeper still.

Finally he came to a single cell deep in the belly of
the broch. The iron-framed door was locked but that
didn't stop the crooning melody from climbing high
into the upper reaches of the cells above. The singer was
on the other side of the door.

The corridor reeked with the harsh metallic smell of
blood.

Heart racing, Sláine put on the earmuffs, stifling the
damned song so that he could at least begin to think
straight. He knew the voice. He was excited at the
prospect of seeing her again, of surprising her and
together breaking out of this infernal place.

Sláine reached out and opened the door.

She was chained to the wall, the black iron collar
secured around her throat.

"Blathnaid," Sláine gasped as he came crashing
through the door. A huge wave of selfish relief washed
over him – this was why she hadn't joined up with him.
Bragg had turned her over to Kendrick and she'd been
locked up in this hellhole like some common thief.

She hadn't abandoned him after all!

He stumbled forwards to free her, sagging to his knees
as he pulled at her chains, trying to yank them out of the
wall or break the metal bolts securing them. He realised
that she was talking to him, but he couldn't hear a word
because of the muffs. He reached forwards, taking Blathnaid in his arms, overcome. She hadn't left him. She

wasn't like the other women in his life. He hugged her close, so close that she began to squirm in his arms.

He closed his eyes.

His hands tangled in her hair, his lips kissing with a passion that could hardly contain the hurt, the anger, the joy, and the pain of all the thoughts that had gone through his head since they had parted. She squirmed beneath his touch, moving more and more as if she was trying to wriggle out of his grip. He just held her all the more tightly.

There was no passion in her lips. The texture of her tongue against his felt wrong. It flicked rather than licked, its movement too frantic, desperate.

He felt Blathnaid's arms coil around him, her fingernails dragging down his back, sinking in painfully.

Sláine opened his eyes.

It was Blathnaid and yet it wasn't, as if some shimmering glamour had been laid over something so hideously evil that even the illusion couldn't quite mask it completely. Blathnaid's face slipped. That was the only way his mind could rationalise what it was seeing. For a moment Blathnaid was there, in his arms, kissing him, and then something shifted and she wasn't and this thing, this scaled reptilian thing was in her place. Sláine recoiled from the beast even as the glamour of Blathnaid's face struggled to reassert itself, a façade over the creature's true and hideous visage.

He tried to pull away but the creature that wasn't Blathnaid held him in a vice-like grip.

The cold-blooded narrow slits of eyes stared back at him hungrily. They were inhuman, the pupils reptilian ellipses. A long forked tongue laved across his face, lingering over his eyes before it darted down, back into his mouth. She held him immobile, her tongue exploring, probing, her fingers sinking deeper into his flesh.

The she-beast – for by no stretch of the imagination was it the cutpurse, Blathnaid – reached up, pulling the muffs from his ears and exposing Sláine once more to her enchanted song.

"What are you?" he yelled, thrashing in the she-beast's arms. Her grip was incredible. Sláine felt his anger rising, but there was no answering surge from the earth in his blood. He was alone, cut off from what made him.

Her only answer was a slithering hiss, her forked tongue lashing across her lips and curling almost seductively around a wickedly sharp fang that dripped with ichor. Sláine recoiled, writhing in the creature's grasp. He felt something cold coiling around his legs. He kicked out at it but it continued snaking higher, wrapping itself around him and, when it reached his waist, constricting.

Sláine tried to look down but the she-beast held him firm.

Her song slipped into a mournful refrain, leaching the fight out of him.

He wanted to be with her, with Blathnaid. He wanted to sink into her, to feel her heat around him. He wanted to give in. Surrender.

She drew him into a kiss, and he sank into it.

He sank his teeth into the creature's forked tongue and yanked his head back, tearing the meat apart. The beast's blood spilled into his mouth. He spat the tip of the tongue out as the she-beast howled and hissed in pain, the hypnotic lure of its song broken.

Blathnaid was gone.

He knew that she had never been there, but her loss was palpable. His own shriek dwarfed that of the she-beast.

Reacting instinctively Sláine grabbed the loop of black iron chaining the she-beast to the wall, whipped it around her neck and braced it around his forearms. He heaved back on the chain and began throttling the creature as it clawed all the more desperately at his face. The beast bucked and writhed desperately, its serpent-like tail tightening around Sláine's waist, choking the life out of the barbarian even as Sláine choked the life out of it. They were locked in a deadly embrace.

The beast shuddered, once, violently and the fight fled its body.

Sláine stood over the she-beast, bleeding where the rough metal of chains had cut into his forearms.

For the first time, he could see what it was – a huge part-snake part-woman abomination. Mannix had told tall tales of such a beast: a creature that lured men in with its seductive charms and fed on their blood and their spirit until they were empty. What had he called it? The word came back to him as he shucked off the dead she-beast's coil of tail.

A lamia.

He dropped the earmuffs on the she-beast's corpse and turned in time for Nudd's club to cannon into the side of his face and send him reeling back. His foot came down on the fat flesh of the lamia's tail, rolling his ankle as it gave way beneath his weight. Unbalanced, Sláine sprawled across the dungeon floor. Nudd stepped over him, grunting as he prepared to deliver another crushing blow with his club.

Sláine rolled to the left, barely getting out of the way as the wooden club hammered into the stone floor. He grabbed Nudd's legs and used them to jack-knife his feet straight up into the looming simpleton's chin. Nudd staggered back. Sláine rolled and came up onto his feet in a fighting crouch. He had no weapon. There was nothing close to hand that he could improvise with.

Nudd's club whistled dangerously close to his ear. The blow smacked off his shoulder and sent a surge of pain bone deep.

"You hurt the princess," Nudd growled. "Nudd hurt you."

"No, Nudd, you don't nee—" he didn't get to finish the sentence. Nudd's club ricocheted off his jaw, snapping his head back.

Sláine collapsed to his knees. The world lurched. There was no focus, no form. Blackness threatened to overwhelm him. Nudd came in for the kill, club raised. Sláine rammed his fist into the simpleton's groin mercilessly, doubling Nudd up in agony. The club slipped from his fingers and clattered to the floor a second before Nudd did.

Swaying precariously, Sláine reached out for the fallen club. It slipped between his fingers but he got it after a second fumble, and brought it round in a vicious arc. The meat of the club split Nudd's skull. He didn't need a second blow. The simpleton wouldn't be getting up any time soon.

He dropped the club and forced himself to his feet. He managed four steps before he lurched into the wall and four more before he fell again. He stumbled along the corridor back to the woodworm raddled stairs and slumped down on to them. He stayed that way, with his head in his hands, until he had mastered the nausea.

Sláine reclaimed Brain-Biter from Kendrick's chamber. The broch's owner was nowhere to be seen, but then, it was night and no doubt the man knew all about the lamia's seductive charms come sundown.

Shouldering the axe he headed towards the drawbridge.

He had almost made it when he heard a wheedling voice cry, "Let me out, you big muscle-bound lummox!"

He stopped in his tracks. "Is that any way to beg, Ukko?" he called back.

"Let me out of here!"

"You really haven't got the hang of begging, have you?"

"Please let me out!"

"Better, but not good enough." He walked five more steps much to the dwarf's consternation. "All right, give me one good reason why I should let you out."

There was silence for a moment, then, "I'll starve if you don't."

Sláine thought about it for a moment. "Nope, not a good reason. One less thief in the world is a good thing, I think."

Five more steps. He stood under the stone arch, one foot on the drawbridge, one on the broch's threshold.

"Don't leave me!" Ukko wailed.

"One reason. That shouldn't be too difficult, should it?"

Silence.

"Got nothing to say?" Sláine called up.

"Every hero needs a sidekick, someone to record their heroic deeds otherwise who remembers them if you go around being a hero all by yourself? Come on, think about it Sláinie, who better to help you dodge your king's hunters and rescue fair maidens and stuff than a thief like me?"

"Pandering to my vanity? I don't think so."

"Okay, okay!" Ukko cried. "I know! I know! I've got it! You need me! See, I know this place like the back of my hand! You're a stranger but I know every inch of the Sourland inside out. I know where the Drunes are, but more importantly I know how to avoid them. You'll never make it more than a few miles without me!"

"I know I am going to regret this," Sláine muttered, turning back to climb the stairs and free the dwarf.

THE THIRD TRISKELL

CRONE

Sixteen
Dry Land

SLÁINE CRUSHED THE dead twig between his fingers. "This place is hellish, dwarf."

Ukko had, of course, lied through his teeth. He had no idea where they were, that much was painfully evident.

"I know, I know. It wasn't as if we had a choice though, your warpishness."

"I don't like it." He didn't say what he didn't like, because it was painfully obvious that the land around them had turned sour. He hadn't felt the presence of the Earth Mother in a full three months of wandering. He didn't like it at all. Danu had always been with him. He felt as if he was abandoning her, although a nagging voice at the back of his mind kept goading him on quietly, insisting that he was wrong, that it was the other way around, that she had left him... like all of the women in his life had.

The choice to turn south had not been an easy one to make.

The Land of the Young had always been his home. Leaving it behind just felt wrong and the wrongness of that decision was making itself apparent in every withered tree and parched meadow. Salt bubbled up from below ground, the earth itself rancid as if nature had become a plague, a pox on the Goddess's body.

It was as if they had stumbled into an endless winter where the Earth Mother had no chance to recover her strength in spring for a glorious summer, but instead wallowed in the depravity of winter as it sucked her dry.

"It is not like this where I come from."

"So you've said, Sláine, a land of milk and honey where the belly of the earth is the most beautiful thing in all creation, the birds fly backwards and the flowers are always in bloom."

"Stop being stupid, Ukko. This disturbs me. Where are the druids who tend to the land's needs? Where are the farmers who work the land, tending to the Goddess's flesh? This is wrong, dwarf. This is wrong on so many levels. Do these people not know what they are doing?"

"I don't think they have a choice, Sláine," Ukko said seriously. "You've seen them. They aren't like you or me. They live in fear. They are always looking nervously over their shoulders as if they expect someone to punish them for some imagined transgression. Well, maybe they are a little like you, because you are always looking over your shoulder as well."

"Then they should stand up for themselves against these cruel taskmasters, dwarf. No Celt should bow and scrape to another man. We are the Goddess's chosen people. We are proud, noble. We are the fiercest warriors, the most passionate lovers, the fastest friends."

"And you've got the thickest skulls," the dwarf muttered. "Take a look around you, Sláine. Do you think… Scratch that thought, of course you don't, that's why you have me. You saw them in Crag Furlough, Sláine. They're beaten men. They slouch around like empty shells sucked dry of vitality. That last village was a graveyard of the living where a town once stood. The place gave me the creeps."

"These are my people, Ukko. Do you expect me to just accept this… this abuse?"

The dwarf sighed. "No, I expect you to bring down a world of hurt on the oppressor's heads with that bloody great axe of yours."

For the first time in weeks Sláine smiled. "You said you wanted to chronicle the feats of a hero, little man. I'm just giving you something to write about."

"I was rather hoping I'd get to make most of them up, I have to admit," Ukko muttered under his breath.

They saw signs of another village a few miles down the road. The fields had been turned but the crop hadn't matured. A few brittle straws of wheat were broken, their seeds little more than hollowed out shells. White stones and flakes of flint were the only crop now.

"Smoke!" Sláine said, seeing a dirty grey plume rising in the sky. The road skirted the barren field but took them more than a mile out of their way. Eyes fixed on the ribbon of smoke, Sláine started to run. He vaulted over a low stile, cutting across the field.

"Slow down!" Ukko moaned, struggling over the stile. Sláine was already two hundred paces across the field by the time Ukko was on the other side. Ten steps on, his foot crunched down on one of the bigger shards of white rock, only it wasn't rock at all, it was a splinter of skull bone; the curve where the jaw met the head. Rotten teeth were still set in the bone. Sláine saw more and more white stones that weren't stone. He stopped running. He looked around the field taking in all the flecks of white on the churned brown of the earth. There were literally thousands and thousands of them.

He realised sickly what the real crop of this field was: bones.

It was a mass grave. Thousands of people were sewn across the soulless earth. They weren't buried. No effort had been taken to actually cover the dead with earth so that they might nourish Danu. The corpses had been scattered carelessly and left to be picked clean by the birds. The bones were white. This slaughter was not a new thing.

No wonder there was no hint of Danu in this Sourland.

It was a foul place and Ukko had been more right than he could have known when he had called the last village a graveyard. Sláine stood amongst the bones, seething.

Ukko stumbled up beside him.

Sláine held out the broken jawbone for the dwarf to see.

"You see, Ukko? You see what these bastards have done to my people?"

"You don't know that, Sláine. Not for sure. It could have been plague or pox or, or, or…"

"The only plague at work here is manmade," Sláine said, bitterly. "Only man is capable of such evil towards his own."

"You may be right."

Looking at the smoke rising from the village he shook his head. "I know I am, Ukko."

"What can you do? You're only one man. Anything capable of doing this has to be more than one man can stop, surely?"

"I am Sláine Mac Roth, dwarf. Be my enemy one man, one hundred, one hundred thousand, I do not think it too many!"

"Soth! You actually mean that don't you? You're a dangerous man."

"Aye, for once we agree on something, dwarf."

"Well, I was rather meaning you were dangerous for me. I'm beginning to wonder what I've gotten myself into."

Sláine dropped the broken jawbone. "They will pay for this, Ukko," Sláine breathed, barely a whisper, and then louder, "Do you hear me?"

Then he shouted, "I am your death! I am Sláine Mac Roth!"

Finally he bellowed, as he lifted Brain-Biter above his head, "Fear Me!"

The world was reduced to two absolutes: pain and anger.

Sláine felt them both as he charged across the bone field. The smoke taunted him. Houses and people were burning and charring, and he was impotent against it. He roared his anger.

The pain of his people tore at him.

He ran towards the smoke.

You're too late, my love, always too late. The ghost of Danu's taunt came back to him, the merest ripple on the wind. It could have been a memory or a whisper from the dead earth.

"No," he said, "not this time."

It stung his eyes long before he was close enough to feel the flame's heat.

He was crying tears of grief and pain, sadness and rage, even before he set foot in the slaughterhouse that was the burning village.

He heard the screams first.

The villagers weren't done dying.

He saw why immediately.

The longhouse was ablaze and they were trapped inside, burning alive. Faces were pressed up at the windows but there was no way for the panicked villagers to squeeze through the tiny openings. Even if they did, the building was ringed by soldiers.

"You picked the wrong day for your butchery!" Sláine roared.

"You and your big mouth," Ukko huffed, coming up behind him. "Never heard of the advantage of surprise?"

"Oh, I think they are surprised," Sláine said, coldly. "Time to die."

"They don't look very surprised, I have to say," the dwarf said, as the first of the soldiers turned to face them. The warrior wore an ugly mask of hair, making it look like some savage shoggy-beast. The soldier wore a horned helmet, and on his shield, the sinister triskele. His sword had a silver skull for a pommel. "Now you, you look surprised."

Sláine showed no mercy. He threw himself at the skull-sword with all the fury, all the hatred, and all the anger of every last one of the victims of the pestilential warriors. His axe sang a funeral dirge as it cut and chopped, and hewed and split bone and brain, throat and gut. The skull-swords were given no quarter. Anger surged within him but there was no answering charge of earth magic.

"You thrive on terror and intimidate the weak," Sláine rasped, disembowelling a skull-sword with a savage twist of the wrist. "You hold no fear for me. I know what lies behind your beast masks. So think on this: where fear ends, that is the land where my hatred begins." An almighty backhanded blow ripped open the jugular of a second skull-sword, too slow to get out of the way. "You die just as well as any other cowards," Sláine mocked, his axe living up to its name.

He was alone in the fight to avenge his people.

He killed twenty-one skull-swords.

Ukko walked through the dead, tallying the numbers. "For your sagas, your warpishness, you understand? Facts? The simple folk like facts. I make that twenty-one skulls and various bits and bobs. A leg bone here, an arm bone there, messy stuff. Let's say thirty-five shall we? It's a good number. It sounds more impressive."

Sláine staggered out of the longhouse, an unconscious woman slung over his shoulder, a slip of a girl under his arm. More survivors emerged, coughing and gasping. "I will not glory in lies, dwarf." He laid the woman on the grass and went back into the burning building to look for more survivors.

"No, no, you shouldn't. I am not saying you should," Ukko called after him.

He plunged into the smoke and flames, blindly, calling out, "Come to me, come to my voice. I will get you out." He heard movements, shuffling feet, coughing. "Come to me," he urged.

Nine more came out of the burning longhouse alive.

"You killed twenty-one. It was incredible to behold, your magnificence," Ukko said, sidling up to the young Sessair, "and you saved all these people."

"I do not think it too many. I do not think it anywhere near enough. There will be more blood when I am through with the demon spawned bullies."

They stayed a day and a night with the survivors.

They were precious few in number but their gratitude more than made up for it. They treated Sláine like the conquering hero he was. Anything they had was his. Ukko took advantage of this mercilessly, collecting trinkets and stuffing them in his sack.

"I could get to like it here, Sláine. They're a generous bunch." He polished a woven silver brooch and fastened it to his tunic. "There, what do you think?"

"You look like a runty little dwarf wearing a fancy silver brooch."

"Just the look I was going for."

They were sharing a small room in one of the newly empty houses. He felt like a parasite living amongst the relics of the dead. He imagined the ghosts of the dead family going about their daily routine, washing, dressing, cleaning, chasing the young ones around to get them organised. It was all too easy to believe that the dead had never left. None of their belongings had been disturbed since the skull-swords had dragged them out of their home. The house – it was a home no longer – would be in mourning for a long time to come.

He moved around the place with respect, not touching anything that he didn't need to.

Ukko, on the other hand, was a thieving magpie by nature. He rummaged through the chests and ferreted out the family's few treasures. He stuffed them into his sack, hoarding anything and everything of any value.

"Don't look at me like that," Ukko grumbled. "I'm just looking to the future, looking after your interests."

"How so?"

"The day's going to come when we need to barter for food or lodging so you can carry on your quest for justice. I'm just making sure you can afford to be a hero."

Sláine closed his eyes. There was no point trying to reason with the dwarf; he had his own unique and flexible set of morals.

There was a timid knock at the door.

Sláine opened the door.

It was Brianna, the old chieftain's wife. Her face was gaunt, haunted; it was little wonder. Sláine knew that not two days since she had seen her man strung up by the guts and left to dangle a miserable agonising death from the hanging tree.

"The tribal council would see you, warrior," the woman said.

"Good," Sláine said, "there are things I would know about this land."

"We will answer what questions we can."

"I look forward to it."

"Misery loves company after all," the dwarf mumbled to himself, licking the palm of his hand and flattening down a stubborn cowlick of hair, making himself presentable.

They joined Brianna and six others in the village roundhouse. It was much the same as Grudnew's hall in Murias. The similarity drove home something that had been nagging away at him since his fight with the skull-swords. This, here, this sour land, this oppression, was what awaited his people if someone did not stand up against the skull-swords.

"Sit, please, warrior." Brianna gestured to the round table where her husband had ruled just two days before. Sláine did as he was asked. "You have our thanks, again, Sláine Mac Roth. We all owe you our lives. It is not easy to be in someone's debt. To this end, we would help you in any small way that we can."

"There is nothing I want, nor need, my lady."

"Now, now, let's not be so hasty, Sláine," Ukko interjected.

"Be quiet, Ukko. The grown-ups are talking."

"I'm just saying..."

"Hush."

"Okay, but I—"

"Hush." Sláine silenced him. He turned to Brianna. "There is something you could be of help with."

The woman nodded.

"I would know more of the skull-swords. They came to my land. They murdered my mother and my friends. I would do to them much worse in return. I would teach them what it means to fear the tribes of the earth goddess, Danu."

"Yours is not an uncommon story, warrior. The skull-swords, as you call them, dance to the tune of the Drunes Drunemeton. It is the Drunes who have done this to the land. It wasn't always as you see it. This was once a good place to live."

"What are these Drunes?" Sláine interrupted. "The word is unfamiliar to me."

"They are the priests of Crom-Cruach, the dark and hungry god," one of the other women said, making the sign of Lugh in front of her mouth as if to cleanse her tongue of the unholy filth she had just spoken.

"Soth!" Ukko spat. "The wyrm god? Sláine what are we doing here? Don't we have to be somewhere on the other side of the Eiru like yesterday?"

"I would hear more," Sláine said softly.

"Well I can't pretend that I particularly want to," Ukko said.

"They are vile priests. They take our young and sacrifice them to the dark god, using the blood to appease the beast. They bleed us dry. They bleed the land dry. Six years ago borders of the sour land stopped as far away as Carnac, but not now. The sickness has a grip of the earth and creeps ever north. Nothing grows here. Our livestock miscarry their foals and calves and lambs. Our wheat rots before it can flourish."

"And this is the doing of these priests? These Drunes?"

"Aye."

"Then they must be stopped."

"There is a simplicity to your words that I like, warrior, but how? How can they be stopped? How can we stop them?"

"You don't have to," Sláine said flatly. "I will."

They told their story.

The Drunes had come from the south, with the bad land, more than twenty-five years ago.

Some few of the survivors remembered a time before the skull-swords and the Drunes, but most had been born into this slavery. It was difficult for Sláine to fully comprehend. He had been born free, lived free, and despite the many tribal wars, had always known he would die free. The notion of being hammered down beneath the yoke of oppression did not sit well with him. He listened, but it was hard not to interrupt and demand how the men could have ever allowed this to happen.

According to Brianna, the skull-swords were the Drune's warriors. They wore their repugnant masks to inspire fear and to pay tribute to one they called the Lord Weird, Slough Feg, but that was not the only reason. Feg was a god amongst them, an incarnation of Carnun himself, they said; part man, part beast. Sláine wrestled with the story, trying to understand how a man could sink so far into dark sorcery that he would willingly shed his own skin – hence the "Slough" of his title, and the need for his swords to wear their masks: to mask the stench of his rotten flesh. Brianna spoke of the Lord Weird in hushed, almost reverent tones.

"He is," she claimed, "thousands of years old, kept alive by dark magic."

The same dark magic that was warping the land here dry, Sláine thought bitterly as the woman explained.

"That's impossible!" Ukko blurted.

"Not so, little man," Brianna said. "There was great magic in the land once. I remember what it was like during my childhood, before Feg found us. This land was beautiful, Ukko. No fairer place was there south of Lyonesse. I made chains of daisies and wore them in my hair while I waited for my father working the fields." Sláine found himself thinking of the last woman he had met who wore flowers in her hair. "He was a proud man, proud of the crop his labours nurtured. We never went hungry. Fruits, vegetables, succulent meat, there was plenty for everyone. Then Feg found us and it changed. Slowly, but it changed. Ours was a creeping death. It was unnerving at first. The first I ever saw of it was a calf, a stillborn breech. Only it wasn't dead, not fully. The poor animal lived on, this eerie half-life, not alive, not dead. My father put the beast out of its misery eventually. He couldn't bear to look at the animal lying there in the dirt of the stable. He ate the cursed meat that night. Nothing should go to waste, that was his motto. He slipped into this ugly half-death himself over the next week, unable to walk or talk, unable to actually die. My mother put him out of his misery."

"Soth!"

"It was the beginning of what has felt like a long bleak winter. My man used to call it 'the Forgotten Season' because it never ended. Feg demanded the construction of the huge dolmen, in praise of his god of wyrms, Crom, and little by little the sickness has spread ever since."

"This Feg, he is immortal?" Sláine asked, cutting to the question that was burning in his mind.

"I don't know," Brianna admitted. "He is a sick thing, but sick enough to live forever? I don't know."

"Well then, if he can't live forever that means he can die. The only question is when. For your people, for this land, for my people, that day must be soon."

"He's going to beat his chest in a minute. He's good like that, very rousing," Ukko muttered to the young woman beside him. He covered his mouth with his hand and leaned in close. "Hmm, you smell good. Did anyone ever tell you that?"

"I will hunt him and kill him in his lair," Sláine vowed, ignoring the dwarf.

"See," Ukko whispered, "I told you. Next is the bit where he promises to rip his heart out and feed it to the dogs or to make a goblet out of his skull and drink to the Goddess's health with the blood of his fallen enemies."

"Tell me all you know of these Drunes."

They were, as far as he could tell, the dark god's equivalent of Danu's druids. They gathered at sacred groves, where their perverted rites soured the land. The most sacred of these, Brianna said, was known as Drunemeton. Sláine thought he had heard the name

before. He would not forget it. He remembered Cathbad's humiliation over the so-called sacred knowledge
the boys had made up. It felt like such a long time ago.
It was hard to imagine the old man having the power
to be dangerous even if he wanted to be.

Without thinking, he said so.

"He holds the knowledge, Sláine," Ukko pointed out.
"That gives him the power over ignorance. I bet he
hoards his knowledge too, doesn't he? Keeps things
secret and hides them in rituals. I would if I were him.
Stands to reason. If you know stuff other people don't
you can get stuff in return for the knowing, but when
everyone knows something, well it isn't worth a pot to
pee in."

"Aye," Sláine said, following the dwarf's rambling
logic. It actually made a certain amount of sense.

"So, what if he turned up one day and said the sacred
knowledge declared the neighbouring tribe of yours
infidels that must die? Said that it was the word of the
Goddess? Said you needed to build a special temple
dedicated to her worship, only it needed to be made
from their bones. Would you believe him?"

"Why would he lie?"

Ukko let out a slow whistling breath. "You and me,
Sláine, we're going to be great friends. Want me to give
you a lesson in why someone might want to lie? Let's
just say they have something he wants. Or hey, maybe
your king is annoying him and this is your druid's way
of having him done in. Send him off to fight a war
against a stronger tribe. He could have a million reasons, Sláine. That isn't the point. The point is you listen

to him. He has power. Power has a way of changing people. They don't like to give it up once they have it, and if they have power, they want more, always more. That's the way of it with powerful people."

"You paint a bleak picture of humanity, dwarf."

"I'm just saying you can't trust anyone. Those Drunes could have been just like your priest once. It isn't unreasonable."

"Our druids protect the land. They serve the Goddess. They would not bleed her dry. It is against everything they believe in."

"Well not exactly the same then, but that doesn't mean I am wrong. Give a man power, he wants more. It's natural. Power is addictive."

"Well it's time someone weaned the Drunes off their addiction."

"And you're just the man, right?"

"I will walk into the heart of Drunemeton itself, the most sacred of their groves, and rip every last heart out of their corrupt skins. I will teach them what real fear is. I will—"

"Bore them to death with self-important speeches probably." Ukko leaned over to the girl beside him and whispered, "See, I told you he would go on about ripping out arms and stuff. I am beginning to think that that's all heroes do. Well, that and kill things, obviously. Can't forget the killing."

"I would see this dolmen that Slough Feg built," Sláine said.

★ ★ ★

The dolmen was a huge construction that beggared reason.

It was unlike anything the druids of Danu had ever constructed: a megalithic behemoth. He could feel it, deep in his bones. It called out to him every bit as seductively as the lamia's song had. It was sweet, but too much so, sickly sweet. It left him light-headed and feeling sick, and it was powerful, there was no doubt about that.

A circle of smaller stones formed oddly spaced arches, and the arches formed a ring around the central stones of the dolmen. He entered the huge stone circle, laying his hand against the central rock pillar. A faint blush of heat ran through the grain of the stone. Sláine stood in the middle of the ceremonial circle, dwarfed by the towering rock pillars. The central stones were more than ten times his height. The capstones holding them firmly in place were at least fifty feet above the earth. The sheer scale of the construction was daunting.

"Feg built this?" Sláine said, marvelling at the feat. The central pillars appeared to have been hewn from a single slab of rock. He couldn't imagine how they could have been transported from wherever they had been quarried, let alone raised in place.

"Him and his Drunes," Brianna told him. "I was just a little girl but I remember it as if it was yesterday."

It wasn't the stones that disturbed Sláine; or rather it wasn't the scale of the megalith. It was something far more primal. He could feel what was happening to the earth. He could feel it bone deep. His link to Danu made the leaching effect of the dolmen something palpable, a reverse of the familiar link he shared with the earth where it fed him. He felt the stones draining the vitality out of his flesh and blood.

He felt the Goddess's pain, and it scared him more than anything had ever scared him in his life.

"Get me out of here, Ukko," Sláine said, lurching back from the central pillar. A moment later the ground tilted, the sky shifting into a dull brown haze and his legs gave way beneath him. He fell.

The next thing he remembered was Ukko's ugly face peering down at him and the sting of the dwarf's hand slapping him across the face, hard. "Wake up, Sláine! Wake up!"

He grunted groggily.

Ukko slapped him again.

"Enough!" he said, reaching up to grab the dwarf's wrists and stop him from hitting him again.

"Soth! I thought we'd lost you there, big man," Ukko said, relieved. "Scary bloody stuff, let me tell you. One minute you were staring at the big stone and then you started acting all weird. I mean really weird and then you just collapsed. I thought your brain had been struck down or something. You were shuddering as if you were having some kind of fit. Your eyes were rolled up in your head. Brianna carried you back to the village. I couldn't lift you by myself. I tried."

Sláine sat up. The world spun again but this time he rode it out. Everything smelled, or rather he was aware of their odours for the first time: the pungent whiff of the dwarf, the rose water Brianna had bathed in, the pollen from the withered grass, the dirt itself, which reeked of corruption instead of loam. It was wrong, unnatural, as were so many of the other odours that reached him. He could smell decay in so much of the natural world that it scared him. Blessedly, it was fading or it would have driven him insane.

You're too late, my love, always too late.

He had shared Danu's pain, felt the world's hurt. He would not fail Eiru. He would not be too late this time. This was why Danu had saved him from drowning in the river, he told himself. This was why she had lured him to Niamh's door. This was what she had wanted him to see, not just a few skull-swords sacking his home. It was all part of an elaborate pattern, a Gordian knot of needs and deceit with him at the heart of it. His exile had a purpose: to save the Goddess from this pain.

"It's all right. You did well, Ukko. The stones…" He trailed off. How could he explain it? How could he hope to understand it properly? "The stones are responsible. They are like…" He was lost for words. "Like voids, like empty vessels… They hunger. They are the essence of all hunger, never sated, like a big gaping maw sucking the life out of everything around them. The land, the people, they all feed the stones."

"We were worried," the woman said, kneeling beside him. "It is good that you have come back to us, warrior."

"You must tear down these stones, Brianna. You must. They are parasites on the flesh of the Goddess."

"But how?" the woman asked.

"Pull them down with your bare hands if you have to. Break their strength unless you want this souring to spread across all of the land. We must root out the canker at its core."

They had carried him halfway back to the village, mercilessly out of the sickening range of the worst of the dolmen's blight. He could still feel it though, an insidious tug on his strength. He needed Ukko to help him stand.

"What will you do?" the woman asked.

"Exactly what I promised. I will travel to the beast's lair and slay it. There is no other way. This is my land, Brianna. I may be far from my home but that does not make the land any less mine. The stones themselves have shown me that, in their own sick way. I will not stand by and watch it wither and die. My mother raised me better than that."

"She must have been an exceptional woman," Brianna said.

"In everything she did," Sláine agreed.

Sláine and Ukko saw more and more of the huge megaliths the deeper into the Sourland they travelled. Sláine felt sure they formed some vast invisible pattern. Had he been an eagle soaring high in the clouds he might have been able to see the whole of it, but walking amongst the stones the pattern was invisible. All he knew was that there were hundreds of them arranged across the Sourland.

At each one the draw on his flesh became more powerful.

More and more frequently he knelt to press his bare hands against the earth but there was nothing. It was dead land, dry.

At first he kept his fears to himself, but as the days turned into weeks he found himself confiding in Ukko. He didn't need to. For all his joking, Ukko understood what the stones meant and feared them every bit as much as he did. As the drain became greater Sláine began to feel a sickening hollowness form within him. In some distant way he understood what it was. The further he travelled from the healthy earth the more distant Danu became. That hollowness was a Danu-shaped ache inside him.

At some of the dolmen they saw people bent in prayer, as if the stones might save them from the damned blight they had brought down on the land. Sláine wanted to shake some sense into the worshippers, make them see that where they looked for salvation there was only more damnation. At others he saw mourners and realised that the villagers had turned the stones into a graveyard of sorts, burying their dead beneath the wyrm god's broken stones. It made him sick to see their emaciated forms hunched down low debasing themselves before the megalith as if some deity might hear them and take pity. They deserved to know that their false gods were killing them day by day.

He wished Dian were with him, and Fionn, Cormac, Niall and Núada. He hadn't thought about his friends in so long but they had never left him, not really, and, he came to realise that he had never left them. They were bonded in ways that not even distance could separate. That understanding gave him strength. He wondered where Tall Iesin had taken Fionn and if their travels had reached these blighted lands. Had Iesin carried back word to Murias of the threat the tall stones posed?

"Do you think there really is a pattern to the stones?" Ukko asked, picking up a pebble and casting it at a broken capstone. The rock missed its mark by a good ten feet, bouncing away across a patch of brown grass.

"What do you mean?" Sláine had been worrying about the possibility almost constantly since stumbling across the second, third and fourth dolmen, so hearing it come from the dwarf's mouth did not help ease his fears. There almost certainly was, but he couldn't see it. He was the river, he was mountain; he was not the eagle flying above them.

"Like, you know, some kind of sacred pattern. These druids–"

"They are not druids. Druids worship the land, they do not defile it."

"Fine, these Drunes don't seem to do much without there being a method behind it, right? So how do they choose where to place their Weird Stones? That has to be the pattern doesn't it, choosing certain sites because they are important, somehow. We know they are draining the land with the stones but what I don't understand is how they decide what areas are worth draining. I mean, I could understand it if some places had more power than others, but dirt's dirt. It isn't as if there is special magic dirt."

"Ukko, you're a genius!" Sláine said, suddenly understanding. There was a pattern to it all, the most obvious one at that, one that he should have seen immediately. He couldn't believe he had been so dense.

"Well, yes, I have my moments. What exactly did I do this time?"

"The leys! The lines of power! Soth! It's so obvious. They are using the leys to drain the earth of its magic." The ley lines were ancient sacred energy lines that intersected all across the Goddess's earthly form. They were a map to the paths of sun, moon and stars, charting their positions come solstice and equinox. What made them special was that they acted as foci or nodes for the earth power, enhancing the magic of the land and acting as a channel for it. They were, as Ukko had said, sacred areas where the earth's power was at its most potent. The tribes of the Goddess often congregated around these foci, drawn by the power. It made a sickening kind of sense that Slough Feg and his Drunes would seek to tap into the naturally occurring focal points, draining the magic from them. They were, in comparison, huge reservoirs of untapped power: the kind of power that Feg would need to stave off mortality.

They found more and more dolmen along the road, and although some of the locals called them by other names, their purpose remained the same.

Again and again that hollowness consumed Sláine.

"Danu, what have they done?"

There was no answer.

Seventeen
Shoggy Beast

THE ENDLESS ROWS of dolmen at Carnac were like nothing Ukko or Sláine had ever seen.

The Drunes had erected thousands upon thousands of the Weird Stones. Field upon field of standing stones stretched as far as the eye could see. Ukko didn't like it in the slightest. He grumbled as they crept closer but he might as well have been grumbling to himself for all the good it did with Sláine. They crested a gradual summit and looked down over a great stone in the centre of ten or more thousand broken and disjointed standing stones. They edged closer. Ukko lay flat on his belly and scooted forwards. Sláine mumbled something. Ukko assumed it was another promise to perform the "blood eagle" on the false priests. He didn't quite understand what the blood eagle was but he was in no doubt it was a gruesome way to shuffle off this mortal coil.

There was quite a gathering down there. He counted easily over two hundred heads. It was some kind of ritual. The ululations of the Drunes chant reached them on the rise. The air around them crackled with life. Bluish veins of energy sparked out of the ground, coiling around the horned figure in the centre of the stone circle. With each sizzle of energy the horned man jumped and twisted, contorting his body in a primal tribal dance, throwing his hands above his head, kicking his legs out, spinning and jumping in time to the venting of the earth's energies.

As the dance grew more and more frenzied Ukko knuckled his eyes, sure that they were lying to him. The horned man froze, threw his arms above his head and began to rise, until he was levitating ten, fifteen, a full twenty feet above the heads of his worshippers.

The blue jags of power snapped and crackled, chasing through his body. The horned man acted as a conduit for the huge central stone, the earth's power streaming out of and into it.

At the horned man's beckoning the sky appeared to darken, rumbling thunderheads taking shape above him.

"Did you see that, Sláine?" Ukko whispered, unable to believe the hideous power the stones gifted the horned man. He looked over his shoulder to see the barbarian in the grip of a fierce fit. Sláine was on his knees, clutching at his gut, a low moan escaping his clenched teeth. Spasm after spasm wracked his entire body. He stayed crouched on his knees as a fresh seizure convulsed through him and then, gasping for breath he collapsed forwards, his bare torso pressed low to the earth.

Ukko scrambled back to Sláine's side. "Not now, come on, not now. I can't carry you out of here on my own."

Sláine couldn't talk. His eyes had rolled up into his head. Ukko couldn't break the contact with the diseased earth even though it was so obviously killing Sláine. He grabbed the barbarian by the shoulders and hauled him backwards. It took every ounce of strength the little dwarf had to drag Sláine ten feet. He hunched over Sláine huffing and puffing, counted to thirteen because at ten the idea of trying to move him another inch still felt idiotic, and hauled on Sláine's arms, managing another five feet.

He slapped Sláine across the face.

Sláine groaned groggily.

"Come on, Sláine. Don't you die on me, you big aurochs, not here. You still haven't told me where that moneylender buried his bloody gold! Wake up, Sláine!"

Ukko hunched over Sláine, folding the warrior's arms across his chest.

"Forgive me, big man, but needs must as Crom drives and all that." He reached under Sláine and rolled him over, and again, grunting with the exertion of it. A third shove and gravity lent a hand. Sláine tumbled down the hill, gathering momentum with each roll.

"Soth!" Ukko gasped, running after Sláine even as he rolled all the way to the bottom of the hill. "Well if the damned stones don't kill him I will."

Ukko jumped and bounced, and skipped and struggled valiantly to stay on his feet as he followed Sláine down the hill.

At the bottom he fell to his knees beside Sláine, gasping for breath.

The barbarian opened an eye. He did not look happy with his lot in life.

"You're a hard man to keep alive, Sláine Mac Roth," Ukko grumbled.

He felt a prickling on the back of his neck, the short hairs there standing on end. It was an uncomfortable sensation. He cast a worried glance over his shoulder, back up the hill, but the Drunes hadn't suddenly appeared at the crest. The feeling of being watched didn't disappear though.

"Wake up, Sláine. I think we're in trouble."

No amount of begging or cajoling helped. The Celt was dead to the world.

"Don't say it's up to old Ukko. I'm a lover not a fighter." He chuckled to himself, and then checked that he still had the small stabbing dirk tucked into the ratty folds of his grubby tunic. "Oh, come then, if you're coming. I know you're out there and I really hate waiting to die. Well, I don't really. I like waiting to die. I just like the idea of it being a long, long way off, in bed surrounded by a dozen beautifully rotund women pampering me with there bare breasts so that I suffocate happy."

Whatever it was didn't come as long as the sun was up.

Ukko rolled over, coming awake quickly.

He didn't know what he'd heard, only that it had dragged him abruptly from sleep with its wrongness.

He lay on his side, listening to the night sounds hoping – and more than half actively not hoping – that it would repeat itself. He looked up at the full silver moon hanging low in the cloudless sky. The stars were bright.

"Sláine? Are you awake? Come on, Sláine, wake up. I'm fed up of being the hero to your sleeping ugliness." The young Celt didn't stir. His sleep was disturbingly unnatural. It had been almost two days since his collapse on the hill overlooking the great stone Watcher of Er-Grah where the horned man had levitated.

Ukko had done all he could; he had dragged, kicked and bullied the warrior to shelter, had tended his visible wounds, a cut on his forehead where he had fallen and cracked it off a rock, made him warm, and kept the small fire going. None of it made the slightest discernible difference to the warrior's condition. He knew some kind of internal struggle was going on within Sláine. The young man tossed and turned, mumbling names in his sleep: Niamh, Danu, and Bedelia, although most often it was Niamh's name on his cracked lips. He was in the grip of a fever. Cold sweat peppered his entire body. Ukko knew that it could go one of two ways. The fever would break or the man would.

Ukko stoked the fire again, throwing on a fresh branch.

"Come on, Sláine. I don't deserve this. I've always been a good companion."

He shivered, moving closer to the fire, but it wasn't the cold that had his skin crawling. He had often joked that as a thief by nature he had an uncanny sixth sense for when things were just wrong. This, here, was wrong. His nerves were firing off warning after warning and had been doing so for almost two days. Someone – or something – was out there in the darkness, watching them.

Then, a few minutes later, he heard it again: the baying of a wolf at the moon. It was a savage sound. He had always imagined that wolves were noble beasts, kings of the wild, their calls swollen with longing and sadness. The only longing in this beast's howl was for meat. The animal was hungry.

Ukko had the uncomfortable feeling that the beast had chosen them to break its fast.

He scurried back to where Sláine lay and pushed the warrior hard in the chest, "Come on, you great lump of meat, time to wake up." Sláine grunted but didn't show any other sign of coming back to consciousness. Ukko tried to lift the barbarian's huge stone axe but it was no use, he could barely get the head off the ground.

"Bloody stupid thing, and why haven't you got smaller weapons, you know, daggers and stuff. Even magic acorns that'd grow into a tree I could climb up and hide in instead of this manly 'look at the size of my muscles' rubbish." He kicked the axe.

He heard the beast padding around them in the darkness. The slobber of its tongue and the *huff-huff-huff* of its breathing gave it away.

Ukko scrabbled away from Sláine, grabbing a gnarled branch and thrusting it into the fire. "Come on, come on. Catch." He shook the branch, stirring up the flames, trying to get the branch to burn. After a moment it began to smoulder. He cast a fretful glance over his shoulder. It was impossible to tell whether the beast was coming or not. Staring at the fire had all but blinded Ukko to the night. He cursed himself for a fool. "You're going to get yourself killed here, you idiot," he said, loud enough for it to sound as if he was talking to Sláine – had he not been unconscious.

The beast came out of the black in a fury of snarling, snapping teeth and raking claws. Ukko launched himself into a backwards tumble, rolling on his shoulder and coming up in a crouch, brandishing the burning branch as if it was the mightiest sword. He brought it sweeping round in a tight arc, the flame making a low whumping noise as it was almost snuffed out. The wolf circled the fire, hackles raised, never for a moment taking its hungry eyes off the dwarf.

"Come on then, let's be done with it shall we?"

The beast inclined its head as if it understood his request. It lowered its nose to the dirt almost as if it was nodding.

"Okay, I mean, I wasn't serious. It was a rhetorical question. No need to be hasty."

The beast sprang, covering the distance between them in a single bound. It hit Ukko high in the chest, barrelling him off his feet. Ukko screamed as its yellow-stained teeth snapped an inch shy of his throat. He threw up his arms, trying desperately to batter the creature away, and then a sickening howl tore from the wolf's slack jowls as the burning branch scorched its fur.

The animal rolled off him.

The stench of burned fur soured the air.

Ukko thrust the burning branch at the beast again, ramming the end of it into the animal's muzzle. A glowing twig snapped off the main brand, piercing the wolf's eye. Its cry was terrible. Ukko sprang to his feet, pushing home the unexpected advantage. He jabbed the burning brand into the animal's face again and again, until the stench of burning was overpowering. With his left hand he drew the stabbing dirk from his belt while thrusting the firebrand into the animal's face again. The beast rolled over onto its back, exposing its soft belly. Without thinking, Ukko threw himself forwards, jumping on the huge wolf and rammed the tip of the dirk deep between its ribs.

The beast stiffened, snapping its jaws around and sinking its teeth into Ukko's arm.

Ukko's answering scream was louder and more anguished than anything the beast had managed. The teeth sank deep into the bone and tore. Ukko dropped the firebrand and dragged the dirk out of the wolf's chest with both hands, ramming the short blade in again and again, with a shocking display of naked savagery until he hit and pierced the creature's heart. The animal bucked and writhed, howling, and then suddenly the fight fled from its body and it lay in the dirt, still.

Ukko flopped onto his back, gasping for breath. He lay beside the dead beast. The heat coming off its corpse was incredible – so much so he thought for a moment that the dead animal was lying on the brand and its entire pelt was going up in smoke – but the brand had died and lay blackened ten feet from where they were. No, the heat was coming from within the dead beast. Ukko scrambled away from the creature.

The wolf's face shifted in the flickering firelight, its snout truncating, and its brow narrowing.

Ukko put the fire between himself and the dead animal, far from happy with this latest turn of events.

Through the flames it was impossible to tell what was happening. He tried to see over them but the corpse had fallen into shadow.

"Just leave well enough alone, Ukko," he told himself. He still clutched the bloody stabbing dirk in his right hand. "Of course you can't can you? Oh no, curiosity killed the stupid thief," Ukko muttered, creeping around the fire.

Instead of finding the beast he saw a young boy lying naked by the fire. He had been a good-looking lad with a nice open face, a scruff of blonde hair and... and his body was soaked with blood. Standing over the corpse Ukko counted twenty-seven stab wounds in the boy's chest. He felt sick. He hadn't been able to stop himself once he had started stabbing. The dirk had just kept going in and in and in, even when the beast was dead.

"Soth! What have I done?" he moaned. The answer was obvious. He had killed the boy. Only he hadn't. He'd killed a wolf, a wolf, not a boy. He wouldn't have killed a boy.

His left arm hung loosely at his side, shredded where the wolf's teeth had torn into his flesh. The wound was very physical proof that he had fought a savage beast, not some wide-eyed boy drawn to the comfort of the fire.

It was only Ukko's blood on the lad's teeth that stopped the dwarf from thinking he had gone mad.

He shivered.

"It's going to be a long night," Ukko grumbled, digging around in his pack for something to bind his wounds, before he settled down to wait out the darkness.

Ukko heard something else grubbing about in the darkness less than an hour after sunrise. His heart skipped a beat. He held his wounded arm protectively to his side. "Please no, not again," he moaned. He peered in the direction of the sound but he couldn't see anything. That didn't make him any more relaxed. The fire was dead. It had burned out during the night despite his best efforts to keep it fed.

The corpse of the young boy was an ugly reminder of the sorts of danger that could be out there.

Ukko crept over to where Sláine lay. He knelt and pressed his lips up to the unconscious man's ear. "Sláine? Sláine?" he whispered urgently. "Wake up, will you?" He nudged the young Sessair, and then again, quite a bit harder. "There's something out there again and I'm not up to fighting off another shoggy beast so just bloody well wake up will you? You're supposed to be the hero, not me. I'm just along for the ride."

The scuffling in the bushes got louder. Ukko looked up sharply. He heard a grunt. "Definitely human," he muttered to Sláine. "Let's hope that means it's an improvement on a shoggy bugger."

His heart stopped in his chest as an old man blundered into the clearing a few moments later. He burst out laughing with relief. The old man was dressed in rags and his eyes were bound with another filthy strip. He used a long stick to feel his way, sweeping it around in front of him so that it hit anything in his path and he worked his way around it. It was slow going with roots and stones sticking out of the ground every few feet.

Ukko watched the blind man negotiate his way to the centre of the clearing and look up, look around, sniffing and turn to look directly at him. "How many injured?"

"Two, one dead."

"How bad?"

"Well the dead one was very dead the last time I looked," Ukko offered, puzzled by the question. "I don't think he'll be getting up in a long time."

"That's usually the way with the dead. I was more interested in the wounded. How badly are they wounded?"

"Ah," Ukko said. "Not good really. In fact you could say badly. I myself have a dreadful bite I sustained wrestling off a damned shoggy beast. That's the dead one, in case you are wondering, although he just looks like a dumb boy now. My companion, the erstwhile hero of our partnership, was unconscious the whole time. Something happened to him at the stones. I've been trying to get him as far away from them as possible but as you can see he's about three times my – ah no, you can't see can you. Well, you'll just have to take my word for it."

"Ahhh," the blind man said, as if that explained everything.

"Look, I don't mean to be rude, I mean, you are obviously, ah, erm, hmm, well, blind. So I mean how could you know we were wounded? I mean... it isn't as if you can see or... well... can you?"

The old man smiled. It was a rather lopsided facial expression. Ukko doubted he even knew what a smile was supposed to look like so he didn't correct him. "I can smell the blood, lad. It's a pretty special smell. It's acrid, like iron coming out of the smith's smelting pot, only more alive."

"Remarkable," Ukko said.

"No more remarkable than being able to see blood... Come on then, lad, let's get you and your friend back to my hut, shall we, before night sets in. I've got some stuff you can use to tend to your wounds."

"Is there a village nearby?"

"Well, it ain't much of one any more. It used to be, maybe a score of years ago. I used to work the flint mines. They're long gone now of course. The whole place has been dying a slow death for years. Domnall's about the only one who gets any business done."

"Domnall?"

"He's a smith. He makes some mighty fine weapons, or so folk say. Warriors come from miles around for one of his creations. Even the Drune priests pay the dwarf a pretty penny."

"Dwarf, you say? Curiouser and curiouser. I might have to go pay old Domnall a visit, make acquaintances and all of that."

"Well, he isn't the friendliest of fellows," the blind man said cagily.

"Ah, but I am sure he'll be happy to see a kinsman."

"Aye, maybe you're right, lad."

Eighteen
Temper

UKKO NURSED SLÁINE for the best part of three weeks, feeding him dubious delicacies like rat's liver and fried toad.

Sláine put up with it just as he put up with the dwarf bleeding him regularly.

"It's for your own good, Sláine. Trust me, I know what I am doing."

"I'm not so sure," Sláine said. He felt his strength slowly returning but for all that he still felt as weak as a newborn babe and he knew Ukko was taking advantage of that. The little rat was up to something, and it was almost certainly no good.

"It's the only way to be sure we get all of the poisons out of you, your warpishness. We don't want you coming over all funny again next time you are beside the dolmen, now do we?"

"I suppose not," Sláine said, grudgingly.

Sláine offered up his arm.

The dwarf drew the tip of his stabbing dirk to open up a fresh cut. The wound was shallow but bled freely, filling the tankard that Ukko held under it.

The dwarf disappeared a moment later.

Sláine stared around Blind Bran's hovel. It was simple. None of the furniture had any sharp edges and it was all within easy reach of the low wooden cot. There was an intricate piece of scrimshaw on the table beside the bed, an effigy of Carnun, the Horned God. The detail on the piece was exquisite. Sláine picked it up, turning it over in his hands. It was impossible to imagine a blind man capable of such craft.

"That piece has taken me three months," Bran said, pushing through the curtain. He didn't have his cane. He didn't need it in his own home. He had memorised the position of every bit of furniture and every ornament so that he could move around as confidently as any one with sight.

"It's beautiful," Sláine said, the surprise all too evident in his voice. He put the small statue back on the low table.

"Thank you."

The pair had sat together regularly, Blind Bran telling the story of his village. It was distressingly similar to the Brianna's tale. The Drunes had come with their perverted rituals demanding sacrifices, animal at first, and then young women, to sate the hunger of their wyrm god, Crom-Cruach. For every mile they had come south Sláine knew of a dozen similar tales. The land was being laid to waste by the depravities of these Drunes in the name of their false god. Nothing grew hereabouts. There hadn't been a bountiful harvest in over a score of years, perhaps even longer.

Slough Feg himself had driven the final nail into the coffin of this small, unimportant settlement, promising to solve their hunger and make food plentiful once more.

"We took him at his word," Blind Bran said. "I mean, why wouldn't we?"

"What happened?"

"He promised us that there would be an end to our hardship, that there would be food aplenty. All we had to do was bend the knee to Crom and our needs would be seen to."

"And were they?"

"Not in any humane way, warrior. The Drunes rounded up the young of the village, all under twenty summers, and butchered them."

"Soth!" Sláine said, realising even as he said it that he was beginning to sound more and more like the pesky dwarf.

"That was more than half of us. He laughed in my face as I challenged him. What are you upset about, miner? Now there is food enough for everyone! You should be happy. I have saved your life. That's what he said to me. He expected me to be happy that he had killed my friends, my son, and the future of our village. There are no children now. Our little place in the world is dying. None have the heart to bring new life into this wretched world. In that Feg and his vile wyrm god have been our damnation."

"I am sorry, Bran. I don't know what to tell you. I am here to prevent this fate befalling my people."

"Then I pray you succeed, Sláine, for the sake of the children."

"I cannot fail." It wasn't arrogance; it was a statement of fact. To fail was to damn the Sessair to the same fate that had befallen these nameless villages all throughout the Sourlands.

"I thought the same once. I was a proud man. I am not so proud today. I haven't always been this way, Sláine. It wasn't just my son they murdered that day, I died as well. This life is a half life. Feg took my eyes because I had the gall to challenge him. 'Perhaps being blind will help you see better', that's what he told me as the branding iron did its work. I remember it so vividly, my boy lying on the floor, this tiny broken thing, and all of the others piled up around him. I can't stop seeing the looks of betrayal on their faces. It's funny how the last thing I saw has stayed so fresh in my mind's eye, almost as if Feg trapped it there deliberately to taunt me. I wouldn't put it past the monster."

"He will pay," Sláine promised.

"I hope so lad, but I have long since past believing it will happen."

"I refuse to live in a world where it doesn't."

"Ah, then don't let Slough Feg hear you say that or he will twist your words and you will be the dead one lying on the stone slab as an offering to Crom."

"I'd like to see him try," Sláine said.

"Again?" Sláine grumbled, holding out his arm for Ukko to cut.

"This hurts me more than it does you, Sláine, believe me. I wish you'd just get better."

"I'm sure you do."

"Oh, I do. Believe me, I do. Nothing would please me more than to see you up and about and back to your old warpish ways."

"Well, of course you don't want me to croak here. I'm not an idiot. I know that stories about the great warped one, Sláine Mac Roth dying in a blind man's hovel won't get you a halfway decent meal in any inn we've been to, now will it?"

Ukko tied off the wound with a strip of cloth. The blood quickly soaked the rag a rich crimson.

"You wound me." Ukko grinned. "Hold your arm above your head, there's a good man. I think I might have cut a little deep this time."

Sláine raised his hand, scratching his ear.

"Good, keep it like that," Ukko said. "I'll be back in a while. Got to go see a man about a cow."

"From anyone else that would be an odd sentence."

"Ah, but I'm not anyone else," Ukko said, grinning as he backed out of the room. Sláine didn't like the look on the little sneak thief's face one bit.

Sláine waited for the outside door to close before he lowered his arm. He stood up. He walked over to the door. He pressed the bandage against his arm but it did little to staunch the bleeding. He stood there for a moment, counting to eleven before he cracked the door open an inch. Blood dripped, a few drops pattering around his feet as he peeked through the crack in time to see the dwarf skipping around the corner of a low longhouse fifty feet away. Ukko cradled the tankard of Sláine's freshly drained blood to his chest. Sláine shook his head. The better he got to know the dwarf the less he trusted the little runt. He was up to no good, of that Sláine was sure, and it had something to do with his blood.

There was only one way to find out. He followed Ukko.

Weak from his wounds and the constant bleeding, Sláine moved slowly, all too aware that the world was precariously balanced and wanted to roll away under him every third step. He kept close to the buildings as he walked. He used them for support when his legs threatened to undo him. The streets were empty, which was far from ideal. A few more people moving around would at least have offered something approximating cover. Still, beggars couldn't be choosers. He inched up to the corner and peered around it. Ukko was whistling and looking far too happy with himself as he ducked into a doorway. The sign above it was of a hammer and anvil.

Sláine crept closer, pressing up against the wall, beneath the window so that he might eavesdrop on the dwarf's clandestine business.

"Excellent," said a voice he didn't recognise. "More of the warped one's blood. This will temper War-Flame, making her the most fabled of my creations, worthy of the Lord Weird himself."

Sláine stiffened at the mention of Slough Feg. It took every ounce of restraint he had not to throw himself through the window and choke the life out of the two-timing double-dealing backstabbing dwarf. He seethed.

"Five bits I think we agreed." He heard the clink of coins being counted out and Ukko's strangled cough.

"I think you'll find it was nine, Domnall."

"Nine, nine, of course, yes. Never try to grift a grifter, eh? Nine bits it is."

Four more coins rattled out of the pouch and into Ukko's greedy hands.

"Sure you can't make it say thirty bits? I mean this is hero's blood, not some shoddy guttersnipe's. It's the good stuff. You said so yourself, Sláine's was the best blood you'd ever come across. Perfect for quenching swords."

"Did I? Well, it isn't bad but it is hardly perfect. It will do. It will be used to forge a mighty sword, the match of any ever wielded by giants, dwarf: a true hero's blade. Slough Feg will reward me greatly for War-Flame when I offer it up to him to wield."

"Soth!" Ukko exclaimed. "You mean the sword is for the horned priest? Sorry, I'll be needing that blood back, and much as it pains me to say it, you can have your coins."

"You think so? The way I see it you aren't in any kind of position to try and bargain. We struck an honest deal. I have upheld my side, and you have upheld yours. That's what we call business."

"You dirty rotten cheat. Give me that blood back or I'll set Sláine on you."

"Really? You don't think he'd have your guts for a hero harness for stealing his blood?"

Sláine didn't wait to hear anymore. He barged through the smithy door.

Ukko and Domnall, the smith, had each other by the throat. Both turned, furtively, to look at the door as he stormed in. Domnall let go first, dusting his hands off on his apron. They were standing beside a huge black iron block that the smith obviously used as an anvil to beat out the red hot metal.

"Sláine!" Ukko gulped. "I can explain! It isn't what it looks like."

"It looks like the smith is trying to throttle the life out of you," Sláine said coldly.

"Well, maybe it is what it looks like then."

"Welcome to Domnall's, armourer to the great warriors of old. What can I interest you in? A beautifully crafted gáe bolga perhaps? Or a razor-edged shield? Your companion here tells me you are one of the fabled warped ones. It would be an honour to craft the mightiest of hero harnesses for you."

"Have you been stealing my blood?" Sláine asked. He cracked his knuckles.

"A helmet, perhaps?" the smith went on, ignoring Sláine's question. "I guarantee anything I craft would make even the most timid of warriors strike fear into the hearts of their enemies."

"Women wear helmets," Sláine spat. "Now, I'll ask you again, have you been stealing my blood? Take your time and think about your answer, both of you. I'll try to ignore the coins in your hand, Ukko, and the tankard of blood in yours, smith, giving you the benefit of the doubt."

"Well," Ukko mumbled, looking down at his feet, "just a drop. Nothing you'd miss, and it was for your own good, Sláine. Domnall here's making you a sword, a hero's weapon tempered in—"

"Don't lie to me, you dirty little rat bastard. You've been bleeding me white for bloody coins!"

"I was going to give you a cut," Ukko said, and then realised what he had said and closed his eyes. "You know what I mean."

"Now's the perfect time to shut your mouth, Ukko, before it gets you in more trouble." Sláine rounded on Domnall. "And you, master smith, have been using my blood to temper a blade for the scum that murdered my mother. This stops now. I will have my blood back. Ukko will return your coins."

"Like I said to your friend, I think not. I bought this blood and now it is mine. It's business. Now, if you don't mind me saying, you look a little pale. Perhaps you should go and lie down?"

Sláine grabbed the iron ring on the side of the anvil and heaved, upending the huge block. Beneath it was a gaping black hole. He sent it bouncing across the floor of the smithy, cracking the stone wall.

"You shouldn't have done that," Domnall said, shaking his head. He moved with surprising speed, stepping back and grabbing a long iron poker from the forge's fire and swinging it around. Sláine barely managed to get his head out of the way but stumbled, his foot falling into the hole in the floor. "Now I've got no choice but to kill you and your damned fool friend."

Unbalanced, Sláine fell forwards, arms windmilling desperately as he tried to catch himself on nothing. His head cracked off the lip of the hole with a sickening thud. He tumbled lifelessly into the pit.

"I know you're going to blame me for this," Ukko said, "but it really isn't my fault, not when you think about it."

"Shut up, Ukko."

"I mean as soon as I knew he was evil I tried to back out of the deal."

"I don't want to hear your voice again before I die," Sláine said.

"That can be arranged," Domnall the smith said, stomping up the stone steps from the midden back up to the forge proper.

The dwarf had strung them up by the hands. Sláine's feet dangled inches above the ground. Domnall's lantern cast a guttering light around the cramped pit. It revealed enough to hint at the horrors that had taken place beneath the smithy. Bleached white bones: skulls, femurs, fibulas, tibias, mandibles and ribs were scattered across the floor. Slick-bodied rats crawled over the bones and under the bones, looking for scraps of meat to be picked clean.

The walls had been scratched with short marks, as if one of the unfortunates before them had counted off the days before he joined the pile of bones.

"Ogham," Ukko hissed.

"I said shut up."

"No, no, listen Sláine. Those scratches, they're Ogham."

Sláine wriggled around, trying to see them better but it was useless and pointless since he couldn't read the old script. "Can you read them?"

Ukko didn't say anything.

Sláine twisted to look at the little dwarf, trussed up like a side of boar waiting to be thrown into the smoke house. "I said can you read it?"

The dwarf wiggled his eyebrows.

"Oh for Lugh's sake! Just tell me if you can read it."

"I'm allowed to talk now? I don't want you to beat me for impertinence or anything."

"What does it say?" Sláine asked, patiently.

Ukko twisted around on his ropes to get a better view of the curious letters scratched deep into the wall. "Hmm, well, that first one says, 'Why me?'"

"Helpful."

"And the next says, 'I don't want to die here', and 'repent, the Ragnarok is coming'. That one's quite big next to the others. And that one there says, 'all dwarfs are'... okay, I'm not reading any more. That's just plain crude, and untrue. We aren't miniature everywhere."

The sound of Domnall beating out the blade of his sword drifted down from above.

Impotent anger welled inside Sláine. Anywhere but this blighted land he would have had Danu to draw on, and then all the evils in the world wouldn't have been enough to protect the toad, Domnall, from his wrath. He twisted around angrily on the ropes, trying desperately to wriggle an extra inch or two of give out of the bonds, but the ropes were having none of it. Domnall had done a grand job of trussing them up.

The steady *clang-clang-clang* of the hammer on the blade haunted him. He could feel it – or imagined he could – each hammer blow ringing through his flesh because the smith was tempering the blade with his blood. They were bonded, just as he was bonded to Danu, her weapon tempered with the blood of the earth. He hung there picturing all sorts of grizzly fates for the dwarf smith. Sláine heard someone rap on the door, and then there was silence. It was unnerving. He strained to hear what was happening, but only caught fractured voices and the occasional word. He couldn't be sure but he thought the second speaker was Blind Bran.

"Down here!" he yelled, ratcheting his body around sharply. Fire burned down his left side as the muscle there twisted unnaturally. "Down here!"

Sláine heaved himself up and pulled down hard on the rope binding him, wrenching the hook an inch out of the wooden ceiling. He dropped far enough for his toes to graze the bones strewn across the midden floor. He nudged them around but couldn't quite grip any of them.

The door slammed and Domnall came stomping down the stairs shaking his head like a disappointed parent. "Now, now, Sláine, surely you understand your shouting just killed that poor blind man, don't you? You as good as stuck the knife in his throat yourself. Of course, I let him leave, but I couldn't let him live, not if he suspects you are down here. Was that really necessary?"

"You're scum, dwarf," Sláine said.

"Well of course I am. It's my nature. Ask the wasp why it stings and it'll tell you because I am a wasp, it is what I do. Now, come on, time to bleed for the nasty dwarf." Domnall came in close. "The blood's all gone to your feet. This is good, Sláine. This is really good. You'll be like that hero, the one who bled to death when they cut his ankle. Gah! I can't remember his name for the life of me. Oh well. Let's get this over with, shall we?"

"Over my dead body!"

"Well, that is kind of the idea, yes." The smith pulled a wickedly curved blade from the belt of his apron and pressed it up against Sláine's inner thigh. "Just one little cut, that's all I need. Open up the artery and that sweet red warped blood of yours will flow like there is no tomorrow. Well, of course, there isn't for you or your pet dwarf."

"Hey!" Ukko protested, "We're equals, Sláine and me. We're a team."

Domnall turned, laughing. "Of course you are, little naive Fukko, of course you are."

Sláine knew he had one chance, and that was barely half a chance. He closed his eyes, trying to touch whatever dregs of power might still reside in this dark pit, and jerked down hard on the rope, gaining another inch of give from the hook. He felt a long jagged spur of a broken femur with his feet, gripping it between his toes, as he would have a gáe bolga. As the smith turned Sláine lashed out with his leg and launched the splinter of bone just as Murdo had taught him to throw the deadly bellows spear.

Shock registered on Domnall's face as the makeshift weapon tore into his chest, the bone ripping out of his back in a spray of blood. His piggy little eyes bulged wide as his hands flew up to the bone piercing his chest, and then rolled up into his head as he fell, his body dead a moment before his brain knew it.

"See how I helped there, Sláine? I distracted him so you could kill him. That's got to be worth something, right? I mean I saved your life, technically."

Sláine stood on the dwarf's corpse, using the extra height to get the leverage he needed to work himself free of the knots.

"Shut up, Ukko. I don't want to hear another word from you if I cut you down."

"You won't—"

"I said if," Sláine cut him off.

"I didn't mean any harm. I was trying to do a good thing. I was thinking about you, Sláine. I thought you needed a hero's weapon."

"Every word out of your mouth is a lie, isn't it?"

Ukko looked around sheepishly as if checking to see who might hear. Satisfied they were alone with the dead, he said, "Not every word."

"Take it, it's yours. It always was," Ukko urged.

Sláine stared at the damned blade, War-Flame.

He shook his head.

"No, let the Lord Weird wield it. I'd rather swing Brain-Biter than some perverted blood forged blade." He tossed the sword into the cooling off barrel. "Besides, for all its so-called magnificence, it's untempered. Only a fool would wield an untempered blade in battle."

"Ah, good thinking, let's hope Slough Feg finds it and uses it eh? And that it shatters in battle when he most needs it, when he comes face to face with you! I knew this would happen," Ukko said brightly. "That was my plan all along. Give the horned High Priest a dodgy sword. I told you I was looking out for you, Sláine. We make a great team."

Sláine cuffed Ukko across the head. "What was it the smith called you? Sukko? No. No. Pukko? No that wasn't it. Fukko, such a great name. I should start calling you that!"

"Don't you dare."

"Fukko," Sláine said with a wink.

Ukko stormed off, slamming the forge door behind him.

"Temper, temper," Sláine chuckled, opening the door.

Three stunningly beautiful, three-quarter naked women waited for him on the other side. An intricate constellation of spirals and swirling tattoos was daubed across their bare flesh. They wore a sash across the cleft of their sex but were otherwise bare. He couldn't help but stare at the curve and sweep of their bodies, the swell of breasts, and the Gordian tattoos coiling around the dark, puffy, aureoles of their nipples and disappearing beneath the pendulous curve of their breasts. Sláine followed each and every swirl of ink with his eyes. The illusion was so perfect that he could have sworn they actually moved. Their muscles were taut, honed, lithe, their bodies like the finest works of art, worthy of the utmost devotion.

He looked up, shaking his head.

"Now this is what I call a welcoming committee," Sláine said, grinning widely. "If I'd known you were coming I'd have made an effort." None of them were smiling. He stopped talking. Something reeked. The smell assailed him. It was like rotten fruit. It well and truly shattered the illusion. He tore his gaze away from the feast of flesh and for the first time he saw beyond the three women: a circle of masked skull-swords stood, blades pointed at him. Behind the skull-swords, the source of the vile stench, a daemonic horned Drune priest cackled.

Ukko was on his knees, begging not to be hurt.

Blind Bran was on the floor, unconscious or dead, it was impossible to tell which.

"Seize him!" the horned priest hissed, and the women came at him.

Sláine wanted to laugh. They were naked, what could they do?

He said as much.

They quickly beat that misogynistic notion out of his head.

Nineteen
The Wicker Man

SLÁINE RAISED HIS hands to defend himself as the first of the women launched a blistering open-handed attack, slamming him quickly once, twice, three times in the chest, face and throat. The third hit had him choking. The second woman sprang, hammering a two-footed kick into his groin. A final blow from the first woman jabbed into his neck. He felt the needle's sting and knew he had been poisoned even before the third woman tumbled forwards. She used one hand to cartwheel around him acrobatically, bounced back to her feet and chopped down savagely on the back of his neck as he fell, sending stars bursting across his eyes.

It was over in seconds.

Sláine shook his head groggily.

He could hear Ukko begging not to be hurt but he couldn't see the little runt. He couldn't see anything beyond his own nose.

"Nuh…" he managed, slumping forwards.

The world was black.

There were no sounds in the blackness, no shapes, no forms and no shadows, at least not at first.

They came – or returned – slowly.

First there were sounds, desperate words: "Mercy! Help! Murder!" and other words, more seductive, promising: "That's what I want, yes, yes, yes. Scream for me little dwarf. I want to hear your screams as I give you the blood-eagle."

"No need for torture, priestess! Please, I'll tell you everything! There will be no secrets between us. We'll be like lovers well not like lovers that way, I mean unless you have a thing for dwarfs. Arrrrghhhhh! That hurt!"

"It was supposed to. That's why it is called torture."

Sláine opened one eye. A Drune priestess – at least that is what he assumed she was, with her macabre tattoos and bare flesh taunting him with the promise of just how enjoyably exhausting devotion could be with her – bent over Ukko, her bare breasts grazing the back of the dwarf's neck. Ukko was bound to a table, trussed up like the Sunday roast ready for the spit. The priestesses must have dragged them to their reclusium, a chamber deep within the bowels of their temple. There was no sign to suggest any form of worship took place this deep in the temple but plenty to suggest that torture and other unsavoury practices were the norm.

"Ah, your muscle-bound friend is awake, perfect. I do hope he'll be more sport."

The tip of a red-hot blade sliced into the muscle of his back, parting the skin and the meat. Sláine clenched his teeth, biting back against the pain. It was the first of four cuts that together made a blood eagle. The pain of it was excruciating but he refused to give the woman the pleasure of showing it. It was a savage reawakening.

He closed his eyes waiting for the second cut. If the priestesses were to finish the blood eagle all they would need to do was pull and his body would rip open, disgorging his heart, liver and guts out of his back. He would be dead before then, although that was only a small mercy.

Ukko screamed again, a gut-wrenching shriek. Sláine didn't want to imagine what they were doing to the dwarf.

"Oh, shut up, you miserable little wretch! I didn't even touch you!"

Sláine wanted to laugh but a second cut ripped the sound from his mouth.

"Drop the knife, witch!" a masked skull-sword bellowed, barging into the sanctity of the reclusium.

"How dare you invade our sanctuary!" the priestess cried, wheeling round on the soldier only for the next sentence to die in her mouth as a sough-skinned Drune Lord came in behind him. The stench from the Drune was overpowering. Sláine gagged. The Drune stood head and shoulders taller than the skull-sword, wrapped in a huge bear pelt. Withered branches took the place of antlers on his hood. Sláine could see the rich red of rancid meat where the pelt fell open on the Drune's skinless flesh. It was like something plucked out of his worst nightmares.

"He dares because I commanded it, priestess. Dare you stop him? No, I thought not. You will relinquish these prisoners into my custody. They are to be fed to Crom-Cruach as part of his bridge's dowry of blood. The Lord Weird has commanded it."

"They are mine," the woman said, but there was no conviction in her voice.

"You know better, priestess. They belong – just as we do – to the Lord Weird. If he would have them burn, they will burn. Now, we both know there is little you can do about this other than hand them over, so shall we dispense with the pretence. You," the Drune Lord turned to the skull-sword, "see that they are taken to the wicker man."

Twenty skull-swords dragged Sláine between them. He didn't make it easy for them. Two more carried Ukko. The dwarf kicked and twisted and howled but the soldiers didn't take a blind bit of notice of him.

The fields around them were parched and dusty, like so much of the Sourland, dead where they should have been vibrant with life and renewal. They passed a farmer bent over a young calf, slaughtering it so that the animal might offer up a few decent meals rather than leave the poor creature to die of malnutrition. Everyone they passed wore the same look of defeat beaten into their weathered faces.

The air was hot, burning his lungs as he breathed. There was only the faintest breeze. The rolling hills shimmered with a heat haze rising off the dead ground.

The wicker man was as tall again as the great dolmen, the Watcher of Er-Grah. It loomed, a giant sentinel on the horizon, towering over the village and the hills that rolled away beneath its feet. The construction was incredible. It really was like a giant man come striding out of myth. He had never seen anything like it in his life. The torso and limbs of the giant wicker man were a patchwork of black holes. As they came closer Sláine could make out the desperate clawing hands of prisoners trapped within the huge wickerwork figure reaching out through the holes. Kindling was banked up around its feet.

It was all too easy to imagine the flames being lit and the wicker giant blazing like a beacon against the night sky.

The skull-swords pushed Sláine forwards, sending him sprawling prostrate at the feet of the towering figure. It was bigger than he had first thought, easily one hundred and fifty feet, each leg thirty feet in diameter and crammed with men condemned by Feg's regime. The figure was so huge that it straddled dry land and foul swamp, one massive leg rooted firmly in each.

"Crom-Cruach cherishes the death of thieves, liars, cheats, murderers, outlaws and other misguided fools who commit crimes against his benevolent rule," The Drune Lord explained. "The Lord Weird has proclaimed that your place is in there, warped one, with the dregs of society, to make up the blood dowry of the bride to be. There are one hundred and nine; with you it will be one hundred and eleven, a sacred number. There will be blood for the wyrm god." The Drune Lord cackled, thoroughly enjoying himself. "Chain them with the others. It's time for the living to burn."

Two skull-swords bullied them in through the base of the huge construction, up the ladders of the wicker man's skeleton until they were high inside the structure. The Drune Lord drove an iron bar into the base of

Sláine's spine, driving him to his knees. "Now, chain him. The Lord Weird is coming. The fires will be lit soon. It wouldn't do to be trapped in here with this scum."

The core of the wicker man was filled with a near constant babble of noise: men begging and crying out, shuffling feet and crazed laughter as fear collapsed beneath manic rage, sour air, sweat, dirty hair and the piss stink of urine. That malodorous melange clung to the air around the antlered Drune Lord, the rot of his flesh plain to see where decay had eaten through his lips and cheeks to expose a cracked and broken row of tombstone-like teeth. The putrescence was nauseating. Flies buzzed around the sorcerer, drawn to the filth of his flesh.

Sláine fixated on the flies as they settled on the Drune Lord's cheek and crawled over his eye. The sorcerer gave no indication that he even noticed the parasites crawling over his face.

The Drune Lord left them, climbing back down the rickety ladder and taking the worst of his rotten stench with him. One of the two skull-swords followed silently.

The remaining skull-sword pulled on the chains, threading them through the wicker frame of the giant effigy, and around Sláine's torso and arms. He set six locks on them, joining the huge metal links. As the last lock clunked into place, Sláine spat in the face of his gaoler.

The skull-sword moved slowly, rising up to his full height. He craned his head as if examining a bug that had settled on his outstretched hand and he didn't quite know what to do with it. Then he drove a clenched fist into Sláine's balls, hard enough to fold Sláine in two, only the chains prevented it from happening, just as they prevented Sláine from protecting himself as the skull-sword grabbed him between the legs, squeezed and twisted savagely. Then again, enjoying the agony it caused.

The skull-sword relinquished his hold and turned to leer at the prisoners chained to the wicker ribcage around Sláine. "Anyone want to feel some real pain before they die?" He clenched his fist, mimicking the vicelike grab he'd performed on Sláine's testicles. The skull-sword had underestimated Sláine Mac Roth, as so many others had before him. Ignoring the screaming pain Sláine arched his back and wrapped his legs around the skull-sword's waist, squeezing mercilessly.

"I die, you die," Sláine rasped. "I can keep you here while they burn us all alive. Not laughing now, are you?"

The skull-sword writhed desperately trying to break Sláine's hold but it was no good.

"Kill him," one of the other prisoners shouted from across the wicker man's torso. "Rip the bastard in two! Him and his kind killed my son!"

"Do him!"

"Show 'im the mercy 'e'd show us!"

"Aye, snap him like a bleedin' twig!"

Sláine raged, his anger seething wildly but no matter how black it became he couldn't tap the earth's power and warp spasm. The land here was dead.

The skull-sword struggled against his grip, which only served to madden him more. Sláine crushed the life out of him mercilessly with his thighs, contorting his spine so that a loop of metal chain wrapped around the skull-sword's neck. It was an ugly suffocating death but no less than the skull-sword deserved.

When the dead man's shudders stopped Sláine let go. The skull-sword fell at his feet.

"Good on you, lad. Give the bastards an account of yourself before you die."

"I'm not going to die here," Sláine said. "Living's far too much fun." He looked out through a hole in the wicker man's chest. The sky was darkening but that wasn't what caught his eye. It was thick with a murder of crows cawing hungrily as they flew above the heads of the spectators. Crows: Morrigan's pets. It took a moment for the importance of this to register with Sláine. If Morrigan's influence could reach this far into the Sourland so too could the other aspects of Danu. He felt a surge of hope. "We aren't damned just yet boys. Trust me."

"We ain't got much of a choice," another prisoner groaned pitifully.

"What did they get you for?" one of the others asked.

"I killed their damned smith, Domnall."

"Sláine? Sláine? Is that you?" Sláine recognised the voice, it was Blind Bran's. He couldn't see the old hermit but there was no doubt it was him.

"Aye, Bran, it's me."

"Ah, boy it's good to hear you! I'm sick of listening to all these cowards warbling on about dying."

"And you, old man. Now let's think about getting out of here, shall we? Ukko? Can you get out of these chains?"

"What chains?" Ukko asked, grinning widely as he stepped away from the wicker wall, the chains in a pile at his feet. He held up a small lock pick and waggled it. "There isn't a lock made that can keep me in or out."

"There are one hundred and eleven in here."

"More," another prisoner said.

"And don't forget the girl they've trussed up in the wicker man's head, Medb. The whole point of this huge bonfire is so that she can become the Bride of Crom."

Someone cried, "Feg! It's Slough Feg!"

Then the Lord Weird's mocking voice damned them all, "Oh, Crom-Cruach, Great Wyrm, welcome on this dark night between living and death. We offer you these sinners who by their crimes have turned their backs on your majesty. We know their suffering will delight you. Accept them as the blood dowry for your bride, Medb, Warrior Princess of the Badb!"

"The bride! The bride!"

"The bride of Crom!"

"The bride is come!"

"Light the pyre!"

The cry of "Fire!" came up from below.

Then the heat of the fire reached them and they knew the wicker man was burning.

One hundred and eleven hearts beat faster.

"You can't leave us here!" Senoll the Scavenger pleaded, shaking his chains in front of the dwarf's face.

"Why not?" Ukko asked, turning his back theatrically on the beggar.

"We'll die here!"

Ukko nodded. "Bound to happen sooner or later, anyway, why worry about it?"

"Untie them, Ukko," Sláine said, holding out his own chains for the little thief to pick apart.

"Oh and you, I seem to remember you were going to leave me in the broch not so long ago. Shoe's on the other foot now, eh? You need Ukko, now."

"Yes, I do," Sláine said. "We all do. Please."

"Ooooh, did you hear that? Sláine said please! Well in that case, don't go anywhere guys. I'll be right back." Ukko scooted up to Blind Bran and pulled the rusted lock down low enough to get to it with his long pick. The pick snicked against the metal tumbler and sprang the lock in a couple of seconds. Next he undid the chains holding Tamun the Stump and Kes the Murk Dweller. Each one stepped forwards, rubbing his wrists as the chains fell away. "See what happens when you say please?" Ukko said, working his way through another row of locks.

"Time to think about getting out of here," Tamun the Stump said, "before things start heating up."

"Where can we go?" Senoll moaned. "We go down there, we walk into an army of skull-swords and Badb priestesses. I'd rather take my chances with the fire."

"Oh, quit your belly aching, boy," Bran said. "I may be blind but I can see a coward right here. Why don't you just sit here and burn then, Senoll? Eh? Would that make you happy?"

"You know," Ukko said, popping another lock to free a young poacher, "I'm starting to like that old man."

"I say we make a stand here. Let the Badb laugh when they see us come streaming out of the belly of this beast. Let's see if they are still laughing when we cut them down!"

"With what?" Senoll spat. "Your tongue's sharp, blind man, but the only thing it'll cut is pride."

"Use the chains, use the wicker as spears, use whatever you can find," Sláine said. "Use your fists and your head. Make them rue this day. Who wants to live forever anyway, eh? Come on, boys, let's grab ourselves some glory!"

"I do," Ukko said, stepping back to let yet another prisoner step out of their manacles. "Well, maybe not forever but certainly until the world runs out of fat women for me to bounce on."

"Go, go, go!" Sláine roared, spurring the others into action.

The heat from the flames was fierce. Black smoke filled the wicker man. As the others ran down, Sláine began to climb up the wicker scaffold, higher into the giant effigy.

"Sláine!" Ukko yelled over the commotion of stamping feet, grunting and the cries of pain as the prisoners forced themselves through the flames and out of the wicker monstrosity. "The fight's down here!"

"I know that," Sláine called over his shoulder, reaching up to haul himself up to the next platform, "but I can't let an innocent girl burn!" He didn't waste any more words. Sláine forced himself higher, gripping a thick wooden spar and swinging his legs up so that he hung from it. He heaved himself up onto the spar and used it to climb higher, beyond the wooden infrastructure of the limbs and support joists and into the effigy's neck.

He couldn't save his mother but this was one woman he could save.

Ukko looked up at Sláine's backside as it disappeared above him, and then down at the thick choking black smoke coming up from the legs of the wicker man.

"How did I get myself into this mess? Soth! Well, it's too late to worry about that. Time to find out just how lucky I am."

"Gaaahhhhhh!" Tamun cried, throwing himself into the fray. Without a sword he was cut down in a matter of seconds, but not before he had torn the mask off the skull-sword he faced and clawed the man's eyes out. A second skull-sword sent his head bouncing across the soured earth and raised his wretched blade defiantly. Four more prisoners took the arrogant swordsman down, tearing the flesh from his bones with their bare hands. It was the same all across the field. The prisoners paid for a few minutes of freedom with their lives, but in those few minutes they won victories that the Drunes would not soon forget.

By sheer dint of numbers the prisoners succeeded in overwhelming some of the skull-swords, claiming their weapons in the frantic scramble that followed their streaming out of the blazing wicker man. The horned Drune Lord and the Lord Weird himself hopped and twisted madly, directing their skull-swords to kill every last man for defiling this most sacred of rituals to Crom. It was bloody and ugly. Fists slammed repeatedly into the masks of the skull-swords until blood sprayed and cartilage ruptured, and then again and again until bodies went limp. Steel flashed and cut, tearing into flesh and bone with impunity. The prisoners were doomed but that didn't stop them fighting with every last scrap of their strength, making the skull-swords pay a price beyond any reasonable expectation for their victory.

Ukko ran out of the burning effigy, saw three towering men going at it in front of him, and ducked and rolled to the left, dodging beneath a swinging blade. He ran a few more paces forwards and threw himself face first into the mud to avoid being decapitated.

"No place for a dwarf," he muttered, scrambling forwards as another sword thrust speared the ground where his rump had been a second before.

The smoke gave him cover enough to hide as more skull-swords came charging towards the fighting. Unfortunately it couldn't hide the reek of their master's rotten flesh. He tried not to look at the wickedly embossed shields with the faces of snarling demons and blades embedded like hooked teeth. It was butchery. The escaped prisoners were weak from malnutrition, desperate with fear and undisciplined.

"Make the moon shine through their bodies, boys!"

"Grease your blades on their foul blood!"

Chains lashed around, slamming into skulls. Swords opened up guts and throats.

Ukko rolled away, scurrying off beyond the fringe of the fighting.

He looked up in time to see Sláine's silhouette crawl spider-like across the face of the wicker man a hundred and fifty feet above him, while the effigy blazed, its legs beginning to buckle as the fire ate through them.

"Now this might be worth a meal or two," Ukko said appreciatively. "Just don't fall off and bugger it all up."

The wood was weak.

Sláine scrambled up hand over hand, his feet slipping and falling into the gaps where the wicker was woven in on itself to form the giant man. He didn't dare look down. The distance was dizzying. The screams of the dead and dying reached him.

The smoke stung the back of his throat.

Sláine coughed, hacking up a lungful of catarrh.

He felt a cold black anger welling inside him.

This was a perversion of all things holy.

Morrigan's black birds circled, flying in close to him, feathers beating at his back and the side of his head as he tried to find a way around the outside of the giant head. Sláine tried to beat them off but they just kept coming, flying at him, trying to dislodge him from his precarious perch. He twisted, lashing out at them but they just flew in harder, their wings flashing at his eyes, making it impossible for him to hold on to the wood. His hand slipped and he dropped six feet, catching a broken spar of wood and dangling perilously over the huge drop.

It took a massive surge of strength to claw his way back to the relative safety of the wicker man's jutting jaw. He hung there, gasping, gathering his strength for one final surge upwards. He couldn't fail the woman trapped inside the head. He would save her. He had to, for himself.

He should have been down there with Blind Bran and Tamun, and Senoll and Ukko, and the others. His battle skills might have meant the difference between life and death for some of those men. Their lives were in their own hands now. There was nothing he could do about it. He needed to concentrate on breaking into the wicker head and rescuing Medb.

The flames were up around the effigy's chest already.

There was no chance of surviving.

He couldn't let himself think about it.

He needed to find a way into the head, but there wasn't one. The carpenters had made the thing like one huge coffin, designed no doubt to keep the woman from escaping before her sacrifice to the wyrm god was complete. He didn't have a weapon. He pulled at the wood, trying to pry it apart wide enough to make a gap he could slip through.

The cruel flames chased him higher.

Sweat and fear made his hands greasy.

You're too late, my love, always too late.

"Not this time," he said, driving his fist through the wicker, tearing up his skin. Ignoring the pain he ripped the wood apart, tearing a gaping rent in the wicker man's face where its mouth ought to have been.

He pulled himself inside.

She was there, laid out on a beautifully carved funeral bier.

Sláine clambered up to be beside her.

Medb: the Bride of Crom.

It was impossible to tell if she was beautiful or even what she really looked like. Thick coils of cloying smoke crawled over her. Her lips opened, drawing it in. Sláine stared at the semi-naked woman. Her skin was covered in an elaborate weave of tattoos, some patterns of art, others darker depictions of the wyrm god and the vile practices of the Drunes. Her hair was shaved at the sides, the centre teased into gorgon-like spikes. Eyes had been painted onto her eyelids so that she appeared to be staring at him as he leaned over her.

"I won't fail you, Medb," Sláine promised, taking her into his arms.

She had been drugged insensate. Her lips moved forming the word Crom over and over again. It was a small mercy that she was blissfully unaware of her plight. Sláine hoisted the woman over his shoulder. This once he was right, he wasn't too late.

He looked around the inside of the wicker man's head.

Tongues of red flame lashed up between the warp and weft of the wicker, licking at his feet. The smoke was suffocating. There was nowhere to go; no way out of the burning tower. The only thing he could do was climb higher.

The entire structure gave a sickening lurch to the left as one of its legs began the slow and irresistible process of buckling beneath the raging fire.

"Soth!" Sláine growled, swinging out of the opening he had beaten in the face of the wicker man. He hung there for a tantalising moment, Medb over his shoulder, legs dangling over the one hundred and fifty feet drop. Then the slow, arduous climb to the top of the effigy's flat head began.

The smoke stung his eyes. He blinked back tears. He couldn't let go long enough to wipe them away. As the flames licked and lashed around Sláine his anger at the sheer bloody unfairness of it grew, and a greater power burned within him. With the moon on his skin Sláine warp-spasmed with such ferocity that his body lost even the most remote of human qualities.

He became a pure creature of the earth: a giant living golem of flesh and blood.

With the tower collapsing around him, Sláine jumped, plunging down through the air, the flames tearing at his warped flesh, and into the shallows of the swamp. The fall would have broken a mere mortal man, but not Sláine Mac Roth.

Twenty
The Bride of Crom

UKKO SAW THE beast that was Sláine fall. The flames fell away from the young Sessair's warped body. The warp was unlike anything Ukko had seen before. Sláine's entire body had tripled in size, the musculature sharply defined even from such a great distance. His hair looked like a fountain of black oil cascading behind him as he plummeted. He clutched the woman, Medb, in his arms as if to protect her form the shocking impact and inevitable death that the pair rushed down to meet.

Ukko stumbled forwards, unable to take his eyes from the sight of the warped one's fall.

Sláine hit the ground hard, sending a tremor through the earth.

For a second Ukko saw a vast outline in the cloying smoke. At first he thought it was a silhouette of Sláine but it wasn't. It was a physical manifestation of the source of Sláine's warp, the true form of Danu, the Earth Goddess.

"Soth!" Ukko moaned as Sláine rose again out of the swamp.

Behind him the figure of Danu shimmered and blurred and was rudely shattered by the collapse of the towering wicker effigy. Blazing brands fell from the sky. Skull-swords and prisoners alike screamed trying to escape from the path of the falling giant. Part of the monstrous wicker man's arm crashed to the ground in a shower of flame and shrapnel, scorching the earth and those unfortunate enough not to have gotten out of its way.

"Sláine's alive!" Ukko yelled, praying his words would carry over the mayhem of the battle to some of the prisoners. "Into the swamp! Run!"

Fifty years ago there would have been a huge river, now there was only swamp. Back then barges would have run the river, bringing food and trade goods. Now the river was gone, mired in a swamp that brought nothing but mosquitoes and sickness. Where there had been life now there was nothing, only absolute stillness, the slow drift of low water and the scabs of withered vegetation.

He didn't wait. He hurdled over a burning wicker finger and ran head down, after Sláine. He didn't care if anyone else heard. It was all about surviving, and chasing Sláine offered the best chance of that.

The Lord Weird watched with disgust as his glorious ceremony collapsed in a pyre of wicker and tortured screams.

The dying clawed at the dirt.

The saccharine stench of burning flesh clogged the air.

The screams were delicious. He was surrounded by such sweet suffering. It was heady.

He didn't care about the prisoners, or, at this stage, the bride.

He only had eyes for the warped one.

"A renegade from the tribes of the Earth Goddess? Here? How is this possible? How can this creature warp the earth force through his body like this?"

"It is a wonder," the Babd priestess said in awe.

Slough Feg sneered. "It is indeed. The warped ones are a thing of the past, like the creatures of the cave that walked upright but were too primitive to be called men. This creature is an abomination, a throwback. It has no place in our world. It is a violation of our master Crom-Cruach's divine law. It cannot be allowed. No, no, no. Such a monstrosity cannot be allowed to live!" Then he spoke softly as if the thought had just occurred to him. "It will make a grand sacrifice to our master. Yes, yes, yes. Its tainted blood will give much to Crom. See, the beast of Danu flees into the swamp. It will die there." Slough Feg threw up his withered arms. The skull fetishes hanging from his waist spun slack jawed. "Awake! Awake! Awake you ghouls! Awake you souls trapped still in the unlife between the Land of the Living and the Nations of the Dead! Awake! Rise! Rise my bitter dead and feast on the giblets of Danu's precious warped one!"

The wind answered; a long mournful sigh that curled out of the deepest part of the swamp.

It was the voice of the half-dead answering the Lord Weird's call.

★ ★ ★

The rotten corpses of the half-dead rose up in front of Ukko as he ran.

Their cries were anguished, worse by far than the cries of the dying behind him. These were the cries of the damned, victims of the Drune Lords' Weird Stones, condemned to a limbo between death and life.

"Sláine! Sláine! Wait for me!" Ukko cried, running for his life.

The half-dead rose between him and the warped one. They came out of the swamp, rising from the very depths, weed and bilge clinging to their bones as the crow-feeders surfaced. Overhead Morrigan's black birds broke into a frenzy, swirling and sweeping low, drawn to the carrion reek of the creatures coming out of the water.

"Soth!" Ukko moaned, scooping up a handful of brackish water and hurling it in the face of an ancient warrior as it surfaced. The creature didn't flinch. It shambled hungrily towards him, spear raised in its skeletal hand. The filth of the swamp clogged in its open ribcage. The rusted tip of the weapon that had killed the creature was still lodged deep in its pelvis where the spear's head had broken off.

Ukko hurled himself forwards, aquaplaning through the shallow swamp water, beneath the half-dead's stabbing spear.

All around him more and more of the wretched souls rose, headless, rotten, broken and bearing the wounds that killed them, eager to answer the Lord Weird's magical call.

Dead voices cried out mournfully:

"We hear you, Lord Weird! We hear you and we come!"

"We come!"

"We answer the call!"

"We who have lain below the water as carrion rise now to feed the Morrigan's crows!"

"We come, Lord Weird!"

"We come, we come, we come!"

"There are too many," Ukko whimpered. There was nowhere to run. The half-dead had surfaced all around him, and still more came, their yellowed skulls breaching the brackish waters of the swamp in a perverted parody of rebirth.

Sláine moved further and further away, splashing through the swamp, the woman, Medb, slung across his shoulder.

Those of the half-dead closest to the warped one surged after him, the water recoiling from their unnatural presence, hissing and sizzling as they splashed on, steam wreathing the walking dead as they waded through the swamp. The others, between Ukko and Sláine, clacked their bones, slack jaws and broken teeth, wailing hideously as they swarmed around the desperate dwarf.

A handful of prisoners from the wicker man splashed into the swamp, fleeing the devastation of the battlefield. They brought skull-swords behind them. The half-dead made no distinction between the living; all were fair game.

The slaughter was brutal, the half-dead dragging the living beneath the surface, downed them in the dead swamp, holding them under until the bubbles had stopped rising and their limbs had stopped flailing.

Ukko squirmed between the legs of a headless warrior, dodging the rhythmic chop-slash-chop of its huge stone axe. He swallowed a mouthful of foul swamp water in the process, almost choking as a spear lanced dangerously close to his side.

He splashed away into the depths of the turgid water, away from the dead, from the fighting and the dying, and away from Sláine.

"Our long iron tongues are thirsty for blood," a half-dead warrior rasped, thrusting his sword clean through a skull-sword's shield and into the soldier's neck, tearing through the heart vein and venting a huge spray of blood. "This pleases us. It pleases Crom! We will sleep if we kill! We will be free!"

Ukko knew of course that they wouldn't. The wyrm god was not a benevolent deity. He was a monstrous one. They would kill, passing their Half-Death on like a plague to all those they fought.

Ukko watched, mesmerised as Sláine turned to fight the risen dead. He had no weapons but he had no need of them. The half-dead surged around the young Sessair, their rusted steel stabbing at his heart, his head, his throat, but Sláine slapped the blows aside as if they were nothing more than flies annoying him.

The others were not so lucky.

Without Danu's power surging through their veins they fell beneath the rusted blades of the half-dead.

Ukko sank beneath the black water, leaning back so that only his nose and lips were exposed, letting him breath as he backstroked slowly further and further away from the carnage.

Sláine felt the rage of the warp-spasm fading as whatever last vestiges of Danu's power that lived in the blasted land dried up.

He stopped running and turned to face the demons that hunted him. He was Red Branch. He did not flee like a coward. He was the mountain. He was the river. He was Sláine Mac Roth.

"Come on then, you stinking corpses! Time to send you back to the death darkness where you belong!"

The emptiness the failing earth power left behind was harrowing. He fought with a savagery that shocked even him. He battered the dead, breaking their bones off to make weapons to club more of their kind back beneath the dark water. He drove one half-dead creature down, grinding its bones with the femur of another.

"Our weapons are useless on this daemon!" a dead warrior with half his face eaten away by the bottom feeders of the swamp railed.

"Then let our teeth gnaw through his flesh mouthful by delicious mouthful!" another mocked.

"Come on then, boys. More dying, less talking!" Sláine said, but they had no answer. Even as the mystical strength was draining from him, the same magic that gave them life faded. Sláine rammed a broken fibula into the shocked face of a collapsing half-dead warrior. The dead, no longer bound by the arch sorcerer Slough Feg's dark magics, came undone in front of Sláine's eyes.

With nothing to hold them together, their bones rattled and fell, their skulls lolling slackly, their arms and legs coming apart at the joints.

"Well that takes all the fun out of life," Sláine said, setting Medb down beside him. She stood on her own two feet and seemed to be coming back to some kind of alertness as the drugs lost their hold. "Stay," Sláine said, holding up a hand. His arm shuddered involuntarily. A convulsion doubled Sláine up. He dry heaved, clutching his stomach. The sudden withdrawal of the earth's power hit him hard enough to drop him to his knees. He collapsed, clawing at his skull as the bones in his body grated and shifted, shrinking back on themselves through agonising contortions until he was himself, gasping, panting, sobbing, and desperate. The dead water lapped around his thighs. He couldn't move.

"You saved the girl, eh? What a story this'll make! Feg must be hopping mad."

He looked up to see Ukko standing over him, looking mighty pleased with himself.

He tried to talk but he couldn't find the words.

"The girl didn't want to be saved!" Medb shrieked, slapping at Sláine's face with her fingers hooked into claws. The blow was sudden and all the more shocking for it.

"But… but… I saved your life," Sláine said, not making any sense of the woman's furious attack.

"How dare you drag me from my bier defiling my wedding! I was going to be immortal! I was going to be joined with Crom-Cruach himself! I was going to be his queen! My entire life has been in preparation of this moment! I have dedicated myself to Crom since I was old enough to think for myself! I live to serve my master, my husband and you, you rob me of my greatest honour! You drag me through this wretched swamp full of ghouls, you wretched disgusting pig of a man! You have ruined my life!" She hit Sláine again and again, across the face and the side of the head as he shied away.

He tried to grab her wrists but moving was agony. It hurt less to take her beating and let the crazy woman exhaust herself.

"I was the best!" Medb yelled petulantly. "Can't you understand that? I mastered tongues, curses, dark magics, shape-changing! I was the best! That's why I was chosen for the honour of serving Crom! I could turn your blood to bile and your stupid muscles to blubber if I wanted to! It doesn't matter! The Lord Weird will find me! He will find me and kill you, you simple-minded fool!"

Ukko came up behind her with a big stick and hit her across the head with it. There was a sickening crunch and she slumped forwards into the swamp water slackly. For a moment Sláine thought that the dwarf had killed her. He pulled her out of the water and laid her on her back. She was breathing. She would wake up with one hell of a hangover, but she would wake up, which was more than could be said for Blind Bran, Tamun the Stump, Senoll the Scavenger and Kes the Murk Dweller. They would be somewhere down in Cernunnos's underworld by now.

"She was giving me a headache," Ukko said, "ungrateful sow. Beautiful maidens are meant to be happy when the handsome hero rescues them. I'll never understand these modern women. Give me a big fat girl any day. They know how to be grateful."

Sláine looked over Ukko's shoulder. The horizon was a bloody red with the wicker man's fire. It was a fitting send-off for so many good men, and so many bad ones.

"What do we do with her? Bring her with us?"

"And go through all that yelling again? Nah, leave her here for her precious Weirdo Lord to find. It's time to get out of here, before more of those ghouls decide they like the smell of your manliness and come looking to serenade you again. Can you walk?"

"I'll manage," Sláine said, grateful for the dwarf's support but not about to say so.

Sláine twisted to look back at the red sky one last time.

Together, they walked deeper into the swamp.

Twenty-One
The Cloud Curragh

COMING OUT OF the swamp Sláine and Ukko crossed into more dead land, soured by the Drunes' foul magic. Carcasses of sheep and cattle rotted in the fields beneath the shadow of a great dolmen. Ogham runes were carved into the base of the great Weird Stone.

Ukko translated as best he could. "It's bad mojo, Sláine. This here, that's the great wyrm, which must be their god, Crom-Cruach. Beside the wyrm these here are conduits, words of power meant to open the earth to the nether world. This is bad magic."

"How can you possibly know that, dwarf? You aren't a druid, and as far as I have seen, you're about the least magical soul I have ever encountered."

"Harrumph! Well it could be bad magic, that's all I am saying," Ukko said defensively. "You've got to pay attention to the signs. Being careful never hurt anyone."

"So you're making it up?"

"It could be a list of the sacrifices they've made to their dark god," Ukko said, pointing a wagging finger at the long list of scratches.

"Do you even know if they are words?"

Ukko grunted and stormed off.

Sláine let him go.

He studied the huge stone. It was peculiar. Since escaping the wicker man he hadn't felt the pull of the Weird Stones draining his strength. It was as if whatever hold they had on him had been broken. His gut feeling was that Feg had drained them when he raised the half-dead, but then, surely, they would have been even hungrier, and their drain would have been exacerbated not nullified. He didn't understand it, but was grateful for the respite. He touched the stone, tracing the curves that Ukko had claimed represented Crom-Cruach. There was nothing, not even the faintest tingle. He should have been relieved, but he wasn't. All he could think was that what little of Danu's presence there had been here in this blighted land was finally spent.

Ukko was hunched down over something in the field. "Probably something shiny," Sláine muttered to himself, setting out after the dwarf.

A bell tolled somewhere in the distance. It was a mournful sound.

Beyond the dolmen lay another desperate village starving under the harsh laws of the Drunes.

After the trials of the swamp it promised blessed relief.

When he caught up with the dwarf he saw that Ukko was holding a bone, a child's leg bone, not fully formed. "They're here as well, aren't they?"

"A child?" Sláine said. "What kind of sickness infects these Drunes?"

"You remember what Bran said? They take the young and sacrifice them to Crom-Cruach. Those marks, what if every one is a tally, one scratch for each child offered to their vile master?"

Sláine didn't want to contemplate it but Blind Bran's words came back to him: "The Drunes rounded up the young of the village, all under twenty summers, and butchered them. That was more than half of us. He laughed in my face as I challenged him. What are you upset about, miner? Now there is foodenough for everyone!" Sláine shuddered.

"We should go around the village," Sláine said.

"Not a chance, I am dying for a decent meal and, no offence, but a change of company for a while. Who knows, maybe there's a nice fat girl waiting to shower me with kisses. That'd be nice." Ukko set a brisk pace, buoyed by the thought of a warm meal and warmer thighs. Sláine struggled to keep up with the dwarf. His mind drifted to the possibility of a real bed and a real woman to share it with him. They were good thoughts.

The village was a pale ghost of what it should have been. Sláine saw a boy grubbing around in the dirt after a beetle. For a moment he thought the lad was playing with the insect until he saw him stuff it in his mouth and chew.

Walking through the houses Sláine had the uncomfortable feeling that they were being watched. The hairs on the nape of his neck prickled and his skin crawled. Every time he turned, trying to catch a glimpse of the unseen watcher, the street was empty.

"Can't say I like this any better than the swamp," Sláine said, looking back over his shoulder at an abandoned street. "The whole place gives me the creeps."

An old man stepped out into the centre of the street to greet them. He was all slack yellowed skin and bone.

"What brings you to Gavra, strangers?"

"The need for food and a bed," Sláine said.

"Well, ain't much of either here. Best you be on your way, lad. This is a bad place to be."

"We've been walking for a week through the swamp, old man. I'm tired, I don't remember the last meal I ate, and I could murder an ale."

"Me, I'd settle for a big-titted woman to use as a pillow," Ukko said, earning a cuff from Sláine. "Hey!"

"Excuse my, ahhh, companion. He's special."

"That's right, I'm special," Ukko said, and then turned to Sláine. "Hey, I don't like the way you said that, you made me sound like a simpleton."

"Is there an inn?"

"Aye, Madaug Stagshanks runs a small place, but it ain't had beer for as long as I can remember, and as to a shank of venison? I think the old fool was spinning a yarn when he claimed that moniker." He shook his head.

"But it has beds?"

"A floor with straw," the old man said with a shrug.

"Sounds like the Summerland," Ukko grumbled sourly.

"Beggars can't be choosers."

"Well, what we have, you're welcome to share," the old man said. "I'm Madaug, innkeeper and what passes as chieftain of this doomed village."

"Sláine Mac Roth," Sláine said, holding out a hand, "and this ugly runt is Ukko. Don't trust him with anything you hold dear. He's a thief and a liar."

"But you love me for it," Ukko said.

Madaug grinned. "Welcome to Gavra."

For all the privation it was a blessed comfort to be in the company of others. The food, while far from plentiful, was filling. The citizens of Gavra had every right to moan and curse the fates but they didn't. They accepted this hardship as their due and waited for their world to collapse.

"How can they go on like this?" Ukko asked, shaking his head.

"What's the alternative, dwarf?" Sláine asked.

"Fight."

"Spoken like true idiot. What is there to fight? Do you see the Drunes here subjugating these people? The damage was done years ago. There is nothing to fight here, no enemy. The monsters are all around but they are invisible. They are hunger and fear, debilitating beasts both. Mother earth is no longer fertile. The essence of Danu's magic has been drained from the soil. This is a dead place."

"And you accept that, warrior?"

"I have no choice. I could avenge these people with my axe if I had her. Otherwise what? You shouldn't save the lives of people fated to die, Ukko, that's cheating the gods."

"Soth! You actually believe the gods care?"

"I know at least one who does, dwarf; one who cares with all of her heart."

The taproom of the inn was warm. A fire blazed in the hearth. A broth that was mostly water warmed in a huge cauldron. Sláine slapped Ukko on the shoulder, and pointed to one of the women stirring the pot. "That should be ample even for you."

Ukko grinned. "Now you're just trying to distract me."

"Has it worked?"

"Indubitably."

"In-what?"

Ukko hopped up and swaggered over to the woman, slapping her on the rump.

"I'll take that as a yes, then," Sláine called over the hubbub of the taproom. Ukko winked and made another grab for the woman. She didn't seem to mind, laughing and cuffing the little runt around the ear.

Sláine sat alone for a while, thinking about what he had told the dwarf. It felt as if he hadn't stopped running since he left Murias, and the more he ran the less he actually stopped to think. It was too easy to just run, lurching from one potential disaster to the next. A time would come when he had to stop running. The day would come when the road would take him back north and he would have to face up to his own stupidity, and, he thought wistfully, when Grudnew walked up to the pyre, return to his people to claim Niamh as his bride. It was a thought he had held close to his chest for a long time. A king reigned for seven years. It was not so long. Grudnew had been king for two years before his exile and he had been gone four already. His days were numbered. Soon he would be able to return to Murias without fear of the headsman's axe.

Did he truly believe what he had said to Ukko? Did he truly think that it was wrong to meddle and save someone fated to die? And if he did, why was he trying so hard to stem the threat of the skull-swords for the sake of his own people. Perhaps it was their time to die. Dare he risk the anger of the gods?

The answer lay in a memory: the smoke on the horizon and Danu's whispered words: "You needed to see, to understand". He understood why, finally. It wasn't about the black smoke consuming Murias. He felt anger welling up inside him. Images of more flames, of innocents burning, of the despoilers pillaging and raping the earth, turning it sour, superimposed themselves on his memories of home, of Murias, and of places he had visited since his exile. He saw exactly what she wanted him to see, and this time he understood. It was about The Land of the Young and the Goddess and the very power of the earth itself, being soured by the evil of Slough Feg and his foul minions in the name of Crom.

Madaug settled down beside him, two tankards in hand. He slid one across the table to Sláine.

"I thought you said there was no ale left?" Sláine said, raising the wooden tankard to his lips and draining a good long swallow from the frothy drink. It didn't taste like any beer he had drunk before. It was bitter.

"There isn't. I call this gutrot. It sorts the men out from the boys. It's fermented like beer but it's got a whole other set of ingredients. You don't want to know, just sup up, lad. It'll put hairs on your chest."

Sláine took another mouthful, feeling the intoxicating rush of the drink go straight to his head. "Potent stuff."

"Oh aye, and then some. Look, lad, no beating about the bush. Are you sure I can't convince you to stay? We need new blood if we are going to survive."

"I'm a wanderer, Madaug. It's in the blood. I can't settle down, no matter how inviting the place, or the woman."

"At least say you'll think about it."

"No need," Sláine said. "It can't be easy," Sláine raised his tankard and gestured to take in the whole taproom. He watched the door. It was a habit learned from paranoia and too long being hunted. Closed doors still made him uncomfortable, "All of this."

"There's nothing here, lad. This ain't the place I grew up in. I love this village but the Drunes have sucked the soul out of it. Gavra is dying, just like every other place roundabouts. The Sourland is spreading. Paeder said he met a bard last month who told stories of the blight having crept as far north as Albion and as far south as Gabala. It's a creeping death. The entire land will fall to the scourge and then what? What will we eat? How will we live? We won't, that's the how and what of it. You know there's talk that we're entering the end of days." Madaug shuddered. He took a deep swallow of his gutrot and wiped his lips off with the back of his hand. "Hark on me, prattling away like a fishwife. Don't get many folks to listen to me these days. That little fella of yours knows how to enjoy himself, eh?" Madaug said.

Sláine couldn't help but smile as he watched Ukko's antics. The little runt had the cook eating out of the palm of his hand. She had scooped him up and was singing a raunchy shanty that seemed to be about small ones being juicier as she swung him round. "Ukko's a law unto himself."

The door of the taproom flew open and a huge horned silhouette filled the wound it left in the wall. The black night spilled into the inn. Utter silence gripped the revellers. The unmistakable stench blew in with the night wind. Ukko hit the floor with a thud as the woman dropped him. He scrambled back towards Sláine's table, ducking under the tabletop as if that would protect him. The Drune Lord stepped into the taproom. He held a limp body in his arms.

For a moment no one moved. Drinkers held their cups to their lips, frozen in place. The dancers stood alone in the middle of the floor. Slowly, one by one, heads turned to stare in terror at the slough-skinned sorcerer as he walked up to Madaug and dropped the dead boy at his feet. Skull-swords swelled into the inn, weapons drawn.

"Murderers," Madaug breathed, pushing the table back so that he could stand. His legs betrayed him. He fell to his knees beside the dead boy. "Caw. Oh, sweet Lug, Caw, what have they done to you?"

"We killed the child because we believed you were sheltering outlaws." Smiling wryly, the Drune turned to Sláine. "It seems we were right."

Madaug grabbed a blunt bread knife off the tabletop and surged to his feet. He threw himself at the Drune, stabbing wildly even before he was five steps away from the sorcerer.

The Drune raised a hand crawling with maggots and jags of lightning streamed from his fingers, tearing into the old man like arrows, punching through his slack skin and spraying blood out of his back. His arms spread-eagled wide, thrown into the air by the black magic shredding his flesh, Madaug Stagshanks was dead before his body hit the floor.

The taproom stank of ozone and gore; an ugly mix if ever there was one.

It all happened so quickly. Madaug's kin were on their feet, screaming as they were cut down by the skull-swords.

Sláine roared to his feet, hurling the wooden table into the faces of the skull-swords charging at him.

"Come on then! Fight a real man! I'll see you in the Underworld, boys!"

The rage that hit him was so vehement, so strong, that the beginnings of the burning fire that marked the warp-spasm tore through Sláine. His face twisted, shifting into something animalistic, bestial. He grabbed two skull-swords by the throat and hurled them into the cooking fire. He broke two more over the back of the table he had hurled, shattering their spines. Another he kicked so hard that he shattered the man's pelvis.

"Say hello to Cernunnos for me!" Sláine growled, spinning around to drop two more, punching the heel of his hand into their throats. They writhed around on the floor of the taproom, suffocating as they clawed frantically at their ruptured Adam's apples.

After that they came at him in twos and threes, swords hacking away uselessly, unable to get close enough to Sláine to do any real damage. He lifted up a table and charged down four skull-swords, crushing

them against the wall. He rammed the table's edge
against the heads over and over again. His body burned.
The fire of his flesh was enough to sear and scorch
them as he fought them back.

He was struck from behind, hard, at the base of the
skull. He didn't see it coming. His legs buckled and he
fell.

"He still burns, lord," the skull-sword said, obviously
afraid to touch Sláine.

Ukko didn't move. He didn't dare. There was no way
he was coming out from under the table now that
Sláine was unconscious. He fully intended to stay
where he was until the skull-swords and the Drune
Lord had lost interest and wandered off to torment
some other poor souls.

"Bring vats of water, icy cold. We must cool his fire
before he wakes or he will throw himself on your
swords in hunger to kill you," the Drune Lord spat. The
fumes rising off his pustulant flesh were noxious.

"Why don't I just cut his throat and be done with it,
master?"

"Because," the sorcerer said patiently, "his death
would be a waste. There are times when it is better to
cage a wolf than kill it."

Ukko winced as the skull-sword drove a boot into
Sláine's side.

Sláine groaned and drew his arms underneath himself.
He turned to look sideways, under the table at Ukko. "I'm
still alive," he said. "There must be a reason."

"There is always a reason," the sorcerer said.

Sláine turned to look up at the slough-skinned mage wrapped in stinking pelts.

"What do you want from me?"

"All that you are good for, warrior: your strength, your tenacity and your fire. I require the services of a bodyguard." He looked around at the devastation Sláine had caused without so much as a weapon. "You bested a good few of my men with your bare hands. I would rather have a man like you fighting at my side, not against me. Oh, dwarf, do get out from under the table, you aren't fooling anyone by hiding under there."

Ukko crawled out grudgingly. He stuck his head out and looked around. There were fifteen skull-swords still standing, as many lying broken on the floor of the taproom. He did not think it too many. In all honesty he would have liked the other fifteen to be down there with them instead of pointing their swords at him. He went to Sláine's side as the big man drew himself to his feet. Ukko ducked in close, letting Sláine lean on him.

"And if I say no? Which, let's face it, I will. I couldn't stand the stench for a start."

"Oh, you'll soon grow accustomed to my mystic aura."

"Mystic aura? My sick aura more like," Ukko muttered, making a show of covering his mouth and nose with his hand.

"Hold your tongue, dwarf."

"I am, and my nose, and it still stinks in here," Ukko said. "P-eeew-eee!"

"You'll be paid well for your services," the Drune told Sláine, ignoring Ukko's hectoring.

"No," Sláine said, "it's not happening."

"Let me put it another way: these people will be given food enough to last them through the winter."

"And if I refuse again?"

"This miserable hellhole will be burned to the ground, every man, woman and child will be sacrificed as an offering to benevolent Crom and you, Sláine Mac Roth, and your cowardly dwarf friend, will suffer the death of the blood eagle. I might even consider dragging your miserable souls back from the half-dead to kill you all over again."

"An offer you can't refuse," Ukko said, shivering at the thought of his ribs parting company with his backbone.

"What do you expect me to do?" Sláine asked. Ukko could read the warrior like a book. He was painfully aware of exactly how hungry the people of Gavra were, and of Madaug's corpse lying amid those of the skullswords. Sláine looked at the body of the boy, Caw. "I won't kill innocent people for you. I am not a murderer."

The citizens of Gavra huddled up fearfully against the walls, bunched together. Ukko saw the slack skin and sunken features of the hungry and the desperate, and thought again of what Sláine had told him: "You shouldn't save the lives of people fated to die, that's cheating the gods." But when it came down to it Crom-Cruach was one god worth cheating.

"I say we do it, Sláine, if it helps these people," he said, "and hey, maybe it'll tick the wyrm off, you know, stealing souls fated to die and all that. So it is kind of a good cause, right?"

Sláine studied the sorcerer. "How do I know you can be trusted? How do I know you won't just butcher three-quarters of the people and then tell the rest they're lucky because they have plenty to see them through the worst of the winter?"

The Drune chuckled mirthlessly. "I see you are familiar with the benevolence of Slough Feg. You have my word, they will all be fed."

"Aye, to the crows," Ukko interrupted, jumping up to sit on the table.

"They will be cared for."

"Taken care of, you mean," Ukko said, kicking his feet in the air.

"Do you want me to flense your hide from your flesh, dwarf? It can be done, believe me," The sorcerer snapped.

"Just negotiating the terms, don't want any loopholes in the contract, that's all, your smelliness. No hard feelings."

"There will be food aplenty for everyone. There will be no sacrifices. You will be giving the people of this village a chance at life. Is that plain enough for you?"

"All right," Sláine said, "but I won't be your butcher."

"Understood."

Sláine didn't trust the Drune, Slough Throt, but the sorcerer did keep his word. Food was delivered by skull-swords, enough to fill the empty grain silo, keeping the mill wheels turning. The morning air smelled of freshly baked bread. Sláine had forgotten how good such a simple smell could be.

Throt came to him that evening, bearing gifts.

"As you can see, I have upheld my part of the bargain, warrior. There is grain and other staples, plenty for everyone. Now it is time for you to earn your life in return." The Drune made a show of taking an oilskin-wrapped bundle from the skull-sword beside him and handing it to Sláine. "Yours, I believe. My men claimed it from the Babd's reclusium. The women were more than happy to see it removed."

Sláine unwrapped the bundle.

Inside was his father's axe, Brain-Biter. The blade had been cleaned and sharpened on a whetstone. He covered the axe head with the oilskin. "Do you expect me to be grateful?"

"I don't expect anything, warrior. Common courtesy would suggest you ought to say thank you, though."

"Thank you for returning what is rightfully mine," Sláine said, grudgingly.

"My pleasure, warrior. I look after my people. Now, we will be moving out in the morning, by Cloud Curragh. Make your farewells tonight. If you could arrange to leave the dwarf behind I would be eternally grateful."

"As would I," Sláine said, "but the little fella is like your mystic aura, he just won't go away. You do get used to him though, eventually."

Slough Throt took Navindar Sark aside.

Sark was a trusted soldier, a leader amongst the ranks of the skull-swords.

"I have a task for you, my friend."

"Anything, Lord. You know that if it is in my power it will be done."

"Indeed. I wish you and three others to remain in Gavra on the morrow. When the Curragh casts off and is well clear, you can drop all pretence at compassion. Kill the villagers. Dispose of their bones however you see fit. Make arrangements for the grain to be returned to Feg's stores before the Lord Weird realises they have been borrowed. When you have done that, make for the peak Shadow's Reach, in Lyonesse, we will meet you there."

"It will be done."

"Oh, I have no doubt it will, no doubt at all."

The Cloud Curragh was a huge longship, a merchant-man, only it didn't sail the seven seas, it sailed the steel grey skies.

Throt and his skull-swords led them up a narrow gangplank behind a cart overburdened with essentials for what promised to be a long journey. Ukko's eyes bulged with wonder. Sláine grew more and more taci-turn as he came to understand the nature of the sky chariot. The Curragh was moored within a ring of sacred dolmen. The standing stones would obviously be used to raise the huge ship, the power of the weird stones somehow anchoring the ship to the mystical paths of the ley lines.

"The rising incantation will be invoked before the shadows stretch another hand's span," The Curragh's pilot called down, "so all aboard who's coming aboard!"

"This ain't natural," Ukko scowled at the reefed masts. "Ships ain't made for flying."

Herdsmen bullied six oxen up the gangplank.

"Sacred animals," Throt explained, seeing his puzzlement. "Their blood feeds the weird stone."

"Blood magic?" Sláine rasped.

"Nothing so crude. The blood merely acts as a facilitator. It is amazing how much more willing the earth is to yield up her power when a little blood is used in offering."

Three horned Drunes hunched over a huge weird stone in the centre of the Cloud Curragh's deck. They were scratching Ogham symbols into the surface of the rock.

"Oh Lug, great god of the skies, look after little Ukko, even if the others get it, just make sure I am right and I'll be a good person from now on: the perfect dwarf." Ukko looked distinctly uncomfortable as he settled down on the deck.

Sláine shook his head.

"Oh and Lug, if you can manage it, look out for Sláine, eh? Thanks." Ukko buried his face in his hands miserably.

Slough Throt joined the Drunes at the weird stone, raising his hands as if for silence. Around Sláine the ship's crew began to mumble in low subdued tones, their words indistinct but growing slowly and steadily in volume and intensity until Throt began the invocation. The slough-skinned sorcerer threw his head back and his arms wide, calling on the spiral energy of the earth, the serpent. The sharp tang of ozone filled the air, strong enough to temporarily mask the stench of rotten flesh that was the Drune Lord's mystic aura.

Ribbons of blue energy sparked and chased up the huge dolmen, crackling with life. The sparks danced and chased across the stones, arcing down and striking the earth all around the longship before they finally lanced into the weird stone on the Curragh's deck.

Sláine's stomach heaved as the deck beneath his feet lurched.

The huge longship rocked sickeningly and then began to rise.

Shaft after shaft of raw energy from the earth's serpent cracked and spat as it was drawn into the weird stone.

The air was cold, clammy, and thick with the smell of Throt's stink. The air shimmered as he looked out over the dried-up fields.

The longship yawed and then righted itself.

Ukko clutched the rail. The little runt had turned a bilious shade of green. "I don't like this, Sláine."

"And you were doing such a good job of fooling me."

"Listen, I've been thinking." The dwarf leaned in close so that the Drune Lord and his crew couldn't overhear him. "What's happening here?" Before Sláine could tell him, Ukko went on, "We're on a ship that is going to sail the skies. That's not natural, Sláine. That's so far from natural it's in the realm of insanity. Why's it happening? I'll tell you why, because of Slough Throt. Are you telling me a man who can make a longship sail through the sky needs a battle-smiter like you? Uh-hunh. I don't believe that for a minute, Sláine. Throt's afraid of someone, or something, and anything powerful enough to make a sorcerer frightened is something that should have the likes of you and me make like the shepherd and the sheep and get the flock out of here. I mean, come on, who's old Dead Meat think he's fooling? You know he had the entire village butchered the moment we cast off."

"How can you be sure?"

"Count the skull-swords, fifteen were left standing when you were done with your little bit of brain-ball battering the other night. How many are here now?"

Sláine looked around the deck, counting the masked skull-swords. "Eleven."

"Eleven, so, unless you bashed a few more heads for good measure, four didn't make it onto the ship. Now, call me paranoid, but I don't like the mathematics."

The Cloud Curragh was aloft, sailors crawling over its rigging like ants, unfurling the sails and bracing the mainstay, adjusting the Curragh's course until she was bearing north-by-northeast.

Morrigan's birds flocked around her bow, cawing raucously. They had been ever present since the wicker man, perched on skeletal tree limbs and the thatched eaves of houses in the village, watching.

Ukko reeled away from him and heaved up his guts over the side of the ship.

"Look out below," Sláine said, forcing a grin. He wasn't in the mood for smiling, but it was important that no one saw his consternation. He knew, instinctively, that the little runt was right on both counts. The people of Gavra were almost certainly dead, and Slough Throt was afraid of someone, afraid enough to bargain with the enemy in the hopes there was some truth to the old adage, "my enemy's enemy is my friend". Sláine felt like a rat in a trap; a rat with no friends and a ship full of enemies.

The secrets of the Cloud Curragh revealed themselves slowly.

She was no merchantman, despite the attempt to appear as one. Sláine found the truth below decks. Slough Throt had assembled a war galley.

He lay awake staring at the shapes and shadow-shapes of Morrigan's crows flitting across the moon. He knew that the witch was taunting him, but instead of despair her birds brought hope. If Morrigan could reach into this blighted waste then surely the maiden could, too, if he needed her.

Deck hands shuffled about, tying off ropes and making minor adjustments for the wind. The low mumble of the three Drune Lords was ever present, their incantations keeping the Curragh aloft. There was a sugary mellifluence to the sound. The sweetness lulled him towards the edge of sleep but the undercurrent of immorality kept dragging him back, heart racing, to the deck of the Curragh and the stench of Throt's rotten flesh.

The slough-skinned sorcerer sat alone. Sláine watched as he ate a slab of old and decaying meat. Throt looked up, aware of the scrutiny. The sorcerer's perception was almost preternatural.

"Can't sleep?" Sláine said, stepping over Ukko. The dwarf grunted and rolled over, snoring deeply again within moments. Sláine envied the dwarf his ability to sleep anywhere. Gorian had drilled it into the men of the Red Branch that a true warrior needed to be able to sleep anywhere and anywhen, because those few minutes might be the last he had for a long time. Ukko's gift for sleep would have made old Gorian proud.

"I have no need of it, my magics sustain my body."

Sláine sat next to Throt. "Then I pity you, mage. In dreams I get to make love to the most beautiful of maidens, I get to wander the streets of my hometown and relive my life. In sleep I am the man I could never be in waking life."

"And you pity me?"

"Aye, I do, because I know a frightened man when I see one," Sláine said. "Tell me, who is it you fear? You're a powerful man, you can make the world dance to your darkest desires, so who is more powerful than you? Powerful enough to make you fear him?"

"There is no one," Slough Throt said, blood from the raw steak dribbling down his chin as he tore another mouthful off the bone.

"Oh, there is. We both know there is. I know who it is. I just want to hear you say his name."

"There is no one," Throt repeated.

"Believe that if you want to." Sláine shrugged. "I have better things to do with my time than argue who's afraid of whom with you."

"Yes, it is your job to keep me alive."

"And you say you aren't afraid?" Sláine shook his head. "You're a rotten liar."

Sláine left the sorcerer to his lonely vigil. He walked to the gunwale and leaned out over the side to watch the soured land drift by beneath the hull of the great Cloud Curragh. He let his hands feel out the extra thickness of the wale, picking away at the seam where it joined the side of the longship. With the wind blowing into his face the chants of the Drunes were muffled to a point where they were barely audible. He enjoyed the comparative quiet of the wind rushing into his ears.

Then he heard them, below decks, moaning, low, beneath the wind and the Drunes' incantations: mournful wails, like the voices of the damned begging to be heard.

Making sure he wasn't being watched, Sláine knelt and heaved up the hatch that led down to the hold. He lowered himself into the darkness. The melancholy lament sent a shiver the length of his spine. Reaching up, he pulled the hatch back over his head, sealing himself in darkness. He listened. Voices, inseparable from one another but distinct all the same, coalesced into a single keening dirge.

He fumbled with the torch and tinder, sparking up a light, and immediately wished he hadn't.

Cernunnos's Underworld itself was trapped in the shallow puddle of light.

Faces of bone and lichen stared back at him, skeletal fingers clawing at the light. He staggered back a step, and then reeled away from the clutching fingers of more half-dead zombies snagging at him. He spun in a circle, brandishing the torch as if it was a weapon. The half-dead were caged. They were drawn instinctively to the light, like moths to a flame. They clutched at rusted spears and battered shields.

There was a small army crammed in down here, enough of the pox-riddled half-dead to bring down any number of villages in the lands to the north of the border where the sour blight ran into rich fertile land.

Slough Throt was flying an army of the dead and damned north.

Sláine recognised one amongst the many, pushed up against the bars of cage, his rough-spun bandage slipping down from over his glazed over eyes: Blind Bran.

Behind him Sláine saw Senoll and Tamun. There were others from the wicker man, he was sure, cursed to this half-life half-death.

"No," Sláine said. "Danu, they deserved better than this. Bran? Tamun? It's me, Sláine Mac Roth, Sláine of the Sessair. Can you hear me?" But they couldn't. Their lips moved over and over, their voices an indistinguishable part of the choir of the damned.

He edged away, up the ladder to above decks, easing back the hatch in time to hear Throt cry, "Assassin!"

Slough Throt was on his feet and raging.

A barrel lay splintered at his feet.

He had a young deckhand by the throat and clenched his hand until his black nails sank into the soft flesh around his windpipe.

"It… it… was an accident, lord," the boy pleaded. "It slipped… from my… grasp."

"There are no accidents, boy. You will suffer for your master's arrogance. Your death will be a message to him." Throt threw the young deckhand across the swabbed planks. He turned to the nearest of his trusted skull-swords. "Strip this traitor and bind him to the mast. I will give his master a death if that is what he wants."

The skull-sword grappled with the boy, cracking him around the head with the hilt of his blade. The hapless assassin slumped in the soldier's arms. They stripped him quickly and bound him, naked, to the main mast.

Sláine sidled up beside Ukko. "What happened?"

The dwarf grunted. "His smelliness was about six inches from being knocked senseless by a falling barrel. He's taking it quite well, don't you think?"

Slough Throt stood in the centre of the Curragh's deck, arms thrown wide, the triskel medallion around his neck glowing a spectral blue beneath the shadowy umbra of his beseeching arms.

"Come!" Throt roared. It was the only word from a stream that Sláine understood.

A cloud of black formed on the horizon, completely clouding the moon as it drew closer and closer. The beating of black wings was deafening as the crows swept in low and hard, beaks and claws tearing at the prisoner's flesh, plucking his eyes out.

Sláine turned away from the feast.

The dying boy's screams were ghastly.

Morrigan's birds flew into his mouth and his throat, stripping the flesh from his lips and nose until they opened the lad up completely and his dead body was only supported by the ropes binding him to the mast.

Even as the last scream was torn from the poor unfortunate deck hand's mouth the mighty Cloud Curragh gave a sickening lurch.

Swollen black clouds filled the sky, hiding the moon.

Throt stood in the centre of the Cloud Curragh, hurling invocation after invocation at the sky. A howling gale erupted around the Slough sorcerer, battering the ship downwards. The Curragh lurched sickeningly again. Sláine grabbed at a trailing guide rope and hooked it around his wrist. An unfortunate skull-sword skidded across the deck and went over the rail, screaming as he struggled gamely to master the art of flight.

Sláine looked over the ship's edge.

No matter how frantically the soldier flapped his arms he only seemed to fall faster.

"I thought you Drunes controlled the weather?" Sláine rasped, struggling across the deck as the Curragh was tossed about violently by the storm. A deck hand fell from the rigging.

"We can. He is," Throt hissed between clenched teeth.

"Who is, damn it? Answer me!"

But the Drune Lord didn't. "The weird stone is weakening. We need a sacrifice. Only blood will have the strength to save us. We must ride out the storm! Hear how the weird stone whines? Yes, yes it needs blood! Only blood can save us!"

The storm surged around them. Lightning jagged across the pitch-black sky. Thunder cracked and rolled.

in behind it. The storm battered the Curragh down, driving it towards the earth.

Sláine grasped the tiller, trying desperately to right the listing vessel. It was no good. The storm was too fierce, its savagery too primal.

"You," Slough Throt rasped. The sailor his putrid hand singled out froze. "Here!" The sailor's face was stricken. His feet dragged him across the sloping deck of the listing ship to the vile sorcerer. The strain on his face was all Sláine needed to know that the man was moving against his own free will. Throt had a wickedly sharp knife in his hand. He grabbed the sailor by the hair, yanked his head back and slit his throat, bleeding him directly onto the weird stone.

Sláine stood paralysed with horror at the murder and the complete lack of emotion exhibited by Throt. "Madman…" Another jagged spar of lightning split the night in two. It struck the earth dangerously close to the Curragh, close enough for Sláine to feel the raw elemental power of it slam into his chest like a clenched fist. It knocked him off his feet. He lost his grip on the tiller. The Curragh buckled beneath his feet and Sláine went spinning down the deck. He dragged himself unsteadily to his feet, bracing himself against the second mast. "You'll pay for this, Throt," Sláine promised, his words whipped away by the fearsome wind.

But Slough Throt heard him. "It was necessary if I am to save us. We can show no weakness against him! I will need all the power of the weird stone to get us out of here alive." The sorcerer made ogham signs in the air, bending the power of the earth serpent to his will.

The three Drunes pressed their hands to the stone, their chant rising above the howling wind.

It wasn't enough.

Another jag of lightning crashed, striking the Curragh high up the main mast. The blow shered the long mast in two. The top segment broke free. Tied as it was to the ship by the rigging, it swung around sharply and smashed into the deck. The belly of the great sky ship began to scream in protest as sudden new strains were exerted on it by the damage caused by the ruined mast. Three more bolts of lightning hit the stricken vessel, ripping the Curragh in two. The dead and dying spilled out of the belly of the ship.

Sláine and Ukko clung on for dear life as the Cloud Curragh tumbled towards the earth.

Twenty-Two
Traitor and Saviour

THE LONGSHIP FELL from the sky. They came down in the middle of a gnarled leafless forest, the skeletal boughs of the withered trees tearing through the ship's hull. The timber frame of the vessel split open like an eggshell, spars of wood and planking popping and cracking, and wrenching free of the rivets pinning them in place. The gunwale snapped clean in two, breaching the integrity of the hull. A gaping wound opened up in the side of the ship. The half-dead crawled out of it, uninjured from the fall.

Amongst the living the carnage was complete.

Sláine had fallen fifty feet from the wreckage, Brain-Biter a few feet away. He reached out for the familiar comfort of the axe. Ukko lay between him and the belly of the fallen sky ship. Skull-swords lay broken in the mulch of the forest floor, the slack emptiness of death claiming their bodies. There was no dignity or care to it. Limbs lay at impossible angles, broken back on themselves. Necks lolled, jaws wide, eyes glazed.

Sláine crawled forwards, towards Ukko.

The little runt wasn't moving.

A stab of grief tore at him. "Ukko! Ukko!" He called, dragging himself forwards. Ukko didn't answer. There was something about the way the little dwarf lay bent over a protruding tree root that sent a shiver through Sláine. He pushed himself to his feet and stumbled forwards, throwing himself on his knees at Ukko's feet. "Oh, my friend, oh, my friend, don't die on me, not like this. We've got such stories to live through yet. Come on, Ukko, don't be dead. Think of those fat women, they need you. Damn it, dwarf, I need you. Don't you dare die on me, dwarf!"

"Wouldn't dream of it, friend." Ukko sat up and stretched. "Damned uncomfortable tree root that. I was beginning to think you'd never wake up and come looking for me." He hopped up and rolled his shoulders, cracking the stiffness out of the bones. "Look at that, not a mark on me. Amazing."

"Oh you little toe rag, you were faking it!"

Ukko grinned. "There's nothing like a brush with death to tell you who your real friends are."

"Don't push your luck, dwarf. There's still time for you to have a terrible accident that leaves me mourning the loss of my dear friend."

"Oh, you wouldn't!" Ukko blustered indignantly.

"Try me." Sláine grinned. Then he turned to look at the wreckage and the grin fell from his lips. The sudden reminder of mortality was hammered home by the sight of Blind Bran stumbling through the withered trees, a low keening moan coming from his lips.

"I've worked it out, Sláine. I know who Throt's afraid of. I mean, who would a Drune be frightened of apart from another Drune? A stronger one? Stands to reason, doesn't it?" Ukko said.

"Slough Feg," Sláine agreed. "We're trapped in the middle of a battle between two sorcerers."

"And by the looks of it we chose the wrong side," Ukko said, picking away at the inside of his nose.

They made their way back to the ship. They walked through the dead, looking for survivors. Deck hands lay trapped beneath huge broken beams, a foot or a hand sticking out from beneath the crush of debris. Only the half-dead moved, shambling around the diseased forest, unaffected by the crash. Sláine found the sorcerer, Slough Throt, propped up against a knotted tree stump. One of the sorcerer's antlers had snapped off leaving a stub of horn where there had been a majestic thirteen points. Throt turned to look at them. "You're alive," he said simply.

"I'm hard to kill," Sláine said.

"A good attribute to have," Throt agreed. "a shame then that we are fated to die here."

"I don't believe in fate, sorcerer. A man defines his own future."

"If your Goddess or my God allows it. The weird stone is finished. The half-dead are on the loose. It is only a matter of time before their curse afflicts us."

Sláine knew that the sorcerer was right. The weird stone was all but drained, only a few blood red lines running through the lifeless black.

"You're forgetting one thing, sorcerer."

"And what's that?"

"We're survivors. There's still some life left in that black stone of yours. Stop feeling sorry for yourself, you aren't beaten yet. Banish the zombies. Prove to Feg that he hasn't gotten the best of you that easily. It is Feg you are running from, isn't it?"

"How did you know?" Throt asked, not meeting the barbarian's eye.

"Oh, I worked it out," Ukko piped up. "I mean who could a Drune Lord be afraid of apart from another Drune Lord? There's one name we keep hearing again and again, the biggest and nastiest of your kind: Slough Feg."

"We cannot hide from him. The Lord Weird's magic is too far-reaching."

"Rubbish," Sláine said. "You're acting as if you're dead before you've even struck a single blow in your defence. When has rolling over and playing dead ever saved the prey from its predator?"

"Never," Ukko said helpfully.

Sláine grabbed the Drune by the wrist and heaved him to his feet. He noticed for the first time that the sorcerer only had two fingers on his left hand, the third finger and the thumb. The others were little more than nubs of bone.

Sláine helped him walk over to the weird stone.

Throt laid both hands on the stone of power, whispering at first, a stream of sounds that might have been words. The stone answered his call, pulsing beneath his hands, and then it died, utterly drained.

"Come to me, brethren of Cernunnos! Come to me dead and half-dead! Come and die a final death!"

They answered his call, crawling out of the wreckage of the broken ship, lumbering out of the withered trees, and dragging themselves across the sour land. They shuffled forwards, weapons hanging limply in their hands. At the front, their pelts soaked in their own blood, their heads lolling slackly on broken necks, came the Drune pilots of the Curragh. One carried a spar from the mast embedded in his throat. Another carried a metal spike from the decking opening a third eye in his head. The third showed no outward sign of what had killed him.

Throt gestured once, sharply, levelling an accusing finger at the first of the dead Drunes. A ribbon of shocking white power arced from his one good finger on that hand. The arc of raw energy struck the Drune square in the chest. It neither dissipated nor caused any noticeable damage. It hung there between the two of them, and then Throt's gaze shifted to the second of the dead Drunes and on to the third. The ribbon of white mirrored his gaze lancing from one to the next, joining them in a web of lethal energy. Throt threw his tangled web wider, drawing in Bran and Tamun and Senoll, and countless others, the shambling creatures and crawling wrecks of humanity, until every single one of the dead and half-dead were joined by the crackling arcs of power.

Slough Throt uttered a single word, a word of unmistakable power despite its foreignness, and the bodies trapped within his web convulsed violently, a series of detonations chasing from one shell to the next as the organs within the corpses swelled beyond containing and ruptured, exploding violently. Eyes burst, kidneys, livers, and hearts. Brains swelled with blood, pressing out on the bones of the skulls until they shattered and blood and brains flew.

"I told you he didn't need us," Ukko said, his face utterly drained of blood.

Sláine didn't move so much as a muscle.

The dead and half-dead jerked and spasmed to the dance of the sorcerer until the raw earth power streaming out of his fingers sizzled and spluttered, and died. The web fell and the unfortunates trapped within it collapsed, utterly devoid of life.

"It is done," Slough Throt said. The sorcerer was shaking. He looked down at his hands, turning them over in front of his face. "I am spent. There is no more until I perform a blood sacrifice."

"Get used to impotence, it comes to everyone eventually, or so I am told," Ukko said. "Well, not dwarfs of course," he cupped his groin and chuckled.

"Are they really gone?" Sláine asked, not trusting the evidence of his own eyes. In this infernal land the dead had a habit of not staying dead. He had no way of knowing how dead was dead.

Throt nodded. "They are dead and their souls have been torn apart and scattered to the four winds. They will not rise again."

"Good." Sláine suppressed a shiver. He couldn't shake the feeling that someone was watching them. He said as much.

"The echoes of my magic will have been felt a long way from here, warrior. Feg has eyes everywhere. He will be aware of our resistance, token as it is. I would bet my life he is watching us even now, through the eyes of the forest denizens."

"Then we'd better get a move on."

"Which way?"

"Does it really matter?"

"No, I suppose not."

"Then north seems as good as any other direction. We have friends waiting for us at Shadows Reach in Lyonesse," Throt said, setting off. Sláine noticed that he moved awkwardly, as if he had spent much of the magic that kept him alive in his conjuration to put the half-dead down. He had obviously risked much to banish the damned creatures.

They walked for a while in silence.

They found a path that led them deeper and deeper into the grim wood. The sensation of being watched heightened the further they ventured into the oppressive gloom of the trees.

"There's something uncanny about this place," Ukko said. He constantly turned in circles as he walked. "It's so quiet, not even the branches rustle as the wind sighs through them. It's wrong."

"Aye," Sláine agreed, "it is." He saw a wild cat hunkered down in the undergrowth, studying their progress. Behind it he saw a squirrel on a high branch, equally attentive.

"Soth! Look at the size of that thing." Ukko pointed up at a huge oil-black raven perched on a thick bough. The bird was three times the size of any black bird Sláine had ever seen.

The further they walked, the more obvious it became that the animals were shepherding them towards some unknown location in the heart of the dead wood.

"Feg has invoked Carnun to come to his aid," Throt breathed, eyes wide. A huge brown bear stood on its hind legs, claws sunk deep into the bark of a dead tree not twenty feet from the slough-skinned sorcerer. "Our doom is sealed. The Horned God will see that none of us leave this wretched forest."

Sláine hefted Brain-Biter. "I've never come across a tree this beauty couldn't fell. No forest scares me. As for animals, it will take more than an army of squirrels to bring me down."

"You're a fool, Sláine Mac Roth!" Throt spat. "If Carnun causes this dread wood to rise up against us we are doomed."

"Have you ever considered the possibility that your damned Feg isn't all that he's cracked up to be? What if these beasts have been sent to us by Danu, to guide us to safety?"

The Drune Lord laughed bitterly.

"There are fools, and then there are fools, and then, somewhere beyond those, there is you. Your Earth Goddess has no influence this far into the Sourlands."

"Yet, I felt her power surging through my veins when your lot tried to burn me alive in that wicker man. Think about it, Throt, if she could aid me there, why not here?"

They walked on for two days.

Hunger and exhaustion ate at them.

They seldom spoke.

The animals were never far from the path, ushering them always forwards, and although they tired, the animals wouldn't allow them to rest.

★ ★ ★

Ukko saw it first, a dark slash in the wall of solid rock. He would have missed it if the animals hadn't driven them at such an acute angle into the mountainside.

"Shelter!" he cried, stumbling and running forwards.

The others ran after him, new found energy in their legs.

Ukko stood and turned in wonder. The cave was light inside, lit by a curious luminescent lichen that clung to the long stalactites dripping down from the ceiling. It was a vast cave but that wasn't what had stunned the little dwarf. The sickly green light played across engravings of wild beasts: stallions, aurochs, bison, fox and hound, owl, fish and bear. Thousands and thousands of them, each one perfectly rendered in the stone. Two stood out, one, of Carnun, the Horned God, the only painted image in the whole cave, and the other of a huge pot-bellied earthen golem. Ukko had seen the likeness once before, as Sláine rose from the swamp after escaping the burning wicker man: a vast outline in the cloying smoke, the physical manifestation of Danu, the Earth Goddess.

The two images, rendered so closely together, were shocking. It went against everything the dwarf knew of the world.

Slough Throt drew a protective ward around the mouth of the huge cavern.

Slowly the beasts of the forest emerged to crowd around the cave's mouth: boar, bear, ox, fox and stag. More and more of Carnun's creatures came: rat and hare, horse and snake, and above them all, the huge oil-black raven that had dogged them since the crash.

"It will hold them off," Throt said, sinking to the floor, his back pressed against the wall. Above him the painting of the Horned God was dwarfed by Danu's huge golem. "Although for how long, well who knows? I make no promises."

The cave bore all the hallmarks of an ancient burial chamber, although who would be interred with the images of both Danu and the Horned God emblazoned on the walls of their tomb, Sláine didn't know. He didn't want to know, either. What might have once been porcelain jars lay in shards, any contents long since gone. Deeper into the cave the walls rose nearly a hundred feet to the ceiling. The floor angled down on a shallow decline. Sláine sifted through the detritus for the makings of a fire while Ukko explored the full extent of the cave.

Whatever Throt had done, it kept the beasts at bay.

With the fire burning, Sláine turned to the sorcerer. The flames danced high between them, throwing erratic shadows across the sorcerer's ruined face.

"You know, I think it's time you told us why Feg wants you dead so badly, Throt? What have you done?" Sláine asked.

Throt's worm-riddled tongue licked across his pustulant lips. "I stole something of his, something I intend to give to those who oppose him."

"So, you're a traitor to your own master?"

"That is a brutal way of putting it, warrior. I prefer to think of myself as saviour of your people."

"You're as slippery with words as Ukko is."

"You have seen what Feg is doing to the world. It is no accident. He is draining the life out of the land itself, sucking the vitality out of it to feed Crom-Cruach."

"That isn't so different from what you would do, I am sure."

"Feg is mad. He seeks nothing more than Ragnarok, the day of doom. He plans to destroy Tir-Nan-Og, turning it to blighted Sourland before he brings about the Deluge."

"But that is madness! Why would he destroy his own nation?"

"Because he is mad, warrior. Crom is his master, the only higher power he hears. He glorifies in destruction. I would warn the druids of the Earth Goddess that Feg schemes to cause a terrible war, an endless winter of raging snow storms, with ice sweeping down from Lochlann, and at last, the killing stroke, the Deluge: vast crashing waves where the sea herself rises up against the sickness of the land, drowning the Land of the Young. Mark me well, it will be our doom."

"I don't get it," Ukko said, walking up to the fire. He kicked a clay shard into the heart of the flames, causing a shower of sparks to fly. "You're a Drune Lord, you serve Crom just as Feg does. Why aren't you looking forward to this disaster like your master?"

"Because," Sláine said, understanding the sorcerer's motivations all too well, "Throt here is a coward who enjoys his power too much. You saw what he is capable of – the magic he threw at the half-dead, making the Curragh soar through the skies. He has power but it is the earth that grants him that power. If Feg succeeds and brings about the end of days the source of his magic will rot and decay like his own flesh, taking his power away, and then what will he be?"

"A big festering sack of rotten meat," Ukko said thoughtfully.

"You may question my motives, warrior, but my gold is good. I will pay you handsomely to see me safely to the lands of the Earth Goddess so that I might deliver my warning before it is too late. Feg must be stopped, for all our sakes!"

"How very noble of you, sorcerer, trying to save them so that they might weaken or who knows, even slay Feg for you. Do you take me for a fool? We destroy Feg so that you might rise up in his place, a vile, cowardly power-mad sorcerer capable of cold-blooded murder on a grand scale. Don't think I don't know what happened to the people of Gavra after we left. I am more than capable of counting my numbers. Some of your men remained behind. Don't waste your breath lying to me any more. The villagers were doomed the moment you walked into their inn. You and Feg are both monsters. I am not interested in your gold."

"I am," Ukko said, quietly.

Slough Throt laughed. It was an unpleasant sound.

"Sláine?"

"Not now, Ukko."

"Erm, Sláine?"

"I said not now, Ukko."

"Worms," Ukko said.

The ground beneath them heaved. The convulsion shook loose rubble that cascaded down the wall to the

uneven cave floor. A huge crack opened up in the flat
expanse of wall. Through it came the probing tendrils of
a huge sightless worm. The floor heaved again, fracturing
in a hundred places, opening fissures in the hard packed
earth, and through the fissures came more worms. Huge
bloated fat-bellied pink things seethed through the
cracks and wrapped themselves around the sorcerer's
feet. Tiny white worms tangled in his pelt and his
fetishes, and coiled around his arms. Purple worms so
huge they were thicker than Throt's limbs looped around
his waist and tightened, dragging him down into the
ever-widening fissures, into the belly of the cave, drowning Throt's screams out as his throat filled with dirt.

Throt writhed against the relentless pull of the
worms, thrashing about, clawing at them, and at the
ground as it closed over his head, and then he was gone,
dragged down into a suffocating live burial. The worms
receded.

"Sláine?"

"What?"

Ukko held a small gold-clasped book in his hands.
Seeing it glitter beneath the folds of Throt's filthy pelts
he had snagged it after he saw the first worm coming
through the crack in the wall. It had been an instinctive
theft. He knew, without knowing why, that the worms
had only come for Slough Throt. "You might want to
look at this."

"What is it?"

"I think it's what His Smelliness stole from Lord
Weirdo." He unclipped the hasp and flipped the book

open. The pages were covered in florid ogham script. The scrawl was barely legible. Ukko thumbed through the brittle pages until he saw the word "deluge". He closed the book, satisfied. "Look!" Ukko pointed at the wall. He hadn't noticed it before but the portrait of Danu, the huge earthly golem, had faded away into the bare rock. Only the image of Carnun remained.

Sláine walked to the mouth of the cave.

The animals had already begun to retreat, disappearing back into the grim forest. The night was cold, and bitter black, but it was not unpleasant.

"Thank you," Sláine said to no one Ukko could see, so he assumed it was to him.

"I didn't do much, just stole the plans for the end of days from a mad sorcerer." Ukko chuckled, coming up to stand beside him. "I probably saved the world in doing so."

"She spared us, Ukko. Do you know what that means? She hasn't abandoned me. I am not alone."

"I've got no idea who you are talking about, there's only you and me here."

"Exactly," Sláine said patiently. "Danu's likeness has gone from the wall because she is no longer needed here. She spared us, Ukko. When Crom sent his worms, she protected us. She guided us to this cave, her cave, a sacred place in this blighted wilderness. It was no coincidence that we found this sanctuary, and in your hands you hold something that might save the Land of the Young, something that might buy my redemption. I have to go home, Ukko. I have to return to Murias. Even though my life is forfeit if I do so, I have to get word of Feg's plans to the druids."

Ukko curled up his lip and furrowed his brow. Sláine going home wasn't what he had had in mind, oh no. There were plenty of opportunities south of the border worth investigating, large-breasted ladies and fat-thighed wenches just begging for a little Ukko-loving and naïve bondsmen looking to be parted from their coin, their chickens or anything else they valued. It was a perfect arrangement. So of course Sláine had to go and spoil it all and do something stupid like going on a damned crusade. Heading north, into "civilised" territory was asking for trouble, but then, if there was one thing the young Sessair was good at it was finding trouble. He had a nose for it. Ukko looked at Sláine, saw the determination in those damned eyes of his and knew beyond a shadow of a doubt that the great lummox was intent on walking all the way back to Murias and throwing himself on the mercy of the man he had cuckolded, convinced that his precious goddess would keep him safe. The lad was a bloody fool. For that reason and that reason alone, there was no way Ukko could abandon him.

Ukko shook his head despairingly.

"Sláine, Sláine, Sláine. Why did I know you were going to say something stupid like that?"

Glossary

CARNUN – The Horned God, Lord of the Beasts.

CROM-CRUACH – The Worm God, Lord of the Mounds. Worshipped by the Southern tribes.

DANU – The Earth Goddess.

DRUIDS – Priests of the Northern tribes.

DRUNE LORDS – Evil Priest-Kings of the Southern tribes.

EARTH POWER – The spiral force that runs through the Weird Stones (Megaliths). It can be used for good or evil. Also known as The Earth Serpent.

HALF-DEAD – Warriors killed but trapped between the worlds.

HERO-HARNESS – Worn by warped warriors, so their clothes don't rip during the spasm.

LUG – The Sun God. The Sun and Earth are worshipped by the Northern tribes.

OGHAMS – Early form of writing. Also a sign language.

RED BRANCH – Sláine's tribe's greatest warriors.

SALMON-LEAP – Jumping your own height. A Sessair battle-skill – like shield-jumping and spear-catching.

SKULL SWORDS – Drune soldiers.

SLOUGH – Drune leader who has shed (sloughed) his skin.

SOURLAND – Land warped by sorcery.

THE LORD WEIRD SLOUGH FEG – Supreme Drune, thousands of years old.

TIR-NAN-OG – The Land of the Young.

TRIBES OF THE EARTH GODDESS – The legendary Northern tribes, including the Sessair.

WARP-SPASM – A strange and terrifying battle-frenzy, much worse than a Berserker fury. Caused by Earth Power, which some warriors can warp through their bodies.

ABOUT THE AUTHOR

British author **Steven Savile** is an expert in
cult fiction, having written a wide variety of sf
(including *Star Wars* and *Jurassic Park*), fantasy
and horror stories, as well as a slew of editorial
work on anthologies in the UK and USA. He
won the L Ron Hubbard Writers of the
Future award in 2002, was runner-up in the
British Fantasy Award in 2000 and has been
nominated three times for the Bram Stoker
award. He currently lives in Stockholm,
Sweden.

Also available from Black Flame

CABALLISTICS, INC.

Hell on Earth

MIKE WILD

**Boswell, on the Yorkshire coast
2.12am, October 15th, 1944**

THOOOM.

Annabeth Jardine whirled full circle as the RAF Mosquitoes droned overhead, banking a second later to bypass Scratch Tor, in whose direction she too hurried. Buffeted by the fly-over's wake she fell and split a palm on the track that ran beside the tor and down into town. The trenchcoat worn over her slight and trembling frame had once belonged to her husband, and its great folds flapped and slapped in the aircrafts' aftermath. She raised a bloody hand just too late to prevent an equally oversized cap being blown from her head and sent tumbling away. Annabeth's dog, Moll, gave chase instinctively, but she ventured only a small way along the path before scampering back to spin in panicked circles at her owner's side. The dog was rarely distressed but tonight clearly sensed there was something horribly wrong not far below.

She rubbed the dog vigorously to ease her fears, patted her solidly. Aye, girl, there was something wrong all right.

Annabeth heard the Voice once more in her head, felt her brain pulse agonisingly as she forced it away. Her breath condensing in the ice-cold air, she continued on, following the planes' flightpath to where the track dropped steeply into town and revealed the panorama below. She gasped and felt her heart seize. Beside her, Moll began to bark and howl.

The town.

Oh dear God, the town.

"We have visual contact, tower. Repeat, visual contact. Oh no. This can't be…"

"Nighthawk One?"

"They're burning, tower. All the people in the town. They're burning."

"Say again, Nighthawk One. Burning?"

"Affirmative, tower. My God. My God–"

"Nighthawk One, radar is showing no enemy air activity in the area. Repeat, no–"

"Tower, Nighthawk Two. Confirming the sky is clear. This is not an air raid, over."

"Then what–"

"So many. God help them, there are so–"

"Report, Nighthawk One. What is happening to these people?"

"Tower, I… I don't know… it's impossible, can't believe it. The people, the people they're just–"

Bursting into flames, Annabeth thought, hand on her mouth. It was impossible but happening right before her eyes. Human torches staggering out of their homes into the streets, screaming, consumed by fire. Others seemingly unaffected desperately trying to douse their loved ones, then themselves wailing in disbelief as their own flesh ignited for no reason at all. Men, women, even children – people Annabeth knew – flailing wildly through the night, collapsing to their knees, onto their faces, then just burning away on the ground. And in the midst of them, those very few who remained untouched, dropping to their own knees, but this time in prayer. And all of them wailing the same desperate plea to the sky.

"FORGIVE ME!"

Oh God, Annabeth thought. The Voice. It's the Voice.

"Mum?"

There was a tug at her hips and Annabeth turned to see her five year-old son. "Judd? By Christ, boy, what are you doing here? I told you to stay at the farm."

"I know. But there's a voice… in my head."

Annabeth grabbed her son by the shoulders, span him away so that he could not see the horror that continued below them. Her heart thudded rapidly. *Whatever the hell you are, stay away from my boy*, she thought.

"Aye, lad, there is," she said quickly. "But you're not to listen to what it's saying, do you hear me? You're not to listen."

"But it wants to see my shins–"

Annabeth blurted a laugh, aware that it sounded hysterical and came with tears, and she drew Judd tightly against her.

"It won't stop, Mum," the boy murmured into her side. "Mum it burns!"

"Judd, I said don't listen," Annabeth commanded and shook the boy. "Whatever it says to you, you must not listen! Promise me that, Judd. *Promise me!*"

Judd reddened and stared fearfully at Annabeth, his own face wet with tears. But he struggled to beat the pain, seemed to subdue it. "I promise."

"Good boy. Good boy."

The Voice, Annabeth thought. It had awoken her at the farm, perhaps fifteen minutes earlier. A sibilant whisper that felt like the remnant of some dream. But then it had grown and grown in her head until it felt like fingernails scratching on the inside of her skull. Not show me your shins, as her son thought. The word had been *sins*.

A command coming from everywhere, nowhere.

Show me your sins.

SHOW ME YOUR SINS.

SHOW ME YOUR SINS!

She had flung open the door of the farm, and it had revealed to her the distant dull glow of the town; the faint cries of despair carried onto the moorland by the wind. She had begun to run, the Voice becoming louder with every stride she took. She had fought it as best she could – agony every time she rejected its call – but passing the road where John had died, it had her.

Suddenly it was six years ago, and she watched her husband dying all over again. Thunder, lightning, the heaviest rain she could remember. The cliff edge crumbling suddenly away beneath John's feet.

"John! Aww, John, no, no, no..."

"Back, Annie... Get back!"

She was laying again on her side on that wet, wet ground, her unborn son in her belly, stretching a hand out desperately to reach John as the mudfall slid her scrambling husband down the liquid edge.

"I can reach you!"

"No, Annie! You can't!"

She had tried. Oh lord, how she had tried, her arms straining in their sockets as she had willed them to grow one more inch, her body arching like a bow until it felt that her spine might snap in two. Then John had pleaded with her to think of their baby, and she had flailed at him hystericaly in denial of the death he knew was coming. But her movements caused her to lurch forward in the mud and, in a moment of vertiginous panic, she'd instinctively grabbed for the safety of the rock. And in that moment, without her being able to say she was sorry, John had slipped away from her forever.

For a long time she thought that she could have saved him, that she had let her husband die. For a long time she thought that she had sinned. But at last the guilt had lessened, and she had found peace.

Until tonight, when the Voice had stripped the time away and again she had wanted to cry, "Forgive me!"

Was this what it was doing? Forcing the people of Boswell into baring their innermost souls? It seemed impossible, but why else were they begging forgiveness? Dear God, no – the question was why were they all burning?

Moll's renewed barking drew Annabeth out of her reverie and she turned to see the cause of alarm, shaking visibly when she did.

Above her, one RAF pilot had already vocalised what she could not.

"Request you say again, Nighthawk One, over."

"I repeat, tower, they are rising. The bodies are rising."

"Nighthawk Two, please confirm."

"Tower, it's impossible, I know, but leader is correct. Sweet Jesus, the people are getting up. And they're dead."

It wasn't just the dead, Annabeth saw, it was the dying, too. The dying and those on their knees, still, in desperate prayer. All of them – every man, woman and child – rising as one. And as they rose, they turned to look out of town, up the hill.

And they began to move towards her.

No!

Annabeth swept Judd up under her arm and pulled the frantically barking Moll firmly by her collar to turn the dog around. She had run towards town in the hope that she could help with whatever had afflicted her neighbours, but this was vastly beyond her ken and she knew she had to get out of there right now. But as she turned back to face the moors, she paused. There was movement in the darkness where there hadn't been before. A shape that was indistinct but seemingly emerging out of the ground itself. It looked like–

Something lunged at her from the dark, appearing and then disappearing in a feral flash of teeth and bone. She span Judd away, screaming in shock, and as she did Moll's collar tugged in her grip. The dog was going crazy, barking and straining on her hind legs, desperate to defend against the attack, and before Annabeth could do anything she broke free and raced into the dark.

"Moll, no girl!" Judd shouted. But it was too late. The aged and loyal working dog was gone, and a second later there was a brief, agonised yelp and then silence.

"Moll!" Judd shouted again. When there was no response, he began to cry. "M-Moll?"

Annabeth stared with horror onto the moor. She couldn't believe it. The dog was dead, just like that. Oh God, Moll, she thought. Please, won't somebody tell me what's happening?

Her desperate plea brought with it an even more desperate realisation. Whatever had just killed Moll wandered out there on the moor, and she and Judd dared not cross it. But equally, they dared not stay where they were. The only way to get her son out of there was to carry on into town.

Through the people.

Trying as best she could to calm Judd, Annabeth drew a deep breath and turned briskly back to the path, swallowing when she saw how far the throng had advanced towards her. Then she noticed that they were not really heading towards her at all. Because halfway up the slope the path forked, and a narrower, less-trodden trail veered up the side of Scratch Tor. It wound eventually to the ruins of the monastery at its peak but, before then, it passed the black mouth of one of the entrances to the labyrinthine cave system that lay beneath the tor. And one after the other, the people of the town were slowly filing inside.

Annabeth stared into the blackness of the caves and sensed the Voice speaking from somewhere deep within. Childhood nightmares of a thing meant to live down there came flooding back. Oh dear God, it was calling these people to it. No, stop, she wanted to cry out, but dreaded what would happen if they actually turned and looked back.

"Mummy, I'm scared," Judd said. "Where are all the people going?"

"I – don't know," Annabeth said haltingly. She knew she couldn't hide these horrors from him any longer. "Baby... I just don't know."

Slowly, cautiously, quietly, she eased Judd and herself down the path, moving as invisibly as she could through the grotesquely shuffling bodies of people who only a day before had been friends and neighbours. Time and again she had to bite her lip to stop herself crying out in shock, and felt there was going to be no end to their number. At last, though, she managed to weave Judd through their ranks.

But there was no respite in the town itself. A further mass of townsfolk filled its narrow lanes and blocked Annabeth's flight at every turn. The screaming here in their midst was horrendous, and it was surely only a matter of time before one or more of their burning bodies came into collision with Judd and herself.

Annabeth looked around desperately. She had to find refuge, somewhere to hide.

There. The church.

She bundled Judd forward, dodging the flailing forms, until the two of them reached the church's graveyard and crashed through its wooden gate, but she made it only partly along the path before she recoiled in horror. She did not need to hear the local priest, himself being consumed by fire, warning in his last breaths of Judgement Day – it was right there before her eyes.

"Nighthawk Two, are you getting this on film?"
"Affirmative, One. Oh, no. that's not…"
"Nighthawk One, this is tower. Report!"
"The graveyard, tower… it's…"

Had Annabeth been able to overhear the exchange she would have had no idea what to say. All that she could think herself was no, oh no, no, no… Every grave in the graveyard was erupting with its dead, and bodies milled about in various states of decay or decomposition. One or more of the more recently interred Annabeth – horribly – recognised. Slowly, inevitably, her gaze shifted to one particular grave in the far corner of the burial ground – and she physically convulsed as she spotted blackened hands emerging out of its topsoil.

No, not John. Oh please, not John.

Annabeth forced Judd behind her, shielding him from the father he had never known, and backed up towards the gate. But other graves had disgorged their dead in her wake, and suddenly she and Judd found themselves crowded by leathered flesh.

It was too much. Just too much. Annabeth felt herself drop onto her knees as frantic bubblings of hysteria began deep inside.

Then a corpse was sent stumbling back, its head shattered under the impact of a huge, hairy fist. "That's quite enough of your nonsense, thank you very much," a rumble of a voice declared. Dazed, Annabeth looked up to discover its origin.

The owner proffered his hand and nodded to her briskly. "Professor Augustus Farralay, madam… My colleague, Winston Bey."

"Good evening," the other man said. "May we be of assistance?"

What, Annabeth thought? She stared hard at the pair, no idea who they were. The first, a huge barrel of a man with a bald head and a bushy black beard might have been a street wrestler but for his smart dress and monocle, while the other, in a pin-striped suit and white turban, sporting a voluminous white moustache and eyebrows, looked like some cheap variety hall magician. But cheap variety hall magicians did not do what he did next. As the one called Farralay battled more of the corpses away, this Bey wrote signs in the air and it was filled suddenly with phantasmal snakes that darted at the dead things Farralay could not reach. Fangs bared, hissing clearly audible over the burning fires, they whipped and lashed at the dead, reducing them to flailing confusion.

Judd stared at them open-mouthed, but they were just too sinister. "Mum, I'm scared…"

"What's happening?" Annabeth pleaded. "Please, who are you people?"

"Best to save your questions for later, madam," Farralay declared. "For the time being, what say we get the devil out of here, eh?" He laughed as if he were Santa Claus and then struck out at the corpses with his fists again, crushing the skulls of – or actually beheading – those nearest. Both Judd and Annabeth cringed each time they heard an awful crunching of bone, and then Annabeth spied John moving through the pack and almost screamed. She knew this was no longer her husband – in the name of sanity, how could it be? – but she could not let him be treated this way. And as Farralay swung, she halted the man's arm, for a terrifying instant becoming convinced he was going to turn the club on her.

"Get out of here?" she reminded him, seeing his eyes widen and nostrils flare.

"Yes – yes," he said after a second. The feral stench coming off him was appalling. "Quite so, quite so."

The four of them backed away from the graveyard and left the corpses shambling in pursuit of whatever was calling them. The town offered no escape still, and as Farralay and Bey hurried the mother and son through its winding, burning lanes the pair dealt any emergent victims of the flames who got in their way the same treatment as they had the dead. But to Annabeth and Judd's horror, many were still very much alive. One old woman – hand on neck and face contorted with pain – came haltingly at them begging for help, and Farralay killed her with a single blow.

"Mum!" Judd screamed as the woman dropped in a twitching heap to the ground.

"Stop this!" Annabeth pleaded with undisguised horror. "For God's sake, they need your help!"

"No, dear," a voice said.

For the second time that night, Annabeth turned and found herself facing strangers. Two more, as strange and out of place here as the others. The first was a short, dark-haired slip of a woman in a low-slung evening dress and pearl earrings who grinned broadly, and the second a taller and much stockier woman wearing a matronly skirt and coat, who tamped down a Sherlock Holmes pipe. At least that was what Annabeth *thought* they were, because though she couldn't put her finger on what, there was something not quite right about both of them.

Bey greeted them as George and Harriet.

"Look dear," George – or was it Harriet? – said conspiratorially. She took Annabeth by the arm and emphasised each word that followed. "There is nothing you can do for these people. They are already dead."

"No," Annabeth said in denial, "she was alive."

"Balderdash," Harriet – or George? – came back. "Utter tripe."

"Don't upset her, darling," George admonished, and she showed Annabeth where the old woman – her whole face gone – was rising up from the ground. "They're nothing more than puppets, understand? All we can do is try to stop as many as possible of them reaching it."

Annabeth stared. "What are you talking about, puppets, it? I don't know what you're saying."

Farralay was suddenly grabbing her by the arm, dragging her to where one of the lanes opened out to offer a view of the cliff-top monastery.

"You asked earlier what was happening," the big man said forcefully. He held Annabeth's chin and tipped her gaze upward. "Look," he prompted. "I said, look!"

Annabeth looked, and shook her head vigorously in denial. "I don't believe it. This has to be a dream."

"No dream," Farralay said. And if the giant of a man hadn't been holding her up then, she would have fallen to her knees. For over the monastery a great golden figure was materialising – looming over the town. Itself seemingly made of fire, it was a vague rather than detailed apparition, but it seemed to be holding out arms as if beckoning to her, and as it did an enormous pair of wings seemed to flex behind its back.

"Impossible," Annabeth mouthed. But impossible or not, it was there, and in her skull the agony began again.

"Mom, don't listen!" Judd urged, but perversely Annabeth wasn't listening. The voice was louder than ever, even more demanding.

Show me!

SHOW ME YOUR SINS!

My sins, yes, Annabeth thought. My sins. From deep within her came the same memories that had tortured her earlier, flooding her mind once more with sorrow and regret. Except this time she was convinced she could have done more. Stretched a little more towards John, arched her splattered, battered body until muscles tore and she crushed her own baby to feel the grip of his hand in her own. Oh God, she could have saved John. Just that little more effort and she could have saved him! It was her fault he died! It was all her–

"No!" Annabeth screamed. This memory was wrong. She had done all she could. She had done everything in her power. And no entity that cared would put her through this again. Nothing that cared would suggest that she had killed her husband. This was no sin, it was an accident and that was all. An accident. And knowing such she rejected it. Rejected it. Rejected it!

"What the hell are you, you bastard!" Annabeth screamed at the figure above the tor. "Leave us alone!"

"A resistant," Bey said impressed, and raised a white eyebrow.

"Few and far between," Farralay agreed.

"But she'll remember," Harriet commented, as if in warning. "Perhaps we should–"

The remainder of her comment was ripped away by the roaring drone of the two RAF Mosquitoes as they turned to meet the materialising figure. Their banking brought them directly over Annabeth for the first time, and she began to wave her hands frantically in the air.

"Tower from Nighthawk Two. I have survivors on the ground. Please advise, over."

"Roger, Two. There is now an official presence in charge of ground operations – please ignore, over."

"Ignore, tower?"

"Affirmative, One. We are instructed to cancel reconnaissance, over."

"Roger that, tower. But there are still people who need help here."

"I'm sorry, gentlemen. But as of a minute ago, this affair passed out of our hands, over."

"Tower, this is Nighthawk One... something in... Oh no, Susan... no, I never meant–"

Annabeth saw the first of the planes wobble and thought, No! It was the Voice again; it couldn't be anything else. Don't listen, she pleaded. Oh God, don't listen. But it did no good. As she watched, the plane veered from its flight path and out towards the sea, and Annabeth staggered back as there was a sudden incendiary burst inside its cockpit. Seemingly without a pilot, the plane nosedived and vanished into the dark.

* * *

"Jesus, oh, Jesus! Tower, what is this thing? Is it causing this?"

"Nighthawk Two, avoid the anomaly, over. Once again I say, avoid the anomaly."

"Negative, tower – I'm getting this on film."

"Return to base immediately. That is an order. I repeat, return to base immediately."

"Sorry tower, no can do. That thing killed the leader. We need to know what it is."

Don't be a bloody fool, Annabeth thought, as she saw the second plane head straight for the figure atop the tor. Then again, what could she do? She could only look on as the Mosquito flew directly at the glowing apparition – then into it, through it. She sighed with relief as the plane emerged on the other side, but the sigh caught as she saw something eject suddenly. Whatever it had been a moment before, it now burned horribly bright, as if it were a sailor's flare.

"Unfortunate," Farralay commented.

"Most," Bey agreed.

The story continues in

CABALLISTICS, INC.

Hell on Earth

BY MIKE WILD